Performance

The Invisible Mile

'Bruising, beautiful and ultimately transcendent. I loved *The Invisible Mile.*' —Markus Zusak, author of *The Book Thief*

'A wonderfully colourful and attentive novel that subtly combines the tangible pains of the race with the echoes of war.' —*Sunday Express*

'Gorgeous . . . Coventry's brooding narrative, in varying parts philosophical action-adventure, travelogue, family drama, war chronicle and psychological puzzler, is suffused with the ever-querying perspective of its haunted central character.' —*New York Times*

'A truly extraordinary first novel.' *NZ Listener*

'A brilliant tour de force of writing talent and style.' —Brian Clearkin, *Landfall*

'It's a book about violence, youth, mythology, history, guilt and love – all set to the agonising rhythm of an inhuman bike race. . . . This has the same feeling of total immersion as I remember feeling when I read David Peace's *The Damned United.*' —Ned Boulting, author of *How I Won the Yellow Jumper*

'*The Invisible Mile* is a dream to read . . . The writing is fierce, a bravura mix of narcissism, masochism and lyricism grounded in the honesty of the unnamed rider's journey into his self and the dawning realisation that the race has become a grand metaphor for the trauma of World War I.' —John Sinclair, *Metro*

'Coventry's masterful *The Invisible Mile* . . . looks closely and intensely at what huge human events do to the mind.' —*The Brooklyn Rail*

Dance Prone

'A magnificent novel.' —Alan McMonagle, author of *Liar, Liar* and *Psychotic Episodes*

'You don't just read a David Coventry novel, you experience it with every facet of your being. Every page is alive. He writes like no one else. This book is astounding.' —Megan Bradbury, author of *Everyone Is Watching*

'The blood, desire, pain and loss . . . all of it feels true, because of the novel's volatile physicality, and the unshrinking vulnerability of its narrator. More than anything I've read in ages, *Dance Prone* feels real.' —Annaleese Jochems, *Newsroom*

'David Coventry's new novel is a gorgeous panegyric to the purity, poison and impossibly high stakes of punk. It's funny, filthy, erudite, and rude.' —Carl Shuker, author of *A Mistake* and *The Royal Free*

'A feverish phantasmagoria of intrigue, *Dance Prone* is a high-tension wire headrush of punk rock, romance and displacement. It bristles with atmosphere and brutal energy.' —Kiran Dass

'An affecting novel about trauma, memory and its fallout where language, pace and tension are expertly pitched and the chaotic music scene notches the decibels up to a level to absorb you in this world. . . . Intelligent, intimate, and raw.' —Scorpio Books

Also by David Coventry

The Invisible Mile
Dance Prone

Performance

David Coventry

Te Herenga Waka University Press
Victoria University of Wellington
PO Box 600 Wellington
teherengawakapress.co.nz

First published 2024

ISBN 9781776920808

A catalogue record is available from the National Library of New Zealand.

Printed in Singapore by Markono Print Media Pte Ltd

For Anna and Rachel

For Francie and family

For Rosalyn and Henry

‘Instead of committing suicide, people go to work.’
Thomas Bernhard (1979)

Contents

The Watcher

It's a habit now, looking west. We fly between Christchurch and Wellington and make sure to sit on the side of the aircraft with a view of the mountains, the Inland Kaikōura Range, where the peak of Tapuae-o-Uenuku hunkers on the side of the Pacific, rising conical from its base. The highest mountain there, the largest upthrust in Aotearoa not a part of the Southern Alps. On a clear day it's extraordinary, peaked and valleyed by graphic, raw geography. Your gaze follows angles, tracks the awe of plummeting ridgelines and their descent into the territory of high-country farming, sheep farming and, lower down, cattle, and then the Pacific. And when we watch it's not for this view's sake, but rather for the hope of glimpsing the geography of past events, of death's terrain.

Sometimes the plane flies near the spine of the range, as if to present alternatives to what really went on there. The ridges that nerve up the neck of the peak, the snow and gullies, the valley—and which valley, which valley was it?

Cook named the mountain Odin, then almost apologetically nicknamed it the Watcher. But of course it already had a name,

Tapuae-o-Uenuku, translating as 'footprint of the rainbow', named for Chief Tapuae-o-Uenuku. Things have many designations in this country, and behind their names are stories and tensions and crimes that became constitution.

Edmund Hillary climbed the mountain in a day as an RNZAF cadet training at Woodbourne. His first real mountain, he'd famously claim years later. Famously, because of what came after for him. Every peak he summited would become renowned for his conquering effort, a step on his way to the absolute of the Himalayas. This shy beekeeper with a body of lanking bones and the extraordinary natural fitness of someone whose blood seemed permanently full of oxygen.

My family, they too were drawn up its valleys and rivers, its snow fields and vanishing ridges. They might've claimed (if they were me) that they climbed the mountain because it was always present, looking down at Wellington where we all lived, saying—*I can see you.* The eye of the south. It was in the logbooks of the tramping club to which they each belonged. They'd climbed in the Tararua Ranges together, stood on Mount Hector and seen the peak. They'd walked Wellington's south coast and seen it rise out of Cook Strait, a deep blackened grey, then white.

You see these things, my father once told me, and you feel you're being instructed to get to the top and, once there, pause and listen. 'And you want to get to the top to halt—*something*.' The mountain's *scrutinising* was what he meant, and how you want to stop it. You want to put an end to its signalling in that hushed language nobody has yet been able to unscramble. And you want to unscramble it. That voice of intangible silence communing with the sky. You unpick it and then somehow it falls, it collapses into the sea and it's no more.

Henry, my father, he wrote a lot, treatises on life.

The three of them—my brother Simon, Henry and David (the boyfriend of my eldest sister)—planned a three-week excursion south, where they would climb Tapuae-o-Uenuku, then head on to the Nelson Lakes arm of the Southern Alps, where other mountains waited.

At the time I was young, sixteen, and had recently made the decision to quit high school. My behaviour had become strange and showed no signs of normalising. I had no idea what my brother and father were up to, which seems odd to me now.

Simon drove the three of them to the mountain, taking his green Mini across on the Cook Strait ferry, all their gear collected in the seat in the back and the miserly boot. He drove from Blenheim up the dust track that navigates the Awatere. Up through the fifty-five kilometres, up and up until they came to a large suspension bridge. Simon parked in the bay between the bridge and a cattle-stop, and they began the walk through the foothills and farmland. It was October, mid-spring in 1985, and the first day was a simple tramp up to the Hodder River. They spoke to a local farmer, a woman who liked to keep a log of who passed by and how long each person was likely to be in the mountains.

Henry, by now fifty-three, spoke in the easy bluster of mountain talk, conversations rehearsed by time in hills. He was a quiet man but knew the obligations of social interaction. He even gave the impression of enjoying it on occasion. They heard the woman give directions to the river, made the guess that they'd need to make close to a hundred crossings before reaching the hut.

'A hundred?' David asked. He had a yellowish beard, long hair that hung in his face. After he dies, his sister will marry my brother.

'Some days sixty,' the woman said. 'It's dependent on melt. But numbers mean nothing after a while.' When she smiled she revealed more gaps than teeth. 'How long you giving yourselves?'

'Three days.'

'Should be fine. Should be. Might get hot. Sun's been unholy.'

'We heard.'

'We lost two goats in the river a week ago to the melt. Pulled them out, gutted 'em on the side of the ravine. Lugged them up home—eating stew till Christmas.'

David said something to which the woman nodded. She searched her pocket. 'Nothing's due,' she said, glancing past them to the mountain. 'Nothing much.'

My father looked at her and paused before giving over details of forecast and prediction for the entire country and the whatever activity out in the Pacific. The narrowing techno-speak of isobar and ablation, barometric and microseism. His face had a shifting stillness to it, animated but serene—he loved the sound of fact and how it tracked into narrative.

'Yeah, the weatherman has his certainties,' the farmer replied when she finished, 'but I've got my own ways of knowing.' She lit her Pall Mall. 'There, I've jinxed you.' She laughed out smoke and said something unheard into the haze. 'But in the end, there's no such thing,' she said, drawing and holding the smoke in her lungs. 'No such—'

'No,' my father said.

'No such jinxes, no curses—though I wish there were.' She laughed again and bent down to her dog, a huntaway, as it slipped across the grass to her side. They exchanged noises as she rubbed its chin. 'The mountain's got a mind, doesn't it?' she said as she stood up. 'That's what I say: Every mountain's got a mind. Give it time and you'll hear what it's got to say.'

The woman had them laughing, stretching them beyond the usual measure they had of themselves. She spoke about growing up in the hills, being a kid on the mountain. Spoke about time and how it felt so different when she was barefoot and ragged; that now it felt like the world was always speeding up, as if trying to correct its mistakes over and again. 'Makes me think I'm just a fork in the road,' she said. 'If that makes any kinda sense.'

'Yeah, I guess,' David said. 'If all we've got is retrospect, forks are everywhere.'

The farmer smiled.

'But I'll tell ya,' David went on, 'retrospect's a pain in this guy's rear, I'll tell you that much for free.'

'I hear you,' the farmer said.

'I got it coming out my—' Despite his rough-hewn appearance, David had an English way about him, his ways of speaking. He found methods around swearing like my father found ways around paying tax on whatever investments.

'I prefer to play the game of avoidance when it comes to sticking your head over your shoulder,' the farmer said. 'Then a thinking woman's beer or two. Or eighteen.'

They spoke on for several minutes before she began walking the conversation past a hay shed, past barns, where she waved goodbye and they headed on, on until they came to a large cairn. From there they descended to the riverbed, a boulder-strewn stream that they followed for several hours, crossing and crossing until the fork. They took the left branch and searched for a trail that departed the river and climbed up the east side of the gorge. They located the track and followed its incline, traversing the slopes before climbing back down to the river for a short period, crossing, crossing. They took to the western slopes and rose to the Hodder huts on a terrace above the valley. This leg took six hours and ninety river crossings.

As they ate, they told tales and rough jokes. Tramping stories, accounts of climbs and the things seen. Old stories about Henry's father and brother in the 1940s and 50s. The huts, the gear, the tracks, the clarity of old narratives, clear because they'd been rebuilt into something perfect by the need to remember. Then, the repeatable romances of epic flights Henry had taken as an officer in the RNZAF. Malaysia and Singapore. The story about the piano, the one about Henry and his fellow airmen tipping it out of a second storey window and incinerating it on the taxiway at Changi. A night of wreckage and drunkenness and indeterminate intent. The one about the ski lodge on Mount Ruapehu that also caught fire, how they all stood around in the snow taking photos. The one made up, then the one about before he was born, and his grandfather in Bulls. The house near where the Rangitīkei exited the plains into the Tasman Sea. Stories of flooding and farming. The construction of a large homestead by his earliest New Zealand ancestor, a Scotsman named Urquhart; deals with local hapū and how they helped erect the homestead out of the silt.

Simon understood our father better than I did at the time, knew Henry felt there was a kind of mysticism to family lore and familial time, in its telling and constant conceiving. Simon knew how to listen and engage and not engage; our father would go on no matter. And this time Simon was listening because Henry skipped the one about our great-grandfather, about his arrival, and skipped the one about that man's previous life in the UK and Russia as an engineer and started talking prosaically about his own mother, how she came to be in New Zealand from Wales. An abandoned child whose parents moved to Canada, taking only her little brother with them. It was something he rarely talked to, this gaping loss in her life.

'It's still a hurtful thing,' he said. They were drinking tea. The tannin and taint of dehydrated milk. 'You imagine so many decades now, time might well be its own illness,' he said. 'If you imagine how it keeps expanding on inside her. It might as well have its own bit of Latin to describe it.'

My brother didn't yet know how to make jokes about family talk, though David did. He and his sister had also been abandoned by their parents, this time in New Zealand, when they were teenagers. He'd always found ways to knock the idea out of it.

'Family's just two people making a roughshod mistake while having too good a time to notice,' he said. 'It's like driving drunk down the wrong side of the motorway. It's gotta be thrilling, but nothing good's gonna come from it.'

'That how you met my sister?' Simon asked.

My father smiled, and they chortled through the tea steam and hut odour of socks and boots and drying canvas. And when finished my father sat up straight, as if the wind outside was suddenly within the walls of the hut.

'Well, yes,' Henry said. And he said his point was that there were these families, these lines of personage landing at peculiar confluences and—'Isn't it strange,' he asked, 'because how many people does it take to make a person?'

'Two, and a bottle of bad decisions,' David said, shooing a mouse from the base of his pack.

'And how many people and how much time?' Henry asked, ignoring him. 'We're all unbearably odd.' He said it without irony. And he said this because the homestead the Scots had built, Poyntzfield, it'd also burnt down. 'There's always so much fire,' he said. 'We burnt down that hut on Ruapehu because we lost control of the gas. It was so cold, and we'd fed it too much and it expanded out into the room. It leaked and was lit by a spark from the coal range. We tried using extinguishers, but the fire spread and it was soon obvious that we were not in control. A strong wind caught the flames and within minutes, the whole building. The floor and wall caught, and the whole thing. We burnt that piano because we'd flown in after a three-night run around the peninsula and there was a party raging and a piano-player going at it all night and we just couldn't take it. We made an executive decision and threw it out of the second-storey window, lugged the remains out onto the tarmac and set it alight. And Poyntzfield, that was burnt to the ground because of a flood. It was in the newspapers at the time. A great flood came down the river and wrecked everything. A cousin thought he'd dry it out by surrounding it in fires. That was the end of something. The house burnt down and now all there is is a cairn marking where it sat.'

Simon asked when.

'A three-metre wave, a surge spreading out down the plains like a plague, and that was that. Eighteen ninety-seven. The Bulls Bridge was wiped out. Three spans of it. The country was cut in two, essentially, and the house was, it was destined for nothing but old stories about this wall of water. There's a cemetery there. That's where I come from.' Indeed, his ashes are interred there, to our eternal confusion.

They dealt with dishes, billies and plates. Sorted clothes around the glow of the fire and went into the wrap of sleeping bags and pullovers as pillows. In the night they listened to ruru. Wide-eyed owls, moreporks in the ridges marking position and place, delivering the same testimony to cousins and kin, that they might understand, might appreciate it when they said: *Here I am.*

The Buckle and Stammer

Over these past years, I've come to relate existence and survival to every aspect of my life. The smallest things surprise me. Making it to the shops and back, showering in the morning. Making dinner. Sleeping, sleeping and waking shock me. Reading a page and the next page is an oneiric revelry I have, and occasionally it occurs, a bright thing in a month of long days in an arthritic mind. I am a writer who willed himself to write. I long for an inversion of this, a reversal where it is reading that comes out of this will to know what thoughts I need to have.

It's not so.

My mind is a small chamber of swollen clouds.

Little makes it through.

I wake and at best I feel concussed.

I wake and have the sensation someone has attacked me in the night.

We live on a hill. People come to the house, they look out and say, *What a view.* And it's true, Laura and I see many things from our home. The Pacific Ocean. The Remutaka Range. The Tararua. Mountains and hills. Mount Victoria, which oversees Wellington's ear-like harbour. Kākā and tūī and the odd kererū frequent the air. People come and sit and look out. They say: *This must be kinda healing for you . . .* And true, true. I did get better once while living here, and I walked in those hills and stood by the ocean and saw Tapuae-o-Uenuku sink in the dusk. But the illness came back, as did the words that follow it around, and each one feels inadequate, given a pulse by a narcoleptic logic.

I have a disease, several of my family have the same.

It has many names.

It has many names, because those who'd name it—they don't know where its cause lies, where it starts and how it ends.

Polyonymy—a condition ripe for fear, awe, ignorance and desire.

Polyonymy—the state of the clouds beyond our windows.

So many names for the same thing.

There, I've used that word again, cloud.

They're always parting, showing off what was always there. Hills, mountains and sea. They are beautiful, and I, of course, want more.

My condition isn't going to kill me, at least it's unlikely. Which you've got to be happy about. Despite this my body does at times appear to be in profound trouble, run deep with trackable distortions to all the mechanisms of homeostasis that keep me alive. We can get technical about it. This disease, this myalgic encephalomyelitis, constitutes the manifestation of intensified nervous sensitivity, one which the science tells us is most likely attributable to a neuroinflammatory etiopathology, one that's associated with abnormal nociceptive and neuroimmune activity.* Possibly we're talking autoimmunity, the body's war, its attack against perfectly healthy cells. Or we're not, and we're talking about something different. It's a kind of hell, not knowing: indeed, the underlying pathomechanism of ME is incompletely understood, but studies suggest there is substantial evidence that, in at least a subset of patients, ME/CFS has an autoimmune etiology.

About my disease: the closer I get, the more I peer at the

* In medical parlance, etiopathology refers to the consideration of the cause of an abnormal state or finding. Nociception is the sensory nervous system's process of encoding noxious stimuli.

specifics, the Latin and numbers, the codes for genes, for IDO1 and IDO2, for cytokines, for facts like we burn amino acids instead of sugars and fats, that there's something called the Ocular Motor Project, which peers into the movements of our eyes, that there's a likely neutrophil malfunction that's a response to our completely dysfunctional immune systems—the more of this I spy the more I believe there is a cure. This isn't so. The one thing we know is it's post-viral. As if the body holds on to the ghost of a virus once it has left the system and this system maintains its immune response at 100 percent. It's like a viral imprint stamped in each of our cells. Long COVID appears, in many ways, to be a version of the same disease—but, again, mystery reigns.*

At best I feel there's been a man, someone with a hammer.

Much of the time, the systems that keep me moving are in a state of unwanted war: the mitochondria in my cells aren't functioning correctly and produce dangerously low levels of energy. Why? We don't know exactly, but mitochondrial dysfunction in ME

* Long COVID is now known to the medical community as post-acute sequelae of COVID-19, or PASC. According to Stephani Sutherland in the *Scientific American*, ME 'bears striking resemblances to long COVID, with symptoms such as immune system dysregulation, fatigue and cognitive dysfunction'. It's been stated that the patterns of neurological, nervous and immune system dysregulation seen in PASC patients is such they often meet the criteria for ME. Hence, it is thought that at least mechanistically the two diseases are extremely likely to be related. The damage caused to the brain by rogue monocytes and macrophages point, it seems, to a similar breaching of the blood–brain barrier in both diseases. It's hoped, also, that discoveries found by PASC researchers will eventually reveal an expanded understanding of ME. It's a guilty hope that sits alongside this kind of statement.

patients is substantiated in multiple studies.* Muscle biopsies taken from patients with ME studied by electron microscopy have shown atypical mitochondrial deterioration. Biopsies have also shown severe deletions of genes in mitochondrial DNA. These are genes associated with bioenergy production. Cytokines spread inflammation into areas of body, cerebrum and cerebellum. There's a likely breaching of the blood–brain barrier by immune cells. Events that produce appalling inflammation: thought and action become beyond difficult. My gut doesn't process nutrients as it should; in fact, eating tends to make me feel ill, as it seems an immune response is triggered if I eat the wrong thing. But I don't usually know what the wrong thing is. Having just two meals a day seems to help things settle and ease, though rest isn't a word often used in my life. It never really comes; there's always a state of bodily agitation in play. And then with each advanced occurrence of the illness neatly describable as a neurological event, I find I remember little of its pains in the eventual aftermath.

The bodily conditions that allow for ME are believed to be hereditary, believed to be in the blood and genes. Some suggest a connection between maladaptive perfectionism and

* According to a 2009 study, muscle biopsies taken from patients with ME 'studied by electron microscopy have shown abnormal mitochondrial degeneration. Biopsies have also found severe deletions of genes in mitochondrial DNA, genes that are associated with bioenergy production'. Another such study on ME mitochondria, at La Trobe University, points to problems with a complex (Complex V) in the electron transport chain. Here, stress appears to be causing ATP (adenosine triphosphate, vital in the manufacturing of energy) to dramatically decline its production when the mitochondria are put under duress. Researchers discovered that the mitochondria in ME cells are using amino acids and fatty acids rather than glucose to feed their energy production chain as glucose appears to be being shunted to a different pathway than usual, making it unavailable.

the disease. Perhaps, perhaps. I'm certainly a perfectionist, maladaptive, too—ask anyone I do creative work with. The default state of my nervous system is a type of aggravation, followed by an inability to stop work, followed by shutdown. My body suggests that some kind of unintended demise is the logical progression . . .

Yes.

No.

One cannot be an expert on ME when one has ME. The patterns and complexities are too much to hold in the brain when broken like this. I can understand for a moment, then, like a sparkling new element created in the lab by white-coated physicists, it vanishes.*

Although the disease has killed numerous people around the world, the likelihood of this being the outcome of my own contagion is mercifully low.† I have moderate to, at times, severe ME, which means I usually get out of bed, but rarely leave the house. Though there are months when I don't leave bed. There are also weeks in which I regularly walk the block. Predictability is awkward. Sometimes I'm on oxygen, but I'm not sure why. It's a prolonged state of confusion and pain, incoherence and exhaustion. For those with severe ME, it's far worse. Patients are often completely unable to process nutrients, needing to be fed through a tube. They are bed-bound, sheltered from light

* Indeed, this book cannot be a breakdown and revelation of all the theories, scientific or social, of how we come to be like this. That's another book, which I hope soon gets written. This one's something other.

† On 13 June 2006, a British coroner for the first time attributed a death to ME. Thirty-two-year-old Sophia Mirza died from acute aneuric renal failure, a condition triggered by dehydration as a result of ME. Since then, the fatalities recorded on death certificates as resulting from ME have multiplied. Suicide remains the most common cause of ME deaths.

and sound and unable to look after themselves. Help is basically nonexistent for ME sufferers: while doctors are seemingly more likely to acknowledge the illness, strategies of treatment and care are mordantly absent.

At best, my life senses itself, feels itself as a thousand pieces of fiction. Something not well partnered in its craft. Indeed, it's not a life that feels lyric-full and prone to poetry, but rather amateur, conniving. At best I'm the typographic holes drilled into each sentence, the holes through which we fall again and again into an undescribed abyss. I desire a state, one without others acting as me.

The smallest events in my life feel like miracles, the effervescent triumphs of survival. But survival against *what* is a difficult question to answer. Right now, people are at Stanford employing nanoelectronic assays against blood plasma and immune cells. They're watching, seeing how these cells process stress, how they strain against it, hopeful the resulting differentiation between ME and non-ME cells will provide a viable organic test. They are yet to misidentify (as of writing) a single ME patient. They are examining MRI results, peering inside brains. They seek out neuroinflammation and find it rife. Right now, they are searching blood, scanning gut, analysing stool and gene. They're finding sickness but not cause—other than the circumstantial evidence of random preceding viral infections.

And right now, right now, I'm at my cousin's home in Diamond Harbour, a house settled in the curved crater of an old volcano. There are views to the golden hills and subdued blue harbour. My sister lives nearby and it's nice to visit here. When I flew south from Wellington, left the winter wind to spend time with family, it was a clear day. The mountains. The valleys and drifts of cloud talking.

I'm here, editing my second novel, *Dance Prone.* I don't know how I'm going to move my pen to change *they are* to *they're*, but the pen moves. Reality is the triumph of the smallest things over the near nihility of energy I wake with every day.

I also started writing about my father this morning.

I thought I'd start this book by gabbing about myself, peer inward at the hysterical cycles of pain, and physical and psychological affect. But Henry kept interrupting, saying: *Come have a look, come and see.*

Climb

My father usually started with his grandfather, Harry. Started there and ended up in the mountains, or Singapore. Or he started with his great-great-grandmother, Caroline—born in nineteenth-century Prussia. Kind of fearsome in that highly racist, pioneering way. There are pictures of her coloniser son, Gustav. Great beard and brilliant, handsome eyes, the son of Friedrich Heinrich Albrecht Hohenzollern—the Prussian prince Henry never started with, because in 1985 this parentage was mere rumour and pretty much a joke. But sometimes he did start with Caroline, saying how she was forced into marriage with a chap named Rockel and they came to New Zealand from Potsdam and somehow, too, ended up in the Rangitīkei. All these people. All these families congregated on a farm. Scots, Coventrys, Germans. This small, illegitimate son of a prince. Henry liked to say that this was the crux of how he came to be: physically, humanly.

This made Simon cringe amid the fire smoke. Our father wanted something out of the dead, a communing people of spectral voice. He wanted us all to hear it. And that was how they finished the night, with this sense of an unfinished language, a fragmented prose drifting in through Henry's voice.

From the hut the climb carried them further up the Hodder as it narrowed and bowed into a tight gorge of constricted rock faces and the odd outcrop of hanging fern and thick moss. At dawn they turned south-east to ascend Staircase Stream, a tributary source that began in the snow fields above. Rock cairns marked the route, sending them on up the east terrace of the stream. After two hours their route exited the creek and ascended sadistic crags. They climbed for several hundred metres until they came to a snow field at which they had a choice of routes to take them up onto the mountain's ridgeline. By then the peak was drifting in and out of sight with the clouds coming in from the north. They made tea and discussed which route they felt was best in the conditions. They decided on the saddle between Mount Alarm and Tapuae-o-Uenuku. They slogged, pushed their way for another two hours to the pass, and from there worked their way north around a sub-peak sticking out of the ridge like the last tooth in the gum of the farmer, her mouth and how she still smiled and smoked through it. From there they were able to reach the upper southwest ridge, smeared in a white wick of cumulus.

It was there the temperatures began to fall, rapidly dropping into the negative. They put on their thick jackets and continued climbing as the weather shifted and the north wind suddenly dropped off. A massive fog, a blanketing haze rose up from the seaward side as they sought the summit, a whiteout so each step became a new and vital decision in the snow, a movement caught between instinct and the diminishing reliability of sight and logic. Each step was held in place by crampon and spike, and those slowly became the line between an unplanned descent and survival. They climbed upwards, stepping on the ice until they were metres from the top and the rumoured view and the silencing of the mountain. The idea that they could see all the places from which they'd eyed the peak in the decades preceding, the ridges and inlets and beaches and ferry rides and flights north and south. But everything was whited out, they would see nothing. The idea of it enough to keep them moving through the white before it came, the other thing.

The unseen thing.

The arrival of the south.

A thick fist of it, weather punching up from behind their backs. An Antarctic air twisting out of the invisible south. A blizzard full of frozen white wind, gale force and the three of them on a ridgeline no wider than their boots.

And it hit.

'Come back this way. This way.'

'What?'

'This—'

They screamed at each other, mouths inches from ears. Screamed and turned, trying to find which way was down because down was suddenly the only choice now.

'That's—where's Simon?'

'No, Dad. I'm here. Where's David?'

'David!'

They weren't roped, because it wasn't that kind of day, not that kind of peak, not so technical as to use riggings and pitons, not so difficult at the end of spring to make it necessary to use the apparatus of proper alpinists, which they were—but now the wind, and they were caught.

'That's east, that's east.'

'Which way?'

'Fuck.'

'Where's the ridge?'

But the ridge was invisible, open and untrusted, the heel of the cyclone force in their faces. And the sudden sub-zero, a numbered air, not a breath of which had been predicted when they set out the day before. Not by the farmer, not by a line on the weather map. Henry knew mountains, he knew all kinds of maps. He knew how to navigate the earth and track its weather systems. He could navigate by stars if he had to. He'd climbed Mount Tasman, Cook and the rest. He was the regional coordinator for New Zealand Search and Rescue. Wrote articles for the New Zealand Mountain Safety Council on weather in the mountains. And now the mountain had disappeared into the white, and all means of direction were being sucked out of the air by the wind and the violent and furious fog.

They were crawling, the buffer and hit and those twins' insistent desire to rip them from the ridge and throw them into the valleys below. They couldn't see, they couldn't move forward or back, until they had no choice but to make guesses and make sure they were good guesses. Simon followed Henry, and Henry in his red jacket followed David, walking at intervals of seven, eight metres. Simon could see his father, could make out the outline of David and the faint edge of the ridgeline. They walked hunched, making themselves into diminished, lapsed creatures.

They continued on through snow-filled air, through space and non-space. They slipped. David slipped. He went off the edge, falling five feet before digging in his ice axe and pulling himself up onto the ridge.

Simon shouted to his father, screamed, told him to stop. Henry didn't hear anything, didn't see anything, not what happened to David, not the faint disparity in the white between the snow's edge and the white of the air. He stepped forward, a foot out into the invisible sky and his body, it followed.

He fell, stepped and fell. A man suddenly airborne. Arms and shouts flailing at all direction, all directions at once, north and east and up and sideways, this man flinging his ice axe, unable to collect it in the rushing surface, the invisible surface. He fell and fell into the white so direction became seconds and seconds became west and left and right and time. Instant and event colliding with time, failing time, time failing at being time. The rapidity of descent, throwing his ice axe at the vertical ice sheet. Throwing the handle of the thing over and over at the surface to arrest this fall, to put an end to the calamity, the coming of calamity. But on and on. His crampons caught in the ice, twisting his legs and flinging him this way, then on his front, then back. He fell, plummeted dozens of feet, hundreds and then more. On, downwards, and his ankles were snapped in his boots and at some point he became unconscious as his head caught rocks.

Time.

Unseen, unpractised time.

Awake, then the other. Undreaming, in black. A void where language had been banished.

Snow settled on his body. His limbs, legs and back slowly lost dimension. Snow filled in the gaps of limbs and torso and made a mound of him, indistinguishable from nothing.

He came to. His body in a valley, hundreds of metres from the voices up on the ridgeline, from the shouting near the summit where Simon and David stood in the utter, sunless and sudden winter. The two of them stunned into stillness, how he vanished in the white, stunned by the sudden eradication of coherence, understanding and direction, by the sight of their hands disappearing in front of their faces, by the fact of the ridgeline, by the fact there was only one possible safe step and its location was unknowable. They were frozen by the sudden stillness of time, frozen by the knowledge of what they had to do next as their own bodies started to shut down.

Half a kilometre away, Henry made to stand and fell.

He stood again. He waited. He stood and fell, grunting. Used his ice axe to dig in and pull him along, dragging himself inch by inch. And as he made short progress, Simon and David made plans that slowly verged on the coldblooded. Plans of rescue and survival. Simon was twenty-one, David twenty-seven. They knew mountains, they knew endurance, survival techniques and the necessity of good decisions. They'd been in mountains for most of their remembering lives, decades of walking in the alpine, days of food rationing, hours of surviving violent cold.

Henry, a veteran of hill and climb and rescue, knew the same. He was retired by the time he fell, was keen to spend his years in the mountains or at home reading and writing. He occasionally appeared on the six o'clock news, bearded and standing beside an Iroquois, saying serious things about the dangers of alpine environments.

Now he walked and fell, and walked and fell, stumbling on rocks as a hardening pain shot up his legs and the messages from his brain told the muscles there to stop and rest. And they did, but he stood again as Simon and David shouted down into the white. The wind took their voices and made them snow and whisper and Henry slid himself along the ground between outcrops of rock and sarsen until he came to a terrace of boulders, a field slowly becoming white with snow fall. He stood then, and believed he'd found his bearings. He believed he knew which valley he'd fallen into. He managed to navigate himself downwards out of the cloud as Simon and David used ice axe and crampons to back-point their way off the cliff, hoping to find Henry at its terminus, though they didn't know where this terminus was. They descended for ten minutes in the blind storm, kicking in steps with their spikes, holding on by the toe of their boots. One ice axe each on the vertical.

It was terrifying and necessary.

The ice could stop and become rock face. The ice could fall away with the spring melt. The incline could continue, then sheer away vertically, could invert and leave them hanging in the air, desperate for handholds, no hope of traction. They too could fall. They too might become equalised by the twist of limbs, by punctured muscle and organ. They inched and kicked downwards, and soon the cliff began to flatten, gradually evened out so they could get in some footholds and rest against the slope. There was fresh snow on crumbling winter ice. They slipped and regained control. Slowly they descended, and the shoot eased out into a valley two hundred metres down from the ridge. A high alpine valley, full of compacted snow and fresh powder. Henry was nowhere, his momentum had taken him on, beyond where they could see.

Simon and David felt their systems slowly shutting down, a loss of sensation as the blizzard grew and raged around them, their concentration slipping and breaking and each of their movements were slowed. They knew they needed time.

They knew they would have to abandon Henry.

They needed to make time in order to mount a proper rescue. To stay in the storm would have, in weighed probability, meant death without proper shelter, clothing and food and protection against the onslaught. And perhaps Simon's father might survive as they collected themselves, perhaps he might die.

They re-climbed the cliff in the furious wind.

The Valley

Six months before my father fell, I was healthy. We lived in Lower Hutt. A valley city shaped by the river draining the south slopes of the Tararua. It was flat, a railway line ran its length. I lived on the line's west side in Woburn, affably well-heeled. It was suburbs, just suburbs and no hint of a real city. Which made it all lonely, in some way. Being the youngest of five meant nobody seemed too concerned what I got up to. I played sport and my other sport was drinking. Weekends had excessive, violent parties in the hills (where, as children, we'd played war amongst the podocarps: partisans and platoons in strange running battles). Parties of gang affiliates and gentle school kids mingling in kitchens. Torn-off doors the marker of a fine event. Standoffs on lawns. It was oddly calming for this outsider, an observer of the great lunacies of youth. Because that was who I seemed to be at that time, an interloper with simple disguises.

School passed by without tremendous effort; I had friends of various sorts. I was fifteen and had already spent a season in the school's First XI and was in my first year of playing for the First XV. I enjoyed sport, rugby and cricket. I was useful at both, played with and against future Wellington representatives and the odd imminent All Black or Black Cap. I was eager, abrasive; I enjoyed my body being hit and my body hitting. I loved the art of evasion; I was quick.

In fact, the thing I was best at was being quick.

I had speed, just a natural event in amongst my genes. I was the swiftest, by whatever measure I can recall, in the school by fourteen. At fifteen, one of the fastest in the country for my age. I won races in bare feet with no spikes or training. I was fast and always had been, and probably would be still if I lost enough weight and regrew the correct muscles. Speed was something I couldn't help. I didn't try; I just was.

A sensation of illusion, a sleight of limb conjuring speed.

I never tried particularly at any sport but was good at a number of them. This combination of not having to exert effort but excelling because of a trick of DNA became a problem for me when, on returning from a quadrangular rugby tournament in Dannevirke, I became sick and spent several months out of school with a somewhat severe stretch of glandular fever, caused by the Epstein-Barr virus. I suspect it was then the disguise diminished to nothing but skin and air.

The illness came after I played my last game of the season at fullback. It was hailing on Strand Park, where we played next to the river, and when not hailing, raining a cruelly cold, slanting south downpour. It came in at oblique angles, as if trying to get past my skin. I left the after-match after half a beer and went home. My parents and siblings were all away for the night.

That half-beer was the last alcoholic drink I was to have for four years.

I sat in the lounge on a chair nobody in our family ever sat on, my wet rugby gear under my dress uniform. When my mother and father returned the following morning from a church retreat in Palmerston North, they found me shivering in the same spot. I'd watched dawn reach mesmerically through the trees, the front yard expanded into an unrecognisable haze of greens and thrashing arms as the storm continued to harass the valley. My mouth open, like a split sky moving air from one pressure system to the void of another. Limbs had forgotten their purpose and I was shifted by my mother and father to my room. I slept with dried-out mud on my shins.

By then life was altered, explicitly.

I learnt about depression, I learnt about the sheer weight of tiredness and what it does to the mind. Both have stayed with me throughout life; I have never known how to describe either disorder. In these states the noetic centres are no longer capable of the kind of abstraction needed to adequately define the pain. And then, once it is over and things blur back into a brief period of normality, who—for godsakes—wants to return there?

I think of my father.

I spent weeks in the same spot staring out the window. Trees and lawn. Days and helical hours spinning, indifferent to the lives of my family and any to whom I had connection. I learnt about the unchangeability of time. Then I learnt how it changes constantly. I have a sense that time, that it morphed the parts of me that once operated easily in the world into something other and ghostly strange. The word I'm looking for is the *interchangeability* of time, of the measures by which its passage went by me and how they were multiple. Time moved in relation to thought and non-thought; to people, to the spectral remains of the people who came to visit with cake and rumours from school cliques and coming changes to relationships and friends.

And the people inside these measures, how odd they seemed.

It would be true to say family and all associates seemed altered; I didn't understand what any were talking about when they talked about the lives that were occurring around them. As quickly as my friendships changed and fell away, my relationship to my body was stripped of its core understandings of itself. I lost twenty kilograms in five weeks. I no longer felt fast. The celerity had gone from my legs; all the agility of concentration, the processes of deduction, these had vanished. I started looking for other kinds of analysis that might give me comfort. Thoughts were replaced by grand summations, teenage exegeses that wanted to explain the world in its entirety. I stared out the windows into the trees and lawn and had the kind of diverging complex thoughts I wasn't yet able to comprehend. It all made me distant, and arrogant with it.

I walked to the letterbox to fetch the paper and felt a slowness that was part robbery and part new reality of time.

Months began to pass quickly; in fact, they didn't seem months anymore but nervous versions of weeks that mattered in ways school couldn't possibly matter by the time I returned. The whole episode feels, in retrospect, as if I'd joined an odd cult of one. Just me, and I had to find a way beyond my body, my body and my old mind.

The simple grades I never had to try for, that had been so easily accessible in the preceding years, these were suddenly unavailable to me. My old bicameral world no longer seemed on offer.

It took thirty years for me to feel I was good at something again, instinctually. Though by then both my mind and body were far worse off than they were in those bare months, those long staring months. I managed to find a way. I do it now through an understanding that time is different for me.

The school, Hutt Valley High, was set beside the sudden bend of the Hutt River as it crossed over the alluvial plain on Wellington Harbour's northern side. The halls, prefabs and buildings sprawled over silt-strewn acres. The sorcery of the magpies who nested in the pines beside the levee sealing off the river from school. Rugby fields, the cricket pitch we rolled dutifully at lunchtime in the summer, these held the young version of me in a specific place. Nothing other than that and a clutch of friends holds much fondness. When gazing back at that self of mine, the one before the Epstein-Barr virus, I see a soul lit oddly by a gentle, easy-going kind of nothingness. A distant but vaguely popular kid who didn't involve himself in school, class or the logic forms we were supposed to learn. I recall classes, but no engagement in the pronouncements, methods and outcomes. I never once did homework, or recall it being assigned.

It's a strange thing: I thought school an overly simple place, that I knew all that was taught already and to gain access to it all I had to do was think, make the right combinations of thoughts and I would know. Just, like: *Hold on—I'll know the answer if I want to know the answer.* And often I did, often enough. Math was fun; I taught myself mechanisms to calculate numbers but never showed my workings because the workings occurred in my head and only partly on paper. Numbers held here, shifted there. I didn't know about π, but at ten I came up with a number similar to the ratio on a day bored by the show of the teacher, and had fun with my discovery. I learnt a few years later it was all a little bit more complicated; everything was.

The only class that completely baffled me was English. I didn't understand anything they were saying. The classes held daily in the new block, a Seventies modernism, a series of mildly brutalist classrooms. A teacher reading and I couldn't follow. A student reading and I couldn't follow. I couldn't blame the texts; I couldn't blame the architecture. Indeed, years later modernism was all I was interested in.

I believed I knew things, unseen things. I believed that knowing was the simple exiting of data, as if all data was already in our minds. The truth was I just couldn't catch a thought. The truth being my mind was, and is, a constant rush of links to unlinked things, of patterns showering un-patterned things. I was forty-five when I learnt I have Attention Deficit Disorder. Nobody noticed something was amiss, and I only notice it in retrospect. I left school once classes became harder than the intuition I was lucky enough to own could take me. Plus, I got a D minus in my sixth-form creative writing project, which confirmed for me—I believed at the time—that I knew something my teachers didn't. I was both arrogant and ignorant of what made me that way. I left and hunted out the meaning of punk rock, which presented itself to me around the age of seventeen or eighteen as a healing music, a form of physical, assaulting balm after the hurt of the illness and my discovered sense of aloneness.

But that was never enough: I had to find a way to write. I had to find a way with words I didn't have access to. I had to find a way to write books, and this book in particular, when twenty-eight years later—as is often the case with ME sufferers—glandular fever seemed to return. This is by no means unusual. ME has long been known to follow glandular fever and other systemic infections, even decades later.* I still need to find a

* Just as I'm finishing this book, a team at Northwestern University have published research that reveals differences in multiple metabolites and metabolic pathways in those who recover from infectious mononucleosis and those who do not. During their longitudinal study, they collected data from participating students before illness, during infectious mononucleosis, and then at six months after infection. By examining pre-illness blood samples, they found significant detectable metabolite variances between participants who went on to develop severe ME versus the recovered controls. They identified nucleotide metabolism,

way to write because it's illusive, not there: the ME mind is a mind that can't know itself. Nor, I realise, is a mind constricted by ADD.*

Sometimes it feels like my body, my mind and self have been lying to me for ten years as they try to correct themselves. As such it feels like a fictive blur of competing realities. This book—just quietly as I leave my dad alone on the mountain for a time—is my response to those lies. It's another country, my body. My mind another world. Often it seems a part of both are at war with an internal me of equal size and wit, a me not recognised by those distant lands. They're also embattled with an external David equally at war with the world of logic. I have one instruction from myself, then, that this book had better be strange, that it be shaped like my mind, like my body.

Flight, One

I think I'll tell you about being out in the world; lying in bed describes nothing but stasis. The articulations of which don't make me feel terribly human (and why write if not to feel human?). Laura and I had the walls insulated and painted recently, but it hasn't changed the fact that they are walls, and

---

glutathione metabolism, and the TCA cycle as dysregulated pathways. These are pathways vital for proliferating cells, especially during a pro-inflammatory immune response.

* I have always been overcome with complexity: my world view is one that battles with and against this. It is, I suspect, the intellectual discharge of (unknowingly) having ADD. Indeed, my works of fiction thus far have each sought out a kind of complexity that desires to project knowability of all utterances and their relationships to all others within the given text. My art project might be regarded as one partially programmed out of illness; might be described as discourses of disease.

walls grow tired of being looked at all day long. They grow restless and move; spread false rumours as they talk. Which is a judgement I put on them; I don't really know what they say. Though I suspect they're saying there are great gaps in things. Gaps in the myths and narratives against which we judge our existence. Wide open spaces, pages where nobody can tell you what to think.

For a period that stretched over four years it became necessary that I fly once or twice a year from New Zealand to the northern hemisphere. I'd make sure at each airport there was a wheelchair in case I'd arrive and find myself unable to walk. I'd also make sure my flight touched down at dawn so my final destination arrived with the sun. I'd drug myself with sleeping pills in the ten hours before, and sleep until landing.

All to trick the light.

So, Dublin. So, Edinburgh. So, Toronto, New York, Austria and Italy.

I've made the decision to include in this telling the multiple episodes of travel I was asked to undertake, the jaunts and flights, legs and stopovers. I went to these places as an author, a person who doesn't exist other than as a function, an imagined soul rearing out of texts. A person not sick but something else, another kind of societal illness. I include these episodes because they seem another world, twilit and impossible to describe. This impossibility seems a way to explicate the state I exist within, open to the inherent tendency of language to destabilise and deform what we seek to know. The bus, the train. Flight. They seem big too, though unremarkable by normal standards. The alert sense that if something were to happen in these moments I'd fall and fall forever. These sensations and events seem queerly linked to living. There, time passes, and countries come and go.

I write these because it is far a more interesting exercise than describing my life on the couch, or in bed. Which, no doubt, I'll get to. And I over-write, over-write everything just to keep my head in the game. Minimalism has me sense that there's nothing on the page. Indeed, I don't read anymore, just sense.

So, writing now, I land and think about my father falling from that cliff. My brother and David, imagining time stretched out in front of them and how they had to spend it in order to live.

Red

So, as it was, I arrived in Ireland, somewhat bruised from sleeping pills. During the flight I imagined the lines on a map, a huge map formed by allegiance to the Winkel Tripel projection, each line curving and bending until something snapped and some part of myself was flung forward into another reality. The body of the earth shaking, vibrating until these frequencies were in my hands and in my arms, in my legs, torso and the infinitesimal operations of my head where synapses speak and then, then seem to forget their own language and don't speak. There's sleep, but it's not really sleep, and awaking from this sleep is a sickness all of its own and standing there in Dublin Airport I saw a woman with a sign saying my name and I felt as thin as the paper it was written on, as light as the ink.

I waved, imagining she'd recognise something in me. She only bent her face in a grin and walked us hurriedly to the van through the throngs like shifting cells, blood cells and immune and the rest. I was just another writer a little sick on touchdown, a little twisted and distorted by the act of arrival. This was ten months before the pandemic entered our bloodstreams, and as if in preparation I saw a large family boarding a bus in masks. I thought: Yes, I might try that later.

I was driven in the pale hours west from Dublin on the M6 to Galway on the Atlantic coast. I was driven by the same woman happy to point out the visual lack of this specific piece of road. She was near my age, had a plain, mardy face like mine. She pointed to gorse tufts, the wilding spurts of green and yellow weed. Stone walls and the odd dented castle amongst the cellular patterning of field and fence.

She asked how my flight was. I said it was as good as could be expected. She laughed, told me she liked flying, that she made the journey to Boston every few years to see her father. She enjoyed it, she explained, but preferred the idea of flight a great deal more than the act itself. She said she wished the whole occasion was somewhat more dramatic.

I told her I agreed.

'They should leave the windows open,' she said, her face as animated as a flat tyre. 'Issue Arctic-proof sleeping bags—only the strong and willing survive.' She gave off a sigh as she overtook a sheep truck, honking as we went by as if it were a loved one at the wheel. 'It should be grand. Instead, I let myself be distracted by all the small events,' she said. 'Like the tiny food. The little screens. I find myself drinking ginger ale.'

I told her my response to all the effort put into making us relaxed was to listen to intense music. Hardcore. Original black metal. Extreme noise. The more life-threatening the music, the happier I am. Punk, post-punk, hardcore. The Fall, Minor Threat, Siege.

She smiled finally. 'This is flying after all,' she said. 'It should be intense, beyond intense.'

‘They should drug us,’ I said.

‘Yes. We trust pilots more than surgeons. Which is for certain insane.’

I laughed.

‘It’s intolerable to me,’ she said.

I said I’d had the thought that on landing we should all be asked what we’d learnt. We should be asked what’d been altered in us.

She took a hand from the wheel and shrugged. ‘Sure, to be honest. Flying, it should be a cure for diseases and pain, should be a source of all-encompassing immunity.’ She laughed. ‘But it’s mostly the opposite.’

‘True enough,’ I said.

‘You land on the other side of the world and you have the most miserable cold.’

The tension in her seemed to relieve as we hit the outskirts of Galway, and in the interior of the bay she dropped me off. Then she began the drive back across the island.

Once in my hotel room I lay in my bed, let the well of travel and time take me until the whole event of half-sleep was interrupted by hammers and saws in another part of the hotel and I went out walking. Up through the park opposite my window and north then west towards the great cathedral parked on Nun’s Island in the middle of divergent black streams of River Corrib. There the city’s dark river forced its way down through to the bay, dragging with it forgotten water and all the wastes of chronology and epoch. Trees leant in, boughs bent in bows towards the flow, listening closely to its various watery secrets as the houses on its edge closed their curtains to it all. I fell for this river. Immediately sensed a living tempo in its thick stream and parallel canals heading to the Atlantic Ocean. It all ran as if in multiple versions of the same thought boring out of the centre of the island. I crossed its bridges many times just so I could watch the dark waterway. It was relentless amongst the houses and churches and the way it thundered on. The sense of enforced determination, a consciousness determined by unseen forces far within the island. I had the feeling I could know something about the people of the county just by staring at the water. History and its viscous distress. This sensation sat seasick in my stomach. I believe we tend to protect ourselves in new places by hunting down easily earned erudition, conglomerated data posing as narratives of space. This emphasis on simple knowledge, I recognised, was tricking parts of me into the false science of privileged speculation. And I let it.

Later that week Alan McMonagle, who I knew through my publisher, sent a photo of the massive airborne *Skywhale*, a many-breasted cetacean designed by the Australian artist Patricia Piccinini. Here it was seen frightening the ocean-going swans from this same thick river on the occasion of the Galway International Arts Festival. But before that, I slept in the cathedral, the stony edifice that wanted to be from the fourteenth century but was in fact commissioned in 1958, on a patch of land separated by the coursing and convergence of the Corrib. I'd drifted and slept there, and then, suddenly awake, I was surrounded by a congregation in prayer. The clergyman at the front cloaked and whispering the secret thoughts of God.

The following day I awoke concussed. A twin of me, the David who feels knocked out of my body, kicked sideways by the hammer of the disease and always present, sat on the bed beside me and breathed strange-sounding air. We didn't move until I was beyond hungry. He'd been there since I'd had a heart attack in early 2017, six months after I returned from my time in

Edinburgh, Austria and North Africa. The illness had returned with it. I'd had a slight remission from ME two years before the heart attack and if my twin had been there prior to the event I don't recall.

After breakfast I found myself back in my room. I had convulsions, I lay on my bed and let them come. They start small, usually in my hands, then my head. My father had, for many years before his death, quite prominent shakes. Slow, long agitations that made the sight of him reading the newspaper quite comical. The whole of the broadsheet would quake, as if the news within had a second physical manifestation. He once reported to his doctor for other reasons and the physician, on noticing my father's affliction, said that he could fix it with the right drugs. My father, being my father and not wanting to be a bother to anyone, said, 'Oh, no. It's quite okay.' Often when I shake, I think of Henry, that he'd passed something on to me, that neural affect that his doctor knew how to fix. And this might be true, but these shakes are not related to him. They come from my mother's flank of the family. I know this because several on her side have this same illness.

On this occasion I let them run through me.

They reached my head so it jarred back and forth and I played the game I often do where I hold my attention on my arm and stop it from shaking and watch as another part of me starts up. It's a result of the nervous system going into overdrive after exertion, and exertion can be as little as talking on the phone or walking to breakfast in the basement of the hotel. Those of us with ME get to a state of extreme muscle fatigue quickly and painfully. It's the result of a lack of energy at a cellular level. Cells require energy to do their work; the mitochondria therein are not able to produce enough of it for our needs. So, we get the symptoms of overexertion after very little effort. Imagine the muscles of a marathon runner at the end of a race that took them beyond what they are capable of, the manner in which their body has used up all available energy and how it goes into shock. Their bodies shaking as if electrons agitated, trying to correct something invisible to eyes.

That's us.

During physical activity, our central nervous system fires signals to contract our muscles. These signals are made by 'motor units' and such a unit consists of a single motor neuron and all the extrafusal muscle fibres it innervates. The firing of motor units delivers energy to your muscles. The longer these muscles are in use, the quicker these signals slow down and lose intensity. At this stage our muscles rapidly alternate between contractions and relaxations, resulting in tremors. Here we lose our ability to use our muscles and that was what I did, let my body be overcome until it was all done and I was able to sit up and watch TV on my laptop. The aftermath is a head full of fluid, or at least that is how it feels.

The cranium awash with a viscous brine.

Indeed, scientists have observed disturbed muscle membrane function in ME patients, even with their motor units involved in low-force generation, such as slowly walking or reading or speaking. They suggest central neural deregulation may contribute to this disturbance.

I'd read about the autopsies of several patients who either died of ME or with the disease. It was found that each of these women (for they were all women) had ganglionitis, meaning inflammation of the ganglia, the incurious concierge to sensations in the brain. This inflammation causes unconquerable pain in the sufferer. I'm lucky—as far as I know the swelling hasn't reached this part of my brain; perhaps it won't. The pain I have is a pain like all nerves have been removed, there is no body, only a void, and a strange, ranging hurt rushes to fill this cavity. Like all the walls of all the tunnels where information flows have turned red and red is the colour now, red is the colour of inflammation. My eyes close and a borderless ache takes the place of organic structure.

Neurologists have speculated that ME sufferers have an immune-triggered metabolic disorder. They've suggested that widespread neuroinflammation provides indications to what's going on. The patterning of inflammation seen in MRIs of ME patients' brains suggests that immune cells are breaching the blood–brain barrier, and doing it in multiple areas, a flood overwhelming a dam pouring through gaps across the brain. Studies also suggest that the high choline signal present in the interior cingulate cortex points to patterns of destruction and replacement, that neuronal damage is likely occurring.

When my cousin and I speak, it's a language of cracked thoughts and desperate trust.

Stone

Quietly stoned on tramadol and codeine, I put on my jacket with the little brooch on its pocket and did a session with Alan that Friday evening in the recently redecorated old town hall.* I spoke about the process of writing a novel, how it is all about making the text remember itself. Recall itself without the writer's constant intervention and once that is done, you're allowed to let it go because at that point it has a consciousness of its own. I explained to the small attendance that a book

* In fact, if I'm talking to you, talking in person, on the street, talking on the radio, on stage, in a magazine—I'm very likely a little bit stoned, sorry. I don't even like drugs.

doesn't need a plot—just a mind, a memory and life.

It's impossible to know how much one can believe of the things I say in these circumstances. They come out in a rush, a deluge I seem to have no control over.

FAST! FASTER!

Despite this I had an overwhelming urge to say in front of the audience: *There's a version of myself, just a small one. Can you see him? He's beside me, trying to remember too.*

But I didn't.

Afterwards I walked as much of the city as I could before returning to the hotel. The traditional roaming of fractured streets and a continual stream of tourist, student and local. Old stone, cafés and the promise of perfection in one of the many bars that lined the streets. Then, after doing a talk in a library situated in a medieval church on the outskirts of a small inland town overtaken by a funeral, I visited Thoor Ballylee. A cold, hard thing in the countryside, five hundred years old and remembered by the culture for the seven stark years Yeats and his family lived amongst its exhausted stone. It sat beside the Streamstown River, which was, I was told, prone to flooding in the winter leaving behind bodies of water on the countryside. I imagined these distinctly as shiny puddles of winding water, spiralling in gentle vortices into the substrate below, pools of time slowly leaching into the vast farmland.

I took photos, the odd compulsion to record the old and failing. I posed beside the building, a series of pictures taken by my driver which, peculiarly, I recalled as a conversation I'd had with an old friend several months earlier at our house in

Wellington. We were talking of ruins and how casually they seem discarded by time and traded empires. We were talking of Rome and Greece and all the rest. Our friend Kristen made the observation that we too lived amongst ruins. In Wellington's hills were the fragments of forest left from the time before Europeans, before axe and fire and gorse and pine and suburb. The culture of replacement was deep in our own land. The fragments of a language left from before colonisation, the stands of trees. Our friend could trace her ancestry back to the great warring rangatira, Te Rauparaha. We'd had lunch and talked, then the three of us watched *I Was at Home, But . . .*, a movie in which time seemed to have no place, only action. We were momentarily overcome by a sense of ubiety inverted as the actors' names appeared on the screen and the credits filled in the spaces left by the cameras. Afterwards we talked some more because we weren't done. We talked about how just one name in our past can prejudice the whole telling of ourselves. I too had a celebrated killer in my family history, and we spoke about how strange it is we use blood to describe our family, as if the same water flows in the same river for centuries, but we know this is untrue. It has long vanished into other parts of the earth, the atmosphere, the sea and all the bodies we lug with us.

Back at the hotel I met Sinéad Gleeson in the foyer, I met Joshua Cohen. They seemed famous, though I was yet to know who they were. Then I had two days, forty hours of which I devoted to the large, soft bed where the pain divided the seas of me, the waking ocean and the sleeping submarine flows.

It's impossible to describe the pain, the weight of it in my head. How each thought since the start has become physical, a variant strain against my cranium. For so long people in white coats didn't believe in the biological existence of this pain. That they couldn't see its locus meant it was psychosomatic; then, in a different line of reasoning, that it was depression.

Let me tell you. Lemme tell you something.

I own an abysmal, life-threatening depression. The lying-in-bed-groaning kind, the kind that has put me in hospital, the kind, the type of misery, the hell in the face sort, the kind that has you trying to cut it out. Remove the source, and source not being life but living within life.

And sure, the appalling pains of both ME and depression are analogous, but also quite dissimilar. With depression it is the fact that each thought hurts in a way that portends great doom, that every simple contemplation is an agony that bars happiness. The sense that thinking itself is going to kill you, and in all truth you can't escape living without thinking.* Happiness is unworkable. With ME, thought too is torture, a deep pain like it has been planned in a lab and injected through your temple, a cruel experimental dose to each lobe, cortex and join. But the hurt is different: I can be quite happy and laughing and amused by it all while in utter, stupefying, unlocatable pain. Blind even—and laughing. Unable to speak but writing a bad joke on my phone to Laura. Their differences are marked as this: one of these ailments is beyond sadness, the other beyond the body—though, seemingly, right at its centre.

The overlap between depression and ME is stark and present,

* During New Zealand's first lockdown I became so dangerously depressed I was delirious. Some parts of myself I thought were dead, others so rotten that I was despised, so infected with hatred that my entire history was one of abject human failure. Everything I'd done in my life, in relationships and art, I deserved to die for. Not much fun. My psychiatrist put me on Pregabalin, and those red and white pills have helped immensely where SSRIs have failed and failed badly (in fact they made me a much worse human being. I lost my thirties to their dire effects. Don't meet me in my thirties; I wasn't myself).

but it is now understood that the co-occurrence of these maladies is explained by overlying abnormalities in oxidative, inflammatory and nitrosative pathways within the brain. They are well understood to be different illnesses. One is allowed to have two diseases. Luckily, I live with this in an age where, from my experience, medical practitioners have, for the most part, been turned around. A time and space in which the old, appalling, hackneyed, condescending fuckery of the medical establishment is no longer the dominant response to the illness (though, believe me, this cock-headed idiocy still exists).* It is not depression; ME is its own illness. But, still, nobody can tell me where the precise root of this pain sits. I can't describe it and at times I feel like I can't because no pathology has been offered. No nouns to situate myself and the disease within, no nouns to apply verb and adjective against treatment.

Most of those hours in that great bed sitting central in the hotel room looking out over the famed Eyre Square where

* Every day I read something appalling that's happening to an ME sufferer somewhere in the world, a situation which shows medical inequity is still rampant when it comes to providing adequate diagnostic and therapeutic healthcare to women and men in far worse condition than myself. People are suffering, some are dying. I also read daily about the dreadful state of funding inequality. The much heralded Ronald W. Davis, professor of biochemistry and genetics at Stanford in California and now at the forefront of ME research, has received hundreds of millions in research dollars for his extraordinary work in genetics. Since his decision to focus solely on ME, his funding has collapsed to the hundreds of thousands. One of his requests for funding from the National Institute of Health was rejected by an initial reviewer because the person believed ME to be merely depression. One can only imagine the ignorant soul was so prejudiced by antiquated psychiatric science he couldn't see the presence of contemporary science's advances. For a time, Professor Davis was likely receiving more NIH funding for his lab's genetic work than the institution was providing for the entirety of ME research in the United States.

students gathered and laughed and knew—these hours were spent in the worst condition, a combined state of both heavy depression and full-blown ME inflammation. And I can't describe it because such a dose clears the memory, wipes at it as if a window blackened in soot and behind it a view of nothing, of chromatic annihilation.

On the last night in Galway, I spent some hours in a bar with Alan, reading and hearing others' stories, jokes and songs. It was a basement bar lit in voluminous light. I drank water as wine was poured and I was offered pints of beer, which, as I have for the last fourteen years, I declined. There was a comic and a collection of musicians, a woman from New York who'd asked a question during my session, the content of which we discussed again. There were other writers who seemed to know one another. I stayed quiet, expecting to leave for the hotel at any moment, to taxi or walk, but conversations came and went like the buses near the square busy with tourists, eager and quickly moved on by other sights and schedules. To get through the night I'd taken my usual thirty milligrams of codeine and some other lesser painkillers. The pills don't so much give me energy as seemingly protect me from breakdown. They seem to have the effect of delaying the effects of exertion, of reducing the uncertain bodily drive that causes the inflammation in various sectors of my brain, as a result making thought a little less difficult. They gift a cognitive flow I neither trust nor rely on but without it the nervous system can at times break down and the agitation I described earlier in my head and hands can become a sight disturbing to some. I was, as a result, fairly intoxicated on opiates, blurred and soon talking in forking lines. So much so that in each discussion, each time my nervousness began to manifest and I felt the urge to leave, I resorted to the

Corrib River as if an unavoidable and permanent topic. The Corrib either came at my prodding or via the natural course of conversations that occur between locals and visitors to towns slung by legend and geographical fascination. We tend to resort to myths, a friend told me earlier in the year, because it's simpler than finding out new things based on facts. 'That takes work,' she'd said. I don't know if this is true. I prefer to think myth is a gift.

There was a piano in the corner. A mic at the front and a crowd of seated listeners.

A Welsh poet, whose name I seem to have lost, recited a piece she had written in the last weeks, a seven-line poem about her visit to Berlin and the Denkmal für die ermordeten Juden Europas a few months earlier. She introduced it by saying there was a comma after the fourth line. She held up the pages and pointed before going silent and reading the words, slow and measured.

The weather doesn't reach here
Only lines measured in light
We remember from the
Places we haven't been,
Except to record the songs
Of memories
Of intolerable intolerable intolerable intolerable intolerable intolerable intolerable intolerable intolerable intolerable intolerable . . .

The room was warm and improvised on the premise that all were here to entertain and be entertained. But here the poet said the word, said *intolerable* for what seemed like forty minutes but were in fact seven. Hammering it until it became a blur, its syllables slipping till indistinguishable, rhythms appearing and disappearing. At times other words appeared, haunting phrases and utterances, but a part of you knew she was only saying this single term of protest. She'd practised this, made it a part of her everyday, a human tape-loop system. She repeated the word until it was as if there were two of her. Then three on stage. I imagined her in front of a mirror watching her mouth, practising its movements. It was beautiful and terrifying.

She finished; a mute silence then applause.

A musician came up on stage.

'I've been here for two decades,' Lorcan Fardel, a friend of Alan's, told me over the top of the compère, 'and this is traditional. Or, you know. What I've come to understand and believe as traditional.'

I asked him how long it had been going on.

'Ah, I think maybe since before any of us were born. It's a funny place. People in the bars and drinking and talking saying here, mark my blood in river and words. That's what some say, but that's just nonsense. I'm a phlebotomist; I know these things.'

He seemed to be shouting, or saying nothing at all. Really he was just moving his mouth and tongue and air was coming out, even and spare.

And I found myself shouting my responses, but it wasn't necessary. It was just the inner workings of my brain, confused amidst stimuli.

Lorcan had a swath of thinning, grey hair and a fervent fascination with classical civilisation. He described his hunger for things Roman and Greek, spitting out vowels and odd arrangements of consonants. He even showed me a small vial of sand he collected from a sandless beach on Lipari, one of the supposed sites of Odysseus's dance around the Mediterranean. He had a dull pallor drawn downwards by baggy eyes. I asked him how he'd ended up living in Galway.

'My father was a doctor,' he told me. 'A well-known and popular man, nice Welsh accent. I was a good student. I liked my classes and worked hard to battle away at the issues that made my lesser topics stand out. I trained myself to learn subjects absent from the classroom rubric. My father and I were an effective team. He loved watching my sisters and I become the people we were becoming; he and my mother doted in ways that might seem unusual to other families, but it was a loving home, both academic and fun. But then at fifteen I became ill, and a peculiar tension came over our relationship. My father was used to illness; it was his life as such. But when my own illness went on for months without improvement, he became frustrated, not with the knowability of the sickness, but with my inability to beat it. It took him years to admit this to me: that he expected that I would remain the same person as the viral infection ran its way through me. I failed school early the next year and left for good when it became clear to me I could no longer cope with classes. I was so far behind I couldn't find a way to teach myself the intricacies needed to make headway. I was also no longer interested and had begun playing the guitar. I liked the mystery of it, but it took me so long to leave the village. I'd visited Galway many times and frankly I was afraid of the place. It's a student town and I was afraid of what everyone knew. I was also afraid I wasn't good enough, not a good enough musician. Not smart enough. You know, just the ruins of me came here. The smart part was left back in my damp old bedroom. But I moved and found I wasn't a musician at all, I was an actor. I was as decent as most and here I am.'

I asked what he'd been in.

'Two TV series. Plays and a minor role in a film. Just local, you know.'

I congratulated him. It's such a thing to be on a stage, on a screen, I said.

He thanked me, said, 'You know what I've learnt? I've learnt that as an actor I don't present facts, instead I present *truths*.' He made a couple of air quotes. 'And it's best, you know, best, to put inverted commas around that word, because you never know when someone will mistake truth for fact.'

Or, I said, knowledge for fact.

He bounced his head in agreement.

I told him I'd visited his hometown a few days before. He seemed to know this and nodded and I wanted to tell him about Thoor Ballylee but instead found myself telling him about my fascination with the river. How thick its water, how unrelenting it was.

'And it changes every day,' he said. 'It has silent moods. Stay here a year and you will learn you know nothing about it. That's why they call it blood and that nonsense, essentially.'

I laughed.

He laughed.

I told him I thought that this was an abhorrent analogy we should try our best to undo.

He tilted his head; a curled smile. Told me he also worked in a blood lab, that they were full of blood talk. He wore a white uniform during the day and collected samples. He was working on a play that involved a character such as himself, a lab technician surrounded by gallons of sick blood waiting for inspection. The character, he told me, takes on the various illnesses via proximity; his existence is reduced to the point where he's wearing a mask twenty-four hours a day. Paranoid, terminally frightened. His colleague, a young, beautiful woman, falls in love with him. 'But it's the new Cillian—that's the character—the terribly frightened creature that she loves,' he said. 'And he rebuffs her advances because he believes his breakdown is leading to a new kind of health. A new kind of perfect life.'

I suggested the text end in suicide and swooning.

'Aha, more or less. He comes from a background of uncertain cultural states and dies in a hospital in Zurich, surrounded by strangers who find him at a roadside, pains in his head. Smart little agonies like they come from another act in another freaking play.'

I found myself watching his face as he talked, how it seemed to change between clauses, simplifying and complicating each idea. I found myself looking away, so it was just his voice and no other intruding, secondary, languages were in effect.

I told him how similar our stories were, only that my father wasn't a doctor but rather an airman.

'Yes,' he said. 'I know your story.'

I stared at him, wondering what he meant. And then I told him about myself. Told him, I suspect, because I wanted to test my own story against his. How when I was young I had sought out physical things that held spiritual significance: guitars, landscapes. I was hunting a shortcut to intellectual enlightenment by placing myself in their proximity. I told him I eventually found a way, one which slowly cracked the door and let the light in. 'Books,' I told him. I said how my girlfriend Deborah and friend Matthew were key in this. I was well into my twenties when I began reading literature, I said. Then I told him about being sick and the lack of evidence in my bloodstream.

'God. Yes. That's a cracker of a disease, that one, isn't it? Ridiculous. If they sort out the name they'll figure out the disease, surely.' He told me he first learnt about it on holiday several years earlier. 'I was in the Aeolian Islands and these people—' He paused and watched the movements on the side of the stage for a moment, a woman with short auburn hair and a man with a grey beard. Two people who seemed to have no connection other than they were about to head up onto the platform to perform, the two of them sudden actors forced into a new, proto-language of gesture and inflection. 'You know, blood's as drunk as a pissed-on priest, you know that? Drunk, you know, with all the evidence of the usual cellular breakdown,' he said. 'Blood knows its diseases. It knows its markers, knows how to hold the traces of illness.' He explained how organ malfunction and poisoning marks blood so well. 'We had a girl like you, I swear a hundred things we searched for. Diseases leave behind traces of their DNA once the immune system has attacked and done its job, so we searched for these things. She was the daughter of our manager; we found nothing that pointed to her being anything but mildly affected by a somewhat benign blood disorder. That and autoimmune responses. She vanished after that, in the way that we never saw her blood again, she vanished. We looked for little circulating proteins and tumour cells for cancers, troponin and serum myoglobin for myocardial infarction, enzymes and bilirubin for the liver. There they go, rushing hither and thither from the heart.' He made quick circles with his hand above his head. He said how these were the happy indicators of impending death or mild inconvenience. The vagueness of this, he found extraordinary. 'We're all dying in our DNA and we don't know it. This is what my father used to say.' He laughed. 'But then there's people like you and that young woman. Your blood's empty. Which makes it the perfect disease: no pathology, no cure. If it's got a language, we haven't yet learnt it.'

I wanted to ask about the pair in the Aeolian Islands, but onstage a comedian made an appalling joke about gay marriage and the crowd groaned and the joke-teller laughed as if he knew this failure was a part of something greater he was taking them all to. He responded with pat responses to the jeers, and took a beer from one of the tables at the front and drank its contents in one swallow.

'Which isn't fair,' Lorcan said.

I asked him how his father felt about him working on that side of the lab.

'Well. My father. When I got the job, he told me all this stuff about blood. He was always interested in miracles, which I found ironic. He loved medieval stories of healing and magic, of religion. He had a theory that medieval magic was the closest thing to science, and religion was closer to what we think of being magic. Therefore, he said, the first scientists were women and the first witches, or what we think witches to be, were priests. He came from a Protestant background. He would have hated your disease. I imagine there would have been a time he'd have described it as fiction.'

I told him my father probably would have offered something similar. 'He was this secular Anglican. No deity, only the phenomenon of combined consciousnesses dedicated to the word. No God, only narrative, story and sacraments, effect and affect. He believed in habits of religiosity, loved them. He didn't read fiction, which I always found strange, considering.'

'Dad,' Lorcan said, 'he once told me blood, that it's always listening, always watching. Which terrified me. Perhaps because I was born near that vaporous castle in Worcester, and all that's left is its watchtower.'

'You're not Irish?'

'Mother, yes. Father, Welsh. I pick and choose.'

On the stage the comedian wasn't getting any laughs. He made another poor joke, and that was the end. Drunks applauded and Lorcan clapped without looking.

An essayist went up on stage instead of me. She went silent, seeking the edge of the audience. A gratifying stillness came over the room, like skin taut against spurs. I looked around for the man and woman, expecting them to be onstage, but they'd disappeared, vanished into the wash of words from the woman's mouth as she warned the room of the invisible pains of silent adversaries, of the political ramifications of not being capable of speaking your pains when the only language left is pain. 'They are,' she said, 'everywhere.'

'You know about veins,' Lorcan said, 'how the body will tell you blood is sometimes blue?'

But it's not, I said.

'No, it's not. It's always red.'

Red because, because when you cut, cut in, cleave and cut, cut the skin and vein, its red, blue because wavelength, you cut and there's no blue, just red, red and red decants because red pours in ways, pours and seeps in ways when you make the incision, you cut and it's red, red like a butcher, red like a sky wrenched out of the day like the hair of the hated, not blue, never blue because blue is death, the colour of death is blue and death means the end and that's when we pretend.

Lorcan explained that light needs to infiltrate the skin in order to illuminate, and some elements of light can reach what lies just beneath the surface and some can't quite make it. The shorter wavelength of blue doesn't make it all the way to the vein, hence is bounced back from its outer surface. So, what makes it back to your eye is the blue. 'There is no blue under your skin, no matter what people tell you. It's just a trick of the light. Unless we're talking about the veins in blue cheese. These are, to the best of my knowledge, blue.'

The essayist began singing in the middle of a poem.

I told him I had a fondness for needles. It was the opportunities they offered me and my mother, I said, to get out of the house in the winter of 1985, when I was incapacitated by that vicious bout of glandular fever. I explained how my mother and I, we'd get in the car and drive somewhere. It was a moment of great excitement I shared with my mum. Then we'd return and I would go back to bed. My mother was an Anglican minister, I explained, and before that a nurse. She had this sense of duty to help, and I was blessed to be a part of that.

He smiled. 'Aberrations from the norm take on spiritual dimensions, no matter how dull,' he said. 'Thing about blood is it's always in observation of past, present and impending dooms, all at the same time.'

I rocked slightly in my chair.

He informed me he didn't think he'd be able to take blood from himself, that he was scared of needles. 'Putting a needle in my arm,' he said. 'That gives me the worst kind of heebies.'

I told him I often inject myself in the upper thigh with shots of liquid vitamin B. He quivered at this.

'I think I'd throw up,' he said, 'honestly, if I had to do that, I really do think I'd throw up. In fact, if I had to take blood from anyone in my family, I suspect I'd have to go to the bathroom and vomit. Anyone I love or have a relationship with, I'd have to take myself off and—'

It's not painful, I said.

I read aloud a chapter chosen randomly from my first book. After several lines I was struck by how I didn't recall any of the events, lines or purpose of the fragments I was reading. It was a third of the way through the novel and there seemed little point to the text other than to hold a space in the narrative flow. I was fascinated by its presence, letting my eyes flick over the page, trying to locate some data that would inform me of the purpose. I read at different speeds, trying to find inflection in the prose. When I found none, I quickly tried to bargain with the text for a dramatic out point, but it wouldn't give anything. I read on until I gave up. There was polite and confused applause. I found Alan and he laughed with me, slapped my back then read something hilarious. Guitars followed, voices and uilleann pipes; a singer accompanied by the delicate drones and honks. I was deeply enamoured of the piper's precise knowledge of squeeze and release, like he knew the total cost of these conversations and nights.

Phenomenology

Sometimes. Sometimes, when in the mood, I tell people it's comparable to brain damage. Which of course isn't practical information for anyone who hasn't been brain-damaged. It's also unfair to me, because I have no idea what actually being brain-damaged is like. I can tell you about the confusion. I can tell you that I don't really comprehend what's going on around me, and if I don't know, my expectation is that others know I don't. Gatherings of people confuse me and I can't cope. This is complex, socially complex. There is a relationship between biological immune systems and an immunity within the cultural: each can be as dangerous as the other. There are the biomedical immune, separated a great deal by gender, by genetic disposition; there are the culturally immune, disconnected again by gender, philological process and the language forms of a patriarchally biased system producing an integument of vast inequity. As Donna Haraway says, 'The language of biomedicine is never alone in the field of empowering meanings, and its power does not flow from a consensus about symbols and actions in the face of suffering'.* No, its power flows from the complexity of our stand-ins for precision and exactness. States that request immunity, but fail and slip because of the nature of their request, because of the nature of immunity.

I can tell you about slippage, about the undoing, about slipping from relative wellness to the state of otherness, about the cultural and material authority that hastens the undoing. I think: Yes, at some stage that'll be useful. I think: But, how? I can say it all but still fear that great fear that nothing will be said, and I fear this because to speak the disease in sensible descriptive terms will not speak the disease at all, only isolate it in one hopeless mode of language, separate it into the culture of the righteously immune.

* And I love how Haraway goes on: 'The power of biomedical language—with its stunning artefacts, images, architectures, social forms, and technologies—for shaping the unequal experience of sickness and death for millions is a social fact deriving from ongoing heterogeneous social processes.'

Amongst the Flowers

After, I walked to the hotel with the Welsh poet. We wandered past Maxwell's Bistro, where the cobbled paths of the old part of the city met with bus lanes and taxi cabs. A stream of people came singing from the bars, neon lit and eternal. A couple argued, red-faced, shouting the things of fallen love. A bard with a colossal beard stood amongst it all reciting poetry, terrifying reports from the edge of language and literature.

When asked about her poem, she explained she was in the middle of a residency in Potsdam, that that was where she had written her piece. 'I went to it, the memorial,' she said. 'We call it the memorial. The Memorial to the Murdered Jews of Europe. Which is a mouthful, so we call it the memorial. I can't describe it to you, that'd be a foolish thing to do. I went and I found it so moving, the way people walk about inside it and vanish, and others appear and they too vanish—I wrote that poem. I read it aloud and now it's finished.'

I asked if she'd ever publish it.

She shook her head. 'Writing it was an experiment. It's not a good poem. I wanted to see what a single comma could do, what repetition. Reading it was the full stop. It's foolishly modernist. You can't write about a place like that. Ultimately all you can relate to is the art of the piece. Out of respect I can't relate to the suffering and violence, I can only keep reminding myself of the unknowability of that suffering. Empathy is finding ways to remind yourself of that every day. But instead of true empathy, we secretly seek protection from it all, from pain, historic pain, from the dying and illness in whatever ways we can. We seek immunity by saying we understand.'

Which is what I was saying. I think.

The two of us entered the north side of Eyre Square, pushing our way through hordes of young men in tracksuit pants. A kind of sexless parade of hunchy vape-smokers lost in their own dialectal spree, arguing and guffawing in a language I could no longer, for the age of me, comprehend.

The poet bent down and adjusted her left heel, hooking a finger behind her ankle and evening out the leather. She stepped back into the shoe and I noticed movement off to the side, a brawl at the east end of the park. An unfocused anger, fists swinging in the near air, missing everything. Shouting, screams that seemed to go on for hours, as if unheard. There was a rush of young men and I was knocked over as we hurried towards the lights of the hotel on the south side. As I fell, a knee caught the side of my head and I found I was bleeding. Once inside the foyer, the poet had the staff bring a towel, which I dabbed against my temple. As I did so, I told her she should spend some of the next day at the river before her panel session.

'Are you going to be okay?' she asked.

'Go and spend time at the river.'

'Your face.'

'It's blood, it'll thicken up.'

'I'll talk to the desk. See if there's a doctor.'

'Doctors haven't been much use to me for years,' I said. 'No, it'll be okay.'

'You're concussed, most likely.'

'Most likely. Go and spend time at the river.'

She asked why and, despite believing I'd had the answer moments before, I forgot, instantly. I had a reason, but as we went through the expensive array of furniture and Americans in specialised travel wear, past towering vases full of magnificent flowers, I realised I no longer had an answer.

Scream

In the scream of it all, of the storm and its fullness, speed and noise, they built a cairn marking where Henry had fallen, rested in the leeward side of an outcrop, and made a plan as frostbite began creeping first into Simon's extremities, then David's. Simon began wincing at the pain of it, a kind of hardened sobbing as the blood stopped reaching the outer layers of his skin, his fingers all waxy and grey beneath his gloves. He stood, smashing his hands together to get the flow back. The pain immense as the warm blood recirculated through into the dying parts of his digits. He and David yelled against the roaring, the fast elements, and fought to make a plan. Two young men shouting as they battled against the threat of wind and snow and the task of dying there in the indecision that was slowly thickening, infilling each of their cognitive processes, thought and speech and sight and breathing. And indecision, because the brain starts to resist. It begins to battle thought, resist the computation of event, of future events they needed to imagine in order to mount an expedition to keep themselves alive and liberate Henry from what was certain to be death in the coming hours. They needed thought, they needed clarity of thought. The exactness of mindfulness that was being sucked out of them by the wind. They needed more clothing, food and equipment. They needed precision and speed and correct decisions in order to stage a rescue, the event that would keep them all alive.

They needed to rescue themselves in order to rescue Henry.

They began their descent.

One hour. Two. Running when possible. Falling, careful in footfalls but slipping and righting themselves. Four hours to the hut.

They sorted equipment, warmed hands, feet and bodies, ate

until they were full and set out with full packs, ropes, sleeping bags, food and tent.

They again climbed the mountain.

They again entered the full cry, the hit and vehemence of a storm still driving in from the south.

Four hours up and at the lower peak they stopped. Simon said, he shouted, 'I can't fucking do this.'

'Yeah—but you do.'

'I can't.'

'But you do,' David said. 'You do.'

They went on, the ends of Simon's fingers greying in his gloves. Nerve death.

Simon repeated himself until David said, 'You. You come along, you do this.'

'. . .'

'Choice isn't a thing here—it's not actually a thing here. You know that.'

Simon knew this, all this. But parts of him were dying, small parts, nerve parts. 'I'm going to stop for a bit.'

'We stop for a bit. For a bit.'

My brother stared at David, a sudden discharge of thought shouting something. An internal pleading within that there were other things they could do other than re-climb this mountain. That there were other things, that this wasn't the thing. Other things. A fire ten metres high and hailing anyone, everyone. A painting of the sky on the sky.

'You do this. This is the option. You stay behind and—'

'And?'

'And don't ask.'

'What if he's dead?'

David shook his head. 'We go looking for him and that's the end. We rope up. We go looking for him.'

Simon was nodding, looking away.

'The question is: *What if he's alive?* In fact, the only statement is: *He's alive.* That's all there is.'

'Yeah. I'm shattered. That's all I've got right now.'

'That's enough.' David said and pulled his balaclava up for a moment. Ice and snow in his beard. 'It's got to be enough.'

'This is, this is fucking—' Simon yelled.

'But beyond being tired,' David asked, 'what are you?'

'Just tired. I'm fucking tired. I'm scared of being scared. And I'm fucking tired.'

'Of course you're fucking tired. But there's something beyond tired and when there isn't, you'll be the one to know.'

They climbed the peak again. After hours in the storm, up and up, they found it. They'd been on the move for sixteen hours, but they found their cairn. A mound of undisturbed rocks in the rushed cloud and snow, the delicate pile saying, *This is the way.* And there the wind died off, reduced so they could see where they'd climbed down nine hours earlier. Again, they began the descent of the cliff face into the eastern cloud bank below. This time they put in ropes, securing them to the ice and looped the rope through the series of carabiners, and they inched slowly down. Fifty metres and the sheerness began to give way, gradually plaining out. At two hundred metres the entire chute eased into shallow sloping valley. Visibility came and went, and eventually they had sightlines of fifty, sometimes a hundred metres. Then something human, a mark in the snow. A single crampon scrape. Now, now they used their voices. They began shouting, calling out with their hands like cones about their mouths, walking slowly through the boulder field, lower and lower, thirty metres apart, calling out for Henry. On and onward, down, shouting out through the freezing air, 'Henry!' and 'Dad!'

The shout and hack of their voices. The fruitlessness of the returning noise, the deadened return. The empty echo humanless.

'Henry!'

'Dad!'

'Henry!'

'Henry!'

Tottenham Hale

The day following, I flew the Irish Sea to Stansted, where I hired a car and drove south to a friend's house in Tottenham Hale. Her sister, twin brother and partners had gathered for dinner and wine and conversation. Originally Hannah was due to fly out to New Zealand the day before my arrival. We were fated to miss each other by twenty-three hours. As a result, I was going to borrow her couch while she was in Christchurch and I was in London. Instead, the journey had been put off a few days and after getting lost multiple times I finally arrived at her house with my suitcase. There was music, and her husband, who I'd met multiple times over the last twelve years, was there. There was family and there was an air of distracted uncertainty. I was intruding on sadness and relief, twin casualties of events back in Christchurch.

My friend welcomed me in, hugged me and kissed my cheek. She introduced me to her sister, famous by now, and I was nervous as I'd never met her. An artist of elementary horrors and extraordinary intelligence.

'You'll have to come to me,' the sister said, and I walked the length of the table to shake her hand. 'How do you finish this?' she said, and I realised she was talking to her younger sister.

'I don't finish this. What am I finishing?' Hannah said.

'Mother. How do you finish talking about Mother? Because we have to leave soon. Trains being what they are.'

'You want me to finish? I can't finish.'

'Well, finish something. I'm out of wine.'

'This has been going on all night,' Hannah's twin said to me. 'Have a seat. Have some food. What do we have left?'

'I'll fly on Tuesday,' Hannah said. 'I'll be with her then and—maybe somewhere over Iran there'll be a mystic interference.'

'What do we do with cancer? We poison and what else?'

'We poison it, cut it, radiate it. We survive in a myriad hell.'

'Christ. Okay. I'll see you Monday night? Yes?' the sister said, and she was up and she shook my hand again without looking in my direction. 'You don't get to donate your kidney. We feel good about this outcome, okay?'

I stood by the back door as most of the guests exited through the front. The long goodbye, the kisses and necessary lingered embraces. Hannah returned to the lounge and gave me an exhausted hug.

'Let's smoke. I have booze to finish.' She ran out of the room and returned with hats and scarves. 'It's killer cold out there, Cov.'

'I don't smoke anymore,' I said.

'But I do, so—outside.' And we went out into the back of her house.

Hannah was supposed to be leaving in order to have her kidney removed and placed inside her mother. Sue was, it is necessary to say, very slowly dying of kidney failure. Years of blood tests and fear and duty and certainty had led to this moment. Hannah was supposed to fly out and would return with one less organ in her body, and that would be a fact for the rest of her life. But life being life, the day prior to Hannah's departure she learnt, after the routine tests the patient takes each Monday as they await a donor, that her mother had breast cancer. All the bleak markers were in her blood, roaming. The transplant was off, and I arrived to find Hannah in a state of rare and full drunkenness, raving between relief and terror, sadness and guilt: all a part of a painful sense of liberation.

'Cov,' she said. We'd given up on full declarative sentences.

'Your life will likely be longer. You will have more energy,' I said, eventually. The air around us hovered with the steam-like questions of breath and smoke. 'These are all positive outcomes,' I said. We sat closer, her head on my shoulder. It was new, unused.

'I know, Cov. But how am I supposed to feel? I just don't understand how I'm supposed to feel. Tell me how to feel, David, and you get a free breakfast.'

'Every time I'm offered a free breakfast, I suspect my life's about to change.'

'I'm desperate to make something out of this but I don't know what it is. I expect a signal of relief. I expect a flag to pop up and say: Live your life! But that's not it. My sister is so pragmatic about it. So much it's killing me. I have no pragmatism, that's my issue.'

'You're highly practical,' I said.

'But that's not the same. Sounds the same but it's not the same.'

'What about Christian? What does he say?'

'He's German; he only knows regrets.'

Back inside the house, Hannah and her brother decided it was time I saw their acrobatic routine. It had become their thing over the last year. I watched as they climbed all over each other's drunken bodies, toes in the clefts between muscles, hands in improbable places. They wobbled and yelled instructions at each other, their faces red, their mouths open from laughter and more laughter, and though my right eye watched, twitched and shut off, I still clapped with both hands. And with that I had an encompassing body sense of the impenetrability of physical forms, their serene language so trapped in what we want to know, that the only way to realise what we need to know is by showing how crude our approximates are. The two of them, these twins, quite beautiful as they pushed towards being 'body', and little else.

In the morning we walked very slowly along the canal, Hannah pushing her bike, me a slug beside her. Old boats, some festooned with flowering plants kept in boxes on the wheelhouse roof, others energised by solar panels, some floating by. Thoughts in a grey, graphite-like light.

She needed to rant. 'Doesn't matter how much I drink, or don't drink, I'm not going to figure this out, am I? Or should I get drunk again, like now on a fucking barge and give it another crack?' She kept turning to me, a red face.

We found ourselves at Markfield Park, there she was to get on her bike and ride off to Hackney where her jeweller's studio sat in the back of her other house. 'There are so many people I think I'm speaking to, but I'm not. I know I'm not. I don't know who I'm speaking to,' she said. 'I feel like one of those old buildings you see in places like Berlin or whatever. You can spot those places, you know, like that were half destroyed then saved. You just have to look at where they connect to their neighbours and you can, you know, spot them.' She said how her husband had shown her years ago, and she couldn't stop seeing them when in Germany. 'The sections that were destroyed by whatever, raids and artillery, you can see where they've saved the remaining sections, they've rebuilt and supported the rest with a new construction. I feel like, I don't know, like the place where they all connect up. Like I shouldn't really be there.'

We said goodbye as that was to be the last time we'd catch each other before I drove out. Our hug was long, needy. She cycled away in the early light. I watched her pedalling, the strong motion of her legs and hips hurrying her through the paths to other streets. Despite the news, or because of it, she would be heading to the airport as soon as she'd finished up some work, and would fly out with her twin and be with her mother in a new, supportive role.

I walked back to her house. I found myself on a couple of occasions standing at corners for long minutes, caught by uncertainty. I have these instances when I freeze. It's not so much a physical freeze, but a moment in which the day's capacity for thought seems over. I can't recall the processes one has to go through to cross the street. It seems like I can't bring up the mechanisms that explain to my eyes to look left and right or explain what the traffic lights mean. This set of instructions remain caught in the neural net, a faint memory of a story lost in the subconscious. It's akin to a safety device kicking in, and I'm stuck on the pavement beside rushing traffic and people until I remember and it's safe to move on. It's particularly useful in the US and Europe, where the rules are quite different. In New Zealand it is just odd, though I'm used to feeling odd in my own town. In London I just felt embarrassed. There's another me, I sometimes think, a mimicked life where this doesn't happen.

In my rental, I drove from Tottenham towards the Cotswolds, hopeful of some hint of England. I determined I could drive two hours at a stretch in the morning before becoming a danger to myself and others. I set off in a peculiar mind. Hannah, her mum and the strangest dichotomy of emotions. I tried to imagine them, attempted to access the middling thoughts of empathy as I struggled to get the car stereo to sync with my phone. I wanted music, a purposeful soundtrack as I navigated my way out of the western boroughs of London.

I drove melancholy for the fact of saying farewell to my friend and the urge of her pain, guiltily relieved to be out of the range of her poor, well-tended anguish. Those plights of nervous energy only time with family could quell or solve. I imagined listening in to her conversation with her mother, hearing every word and understanding none of it. I wished to hear one of the songs that played on my phone, a song disregarded by the car. I wished its invisibility might blink out some of her anguish, flash it with untenable light.

Waiting at roadworks near Harrow, I received a text from Hannah as she sat at Heathrow trying to waste time before her flight:

Relieved is a strange feeling, isn't it?

I couldn't reply, and the message sat on the face of my phone as I drove out, easing into the series of A roads leading me towards Oxford, where so many things have been asked and answered, so many lost in the act of being thought.

East Atlantic

Soviet psychiatrist Bluma Zeigarnik once argued that when one refrains from naming a phenomenon, the idea of it stays dynamic in your thoughts. She postulated that individuals and societies recall incomplete or interrupted undertakings better than accomplished, named tasks. Specifically, Zeigarnik discovered that we have better recollection for the details of an unresolved task, an unfinished riddle, an unnamed psychological phenomenon, than an explained or labelled entity, item, thing.

As I headed west to Oxford and glanced about the city this idea expanded its perplexing dimensions within me.

I had lunch in a square overlooking the Radcliffe Camera. That domed Palladian arm of the famed Bodleian Library that seems a part of every British TV show featuring Oxford. I don't recall getting there. But I did take several photos, surprised how determined I was to access the dimensions of the edifice as it narrowed exquisitely at the top of the dome and its nippled peak, accenting certain mathematics of curvature. As I ate, I imagined the mind of the architect in the deep concentration. His mind visualising all the thoughts of all the learned and learning souls inside. I tried to envision his imagining of the finer particles of ideas and cognisance, all of the scholars congregating, reading and noting grand thoughts, how those ideas rose, squeezed into the dome above; then in a kind of cognitive precipitation they cooled on the sheets of Derbyshire lead used for the roof, and fell on the floor, a clattering sound in recompense for their failure. For all thoughts are failures, I supposed, all thoughts a form of calamity. Except for those shy ideas that make it to the end, unnoticed and complete, and mark a new element amongst the mind's shining rows of developing technologies—and then all the schools of thought claiming it was there all along. I imagined these individual thoughts pushing up through the aperture of the apex at the top, released to the world via this grand syringe fashioned by the will to knowledge.

I was soon awash in it all, in the thought that symmetry is somehow immune from criticism, from judgement; it is adored on all levels. We seek it. We seek it at miniature and grand scales. We crave impeccable forms both in nature and by our own hands. Desire Hawaiian isles, giant conic symmetry rising from the sea. Such a sight tells us we have somehow arrived at safety and assured protection from the end of structure. An immunity from the frailties of human instinct to pattern. And as soon as we believe we have seen perfection, something vanishes.

I supposed this is what Zeigarnik was getting at—the vanishing.

During moments of extreme beauty, the disease feels almost fiction. Such is the sudden clarity, such is the indeterminacy of its language, such is the indeterminacy of the response from the world, from GPs, research dollars and populace. And my life, my life feels analogous to the whole unstable telling—a narrative space I enter into without trust for the structures of account. But then, in the moments when the clarity is rent asunder, my life is, in truth, the dubiously shaky pillars of narratorial erection, always ever in the state of collapse until something seems to hit.

Perhaps I let these thoughts in because one of my ancestral namesakes, Sir Henry Halford, went to Christ Church at Oxford University. He was a baron, physician to kings and the president of the Royal College of Physicians for a quarter of a century. Oversaw the lives and deaths of King George III and his successors—George IV, William IV. He also saw to the health of a young Victoria. My niece, Danielle, found a copy of his biography in Leakey's Bookshop in Inverness. On the same page that he mentions his interest in euthanasia he discusses being present for the ghastly death of the rather pitiful George IV. Danielle made the supposition that perhaps there was a connection and perhaps, perhaps there was regicide in the family. We made the decision to run with it.

I wanted to tell my phlebotomist friend in Galway about my strange visions and what kinds of ill those sights might make him and his play's characters. Instead, I messaged Hannah. Asked if she was okay heading home. The first time I met her, in the early 2000s, she was in recovery from a brain haemorrhage she'd had when she was just twenty-two. There was a likeable oddness to her then, something removed but intense. For reasons related to this I found myself more concerned for her health, her mental health and its peculiarities, than I did most people.

It's sort of a relief.

And it's sort of sad.

She was in the aircraft, typing this out and taking her seat. She went on, describing all the free stuff they give you.

Headphones. Blanket. There's a little pillow that I can just about stuff in my mouth.

In the Park

The next morning, I drove west from Bidford-on-Avon, a village a few minutes' drive from Stratford. I'd rented a room in a cottage there for three nights. Drove, jagging in and out of the small towns towards the heart of Worcestershire wherein sat the land and house I'd made a deal with myself to visit if I ever had time in Britain. My father had spoken about the estate when I was a child. And he spoke about it again when he was aging and his mind was failing. He was only in his early seventies, but he struggled to remember where he was if he was interrupted when telling a story. He had to start again, as if the only marker in his tales were there at the start, a post in the unremembered earth. I think now that this was the reason I went, for his memory rather than mine—his failing memory.

I left the rental in the car park with the hundreds of others. Pilgriming mums and dads visiting with their children and prams.

And pilgrimage is not a word I would use for my visit to Croome Court, more an exploration of intrigue. The estate had been inherited and developed by an ancestor of mine and transformed into a Palladian manor of ridiculous grandeur. George William Coventry, Tory MP and earl, had employed Lancelot 'Capability' Brown to transmute the swamp-laden park into a flow of hill, river and dale. Brown drained the surrounds by means of immense culverts reaching from the site of the new house to one of his artificial rivers. He then dotted in eye-catching conceits and ornaments in the shape of buildings, bridges and fountains. The park was entirely fake, a facsimile of the rise of idealised elevation, the fashioning of formalised omnipotent power. As I emerged from the trees that separated the entrance to the estate, I felt a slipping, a divergence from my cynical expectation.

Simply, I'd wanted to know what I would experience by visiting this curious old seat from which my family gets its name and elements of DNA, what the encounter with all this illusion would place on my mind and body. The visit was an experiment in familial inheritance and I expected nothing but cynicism, perhaps anger, perhaps bald annoyance and a quick exit. I live in a country whose colonial origins are raw and necessarily questionable. I felt there was a false equivalence between familial sequences and who I am. I've always been comfortable with the uncomfortable sense that I am a permanent visitor to New Zealand, that my history is one of émigré intervention, that I am a caller. I am an outsider, and that is a necessary cultural truth. One marked by white sails and a promiscuous obsession with ownership by men such as George William Coventry. I am a pallid intruder. I live on land purchased by my wife and me through means and mechanisms of law whose roots are in the misapplication of treaty and trust. I am a visitor and like all visitors, we have obligations that are impossible to articulate. My history isn't grand homes, but uncertainty and disquiet. It is the land of Kristen's ruins, the tracks of bush and people marginalised by expansion. Every city in New Zealand is a ruin at the moment the first pile meets the earth. I like this sense of subjective dissonance. It signifies there is always a hunt for knowledge of cognitive and bodily locality. I belong within the complex arrangement of place, a word I have always failed to define with adequate effect, or affect.

But now this park. All the effort to make a statement, of place, that place is beyond thought and debate and consternation, that it's eternal. A marker against time and the meagreness of DNA strand and all else.

During World War II, Croome Court was used as an officer's mess for the nearby RAF station, Defford. The earl from that age had died at Dunkirk, and his young son did not return to live in the home once the war was done, instead settling in the village of Earl's Croome. The manor was then sold in 1948 to the Catholic Church, which used it as a school for intellectually disabled boys. A Hare Krishna sect moved in during the Seventies and it was then bought by a developer who made a severe wreck of the building's structure—the roof removed, the elements let in. Finally, the National Trust took over, and a slow restoration had been underway since the mid-2000s—this is the version of the home I visited.

On arrival the first thing I saw was the perfect sculptured

view, a long field sheering away from a fake medieval chapel in a perfect arc downwards to the rectangular house, enormous in the fields below and seemingly held in the shape of the landscape by the curve of the Croome River drifting slowly by until it eventually surrendered itself to the Severn some miles distant. I entered the chapel first. It was cool in from the warm, vernal air.

My father had been here.

'I visited Croome Court in 1963,' Henry wrote, a few years before his death. 'I was stationed in the UK for six months and drove from southern England. It took me a long time to find the place. But I got there and spoke to the sister who was house matron for the school. I introduced myself but I didn't give my name. I said merely that my family once lived there and asked if I could have a look around the school. It was strange and I couldn't have anticipated her response. She immediately took me to meet Mother Superior, introducing me as "the earl's cousin from Australia". It seems now to me,' my father wrote, 'that this Mother Superior was being presented to me rather than the other way around. I was then taken on a tour of the school. In the reception rooms there were still portraits of family members and in the front entrance some recent photographs of the earl receiving a gift from the local community on the occasion of his marriage. When I came to leave, Matron said it was a very sorry day when the family sold the home. She said that most of the local people had been employed by the family. The family, along with Croome Court and the surrounding park, she said,' my father wrote, 'was a source of pride and a focal point in the local community. She said it was an institution that provided the intangible threads that held the community together.'

He was writing all this from thirty-nine years out, and he sounded so sure. To me it sounded like the memory of a man desperate to recall the light of a day he wished to return to. Words slowly altered in his mind from the matron's mouth to that day in 2002. A kind of request to his younger self for the depth of supreme connection. Two years later Dad told me this same story when I was visiting. He lost his track and started the story twice over without noticing; that was the state of his memory then. Memory determined to complete itself. I felt sad for him, that there was something he believed to be there, something intangible and waiting. I learned many years later from my elder siblings that my father's father had always forced on him the idea that he was somehow different for having been derived from the aristocracy. And that kind of enculturation can't help but affect a person's approach to selfhood. But, as I wandered through the chapel there on the hill, I soon realised the reason for this. I turned left at the end of the seating and immediately saw his name on a five-hundred-year-old gravestone set in the wall. In pomp and Latin. My name, too, if you remove a couple of add-ons.

At the sight of this I stood quite still, uncertain and suddenly nervous. I was there for half an hour and nobody entered the chapel. I let the silence of the place play out again as I looked around the sanctuary and saw versions of my name on various other tombstones and plaques. I looked at dates and waited on something, an interruption, a buckling of some kind, children perhaps, loud and violent. I sat and began to wonder about all the things, the names and objects.

My brother by then was in ownership of a watch passed down from eldest son to eldest son. It was originally owned by Baron Henry Halford. The watch (along with a pair of pet emus) were the king's gift to the doctor on retirement. His daughter married George William Coventry's grandson and they had my great-great-grandfather, on and on. We can see it all typed out by my father. These networks of things and words were supposed to enhance and engage me in my relationship to a certain world, but instead did the opposite. I felt diminished and lax.

Eventually I went out the door and ambled slowly down off the hill towards the huge house. I saw swans on Croome River; I murmured to some part of myself how they were particularly reminiscent in their white plumage of my father's own white hair. I never asked him why the emphasis on this part of his family; there are, after all, many other versions to trace—the Scots, the Welsh, the Germans. I suspect he would have told me history is made first by our inability to resist grand elevations. But I had a sense then of the power of arranging the dead in this way, of prompting the beholder to seek connection to something as old and futile as the royal family. There seems an imperative within certain cultures to elevate specific individuals or groups of humans so that we have a sense of command and directive, a knowledge of stratified space outside of physical capacities. A part of us despises the royals, another is roused by the queen, applauds her in the same moment as hating all she stands for. I put this to one of the National Trust staff, who sought me out after I was found bewildered in the grounds to the south of the house.

I'd left the chapel and walked slowly down the large sloping field towards the manor. It seemed to gain size as I got closer, the imperialistic double staircase leading to the front door and the overwhelming number of windows. I was circled by teeming children and heated parents as I climbed the stairs. Then I was at the door. I opened it and stood in the front entranceway, where immediately I was surrounded by members of the Trust, who asked if they could provide me with any assistance. Confused, I told a tall, thin man my name, the whole four barrels of it, and they said, 'Oh—you're from the family!'

I told them my relationship to several of the figures on the wall, painted in that nauseating classical style of imperial import, each hung there as if to suggest we were all there waiting on their return. Three of the volunteers came at me from different directions, each began telling me histories of the rooms, insisting to be sure I saw the Long Room, to be sure to see the Tapestry Room, to be sure to take in the second floor, that I was welcome to enter the Red Wing if I was willing to wear a hard hat—the previous owner had removed the roof and things there weren't ideal.

Left to my own devices I walked west through a series of dilapidated halls until I reached the Long Room, where scaffolding lined the walls. It was a hall of light and hearth, window and spectacularly moulded ceilings lifted above the multiple arched alcoves once home to statue and vase. It was beautiful despite the restoration work still underway. It spanned the length of western extent, windows showing off the grounds and letting in grand, thick rays of dusty light. I walked slowly down its length and stood waiting until it was empty of people for a moment.

I stood trying to recall something, because that seemed to be the point of all this, trying to remember something unspoken, unexperienced, untrue. People poured into the hall and I went east through several rooms until I was surrounded by squabbling and shouting, and I saw a door that informed, via a crinkly note in a plastic bag, that it was not to be opened under any circumstances. I felt my head become heavy, the width of my vision shrink and I knew what was next. I had to sit down, and I needed to quickly. I needed to either take some pills or sleep or find somewhere my body could convulse.

I pushed through the doors. Despite the warning they opened freely, and I escaped out into the South Portico and down the wide stairs. I stumbled slightly, despite the symmetry of it all.

I wasn't convinced about my reasons for walking the grounds with such abandon. Whether there even were reasons. I have to push myself towards complete collapse in order to get to the point necessary to write certain things, even this. All activity in my life has its own metafictional element, but what limned thing lay at the end of this wandering I wasn't sure, and I kept walking. There were picnic tables in the near distance; I made my way to them and sat. I let my head sink into my crossed arms and felt my heart run agitated and uncertain on a sudden excess of adrenaline. I counted in deep breaths and to my relief the effect left me and I stayed in that position with my eyes half open, the house blurred as if time was a real effect and not just a reading of the arms of a clock in some massive Horologium, that time really bent the things erected in the ages before now.

I liked the vision, the twisting and bending of line, roof and window that no degree of scaffold could contain or rectify—as if time were an element of gravity, a force of warping capacity and continual change.

I slept briefly and woke and ate a sandwich I'd made that morning. I felt better, which was unusual. My eyesight came back and my head didn't feel so full of expanding materials.

I stood and walked away from the house in order to get a perspective I could capture on my camera. I took several photos and sent them to my wife. I stood there hopeful Laura would write back immediately, a little *Wow* or *Where on earth are you now, honey?* But it was 1am in New Zealand and I knew she was asleep and adrift in our bed. I stood a hundred metres from the house and tried to put myself into it, as I knew that was the trick of all this: it asks you to ignore all other lines of inheritance and believe this is some kind of birth right. An imperialism of blood, the cult of name and DNA. It slowly came to me that the awe I was experiencing was for the situation, for the power of the place.

I wanted to be revolted—but wasn't. It was something else I couldn't undermine with thought until I realised it was a sense of ownership, not on my part, but on the part of the effect of all this awe, how it bombarded me with an empty insistence of familial permanence. I wanted to leave, then, but was given pause by the appearance of a slender figure exiting the same backdoor and descending the portico's steps. It was the man who had greeted me at the entrance and had asked if I was all right. He slowly covered the ground between the building and my position in the middle of the field where it had begun to drizzle.

Sl—slen
Slen
Sl
Sle
Slen—d
Sled
Slen
Slend
Slen—der

'If you speak to Meredith,' the thin man started once he was within range, 'she says she'll take you up to the out-of-bounds top floors. There's many paintings and hideaways. Most of the old furniture is in storage up there, you'll get a good idea.' He came and sat beside me and we talked about the house in front of us. After asking if it was my first time to Croome Court and hearing me reply that it was and explaining that my father had been to the manor in the early Sixties, he nodded solemnly, as if the fact contained traces of uncovered tragedy. I told him my father's name was Henry and that seeing the mounted tombstone in the chapel had been a shock to me—it felt like a trick of the light, all this grandeur, and I was struggling to see my real place in it. I said that in all reality I had no part in it whatsoever, apart from strangling elements of DNA and stories, neither of which I thought had any hold on me. I was seeing and feeling what the estate wished me to feel.

I felt manipulated by this giant museum of self.

I told him this was my first time in England outside of London, that I was there because I was intrigued to know what my reaction would be.

(I felt manipulated.)

'I understand. And your last direct ancestor who resided here?'

I told him I wasn't sure and admitted it was overwhelming. But it shouldn't be. It should just be a place.

'Indeed,' he said. 'After all, every person on the earth surely has some claim to generations going back and back to—it's just that not all have the means to mark them so conspicuously.'

I nodded.

We discussed how most of us don't have the means to so ostentatiously arrange our dead, to do it in a manner that places a sense of ourselves into the arms of an overtly privileged composition of cultural entitlement. Something so old and entrenched that there seemed a nascent spirituality invoked when letting ourselves get too close. He described a filial religiosity, something formed by subjugation and the elevation of the moneyed into a sphere of uber human. He glanced at me to see if I was listening. He pinched his eyes. 'It's nice to have connections, as the saying goes. It's nicer to think that connection means something beyond the everyday.'

I was unsure if he agreed with his own comments, or was just making an observation from afar. That was when I made my comment about the queen and order and directive, the whole thing about elevating specific groups of individuals into a class touched by God. That in the name of bullshit we charge them with specific capacities.

At the age of twenty-three, I went to stay with Henry for a few months. I'd left home at seventeen and hadn't really spent a great deal of time with him as an adult. This held both a convenience and a concentrated purpose: I had a small and secret intent to get to know him. He was a distant man who my entire life had had sparse grey hair and an air of age, of having always been old. Gently mild-mannered but also outside of the normal reach of the family. The plan was that I'd stay with him while my girlfriend, Deborah, moved to Auckland. I'd join her once I'd helped him move house with his new wife to a rural property out towards the south coast of Wellington. It was a pleasant time, but I got to know my father's wife, Anne, much better than I did my father. I left eventually, having helped my father plant stands of wattle and pine at the rear of the property. But I left having discovered very little of Henry aside from several stories he told my friend Matthew and me about his years in the air force. These stories came out unprovoked one gentle autumn afternoon. He told us how he used to fly his Bristol Freighter around Southeast Asia, the car he'd bought in Singapore in the cargo hold so his air crew would have something to play in when stationed up in Kuala Lumpur or over in Borneo. How they flew drunk, raged on the long nights at the officer's mess that emptied into the morning's operations. I explained how my father told us that on a flight up to Bangkok he was smoking a cigar in the co-pilot's seat while the co-pilot napped hungover at my father's station behind the front seats. An hour passed in silence, with the pilot plotting their way north on my father's instructions. Henry knew navigation, how to plot the globe and track its weather systems and whatnot. He was a navigator on board Hastings, Blenheims, Devons, C-140 Hercules, and these shaky Bristol Freighters. He directed aircraft from Whenuapai in Auckland to London via compass, map, sextant and watch, dead reckoning and radio beacon. He flew to Antarctica, Texas, Singapore and Vietnam, and during the Malayan Emergency—in which this story of his was set—they flew all over Southeast Asia as uncompromising colonisers dropping supplies and propaganda from the hold. He told us how the pilot eventually stood up and came across the cabin and opened my father's window, saying he needed fresh air. Then, a few minutes after my father lit up his next cheroot, the pilot took out his service revolver, aimed at the glowing tip of the cigar and pulled the trigger. The cigar burst and the bullet passed out the window. My father didn't move, he told us. He just sat in terror trying not to show his fear as the pilot went calmly about his business, flying them north. Matthew and I laughed like eight-year-olds as he began telling another story involving hangovers and the burning of a piano in the middle of the Changi taxiway after it woke his crew in the early morning after a long night. He told us these stories and more, and I realised how simple it was for him to relay this information. I heard nothing of what it was like at home for my mother, what it was like when he was at home with my mother and older siblings. I began to wonder, I told the man. I began to wonder too of his relationship to these stories, whether he was there or had himself painted in. It didn't seem to matter and couldn't matter: this was the factor of his life before I knew him.

Henry was thirty-eight when I was born and he was beyond flying days by then, stationed in an office, becoming this strangely silent man, waiting. Waiting on this link to the old aching past, for it to be made skin and vein in the invisible act of story. That was what I took away when I moved north, nothing of the father I spent time with, but the one he wished for, to appear again in the act of storytelling. Indeed, the archive of his writings came to me when he died; I've never been sure who they were for, himself or the remembered self we all hope carries on in the after.

Three years later, I moved back from Auckland to Wellington. This time Henry went looking for me; I'd made the decision to disappear off the family's radar. He'd broken up with his second wife and wanted to talk with someone. It was the first time he'd come looking for me—and without luck; he didn't find me for months. I'd gone missing, hiding at my friend Matthew's house in Mount Victoria while I tried to reason with what had gone wrong in Auckland. And I wondered then, and wondered often, what my father was looking for when he thought of me.

I told the tall, slender fellow I felt closer to Henry now he was dead. That I'd figured him out a great deal more. More than was possible when he was alive.

'When did he pass away?' he asked.

2006.

'Well, you know the date to return to. Now you have a place.' He smiled then, fatherly and offering, though he was likely my age, or just a few years older. I walked back into the house and he called out after me, 'Look out for Meredith.'

But just as I was wondering if he meant I should watch out for her because she had undesirable habits or because she would show me something I really needed to see, Meredith found me.

'Mr Coventry,' she said, and we went up the stairs of this vast Neo-Palladian mansion, creaking on every warped step. I saw paintings and rooms of wonderfully odd shapes. I saw servants' quarters and furniture of astounding beauty, objects I couldn't date for they seemed at once modern (Modern) and classical. Items sold off after World War II, then recovered by the Trust. Here and there Greek statues and Roman, men and boys with their genitals smashed off by zealous hammers.

I met a chap named Dafydd, a slightly hunchbacked young man with what I suspect was cerebral palsy, working in the upper floors. He was knowledgeable of each space and knew how to get the sticking doors open, the jammed four-hundred-year-old wood and how to twist giant keys just so.

He intimated to me that there was something beyond science in culture, in heritage. We were standing in a room full of paintings and the most extraordinary red-stained bureau hidden away from the fading sunlight. 'That's why there will always be homes like this,' he said. 'That's why there will always be supposed gods and royals and apparently ordinary people willing to spend their weekends in mansions. I think we're always trying to understand something of the gap between the past and what we know of it.'

Though I wasn't quite as certain as Dafydd, I wanted to listen to him through.

'We like to wallow in the misery and mystery of how we

got to now, then call it mastery. That's why there will always be those willing to call themselves Britons.' It sounded practised, but I already liked him a lot and was disappointed when he told me his shift was ending and he had to leave.

'We come here,' I said, 'we create a story about something or other, take it out into the world, filling it with enjoyable apocrypha.'

He nodded and smiled. 'And it's troubling at times, being here—feeling the fictional aspects of the place overtake the lineage of facts. It's an odd dissonance, between fiction and what you hope to be true. It's an anxious thing to be on these grounds every day. That's why I like it up here.'

Now I nodded. Frederick William III, I said. The Prussian king. I told him he was my great-great-great-great-grandfather. That I have dubious relatives on both sides of my father's family.

'Yes? Indeed, well—'

I explained that this was hearsay for 170 years, that when we were kids it was a ridiculed rumour run through with jokes, as if all of history were a prank. It came from myth, stored in the warm letters of my German great-great-great-grandmother to her son, warmed in the mouths of her descendants, then it became truth via DNA matching. Cousins I've never met put it together. The Kaiser's son had an affair with a woman named Caroline Wagner. She had a boy and moved to the Manawatū in New Zealand. This boy's daughter married a Coventry. Then I'm born a thousand years later, I told him.

'Just like that.'

And all of it's meaningless, I explained, until you say it, and something happens. Suddenly it prejudices all the other lines of descent and they disappear, which makes me angry. I find it revolting, I said. I told him how Hannah's German husband calls me the Prussian fascist. All because of an illegitimate affair. I told him I have boxes of photographs of that side of my family, images I inherited from my father, the Germans. Nineteenth-century black-and-whites. They lived somewhere near the mouth of the Rangitīkei. I'm afraid of what's in the boxes and I've never opened them.

'And who knows the nature of the affair. I mean—'

My father had an obsession with family that went deep to the substrate of his distinctive self. He believed, I said to Dafydd, that family had a spiritual quality, which was odd, because he hardly ever talked to us.

'Fathers be fathers.'

Shortly before he left, Dafydd showed me several paintings of my father's close cousin, the ninth earl. Here on his horse in a red hunting jacket, beside him the countess, their two steeds surrounded by hounds. In each painting he had the same identical features, despite aging greatly between the nineteenth-century renditions and the twentieth. He had the same balding head and tight eyes. He had the same handsome nose throughout. Slightly Roman, and distinctively—and distractingly—the same nose as my father. The same nose my eldest sister inherited and at least one of her children carries about every day. That they were both now dead seemed suddenly heightened by these images.

On seeing this I decided I had to leave. I descended the eastern stairs to the ground floor and walked through into the old tapestry room once draped in great red works of woollen art detailed by the intricate and extraordinarily melancholy renderings of great classical myths. I paused there beside the white walls of bare wooden frames and read a message on my phone from Hannah. She was in Singapore, where she'd stopped off for two nights because she said she hated the way she felt after landing in Christchurch, feeling her body flipping its circadian rhythms 180 degrees.

I'm not sure I'm off the hook, Cov.

I took a picture of the room and sent it.

Mum says it might be simplest to have a mastectomy. Ding, and then she can have a new kidney. There's precedence.

She sent a picture of herself looking de-stressed beside a Burger King. I walked the old drained park back to the car in the quickening drizzle, a rain hoping to come and flood the fields.

I arrive and I'll have further tests.

I walked on past the stables, past horses in immaculate presentation. They seemed the playthings of nobles, the machines of the peasant other. I walked out and visited the RAF museum near the car park. I spent an hour there, seated in front of panels of pictures explaining the history of radar, whose development was a part of the story of the grounds. I read none of the text, just let it all blur until all I can recall now is the displayed nose cone of a Wellington Bomber, its telemetric systems and whatnot that once scanned the area for incoming threats and possible targets. I waited until closing, by which time I had a shadow of the energy I needed to stand and drive back to Bidford-on-Avon.

During the drive back east I was passing a cut in a low ridge, a path beside a conical architectural piece made out of piled stone at a farm's edge. It was quite beautiful. As I took a glance a man was suddenly stepping backwards out of the cover of brush. Time dilated and so too did the space between us. I felt a sudden shock. In my eyes he hit the front of the car; in physics he seemed to pass right through. I braked hard and rubber smoke immediately filled the air. I stopped, wound down my window.

I yelled, 'You okay?'

He was standing quite upright, none the worse for wear. I turned and drove past him once more. He was still. Others—farmers at a guess, or villagers—were now standing beside him as if they'd stepped out of the structure, and they watched, watched me. My mouth open trying to say something. A toddler in the arms of his mum and only the little one seemed to be hurt because he was crying, a long internal ruin. My mouth opened then closed and eventually, eventually I drove into the low hills with the sense I'd just caused a great pain.

Once in Bidford I was forced into bed for the next two days, writing sporadically to Laura about all this, the near accident and Croome Court. I waited for the inflammation to disperse from the secret parts of my brain as my body began to dream of never waking again. I called her when our hours crossed paths and it was late at night in New Zealand. I described the manor to her as a museum of itself and she reminded me how I once complained about castles and the such being made into museums, that they should just be left to rot on their foundations. And I reminded her she's always quick to point out my contradictions.

'But hon, why else would you have them if not to be commented on?'

'To be ignored, L, as a quirk of great but dubious intellect.'

'Idiot.'

'Did you, did you—'

And I didn't manage to form my question and somehow we ended up talking of other things, linking things. Things in the blood and in the numbers. She went to sleep and I stayed in bed after sun-up, reading fragments and learning facts of the estate I could never take on board by merely being present. I tried to find the small stone building and found only images taken on the same date on Instagram. Nothing about its provenance.

You can see Croome Court's tapestry room in New York when you visit the Metropolitan Art Museum. The red tapestries, red seats, the ceiling with its ornamental wheel mouldings and garlanded trophies and various red-themed artworks—these were stripped out at various times last century and exported in the 1950s to the New World. What remains in the original room in Worcestershire is a replica of the ceiling and a photograph in the corner of what was once there, but now in place across the Atlantic, up the Hudson and settled beside that other great parkland in the centre of Manhattan. Indeed, on a trip eighteen months earlier I visited the Met and saw this rubicund room, not knowing where its pieces had come from. Not knowing that a copy of the original ceiling sat in the original's place, looking down on tourists like me who thought they knew something. I'd glanced in at this room and moved on, eventually leaving and walking north to the 97th Street Transverse, where I crossed to the westside thinking about the exonerated Central Park Five because I'd recently watched a documentary and how sad I was for the woman, for the boys, and how in some instances blood tells you very little, so little. Indeed, there is no test for any of this.

Incline

Henry was asleep.

He was dreaming, adrift and dreaming behind a shelter. A

pile of stones like a small two-sided house he'd made himself out of scattered rocks. Rocks drawn to him once he'd crumpled down into the spot. A bivouac of stacked chips and shale. Sleeping in the snowfall and dreaming voices, distant voices, oneiric and vanishing. He heard their calls like the wind-shifts making their way under his clothes, diminishing the blood and slowly shutting every last thing down. Their voices wafting as they came, carrying their pleas from the mountaintop. He dreamed of people then. People in his skin, living in his skin. Dreamed of faces and fractured figures, people but they were the wrong people. Features quivering in black-and-white, animated forms stretching out of the snowfall; each flake fell with a tale, a telling desperate to be decoded. Voices, and he saw people in a meandering march. The long line of humans. Voices too, but they were the wrong people. Everyone was the wrong people. There was only one set of people.

Voices, and they fell like fading footfalls.

'Dad!'

'Henry!'

He woke, still dreaming terrene dreams. He woke with the sensation of blood somewhere on his body, warm and cold. He shook himself, banged his hands against his arms and chest until he was awake and pushing himself to stand, and Simon and David, they were walking on, downwards. They were past him now, deeper in the valley, and he stood up on his wrecked ankles and shouted. Snow outing the shape of the valley, then disguising it in a silent weight. He shouted until David caught a bare human syllable, turned in the same instant and caught a neuronal flash of him over his shoulder. An old man frozen, an icicle of snot and tears hanging off his nose.

They ran against the incline.

Tent

Then walked. An hour, three hours. The three of them slowly down the valley, seeking shelter. Henry with two ice axes as support. Sunlight began to diminish as the valley began to steepen once more. They pitched a tent. Put Henry inside and organised food around him. Simon watched Henry as he began to peel off his layers, his PVC over-trousers, gaiters and leggings. He took off his boots slowly, edging them from his feet. Then his socks, and from his toes to his mid-shin the skin was black and swollen with bruising. He revealed the calf of his right leg. The muscle was split and was just raw meat, two steaks separated by an inch-deep incision. Muscle hanging by tendon. Henry made no sound, just watched the space beyond his son's eyes as Simon felt vomit track its way upwards then retreat.

'It's a wee bit sore,' Henry said.

They bandaged him, fed him, and then they slept.

In the morning the sky had cleared.

They put it to Henry that they had two choices. One, they reverse their direction and re-climb, head back up the mountain, make their descent and return to the hut. Or, two, they continue down the valley into the unknown. They had limited food, there was no track and no facilities between their position and a hut a day's walk to the east on the Clarence River. Henry admitted the climb was beyond him and they would have to continue downwards.

The next morning, they went in an agonised crawl down, headed on until, after an hour, Henry admitted he couldn't continue. His legs no longer functioned, the two limbs open and nerve-busted. They were at the edge of the treeline and it was agreed then that Simon would stay with Henry, and David would walk out and try and get help. How long he'd be no one knew, but he began running, boulder-hopping with barely any gear and the knowledge he had to survive on nearly nothing for unknown time. He could be days, he could be a week: the nearest settlement was sixty kilometres of alpine valley, high-altitude sheep farm and a long, winding river valley away. He ran and disappeared and Simon pitched the tent away from the wind between two southern beech trees. He took Henry's red parka and displayed it on large boulder, weighing it down with rocks. Now they were visible from the staring sky.

Simon had a day's worth of food remaining. He prepared minuscule meals and made sure they were both warm. He looked around for any esculent offerings in the valley and found none.

That night the storm returned, tearing at the tent, snowing them under and threatening any sense that they might survive. Neither slept properly, woke constantly to winds rocketing up the valley, snow and sleet and fear.

And they waited. They barely talked. Just waited. They expected days to pass, expected the experience of time to waste itself upon them like an impossible voice neither of them could hear but seemed to understand. Theirs was a gradual entry into the purpose of time, its collapse and relapse. Henry lay in the tent. His eyes open, then closed.

'You hungry? You want rice?' Simon asked his father from outside.

'We shouldn't talk about food; it'll last longer that way.'

Simon put the billy on the primus. Used the blackened cloth to protect his deadened fingers as he lifted the lid. 'There's enough tea,' he said through the tent flap. 'There's enough for two months.'

Henry closed his eyes. The tip of his nose black.

'You sleeping, Dad?'

Henry's eyes were open, then shut. He talked slowly. Measured, pauses ridiculing the centre of sentences. Words waning, cut. A language in agony, languishing, lying. A culmination of exhaustion, phrases knocking at his teeth like stones.

'Tea would be nice. Thank you,' he said finally.

Simon wound down the gas, the vapour nozzle slowly reducing the flame so it went through a series of colours before vanishing. He removed the pot and placed it on a flat stone beside the tent. There wasn't room for the two enamel cups so he set his father's on an even spot next to the stone. He poured the tea, but as it hit the bottom of the cup the mug started to tip. He put the billy back on the rock, squatted and set the cup between his boots. He lifted the pot once more and poured until the cup was full. He put the billy down and bent to pick the cup up. His boot moved and knocked the mug so half the tea emptied onto the ground. He took the tea into his father.

'You not having any?' Henry asked after thanking his son.

'Maybe. Maybe.'

'We can share.'

'No.'

'It's just that it's quite hot.'

Simon took the cup from his father.

They sat like that. The steam rising, ebbing the heat into the tent. It cooled until Simon handed it to Henry. The old man drank from it silently. Though not so silently; the sound of his father sipping from the cold tea started to irritate. The drink had cooled off and was only half full; there was no reason to drink so delicately. He looked at his father, watched as he brought the cup up to his grey face and took his sips. His mouth hovering over the fluid as if it were still ninety degrees. He blew down into the tea, his mouth pursed into a small funnel. Simon imagined the surface of the liquid rippling, waves, tiny waves shivering on the surface. The smallest of movements and it was all he could hear. The faint whistle of his father's breath, a jet of fine air and it seemed the longest breath and all those rivulets and he began to wonder, he began to hear something as he began to wonder if he could hear those waves and it became louder, louder, a form of rumble as if all around them the mountain was coming down. He thought: avalanche. He thought snow and the spring melt and the slippage and the tiniest of things can set anything in motion. The sound of sound against sound, sound smashing sound, sound striking against the air.

'Dad?'

'It's okay, I'm just sleeping.'

'Dad?'

'. . .'

'You hear it?'

'I'm just sleeping. It's okay.'

Noise flooded the tent and all else seemed to vanish.

Simon unzipped the flap, stepped through and zipped it to the top. He stood to the right of the tent. The noise gathered then condensed in the air. Heavy, rotary, brutal and cutting. Then speed, then the sight of speed and immediately slowing and hovering and lowering. The dark military green mass of an RNZAF Iroquois, the machine swooping up the valley. Simon jumped and signalled and waved. He shouted in the storm of violent air, of jet noise and rotor wash debris.

The pilot brought the machine in low, settled a skid on a boulder. Simon pulled Henry from the rippling tent, shoved the limping man up into the helicopter. Immediately the machine rose and they flew, with Simon standing beside their gear watching them climb, then bank and peel, speeding down the deep valley. He watched until the Iroquois had vanished behind the walls of the ravine, and he continued to watch the same space. The slight indent in the hill where the helicopter had disappeared into unseen sky. He watched until he realised what he was watching, that he was waiting for that same piece of sky to reveal all the things that had occurred in those last moments. He stepped back and looked at the tent and the strewn display of equipment. The ropes and harnesses, discarded gas bottles and packets of dehydrated food. He found himself moving then, sorting the gear into his pack and his father's, then he waited.

He lay on the boulder beside the red jacket. He closed his eyes and waited. How alone. He opened his eyes. The massive skies and rock. Silence. How alone he was without the sound of another, without another sucking up the reverberations of his movements and creatural complaints. The rock cracked in places, split, the lines running in predicable patterns. The staring sky and the sense that he'd know, that soon he'd have knowledge of the future, not just the possible and plausible futures, but *the* future, a singular point in the coming history. He closed his eyes and listened. He found his ears beginning to go soft and the red light that found its way through his eyelids reduced down into a black. He asked what kind of sleep it is when there is no sleep but everything else is turned off. He waited there, certain and sleeping under the dance of phosphenes telling their tale.

When he awoke he built a fire. Small, just a few pieces of kindling he'd found around the campsite. He stared at the fire, waiting. He stood, started looking for more wood, larger pieces. Logs and branches. He dragged them from fifty metres away and threw them on the fire. He heaved great wedges of wood down and watched the sparks leap and grab at his bush shirt. The smoke rose, spiralled and rose and so thick, thick like wicker, and he was barely breathing in the size of it all.

Iroquois

The Iroquois returned, floating in with its storm of downdraught. Rotors cutting through turns of smoke so all was shattered. It hovered over the valley floor, a monster above the flames. My brother crammed all their gear into the pods on the side then hauled himself into the cabin and they rose. Simon looked down at the fire, the sight of smoke and his father's red jacket laid out on the rock. There forever until, until. Then out of sight. The machine sped down the valley, rushing between cliffs and gullies, over snow deposits and debris falls, until it reached a flat piece of farmland several thousand feet below. There Simon saw his father standing alone, balanced on walking sticks in a paddock, in bare feet and long johns. Several dozen steers ran in loops around the old man. He looked ridiculous, the work of a madman set in the hills. Simon began laughing at the sight of his father, bedraggled but clearly alive, a survivor standing amongst the cattle running in circles. The pilot landed; they got Henry back on board and began flying west, up and up over the mountain, over the peak where the storm had reduced itself as it shifted north. They landed at the hut, where Simon collected up all their gear. They flew back down the Hodder Valley to my brother's green Mini. The Iroquois continued on without him to the hospital in Blenheim, where Henry was rushed into emergency and stitched up, casts set on his smashed ankles. There at the car Simon took pause. The Mini was exactly as he had left it. The tyres set in the gravel, the same skid marks where the front wheels had locked up briefly as they came to a stop. He stared at it; how impossibly ordinary it was. The door unlocked with the key and this all seemed a kind of trickery, that this world was the same as the one they'd abandoned days before. He opened it and the car breathed out. He smelt the heated vinyl smell of days in the sun and cold and night.

He drove out of the valley, slow at first. Clutch, accelerator, engine. Then not slow; he drove at speed. Powering out of corners, the rally tail flick and blind pace. Gears, first, second, third, fourth. Down, up. Faster, faster. A trail of white dust behind him as he pursued the helicopter. He raced through the valley until he was paused at State Highway 1 just north of Seddon. He found himself panting, as if he'd run the distance, sprinted, and now here he was at the end.

He drove to the Blenheim police station in traffic. There Simon found David; grinning stupid, he told his story.

He'd run out of the alpine valley, down Branch Stream until he came across farmland, traversed the fields where Henry's steers had stood eating grass, then crashed through a small cut in the foothills till he was finally in the Clarence River valley and making his way north. He ran and walked and fell and jogged until he came across the New Zealand Army, there on manoeuvres. They'd accidentally sunk a boat the week before and were back, trying to rescue it from the river. They got him out of there and brought in the air force to find Simon and his father.

They laughed, joked.

They bought cigars and steaks. Afterwards they found Henry in the hospital chatting to the nurses, high on morphine and quite happy. He told them not to worry about him, to continue on their trip. So, they did.

They spent two weeks climbing the Alps in Nelson Lakes National Park. Within ten months David would be dead: he would fall during another whiteout, this time from a cliff near Chancellor Hut in Westland National Park while plotting his climb of Aoraki. But before that, before those awful days, Henry made his way back to Wellington where his wife Francie and I were waiting.

I was sick then, the first time sick. Cornered in the lounge considering the wide pane of glass that drew in the outside, the gardens and trees my father had planted over many years. Pōhutukawa beyond the front fence, then a series of old established pines, then the smaller bushes and roses. On the eastern side was a kauri I had planted when I was eight. It was Arbor Day at school and I'd brought home the seedling. It was the tree I believed most likely to take over the garden and dominate the rhododendrons and other flowering shrubs. By now it was a slender sapling hidden behind a recently planted ponga always excited by the wind and throwing shadows on the lawn and across the face of the house, flickering remarks to those who sat watching from the lounge. There, Henry and I convalesced and considered each other. We sat in identical chairs spaced by the matching sofa and waited on our bodies. Wide windows and unusual heat. Conversations began in moments cued by uncertainty. Neither sure what the other was saying, what languages were being spoken.

Seven weeks later Henry had his casts off, but he existed in the lounge, bored and reading. Then, once the muscle fibres knitted themselves back together and he had movement in his legs once more, he again planned to leave the house for a tramp, his pack full, his ankles barely taking the weight. I watched him at the top of the steep staircase that led down from the upper floor. He was ready for a two-week tramp in the Tararua Range, his pack strapped to his shoulders.

'He swayed,' I said, 'and reached out to the walls to balance himself. Then took his first step and he, quite simply, fell.'

'He fell?'

The Listener

'He fell,' I nodded. 'He fell. Just—toppled forward and went down the stairs. This awful noise, body and carpet and backpack. I stayed in the lounge listening. And, you know—God, after all that noise, my father still left the house. He went tramping in the hills. In the fucking mountains with these destroyed ankles and dead fingertips.'

'Families are dicks, eh?' Hannah said. 'What was he like? I don't imagine you having a dad.'

'That's a strange thing to say.'

'Because I've met your sisters and mum, but your dad was always—absent.'

'He's mostly been dead, I guess.'

The people around us around ate unrestrained on the roof of the old radome overlooking the city. They gnawed at burgers and gripped sandwiches fiercely, forcing them into mouths. The grotesque, near-silent voicing of mass ingestion. It was a Sunday and people came to the top of the hill to hang out in these old buildings, to eat looking out over Wilmersdorf, Charlottenburg and all the way across to Mitte in central Berlin. Hannah was sitting on a large piece of masonry beside me, her feet tucked up under her thighs, wearing a jumper three times too big for her. She's small, compact and easily situated. She was in the city on business, a proposed exhibition of her jewellery work. A collection inspired by her donation of that kidney to her mum many years earlier. We'd landed in the city separately, timetables aligning so we were able to have this afternoon to hang out.

'There's a few contradictory versions,' I said. 'Laura never met him, which breaks my heart some days.'

I took something cold from the little hamper she'd put together at a Lidl near where she was staying on Karl-Marx-Straße.

She asked for the sorts of things he used to say, and I explained how he used to talk in an almost official tone. He'd talk about things like religiosity openly. He'd say this and that, that his spirituality was not bound by normative statements of belief or philosophical logic, rather the experiential and relational. 'Which was nice, you know.'

'He sounds nice.'

I explained how I'd recently found a piece of writing explicating his relationship to the various family trees, that this was the one thing for him that transcended mere knowledge. That it was something intensely personal, culminating in personhood. 'Which made me uncomfortable, you know?' I said. 'He wrote something similar about mountains. Maybe it would have made sense dying up there.'

Hannah said it didn't make sense dying anywhere.

'True enough. Though you could invert that and it would be equally true.'

My friend smiled whenever I tried to make sense but missed. Hannah has always had a generosity I wish I knew how to match.

I told her how Dad had referred to himself as a post-modernist. 'Which was odd in many ways. But, he was the first person to tell me Nagasaki was the opening event of post-modernism, that Hiroshima was the last act of the modernity. Which was reaching, but it all sounded cool.' God and gods, I told Hannah, weren't dead, just a series of marginalised cultural constructs, yada, yada. Which I kind of liked. 'I found him deeply religious—more so than any evangelist. My mum too.'

'He sounds almost relatable, weirdly.'

'Yeah. Only he wasn't. He just had this, like, drive. And my sister too,' I said, 'and another cousin, which shocks me now.'

'Which one?'

I told her about my sister and then about Kimber, my cousin's daughter. That she got sick in 1996, thirty-one years earlier. 'We didn't know what was wrong with her, just that she'd stopped suddenly.'

Hannah looked out at the view and nodded, and we paused.

I was in Germany to do research on a new book. A book about Caroline, the young woman who got pregnant to Kaiser Frederick's son. About her own son and his daughter and the Coventry she married. A pioneering family tale to be cut through with contemporary tellings, comparative and ridiculing of the method I was engaged in. I arrived and found I wanted nothing to do with the story. I just wanted to be in Berlin, in the furnace of the faceless modern. And I didn't even manage that; most of my time was spent in my apartment watching television, waiting for clear health and summer. It arrived at the same time as my friend and I found myself talking about Henry, trying to find an angle into him, because he, I realised, was why I was there.

'What was he like when he talked? Because I'm wondering if he was the same as you.'

I shook my head. 'He didn't believe in illness.'

Hannah laughed. 'And illness is like your religion, eh?' She put a finger into the corner of her eye and scraped out some sleep. 'I wonder if he sounded like you when he talked.'

I stared at her for a moment. Earlier, we'd taken a taxi from the Jewish memorial across the city and up Teufelsberg. We had the driver drop off us at the car park and then ambled our way here. The hill, and how we took many breaks during the short walk. Stopping every twenty metres and sitting, or just standing, looking up at the abandoned buildings that made this hill, a chunk of post-war orogeny, so interesting. We'd walked in the halls of the old American listening station, a spy post constructed on the crest of a hill that didn't exist before the war. It was built by piling up all the ruins of Berlin. They infilled it with soil and planted a million trees.

We walked among the artworks open to the elements. Impeccable ruins laid down in the near forty years since unification and the vaporous end of the Cold War. The decay of the modern, geodesic radomes disintegrating on their graffitied platforms, the manifold structures all once part of a great metallic ear bent to the east. They were now weighted in paint, in the inscriptions of street artisan and tag. Partial names, full names. Names and the po-mo pseudonyms of logogram and reclamation. We'd walked slowly, sitting sometimes. I watched, gazed ahead and listened to Hannah talk about the hell she went through after she finally gave her kidney to her mum.

She spoke then stopped, pointing at the tags and images spraypainted on the walls. Some of the works adhering to the shape of the buildings, others rudely against it. Stylised, anti-style. The half-revealed breasts of a woman with her camouflage T-shirt pulled up to nipple height, comic grimace on her mouth. A child with his finger in his nose. A still-warring Waffen-SS officer, now a skull and hat screaming, yelling instructions to a sudden post-cubist machine-gunner. A photorealist of an attractive young woman with her middle finger shoved into her mouth, lips and teeth glistening, a beatific middle-class *fuck you* shining and shattering. Behind her an endless scree of bulbous and colourful declarative repetitions. *Fuck Facebook. Fuck Steroids. Fuck NSA. Fuck Osama. Fuck elders. Fuck Imperialism. Fuck Taxes. Fuck pickles. Fuck Dogshit. Fuck USA. Fuck 7am. Fuck Fame. Fuck Cocaine. Fuck me. Fuck haters.* On the floor in front of the piece 'Punk' was scratched determinedly into the concrete, multiple iterations put there by the same hand. All as if the impossibilities attached to any interpretation of the word were understood suddenly, that its meaning had finally landed there exact at that discarded border, that frontier of sound where cleverly routed electricity once sought evidence of the other on the far side of the Berlin Wall.

Now we sat and ate, looking out over the broken lattice of the city, its electricity and drone.

'Two stories about Kimber,' I said. 'She must have been twenty-six or seven and she returned home from work unable to use her fingers. Her hands had become soft and unmoving like empty, wet gloves. She sliced her thumb open cutting up vegetables. She went to work the next day and the day after that but was eventually let go because she just kept turning up and collapsing. She was determined beyond determined until determination didn't have an effect anymore. She was sick for over a decade. But before that, you see, she also climbed mountains. She knew the end point of pain, because to be good at climbing you have to look at it every time you put on a harness. She also knew it from the other end when she couldn't get up from the floor one day after collapsing in full sight of her partner.' She had it for twelve years, I told Hannah. 'And my cousin, Rachel, she's had it over three decades. Thirty years with an undiagnosable disease, despite us knowing its name. This is my connection to living, fighting this contradiction. The way I have to fight for every moment.'

'How many years does a disease need?'

'I don't know,' I said, 'it's a dick.'

'I can't imagine illness without my twin. I just can't do it.'

'Yeah. I'm sitting here and I miss all the people we could have been,' I said.

'I know what you mean.'

'You know what I mean? Like this has become my particular belief system. It's like I've begun believing my family put themselves in these positions, that they climbed, they climbed to that height in order to search for the thing I can't actually escape. Which isn't a fair thought, but I keep thinking it. Another sister, Adi, wants to write a book about her cycling feats, continental divides and all. She's the oldest woman to complete the Trans Am, this mad unsupported race across America. She got her hips and knees replaced and first thing she does, before she can even walk properly, is get on her bike. It's a familial disease.'

Hannah laughed. 'Anyway, where are you going after this?' she asked.

'Meeting Laura on Isola della Scogliera Rossa.'

'Really? Cratere? Great. The painting . . .'

'Yeah. And the new exhibition.'

'I went there, the same time as they found the form things.'

'Right. I don't think you can actually see them yet.'

'No. But there's the old steps and there's the painting.'

'Yeah. Laura does the research. I turn up and walk blindly into museums.'

'See the painting.'

'I know. There's also a rumoured family thing there.'

Hannah shrugged.

I told her how my great-great-great-great-grandfather was

kicked out of Prussia for an indiscretion back in the 1840s. He went to the Sudan on an expedition and apparently stayed on the island on the way back through Genoa.

'Well, I guess go stand on a beach and wave.'

We ate. The air shuffled the old sheets of canvas set between the geodesic framework of the radome's encloser. The strange monster that once kept the electrics of the listening machines from element and view. There was no equipment anymore; the radar units had all been decommissioned and removed in the 1990s. There was just us and the talking breeze and the frames.

The hill was close to the size of Mount Victoria in Wellington, which I look out on every day from our house. It's the first place in Berlin to get snow in winter. All is measured in ash.

I said then how I'd say goodbye to my family and off they'd go, driving down the road and then onto the ferry, or north, and they'd walk in valleys and then up a specific ridge. They'd climb up higher until they're only following a thin, impossible edge. Sheer space below them. And beyond the edge is the shutdown, the body shutting down, the brain retreating into a state marked by severe bodilessness. Then they'd retreat back from it. And occasionally they'd fall. 'And,' I said, 'who can blame them?'

'Your family are idiots,' Hannah said, wiping at a stifled laugh on her mouth.

'So are yours.'

'Yeah, but mine are artists. They know how to do it with detached irony.'

'My sister was the real thing, before she got sick. A proper mountaineer. I'm in awe of her, the things she's climbed and everything.'

Hannah got out her phone, ran her finger over its surface. Over her shoulder I watched as a man came up the stairs, cane and guide dog. A blond Labrador guiding him through descending tourists. I kept watching—the simplicity of their movements as the dog directed him to a clear space, where he sat. I wondered if there was a mental map the man and dog shared. I watched this animal, its soft eyes and wet nose. Tongue contentedly out and waiting. I continued looking until I sensed that by staring I was further reducing the man's vision by making his dog a pet. A thing of jump and play. The two were intimately linked and I was reducing their connection down to that base knowledge of interaction we carry everywhere.

'I'm ashamed of this,' I said to Hannah, 'but. But you know, when COVID hit I got strangely excited.' I paused. 'Thought, stupidly, like: I might die! Excitedly. That I'd get out of this thing. All this—whatever and exhaustion and—'

'Yeah, I know. I know. I had the same response.'

I didn't say anything. Seven years earlier, Hannah made it back to New Zealand two months before the first COVID lockdown. The operation and kidney donation occurred just as the world was preparing for the worst.

'But I don't feel any shame about it,' she said. 'It was the same when I had my brain haemorrhage. I was like: God, I almost got away with it. So close. I almost escaped and got away with not having to go through a whole life.'

'Because life is—what is it—life is fractious.'

'Fractious.' She laughed. 'Because it's incredibly difficult,' she said, cheerily.

'Do you feel like you're in a stasis, Hannah? Since your mum and kidney? Between life and whatever?'

'A bit, yeah. Ask me again in a few years and I'll have another answer. I'm not really all that enamoured with life, you know? Right now.'

We'd had this conversation numerous times. She was the only one who understood it when twenty-four years earlier I'd tried to do something about my life and the depression that anchored it to the depths. That I tried to take it by swallowing two bottles of pills. She'd laughed at the event, which didn't endear her to my family particularly. But I knew why she'd laughed. She'd had that subarachnoid haemorrhage eighteen months earlier and her life was like a permanent (and years before I began using the word) concussion. She didn't feel like who she was, didn't know who she was supposed to be. Played out this new life on assumptions of how a twenty-three-year-old woman was supposed to behave. Ideas taken from uncoalesced memories. Which was in strong opposition to the person she used to be.

'After the kidney donation, I entered that world of yours,' Hannah said. 'It was the same, post-brain-haemorrhage. The clarity of signals kept diminishing until I didn't know what was causing anything, the world was non-causal—and I was thinking: Maybe I'm just tired. And with the kidney thing it has been the same. Maybe I ate something wrong. Maybe, maybe—what? I don't know what's a sensible answer to things.'

I asked her what it was like, having a part of her living inside someone else.

She shook her head, and the blue in her grey eyes brightened. 'It's normal. I'm a twin. A part of me has always been living inside someone else.'

'I didn't think of that.'

'You wouldn't. Like, the boundaries of my body, they have never been the same as the boundaries of yours. Someone asked me once if I'm competitive with Willie, and I just laughed. It would like competing with my elbow. You ever got in a tussle with your elbow?' she asked. She laughed a little at her use of this specific analogy, like she'd been wanting to make the joke for years. 'It doesn't work out. It's—a. And, like, with my mum: I am *of* her. I'm a part of her. So my habits, sense of self, my body. I felt like was putting something back in her. She asked for it, and I gave it back. But I think this sense is heightened because I'm a twin. It feels like a return rather than a gift, you know what I mean?'

'I would never have thought,' I said. I glanced at the city, its faint hum, the odd distinct word that hikers made on the hill.

'Fictional Hannah would never have thought of this,' she said.

'No.'

We talked over the quiet of the view, the haze of Berlin in the distance. I had the brief thought that perhaps my reasons for being there, for heading to Charlottenburg, Potsdam and also Croome Court those years ago was also to put a part of myself back, back into theoretical places that had only existed in my mind. An unwanted part I couldn't distinguish from the territories of myself that were vital and necessary.

The man with the cane reached to touch his guide dog's head. I saw a couple sitting cross-legged reach and hold hands. I wondered if they'd been arguing, I wondered if this was something new.

'But, you know, this recovery has been hell,' Hannah said. 'Absolute hell. My mind has gone. I can't read a book. I can't do a crossword. I'm as bad as you.'

'But you can walk and run and do acrobatics now.'

'But my head is still mulch. This is my inheritance.'

I said I wished I knew how I'd inherited mine. That I too would give it back. 'Like, here you go Mum, have my immune system, have my gut and ganglia. The immune is a bit bung, it doesn't seem to switch off.'

‘That’s not really what I was talking about, Cov.’

‘I know.’

Hannah tilted her head. ‘Yeah. And seeing how hard it was on my mum. Just how hard it was on her. I’d no idea. Her life is worse with my kidney in her than it was before. She just used to get tired, but now. Oh my God, she gets so sick. I can’t understand. I know you know it. And only you out of all the people I know can know it. The depth of sick she experiences. And I feel weirdly responsible for her being this sick. She asked for the kidney, but she didn’t ask for this. Before the operation she was so exhausted, and even then I thought: I don’t think I can ever understand that level of tired.’

‘That’s why I told you about my father, about my brother. I imagine it’s the only way to understand how deep this tiredness gets. All analogies are hopeless. But I’ve been wondering for years if this illness was the result of some stupid, out-of-control thought at some point,’ I said. ‘Not by me, but some ancestor.’

‘Which is the best analogy.’

‘What?’

‘That all analogies are hopeless.’

We were quiet for a moment.

‘Yeah—I can’t comprehend mountaineering,’ she said. ‘It’s all the unnecessary being right up close to cliffs, heights. And the cold. I can’t abide cold. It’s the brink of death stuff.’

‘And I guess that’s the point. That’s what my body seems to mimic. Hey, it says, death’s just there, you—like—wanna? That’s what it feels like. It’s like I have a ghost already. Follows me around, pointing things out.’

‘We need to give it a name.’

‘Really?’

‘Call it Allison.’

‘Call yourself Allison.’

She laughed. She told me about her guilt, all the complications that come after receiving a donation. That it might only buy her mum two, three years. And maybe Hannah had only given her mother a few years of pain. So, guilt. 'I fear so much about this, feel terrible and I can't see an end to the cycle. God. This is what it is loving someone, it's so complicated. I'm complicit in her hurt. I gave her life, I gave her pain. Very Buddhist.'

I looked again at the guide dog, its ears like a child's gloves. I imagined them hearing in the same way a child's fingers touch, always touching things of tactile intrigue. I had a sense the man knew I was looking so I glanced away, then back at the Labrador, then at the man eating his cake.

'Do you need to lie down or sleep or whatever?' she asked.

I shook my head. 'You know,' I said, 'I've tried to spot my dad's red jacket, like a hundred times. Flying to Christchurch and—'

'Why? You ever spot it?'

I said no and I did lie down, my head on a smooth stone.

Two hours earlier I was supposed to meet Hannah at a café at the west end of Spielplätz, in Kreuzberg; instead she'd found me at the bus stop in Hermannplatz. I was caught in a moment. One of my frozen set of minutes where people and cars become a surging event I can't comprehend. I can't comprehend how to cross, or why I am crossing and where to. The interiors of specific thoughts and their related actions are lost to me. I'd sat down outside a bank and I don't know how many minutes passed until I heard her saying my name. She took me across the street, through the market and to the other side when I had to sit again. We entered the Starbucks, where we ate a muffin.

'I've never been to a Starbucks,' she said as she inspected the dismal muffin, the dryness and specks of wan blueberry. 'This is literally, literally my first time. I was hoping for something, I don't know what.'

Know.

Know.

Know.

Know.

'Do you know?' I'd asked her. We'd stood in line to order and I'd asked if she knew how much of a different person she was after her haemorrhage.

She shook her head. She told me about reading. How she used to read books, and the book would be in her mind. If she had a connection to a book, she would almost have memorised it. The consciousness of it. 'The book was in me,' she said. 'And that trait, skill, ability, it left. Like I lost all these things that lived inside me. My ability to do special things with books and text vanished. But, but it made me more—analytical, I guess. I had to think about books more. Like I had to talk about the nature of words more. How we shape them into realities that—you know. I was at the end of my honours year when it happened. I had to learn to be a reader again. And I became more precise in my readings because I didn't have the books memorised. So, it was a different me. I was resentful. I missed myself. I just wanted to be me, but I was aware it wasn't coming back.'

I asked if she felt like there was an absent person, someone she missed from then. 'Because I do,' I said. 'Even though I have achieved pretty much everything I have achieved in my life with this illness, I miss myself.'

She looked at my face, and off to the side. She smiled a little.

'There's that person,' she said. 'The one who fell in love for the first time, you know? The person who, for the first time falls in love and is *altered* by falling in love. By the beauty and heartbreak of falling in love. You can never be that person again. Do you know what I mean? That person vanishes. And that's how I feel about the person I was, I can never be that person again. But I feel love, and that's what matters. How I feel about my body, I don't know.'

'How I feel about my body,' I said, 'is it's a traitorous fuck.'

After a time sitting in the Starbucks she asked me again if I was okay, if I was all right to walk and I told her I was. It took some minutes for the event to occur, movement and ambulation, but I made the right combination of words in my head and, as if in the unlocking of those thoughts, my body moved. I stood, my limbs capable. We headed to the U-Bahn outside the Starbucks. I was dazed still, but it felt necessary that we leave the restaurant and travel into the inner districts of the city, the pockets of deliberately contained culture. The museums, the galleries and strict lines of street. During my first visit twenty-eight years earlier I was told it was a place of multiple hives, the whole place hummed by a desire to maintain the island status of the city, a world of otherness and odd social invocation. These events were everywhere, transferred through scene, building and border. That was in 1998 while travelling with Deborah's sister and her husband as their band's sound engineer; I've no idea how true that quixotic summary was, it felt over-simplified but I wanted it to be simple, simple and true.

At the U-Bahn, Hannah and I took a seat on the platform amongst all the movement, the performance of transience and passage. The masses vaporous, all scattering and body shift. The sense of their circling movements, this rush and turn through the boroughs.

We waited; a haze of heavy non-thought sat in my body;

trains passed hissing, the rush and metallic hullabaloo. Yellow steel and bright windows. I had that memory of catching the train twenty-eight years earlier: the process had seemed simple enough. We'd boarded, sat and talked, then exited. We went from one unnamed part of the city to another. We'd board and travel several miles in closed conversation with our tour manager, Michael. Now Hannah and I sat alone. I watched others, remembering what it is with others. That you watch and remember, or you watch and take on new processes to practise and repeat. Men and women passing the ticket machine. They pressed buttons labelled in German, followed instructions written or remembered in German. Two more trains. Graffiti and its codes of colour and form. An almost theatrical passing of time, a flashed life staged by uncertainty. I hoped by just waiting we would know how to purchase the ticket.

'Can I see him?' Hannah asked.

'Who?'

'You know.'

'I know?' And I did know. I just didn't.

'Can I see him? Allison.'

'Of course you can see him.'

'Awesome. When?'

'I don't know.'

'What do you mean, *I don't know*?'

'I assume you see him all the time.'

'How do I know?'

'I don't know, I don't know what you see.'

'Where is he?'

'Hopefully on a beach somewhere.'

The train took us to the eastern extent of the green sweep of the Tiergarten. Hannah asked again if I was okay. I said nothing and wandered, slowly stepping into the rows, the hectares of granite slabs, the quadrilateral standing stones, the massive rectangular hunks of rock. The mark of the Holocaust-Mahnmal.

I'd visited there eight years earlier, after I'd spent time in Galway and Croome Court. Seen the same stones, or not seen them at all. I'd walked slowly through a fraction of the millions of turns and the possibilities of turns. Lost myself, found myself, then purposely turned and turned until direction was lost again. And Hannah and I did the same. We walked slowly into the shaping and rising of the blocks, the way they ached from the earth and the alleys between talked of dimension and order. I felt myself speaking, then not speaking. We walked until we passed out of sight of each other. Walked in stillness, quietness. Then a noise, a flash, a man nearby, then distant. Voices, kids yelling. Children and young couples making a game out of the hundreds, the thousands of irregular stelae the size of humans and beyond humans, the size of cars, each orderly arranged, perfectly arranged, perfectly ordered. Ordered perfectly beyond sight for she was still in there, walking, walking as I was, walking and stepping amongst stone, perfect stone, perfect order, and my friend vanished amongst this strange edict of stone, beneath the surface of order and pillar. Beneath the word. The one word the poet had for the memory of this place. How she'd repeated it over and over, over and over until it was perfect and sustained by its imperfection. *Intolerable.* I thought of her and sat at a junction of two colossal pieces of stone. As I sat, I thought of the very place I was within, its size and intent and how once inside you are utterly alone.

From Mitte, we took a taxi up Teufelsberg, and to get to Teufelsberg we drove through Charlottenburg, through the endless spree of five-, six-, seven-storey buildings in a new drizzle. The stucco seeding of outer Berlin. It was near where Kaiser-Friedrich-Straße intersects with the dedicated straightaway of the B5 that Hannah began pointing. She was nodding at a building, then older buildings, stayers, survivors, as I sat with my hand out the window, catching rain. Hulls and remains from World War II and here they were, rebuilt and rescued from a future propping up Teufelsberg in the west.

Hannah said she had a problem when in Berlin, that she could never stop looking for those buildings that had only somewhat survived the war. That were partially rebuilt in strange shapes. She said she was always staring up at them, looking for damage. She said you could walk by a place for a year and not realise, and then you'd see. 'Suddenly you see an arch cut off before its end. A single window missing, and you just think it was all part of the design, that that was all the architect's pleasure. I find it disturbing, upsetting even that this was a practice. I'm not sure why this is.'

'You expect destruction to be destruction. You expect ruins to be ruins,' I said, and closed my hand about the rain, held it in my palm.

We passed through Kaiser-Friedrich-Straße, the lights green and the traffic sudden in movement. I nodded at the street sign.

'You wanna go to his palace?' she asked, and screwed up her face. 'It's around here someplace. I think.'

I shook my head.

'Yeah,' she said.

'It was flattened anyway,' I said.

'But they rebuilt it, right? The palace?' she said. 'They rebuild everything, eh?'

I opened my hand and let the water slip.

'They rebuild everything.'

Eighty

The literature tells us that over 80 percent of ME sufferers are women. A 4:1 ratio that is so far mostly unexplained. However, a recent Barcelona study suggests that as a neuro-inflammatory process the divergences in male and female ME patient numbers could possibly reflect variances in the disease and how it advances. This is because there are neuro-immune differences between sexes. Uncertainty rules here. But what it does also suggest is that this book needs another voice, in fact multiple voices, multi-generational and representative of all who aren't me.

I ask those in my surrounds how I might do this.

Further uncertainty, further doubt at this book's capacity to show.

Do you want more facts?

Okay. Okay, more facts.

The name of the disease refers to both the muscle pain and the inflammation of the brain. The resulting effects are often extreme, debilitating body fatigue and cognitive dysfunction that can replicate the symptoms of patients presenting with damaged brain tissue. There is definite reasoning for this supposition: the functional cognitive profiles of ME are similar to those presenting in patients with traumatic head injury. Imaging studies at Stanford have shown distinct differences between brains of patients with ME and those of healthy people.

It's terrifying.

Terrifying.

In fact, I'm afraid every time I talk with a friend I'm going to somehow infect them just by trying to remember facts like these. And perhaps I do. My memory doesn't seem to belong to me, but to that other *other* always trembling nearby. These bastard twins haunt the strangest of places.

My fears are continual.

In the Salzkammergut

During the waning days of a period of reasonable health, Alin and I took the train west from Westbahnhof station towards Salzkammergut country in upper Austria. We rode from Vienna with her youngest boy, Kaspar, on a Friday morning in the northern autumn of 2016. We sat across from each other, Alin and I, talked through the odd aura we'd create about ourselves when we were in the same physical space, the mechanism of friendship we'd managed to protect for over a decade. We were kind to each other, gentle, because that was what the relationship was, delicate and infrequent.

She pointed out sights to Kaspar.

'See, look,' she said in German. Then repeated everything in English for my sake as we ploughed through swathes of land bordered by high places whose peaks' elevation were hinted at by snow and bent light. I asked what a specific phrase meant when she gave the name of a hillside leaning upwards away from the train.

'Oh, I'm guessing some hilly castle. A count, a baron or prince.'

'Sure.'

'Then occupied, of course. Nazis, so we hate it.'

'Of course.'

She leant her head forward to look out beyond the window, to things invisible to me and her son.

'Really?' I said. 'Nazis.'

She shrugged. 'This was brown shirt country. It's best to just look at the scenery, you know?'

'I have morbid fascinations for these things,' I said.

'Oh boy, you.'

We talked artlessly for the most part, the small fascinations of our lives that were easy to share. And in doing so we let ourselves slip inside the tremors of narrative that let us learn and listen in a way that was outside the simplicity of the words. There was a child in the seat beside us—I have always struggled to lift the level of conversation when the ears of a kid are open.

She turned towards me while explaining a little history of the area.

And me, I'm a master of nodding. A master of extracting the subconscious hints and taking them to be dialogue. I pick up on tone and scattered nouns and generally get the idea. ADD, you see.

The history of Alin and me seemed at the time to be a search for the measurement we might apply to our specific connection. We'd never had this much time together and there were some things we needed to learn via the way we spoke, how words landed and repeated, amended their meaning over and over until I'll admit I felt a kind of fear we were running out.

‘When’s the sun coming?’ Kaspar asked. The sun was dimmed now by the grey.

‘It’ll be sunny as soon as we get to Oma and Opa’s, bubby,’ she said, then corrected him for some fault in his speech. She then shrugged at me in that conspiracy adults keep for themselves, that they lie to children because they can.

I lay back against the window and let them talk and play.

In extremes of climate, I develop a sudden ache for the ordinary, for shirts and that jacket I pack in my satchel just in case. On my arrival in Vienna two days earlier from Morocco the sky had hung dented, clouds punching black into the white, and there was a dank hold on the air. A smell of fallen leaves. In Marrakech the heat had caught me out. Forty-five degrees, a kind of white, piercing centigrade that saw every patch of shadow populated by animal, child and adult. Men and women intent on remaining stationary, for their bodies to produce as little heat as possible. But there in Austria it had settled down into something closer to the known. I was wearing jeans for the first time in weeks and as a result felt a control that had been lost in the titanic heat. And I mention the weather because of its monotony, its comparative sameness during our time in Vienna. It was massively dim. I mention it also because Vienna was the first time since leaving New Zealand that I’d noticed my energy dissipate in a worrying manner. First time since January 2015, when I’d begun a remission of sorts. The drop in energy was almost immediate. In Vienna my muscles were suddenly heavy in my skin. I could feel my bones. I could feel the expansion inside my head, the urgent need to lie down and wait for what came next. Instead of what came next, I’d met Alin and Daniel and the kids. The beauty of them all. They buoyed me until it was time to sleep and let in the nervous system's uncanny imitation of a frightened child, the way it begins to shake in the most minute ways as the adrenaline drive takes over. The familiar desire of my body to undo all its hard work getting me to the city as I lay awake with my heart rushed by a chemical efflux symptomatic of illnesses I did not have.

I nodded at Kaspar and told Alin about my tendency to be fearful around kids.

'Don't be. It's silly. Why?'

'I'm always worried that I'm likely to ruin something.'

'You can't ruin kids. They're self-actuating.'

'No. What? Is that something?'

'I'm teasing you. Of course, you can ruin them in many ways but probably not like how you think.'

I told her how I worry something great and important is about to happen in their lives, and I'm like some awful, giant potential fork in the road of their *will-to-selfhood*.

'There's no such thing,' she said, though the look on her face told me she believed the opposite. She then repeated those last words and laughed, kindly. 'It's like, it's like there's a kiddy bill of rights no one's ever written down. It's much more powerful than anything we can understand as adults, its ramifications quite enormous.' She nodded at Kaspar pointing and examining the intrigue of his toys as they fought climactic battles of resolve and reason. I felt appreciative then for the days I had to spend with Alin, for the train, for its speed through the country as we headed for Attnang-Puchheim, where her father waited in the car park. A small, unattractive town in the mid-north of Austria, twenty minutes' drive from our final destination at a lake town among the alps. Angular and brutally, beautifully cleaved. But more than that, I was shocked that we were there—actual, physical, undreamed and potentially difficult.

We let the high-speed rip of suburb and dorp, castle imprints and old vehement empire, come and destroy itself in the blur. We watched the colour fade of early autumn, let the light-gash of stations flash by. The breath and breadth of it. Felt the compression when the tunnels came, the way air expanded in the cavities behind our eyes so we were each opening our mouths and forcing the air out into somewhere.

We drew pictures for her boy—crayon fish and jelly monsters.

She wiped his nose with ultra-light tissues.

Alin, I liked to say, was an old friend, though we barely knew each other, not as breathing, aching, touching humans. Prior to this trip the total time spent in the same room would have added up to a few hours. We were squared-off by text, by keystrokes and the tapping of fingers. We were, proudly, epistolary. Linked by data stream and news feed, and there we sat in the Kinder carriage, a partition on the train for parents and children extant with all the noises of infantile Deutsch and Czech. The full-blown sirens of childhood and its related panics.

We were also quite certain one of us was about to die.

Alin's husband, Daniel, had had a weekend planned in the south of Germany. He'd taken their eldest for the days we'd be away in the country at her parents. Kaspar asked over and over where his brother was. Each time she explained to him, he'd say *Scheiße, Scheiße,* as he sipped on his straw sticking out from his mug. Alin would turn to me with a grin and translate: *Shit, shit.* Which was funny, because it was one of twenty or so words I could understand in German, but Alin enjoyed saying it back to me. It was as if within this short phrase, she was able to share a part of her life she wasn't able to translate through simple explanations. Because we were simple, the two of us, bordered by language and connected by the belief we had in our friendship. Sometimes noisy, sometimes absent, it had an age behind it that was permanently caught in slow motion. Things mature at a more leisurely pace when its contents are logged by epistolary means, when constructed via the words we wish to hear.

The boy had picked up his swears somewhere along the way at their flat in Leopoldstadt, or his kindergarten, and now took it across country pulling in looks from the other parents and those curiously blank stares only toddlers can put across their faces. He said it quite often and Alin would laugh and say to me: *Shit, shit.* And it seemed to me then that there's something in motherhood, in fatherhood, that doesn't translate into the world of the childless. Something, perhaps, about the impossibility of fully understanding one's child, but loving him with greater zeal for the fact of that self-same distance. I came to know Alin more in those exchanges than I had through all the gestures of text and translation we'd built ourselves upon. Everything for her was translated, marred and questionable. For me, though, this was the suite of my language and I felt a responsibility to keep us naïve and inexact.

Earlier in the year, when I learned I was being flown to Edinburgh for the festival, Alin made plans to meet me in Scotland. I also made arrangements to travel to Vienna and stay a few days and meet her young family. We organised a time and day, and when that was reached we ran at each other on Princes Street, pushed past pedestrians to get to that place on the pavement where we'd finally meet after such a long time contriving and stoking our nearness with what-ifs and the small fictions of possible lives. We'd stared into eyes, held each other's faces like the lost paramours we'd once thought and pretended we might've been but never were. We laughed a lot, kissed and hugged and laughed more, because there was no other way to be when the reality hits and says the person you've been longing to see, that you and she, you don't really know each other. There were presences and absences never thought of.

And, as with most of my relationships during this time, things quietened quickly when it became apparent I had little to give beyond mere proximity of company. The sickness that had been with me for four years by then was growing once more. Thickening and laying me out as if a dawn drifting above the water line. It was a hospitalising thing, but then it retreated into the background enough for me to write a little and mutely attend to the things life had created. And, in the case of Alin, attend to the things my previous life had borne to us as two unusual but grateful friends. But, as in Vienna, I understood my energy was waning, repeating its tendency towards self-annihilation, correcting the body's desire to be well and sure by sending the adrenals into a quiet overdrive.

I wanted to say, but didn't know how to say, that I was tired.

We clocked towns, and Alin told her boy little facts about buildings and spans. Whether true or not, he pointed and looked and uttered some new phrases. I had the thought that a parent's tales are always true, always necessarily so. I found them fascinating, mixed by ruins of old futures and damned pasts. This was Nazi country after all, deep in Catholicism and the horrifying grandeur of rumour. As a result I felt the presence of old family, though none I knew of had ever lived here; I felt the violence of the Hohenzollern name, though we're talking different empires, different dialects. Alin's stories also drew us back to another time, drew us back to Scotland and the worst thing, the worst of things.

We were trying to get up to Milne's Court and a car. A car, an Audi, tore out of Mound Place and into the descending traffic. It happened right in front of us. Audi into taxi then bus. We saw the whiplash of the driver entering into the traffic, the way his vehicle collided with a taxi. His head whammed and settled. Alin grabbed my arm, then—*Oh*—then we saw. Then the bus and the way the man's car was crushed between its bumper and the shining black of the taxi and then we saw his body twist in queer angles as if asking, demanding an answer to a new question of what it's like to be living. All around the high noise of car tyres, of engine revs and ticking metal. Slowly there was only shouting and one noise, the screaming from the back of the cab. A pair of tourists: one of them banging at the windows, and the body next to her. The blood-matted hair and slumped head.

Alin grabbed me and started to pull me away.

'David. David.' Her face was wet and red. I'd never seen her cry. Why would I have seen her cry?

We walked, up, down. Stairs and alleys. Just the act of walking. We found ourselves at a café on the far end of Middle Meadow Walk. I don't recall getting there, arriving, anything. I had water and watched her drink an espresso. Cyclists parking their bikes.

She held herself like it was cold and she was wet from rain, but this was August, and all wore light shirts and shorts. It was only us who couldn't feel the temperature. She shook and kept looking back up the path towards the old city. My gut hurt and I watched the tabletop.

'Imagine if that was us,' she said after a long silence. 'Imagine if that was you.'

'Why me?'

'Imagine that was you and you were running down off the hill to meet me and you caught a cab and it was you. And we don't meet. That this was just some appalling fate we were never meant to have.'

'But nothing of the kind—'

'No listen. Imagine.'

'Why?' I asked.

'Because—listen.'

'. . .'

'Because.'

'. . .'

'Because all of this is so, so unlikely, after all this time—isn't it almost certainly most logical that we didn't get to meet again?'

'But here we are.'

'Yes. But does it feel real?'

'I'm not sure yet.'

'See? Perhaps it hasn't, hasn't happened.'

'What an awful thought.'

'Yes,' she said.

'What an awful but interesting thought. And I'm dead in a car crash. Just over there.'

'And I'm over there,' she said, pointing back through the hill to where we'd sat beside the coffee cart after first spotting each other and hugged, 'oblivious.'

'We should never have done this,' I said.

She laughed then, very softly, covering her mouth. 'Oh, David.'

We began joking and making up scenarios over and over

until we felt ourselves drift into a shallow and deepening sadness, convinced of something untrue but real. Real because of the way she looked at me. The way two strangers can't look at each other, for we were strangers.

'One of us, one of the two of us is going to die.'

We both nodded.

'We can't tell anyone else.'

That was our story. Though mine continued on into the night. The sense of the car, the engine and bonnet, the radiator grille smashing, the hit and grunt of it, of the bus. The face of the man became the face of another, the gradual other, the other who follows me, who sits beside me, half inside me, the terror version of myself.

I didn't sleep, and after sunrise lay through the day in bed. The truth of me bare in the stone-walled hotel room opposite the gardens where the festival took place, full of expanding thoughts, of people having primary, opening inspirations. The day after, I had to speak. A small audience oblivious to how we die every day and know it only in the things we forget.

I spent most of that night near the bathroom. Dysbiosis. The leaky gut we have. The sense that some small hint of history is seeping in. My body shook invisibly and silently. I thought of the grotesque, the proliferation of genetic glitches bought on by a thousand years of my ancestors continually marrying their cousins. Haemophilia, porphyria. I wondered if there was one such moment of lust that triggered this propensity of my nervous system to fire in the way it does.

Then Kaspar, after one tale too many, fell drifting into sleep and Alin put her forefinger to her mouth and *Shhh*-ed. She watched her boy until she was sure he was asleep and eyed me in the sudden draw of conspiracy. The pair of us, narrowed eyes and uncertain.

'What do we do now?' I said, whispering as if ash was on my mouth and tongue. The table between us was strewn with crayons, torn paper, tissues and crumbs.

She gave an exaggerated shrug as if this had never happened before. We were alone for the first time since Edinburgh.

I hushed. Alin knew people like me, had three friends with the disease, each of them women. She knew what silence meant to them.

'Ask me something,' Alin whispered, part question, part request.

'Ask you something, why?'

'Just—anything, something. Quick.'

She had this look that was like a frown but was actually a kind of grin. I'd learnt this look in the first few minutes of our meeting twelve years earlier. It said: *I'm smarter than you, but I like you already.* I felt like we were about to have our first terrestrial argument.

'Hurry up with something,' she said.

'. . . ?'

'Come on. The thing you can't ask, you know, in a fuckening email.' *Fuckening.* 'The thing you'll only know my answer to by the way I do, or don't, move my chin or whatever. You understand what I'm saying?'

I laughed.

'What?' she asked. 'I'm serious. We should get familiar with the way we actually talk. This is what I'm saying.'

'This is probably true.'

'The way we lie and don't lie? With our physiques and hands. We need to do this. You think, right?'

'Okay. Okay, I agree.'

'Thank the Lord he agrees.'

'I'm in agreement,' I said and put my hands in the air, a surrender like sand to the sea.

She pretended to prod me with something long and sharp. 'We need to know the language of this.'

'How long will he be out?'

She nodded at Kaspar. 'This little strudel? This boy's out until we get to his grandparents, I think. I slipped Valium in his sipper. Morphine in his—anyway.'

And as we sat grinning Alin asked me several questions. Each, I quickly realised, was aimed at a specific age. It was an odd request, one that desired to learn what was happening in my life when I was the age she was when we met. In other words, what was I doing when I was twenty-four? I was ten years older than Alin, in my mid-thirties, when we'd met in Wellington. She was the first visitor to the new video library we'd built in the Film Archive's basement where I worked. She'd stood near the door with that wakefully impish grin, staring at me seated behind the desk. I froze, before I started laughing. She was imperiously Teutonic, over-iced eyes and white hair settling on the shoulders of her great woollen coat. She wore the biggest smile. The first thing she said to me was: *What?*

'What were you doing at twenty-four?' she asked on the train.

'Not a lot.'

'Come on.'

Recounting this now, I recall another moment. It was a few months ago in Tāmaki Makaurau and I was thinking of this same conversation between Alin and me. This time I was on my way to visit my old manager, Mena. I was walking the promenade abutting the Auckland downtown to the wharfs as

I made my way to the ferry terminal. Mena was a friend from this time Alin was requesting information about, from when I was twenty-four, and I thought about our conversation on the train. How we need to lie sometimes. How we need to place fiction into our lives, into the narratives that keep us satisfied we're us. A purposeful unreliability, I'd thought, that corrects our instinct to believe each memory as fact, whereas they have been rewritten over and over through time.

My intrigue about this thought is in the manner in which I have dual visions of this day, taken from months apart. Competing memories, almost exact, but different enough to create a kind of three-dimensional impression of this train. And what I'm thinking of is not Alin and me, not Kaspar swearing in his remote dreams, not speed—but rather the photographs that Spitfires, Mosquitoes and other aircraft used to take with dual cameras set in the aircraft's body during WWII. Photos of Germany, of the Lowlands, of Austria, Italy and France. Two cameras a foot apart set in the side of the body, in the undercarriage of the body, snapping at industry and fields, houses, barns and secret things. How young women back in England scoured these photographs with strange glasses that pulled the images together to create a complete, three-dimensional impression of radar site, of hangar, of rocket launch site and airfield. And I think how such an image is a lie, a ruse of reality caught in haphazard moments, days, weeks, inches, feet and months apart. Out of these lies we seem to understand the world so much better. We need them so we can know (and claim) objectivity. Illness reduces this capacity to such an extent that it is rare anything is but an object. Language is at times reduced to the extent that the object fails, loses all shape, merges with the words around it.

'Twenty-four? I was living in Auckland,' I said as we hit

Linz. We rumbled across a bridge, the river to our left, ancient and always hunting out the sea, the Black Sea at the edge of the East. 'Was living on K-Road above a porn shop. This was mid-1990s, right? I was trying to learn how to be a sound engineer, studio technician and so on. Living with other audio engineers. My girlfriend was learning how to be a journalist. She left me for another journalist. Which killed me because, you know, I only ever read the sports pages.'

'Is that true?'

'I think so. But then I moved back to Wellington, and I don't know what's true about that time in Auckland anymore.'

'What else?'

'What else? I drank beer. Quite a lot. Played guitar in a band and played pool. Listened to music, played punk rock, actively deafened myself. Et cetera. I watched friends become junkies. It was a time when we were moving from simply being in bands to being in bands with wretched drug habits.'

'You?' she asked. 'You too?' It was a question that seemed, from both of my memories, one that desired something wicked. She asked it in a way that desired her friend to be worse than her in some way.

And in both these memories I shook my head and nodded out the window, said, 'Do you know "Danube", the actual word, is related to the Rigvedic Sanskrit, "dānu"? Which means *fluid*, or *drop*.'

'You too?' she asked again, a little deviousness in her accent.

I shook my head once more. 'No. I thought it was more punk not to. I thought drugs had a hippy whiff about them.'

She laughed, as if she knew this all along. But before she laughed I saw a hint, a small look of disappointment, one that might have asked how deep I got. How far down, how far into the end of it. Had I ever shot up so I saw stars turn red then black then nothing. Had I, had I ever died and come back. Had I, because this would get us out of our Scottish nightmare—that one of us had died and that was the deal done.

'See, this is good,' she said. 'I didn't know you ever lived in Auckland. With drug abuse and idiots.'

I nodded and shrugged. 'They were idiots, yeah, but mostly very, very smart idiots.'

'I was there, too, you know,' she said, almost accusing me of something. 'Same age.'

'When were you in Auckland?'

'When I was twenty-four. But I didn't live above a porn shop. That'd have been educational. Did you ever go in?' she squinted, asking some other questions I couldn't quite grasp.

'Only when the washing machine overflowed, and I had to go down and clean up. Three-hundred-and-sixty degrees of dicks and vaginas. It was a seedy area. A little dangerous. Our friend Tim was so badly beaten outside our door one time we didn't recognise him when he came hollering for help.'

'That's horrible. I'm sorry,' she said. 'Is he okay?'

'I guess so. Some girl he knew had his baby and he moved away.'

She looked surprised for a moment. She wasn't someone who often looked surprised.

'How are we supposed to bear what we do to other people, you know, David?'

'Things happen all the time, Alin, and we don't always know they're going to happen and they happen and we're that person that awful thing happened to.'

'Things either happen less or more than we think. I have two kids, and who'd have thought?'

'Me and my girlfriend Deborah had a Mini, we killed it driving back and forth between Wellington and Auckland.'

She smiled. 'One of those little, little cars? Sweet little cars?'

'And we'd take our cat all the way. She'd sit on my shoulder and watch the road. This is when I'm twenty-four. Which is a better memory than most of that time.'

'We should stay away from cars,' she said. 'I think of cars and I think of—and I don't want to think of Edinburgh.'

'I know, but it just feels nice to think about. My cat purring on my shoulder as I drove 660 kilometres. That doesn't happen now.'

'But a better memory?'

It was a fair question. Both of my recollections of this, these twin images of us on a train, taken from that deep body part of my mind, are at odds with the tone of my answer. I'm in Wellington as I write this, winter. I was in Auckland when I thought up the same scene. Cities separated by so many miles, so many swathes of emotion, by summer and winter. I was walking the road towards the boat; it was at the time the longest walk I'd taken in months. My body is a liar, a bastard, a scoundrel, but there it was, letting me walk towards my friend and a day on Waiheke Island.

'No, I mean,' she said, 'is it better because it's clearer, or because it's a cheerier thing to think about?'

I admitted I didn't know. But in the Auckland memory of this, I said that I did know. I knew clearly, I knew well that I knew it was a better memory because in Auckland I recalled I was once in love, I was once drawn forward into life by love and nothing much else mattered.

Alin and I sat quietly drawing pictures and feeling the land flare. The running green, the flashed edges of township and city, the fence wire and the rocks and stones, their rust dust cover and the point beyond the near, the place in the centre of a field where the grass threatened to stop blurring, where it loomed as we flew by. And in the distance beyond was a kind of still. Seemingly. Complete and lying. I felt glassed in and aired out by the unstable light. The train hit, crashed through the dark hole of a red brick tunnel as I started to speak of another car—and another death.

These Thieves

It was late summer when the destruction began—Joanna and I at our end in the empty sunroom of my parents' house just after the movers had come through. And with the devastation almost complete, I left town. I stood like an actor at the side of the road, thumb out, asking something of my audience, that they take me wherever they were going. I stitched together lift after lift until I found myself with Martin. A thin, windswept man in his forties, newly grey and cocooned in a sleek German saloon. We hit 150 in the wides of straight and camber, in the violent wind shifts of being overtaken and overtaking. The whooshed doppler effect of fast metal and close air as we headed into the warm geography above the Waitematā.

Brief moments of talk, then—quiet like a vice, silences gripped between the first and last words said in retaliation against the smallest talk. Things disclosed, woken. Martin was separated from his wife; they'd been that way for four years and hadn't spoken since they'd figured out the money. I learnt that the man lived in Island Bay, close to where Joanna grew up. The last suburb, Martin said, in the entire North Island.

'I know,' I said, 'I'm from—Wellington.'

'Okay then, yes,' the man said. There was an unspoken strain on his face. 'Where in Wellington?'

I put my feet up on the dashboard. 'Miramar. By the airport.'

'Okay.'

'Though we never seemed to fly anywhere.'

'No.'

Martin glanced at my sneakers and told me he'd left his house on a whim two days earlier. 'Although,' he said as we passed through near, staring bush outside Kaiwaka, 'I'm generally a little weary of that word.'

'What word?'

'Whim.'

I said nothing, uncertain I knew the word well enough to have an opinion on it. Joanna had recently pointed out there was a whole world of words at war with my ignorance of them. It had at once depressed and invigorated me, or at least the parts of me that I'd left behind at school eighteen months earlier. Whatever the case, it had kicked the arguments into gear.

'Saying something is a whim,' Martin said, 'has the inglorious effect of suggesting caprice is my only motivating—my only what's-have-you. But, well—it's not.' He wound up his window and wound it down again. The smell of silage as he worked the gears and overtook a sheep truck. A moment and then the car smelt expensive once more, shop-floor new.

I thought, *There's an island somewhere nice called Caprice.*

'I decided Cape Reinga would be good,' Martin continued. 'That was the whim, but I soon knew I left for good reason.' He paused, glanced at me. 'Sorry,' he said. 'I haven't spoken to anyone for two days. It's strange hearing my voice again. I sound slightly . . .'

I said I thought he sounded fine.

'Thank you. That's sweet, but God knows. You've been to the Cape?' he asked. 'Everyone's been, of course you've been.'

'No.'

'How old are you?'

‘Eighteen,’ I said.

‘Eighteen. The age of rank foolishness. The weather doesn’t reach there.’

I again said nothing, felt a sudden regret for putting out my thumb in Wellsford. I’d been standing beside a phone booth after being dropped there by a farm boy and his cousin, a girl, a teenager like me. She’d kept turning to the back of the car as if to ask a question, staring with one squinted eye then turning away. After they dropped me off, I stood in the shade for forty-five minutes, wondering what she was going to ask. I felt like I missed her, or not her but the fact she seemed to want to ask me something. I forgot about the traffic until I saw Martin’s machine and reached out my hand, and it was answered by gear change and brakes.

‘I’m sorry. I guess I say foolishness because of certain wistful things,’ Martin said, turning to me slightly. He was, how old? Mid-forties, that was my guess, but I didn’t really know.

‘It’s all right. I’ll be foolish, too, when I’m your age,’ I said. I found myself telling him about my father, how he survived the mountains a couple of years earlier. How as he sat there dying he felt himself slip inwards, and not inwards of himself, but of the whole great mountain. That he was being consumed by the rock, swallowed and made nothing. That all his thought was stone. That was the sensation of the dying.

The man stretched his neck. A pain seemed to roll through him.

‘Your dad?’

‘Yeah. He used to be an airman but ended up near dead in the hills.’

‘An airman?’

‘. . .’

‘You know, flying. I’ve always thought it should be a

treatment for bad things. Don't you think? Such is its wonder. We trust pilots more than surgeons. It really should be a cure for diseases and pain.'

'. . .'

'Anyway. Perhaps you're one of those blessed kids.'

'I'm definitely not one of those kids,' I said quickly.

Martin just nodded. 'One of those kids who hasn't yet found foolishness, or—maybe—is too silly to recognise it. Or, perhaps, perhaps you're not eighteen at all. You're one of those unknown ages.'

It sounded like he was trying to make a joke, something light, but instead of smiling Martin grimaced and his mouth seemed to fill with something. I felt momentarily ill. A sudden revulsion, and I turned away, watched the scorched fields.

'Excuse me,' Martin said, sounding grey.

'What's going on, sir?'

'Sir? That's an odd word,' he said.

I shook my head, I'd never used that word before, at least not since I was at Wellesley College when I was ten and it was all *sir* and *ma'am*. Saying it now hurt something, the way I felt about myself. 'I'm sorry, are you okay?' I asked.

'Let's just get where we're going.'

The stretches of hills and housing, horses and kids. Boys calling out at Martin's car, the sleek Euro steel and effortless speed. At Ōhaeawai, Martin seemed uncomfortable, said that he'd had a pain in his neck, that it'd been going on for weeks. I looked at him and began to see his face for the first time.

'You okay?'

'You'll have to excuse me,' Martin said. 'This has been going on and on.'

'I've got some Panadol,' I said.

He shook his head. 'Just wanted to see where the Pacific

ends, see its last horizon,' he said and sat up. 'It's always been a thing. When I was small, when a boy, I used to wonder if the horizon was perhaps a hidden thing of the weather, do you know what I mean? Or perhaps a some special illusion of the heavens. I couldn't know.'

'Sorry?'

'At the Cape.'

'What's at the Cape?'

'The horizon. Then later I wondered if it were actually the gap, the true gap between, let's say, knowledge and unknowledge. I'd say: *You're not even vapour, are you? You're just a bloody noun. Just sandwiched there.*'

'Maybe. I don't know,' I said.

'Anyway. I need codeine if you're offering pain killers.'

'Codeine?'

'I need some—' He bent over the steering wheel. 'It's the biggest thing on earth,' he said.

'What is?'

'And I just wanted to see where it ends. The Pacific.'

'Is it?'

'What?'

'The biggest.'

'On earth, yes.'

'And where does it end?' I asked.

'I can't know,' he said. 'Not really.'

'Okay,' I said. I realised then that Martin's voice, its odd formality and precision, was a result of pain. That each word was thought through an aperture narrowed by something unsaid and gaining strength.

'Which is the thing that seemed beyond a whim, to me at least.'

'What do you need?'

Martin told me this wasn't a pain relieved by shop-bought palliatives. He'd had massages and acupuncture but nothing had dulled it. He said he lived with the pain, drove north in distraction. I sat beside him, rolling cigarettes. Martin continued to reach around behind to stretch out his neck, giving an on again, off again moan.

'You break up with someone, huh?' he asked suddenly.

'Why don't we find a chemist?'

'It's okay to hurt,' he said. 'What's her name?'

'Joanna.'

'That's a nice name.'

'Yeah.'

'Can you tell me about her?'

And after a pause I did, said how we'd been together since we were fifteen. How full we were of each other, full until we began to understand why we were always sad and crying.

'We met the last week of school. A summer party. We were the only ones not drinking. We just talked, then walked. Just everywhere. Talking, walked through the gardens, waterfront.'

'She's special, I'm sorry.'

'Why? Why are you sorry?'

'Because it hurts and you're on your own. You're on your own and that's something—suddenly.'

'I can drive,' I said. 'If you wanna take a break.'

'You can drive? I'm okay.'

'I've been driving for years, if you're worried.'

'No. It's—you know how much this car costs?'

'If I knew or cared I wouldn't have put out my thumb.'

'What does that mean?'

'It means I just think you should let me drive, 'cause I'll drive it like any other shitty car.'

We traded places. Martin sat calmly, twisting his neck,

wincing. We were in from the coast, and I saw signs for the turn-off towards the kauri forests. I had a hankering to pull over and get out. Hitch to the park with a different driver on a different road. That was what we used to do, Joanna and I. We'd ride with people until we saw something we thought we remembered, or something we thought we would want to remember later, and go. Martin kept very quiet, mute almost. He made a series of gasping sounds and we drove into the evening with him breathing like something was awfully wrong.

In Kaitaia I went straight down Redan Road, barely lifting my eyes to the traffic. Soon I had Martin in Emergency. He was lying on a gurney, panting. The hospital staff asked for his name. Then, then he was convulsing. Somehow they got a needle in him and pumped him full of morphine. I was surprised when Martin remembered my name. He grabbed my hand and said my two syllables softly.

I had nowhere else to go, so I stayed with Martin. I looked through his wallet to find out anything I could about him. Martin Yare. His business card said he was an orthopaedic surgeon. It had a line drawing of hands clasped together. Nurses came through, asking me the same questions over and over. I spent time looking in the White Pages for matching Yares in Wellington. There were only two entries. I rang the second number; it was Martin's younger sister. I told her what I knew and she said she'd get a flight up. She asked me everything she could ask. I said I had nothing to offer but the fact I would stay here. She asked why. I said because I had his wallet and keys and that I didn't trust the hospital to keep them safe.

Back in the ward, doctors were hovering and orderlies were taking away machinery. I wasn't allowed into the room until a nurse recognised me from earlier. She put her hand on my shoulder and walked me into the room humming with equipment and lighting that felt suddenly inadequate. Martin, they said, was dead.

A sheet had been pulled up over his face, his feet showing at the end of the bed. Small toes, bluish, boy-like, as if he'd just been swimming in the cold water at the end of the country, but he hadn't been swimming, he'd been hanging on for the doctors to do something. He was as good as dead many hours earlier, they told me. A cyst had burst in his neck. Another was drilling into his cerebral cortex. He'd had a seizure, and that was it for Martin. He died at 8:20pm.

I remembered I hadn't eaten since the morning in Devonport where I'd slept the night in the shell of a house still under construction. The last of the sandwiches I'd made in Joanna's aunt's kitchen in Hāwera two days prior.

I found a mirror. My eyes looked like cold stones. There seemed so few people suddenly, and then too many, too many and they were all staring in, all wanting to know how I got to this instant, how it seemed made out of me and only this lonely me.

Michelle arrived late the next morning. She organised for Martin to be shipped back to Wellington. I gave her the keys to her brother's car. That was all I had, after everything: keys, wallet and the strange lightness of them as I handed them over. We were standing in a hall in the hospital, we were all alone, and Michelle told me she didn't have a licence.

She was five foot two, and just so and I was standing over her thinking how pretty she was. Which was just awful, but it was the thought that came into my head. Which embarrassed me. She was six, seven years older than me, and I couldn't help this thought. Without thinking, I told her I would take her and the car back to Wellington.

And I did, we got in the Audi and went. Drove south out of the town, back past the forests, past all the turnoffs. I pointed out the signs and she nodded, kept looking straight ahead. I took glances at her and later all I would remember was her ear, how it looked like a question mark amongst her hair.

We stopped, ate in Taupō. Dinner in a restaurant looking over the lake. Any tranquility was disturbed by jet skiers out smashing, thudding through the shallows on their black and silver machines. Michelle knew I'd no money and bought pizza and we shared a pint, shifting the glass back and forth across the table.

'What'll you do when you get back?' Michelle asked.

'Back? I don't know. Start again.'

'Start again?'

'Find another place to hitch to. Māhia, maybe.'

'You just up and leave, right?'

'You'd think,' I said.

'I'd think? I don't think much of anything.'

'No, I mean, there's like a procedure of thought I have to go through before I make the decision to do anything.'

'What, like brush your teeth?'

I nodded. 'Yeah. You'd be surprised what processes I need to go through, you know, in order to do anything worthy of getting out of bed.'

She gave a tight laugh. 'Sure. I hear you. Life's—it's frightening.'

'Life's terrifying.'

Michelle had the same eyes as Martin, the same mouth shape. The difference was in years and speech patterns. She had a knowing voice, small but specific.

'What was he like?' Michelle asked.

'Who?'

'Martin.'

'Martin? He was—why are you asking me?'

'He's—he's like years older than me. I don't really know what he was, I don't have a sense of him. Which is terrible.'

'I liked him.'

'I mean I knew him, kinda. I loved him like a little sister does and, I don't know. He was just this mystery to me, like most of my life.'

'I liked him. Not at first. But when he admitted something was wrong.'

'When something was wrong?'

'Yeah.'

'You're eighteen, huh?'

'Aha. Actually, nineteen.'

'What do you know about something being *wrong*? Things being *wrong*?'

I stared at her till we both looked away. I sipped the beer. It was my first drink in three years, and I feared it. I'd stepped out of drinking with my rugby boys, my mates, because I realised I was looking for something that nobody seemed interested in talking about. That was until Joanna. And with Joanna, no matter where we wandered in Wellington, we just seemed to discuss that exact thing, though it wasn't exact. We were thieves of something beyond the powers of exactness.

'So, you got out of this alive?' I asked.

'Of what?'

'Nineteen.'

'I guess so. Not everyone does.'

'No. *Everyone* is way too general anyway.'

'My nineteen—I was like, I was in jail, like for seventeen months,' Michelle said.

I stopped chewing.

'Manslaughter. At nineteen. That's my nineteen.'

I laughed. I'd never heard anyone say that combination of words before. 'Fuck,' I said.

'I went away for seventeen months and, I came back. A year and a half, and now I'm here. That was seven years ago. I killed a man and his kid. Crashed into them in my car while talking to someone on my dad's goddamned car phone. It rang and I bent over and hit answer and I don't remember not looking at the road, you know?'

'A car phone?'

'My dad's a—like, you're talking to someone next to you in the car. And this man and his kid. Talking and then this man and his little kid. I looked away, hit the answer button. Then—' She stared at me. 'I used to wonder why nothing else happened,' she said. 'I mean, I wondered why nothing really happened to me. It was just time and space they took away and I also wondered why nothing else happened at the other end of that call, you know?'

I shook my head.

'Like, nothing else bad happened at the other end of the line. I was talking, talking, and . . . I wondered why nothing happened to the person who called me. And now, maybe it has. Maybe something else has crept in, I don't know. All they took away was time and I barely remember.'

She sat silently, looking behind me. I felt like there were two versions of me then, one mussy on beer and the other silent and still.

'Who?' I asked.

'Who what?'

'Who were you talking to?'

'I knew you'd ask, didn't I?'

'I don't know.'

'It was my brother.'

'Fuck.'

'It was Martin calling to say he was gonna meet me to talk about Rachel, that's his wife. I hit the answer button and . . .' Michelle sat still, her face marred by what comes after such silence.

That evening we lay in our underwear, spread out under a fan because there wasn't any aircon. Outside was the sound of water, the light shoreline splash and draw. I woke up in the late night to the sound of Michelle crying. Her skin was wet and warm.

In the morning I ate a buffet breakfast at a table sitting opposite her, looking out at the lake. The terracotta-tiled room echoed with children and dank conversations. I was nineteen and sitting with this woman who was seven years older and she'd said these words to me the previous night and I remembered how her skin had felt because I'd held her. Held her small self and how she'd quaked and there was nothing I could do about it. I'd wanted to call Joanna and explain the moment and hear her voice, hear the way she thought around everything to a place in the universe nobody had ever thought their way to. But there was no phone she'd answer without being certain it wasn't me on the other end.

I buttered my toast and remembered Martin in the hospital, how he'd said: *You're one of those sad boys, aren't you? Always sad. Makes me happy you're here.* And then I remembered something else—that I'd woken up, and something new and strange had entered the hotel room. I'd stirred just before dawn, Michelle was standing fully clothed in the middle of the room. She wasn't moving, just staring at the door, crying. I'd wanted to say her name, but in the moment I couldn't remember it. I couldn't recall its syllables and sibilance. I fell back to sleep and when I awoke, she was beside me again. Naked, uncluttered.

Then 10am and she sat opposite me at the table.

'What were you doing, anyway,' she asked. Her plate filled with eggs and hash.

'What?'

'Up north.'

'I don't know.'

'You know *something*. People say they don't know, but they know. They know something.'

'Just wanted to see where the Pacific ends.'

I looked away. I knew where I'd got these words: Martin. Martin, dead in a morgue waiting to be shipped back home. I hadn't realised I needed a reason to be heading north. But suddenly it seemed I required one, and these were the words I chose without Joanna there to explain. It was Joanna who always figured out what were the right answers. I felt suddenly sick at stealing from the dead. That I'd breached a barrier.

Michelle looked away, frustrated. A waiter came by, gave the word the buffet was closing soon.

'I wanted to see where the ocean seams up with the Tasman,' I said.

'Yeah. But it doesn't end, eh?' she said.

'. . .'

'It just goes around and around and you're trying to figure out if it really ever started.'

'. . .'

'You're just—always trying to figure out where it started.' She winced slightly at her words and took my hand. The way her thumb touched the back of mine.

'Do you ever get the sense that nothing ever really starts?' I asked. 'Like it's always been in motion and we just haven't figured out the science of catching up with it?'

Her fingers shifted. I could feel the life of them, the slight movements, the relaxing muscles.

'You didn't know how to look at me this morning, did you?' Michelle asked.

'I did,' I said. 'I did, then.'

'No, you didn't.'

We sat still. I glanced, the sound of metal. A waiter lifting the buffet trays from the server, steam rising pale into the room.

'I don't care about nakedness,' I said. 'Unless it's specifically for me. Then—'

'What? No. I don't give a shit about my body—about. Don't give a rat's. No, when I was standing waiting. Trying to leave, 'cause I was trying to leave. You didn't know how to look at me.' She paused, watched the food on her plate. 'I don't care about being naked. Not anymore.'

'The body only tells what it wants to tell,' I said, suddenly certain.

'I don't care about being seen naked, I just care about how other people *see*. That's how you learn if they're fucked or not.'

Michelle's sad small mouth, its question, its inquiry—then suddenly the clang and clatter of metal on tiles. We both turned. The waiter had lost his grip on the trays. Now food and the sight of it, eggs and meat were spread over the floor. People standing up. Laughter, a small scream. Michelle grabbed at my arm. The room full of people staring at the mess and a phone ringing at the counter, decibels and voices.

'Everyone's staring,' Michelle said. My eyes, the phone ringing, pale faces and my eyes and then Michelle's too. In the end Michelle spoke.

'You gonna, like, you gonna pick it up?'

I stood then, the sound of my back clicking. I went to where the staff waited for their moment and bent with them to the floor. Someone was saying and organising but still, it took the longest time before all the food was scooped into the trash bags and the smell, the high smell of the cleaning product, tomato and beans, it took many hours before it left the long empty room.

Probably

The train ran on through the light, curved by speed and time and track. Alin watched me as I finished telling the story. She watched the people behind me, tracing their movements through the carriage. I turned and realised she was watching her son playing with other boys. Perhaps she knew one of the other mothers, perhaps she was trying to recall their names, but then I realised she was watching her son because watching someone so close and dear operating among the unfamiliar and plain is like watching them anew.

'So, that was the last time I went hitch-hiking. I'm someone else now.'

'So it was.'

'Someone gone. Someone very likely tedious.'

'Is that true?' she asked.

'Oh yes. Exceptionally tedious.'

'No, I mean for me. For me, I don't know if it's true. It's more like—I know who you became. I know you became sick when you were trying to be well. I know you got to come here, we got to be who we are together. I got to watch you talk onstage, and I loved the way you were onstage because you were no longer sick.'

'Yes. It's the performance of a me. I should get better known, write better books. Then I can be onstage more.'

She smiled and then frowned. 'But me, I don't know who we become. And that is very sad. I know who I was when I was young, but now.'

'Yes, now,' I said.

'Now is so much more confused.' She nodded at Kaspar. 'Now we have no choice but to love, but back then.'

'So, many years later I came to the realisation about something, Alin, that it was such a thing that I did, holding her like that.'

'Back then love was an experiment. Who? The young woman?'

'Yes. And the thing I realised was if I had been her age or older, we'd probably have had sex.'

'I'm sure she'd like to have had a say in that,' Alin said, and laughed.

'Hear me out. I know sex isn't that simple.'

'Well, sometimes it is.'

'But this was my later realisation. That we might well have done it as a response to all we'd just been through. That for some reason everything was heading us towards this. This true and disclosed horror of losing her brother in this way. Our proximity to it. And this warmth and cold confession. The giddy closeness and damp. But the thing is, I knew *not to* when I was that age. I wouldn't have known not to when I was older, say in my late twenties or thirties. I suspect I would've slept with her, you know, if she'd wanted to. That seems the likely outcome of such a moment. The outcome of comfort and dissuasion from grief and its awful confusion. She would've slept with me. Probably. Which grosses me out now, it grosses me out, completely. It would've been the only way to have coped with the fact it was a *thing* between us. But at nineteen,

I knew what to give, what was needed.'

'I thought you were eighteen.'

'It was my birthday.'

Alin watched me, uncertain. Then watched the people behind me, and I realised she was watching her son playing again.

'We were mistaking grief for attraction,' I said. 'And I just don't know if I'd have known to separate them later on in life.'

'But you know now, though.'

'That's because I have white hair and I'm very wise. My point is,' I said, 'things become so much more confused the older you get. She, we, we still write to each other. You know that? I haven't seen her in twenty-eight years, but I miss her in the strangest way.'

'How did you tell her about your health?'

'I haven't.'

'You haven't. You'll send her this book?'

'She doesn't read novels; she hates reading things she doesn't think she can do something about. Besides, Michelle got sick, a while back. More than a while back. She's been ill for fourteen years and I just can't tell her.'

Gmunden

In Attnang-Puchheim, Alin's father collected us at the station and drove us through the countryside towards their home in Gmunden, a town pinched at the shores of Lake Traunsee, below Mount Traunstein and surrounding peaks. As we headed towards the lake Alin pointed and said, 'David.'

My eyes followed a ridge up from the waterline, through forest and finally snow.

‘We walk there tomorrow. It’s my favourite place.’ At my nodding, she continued, ‘We take the gondola and up above there’s tracks. We can go tomorrow if you’re feeling well enough.’ I said I would love to.

At the house I met her mother, Alena. She was in her late sixties and quite striking. A lean concentration. Her father, Jörg, a tall, good-looking man in his seventies. Alena spoke no English and instead used her hands and shifts of her head to her daughter to talk to me. We did just fine, locating the moments to laugh or nod in that way that meant we understood something we hadn’t sympathised with before. She liked that I didn’t say much; it meant she didn’t need to keep asking Alin for translations.

I slept heavy for five hours that night in a small room below the kitchen where we’d spent the evening talking. The house was four hundred years old, giant and full of old, querying sounds and cracked wood. The white walls were full of Alena’s paintings and framed photographs taken by their famous son—nudes in black-and-white and splashes of red. The house once sat flush against the lakeside, but in the early twentieth century an apartment building was built in front on reclaimed land just metres away. Now only a part of the veranda above gave a view to the lake, the mountains and black trees. I tried to imagine the view, correct it so it replicated some unknown origin. There was a weight to the residence, like it had shifted at some point in the past and was now continually resettling, like the lives of all those who’d been through it previously, who had died, woken and found birth in some other dark place. When I woke I found myself thinking about a story Jörg had told the previous night as we smoked cigarettes on the back veranda. It was an East German story, about travelling through the GDR from Sweden to Austria in the early 1960s when he was young and equally tall and dashing. It was a six- or seven-hour drive, but five hours into the journey, near midnight, his car broke down near Leipzig, south of Berlin. He described the countryside. Remembered for us what a paranoid country it was. Phrases such as *Staatssicherheit*, *Trabant* and *Ostalgie*. He said the only familiar thing was the language, and even then it felt full of suspect agendas. The country was, in his mind, a delusion of completion, of totality.

'I'd drive past people on the side of the road,' he said, 'and I'd wonder what would happen in their lives if I was to stop. I wondered what we'd understand of one another. These mirrored people. What the differences were between us, what effect these would have. But I never stopped, not until the car broke down.' When the rotor in the car's distributor cracked he was suddenly isolated at the side of the road. He explained that he felt like an island in the centre of that near-dark state where everyone seemed to be watching him. The whole country was set up to watch, he said, and to record movement and motivations via machine, eye and ear. These were its only sources of light, and you had to tread carefully under their gaze. 'It was like I was famous,' he said. 'But for the worst reasons. And nobody, nobody could tell me what these reasons were. Just that they were diabolical.'

He was put in jail for two nights as his papers only allowed for the hours of his planned journey.

The thing about the story was that Alin had never heard it before. She complained to her father that he'd never told her, and why not? And he didn't have an answer. He looked nervous, waiting for something. And that was the thing that woke me in the middle of the night in the middle of the house half the size of Europe in old Austria—the way he didn't know the answer, though the answer was obvious.

I went up the stairs, found myself in the kitchen. I sat there for a time drinking cold tea. I heard a noise and saw Alin at the door. She was in an old nightgown, a Seventies thing that sat comically large on her like a tramp's coat. 'You okay?' I asked. She gave her best attempt at a smile and sat with me.

'Super,' she said.

'What keeps you up?'

'This and that.'

'This and that,' I mimicked.

'I started smoking again after I had the kids. Maybe just something for myself, I'm not sure. I never really learnt how to sleep again.' She put her head on my shoulder. 'And it's fun creeping around the big old house, no.'

'There's something in it, sure.'

She smiled. 'It has a series of quite musical creaks. It's slightly rotten, a little dying, but I think this is what gives it its song.'

We stayed quiet for a while, as if to listen.

'Are you still annoyed at your father?' I asked eventually.

'A little—but I'm not a girl born to hold a grudge.'

'Don't you think it's obvious why he told the story?'

'I know why he told the story. Of course,' she said.

'Of course.'

'You,' she said and pointed at my chest.

'It's all about me,' I said.

'You're new, foreign. You're sudden. An occupying force in the house. You force out the unsaid—which makes you popular and a little despised.'

'I like your nightgown, talking of despising.'

She laughed.

'Of course you do, it's 1978 rayon. But I'm just a little irritated, yes.'

'Irritated is your right.'

'Because that's a shaping story, yes? And it shapes me, the parts of me—who knows what parts of me. I'm the daughter who wants to know everything about herself so she can make adjustments. About herself and the previous versions of herself living inside her father and mother. So—grrr, grrr. I want to get to know the invisible versions of myself. I demand pre-Alin data. It's annoying the way this comes out sometimes. So, grumpy.'

'If a little sleepy.'

'Yes, a little sleepy grumpy. You know why I couldn't sleep? You know?' She gazed at me. 'I kept having visions. The man.'

'The man.'

'The man in Edinburgh. I kept having visions that the man was here. That he was in the house. This stalking thought of him here.'

'. . .'

'But my father, see, as he was telling us his story I couldn't stop thinking of the man in Edinburgh. I kept thinking my father was going to crash and I thought of the look on the man's face suddenly on my father's. Dad's face just—' She put her hands up to her cheeks.

The house moved, a major shift in its harmonies.

'You remember the man with cancer,' I asked, 'in the car?'

'Of course the car. Always cars.'

'Well, I think this quite often—I think about if I hadn't been there, you know? Think of him dying as he drove on. Think about not being there in the car and taking over the wheel, about him ploughing into other people. Him dead in the driver's seat, the car at 110 kilometres an hour. I think there must be a connection between me as a young man and this not happening. That those two days and nights were my moments of grace. Those were my moments and I did good. And now. I don't know. Here we are and I don't know.'

'This is what's keeping you up?'

'One of the things.' I didn't tell her about my twin, my strange echo.

Alin looked up momentarily. 'My mother Alena, she believed quite strongly that she knew something after a close-run thing with her heart a few years ago. An operation at 4am in the morning. That she knew about the future. From what I heard from her the future, it's just this place we want to inhabit. It's just people you've met. It's the lake and the boats, the hills you've walked, whatever. It's the sense that we carry them all, each individual, each voice of each individual, the hunger of each individual's desires. They come with us. They're all waiting for you in the future. But you'll probably never see them again, but they're waiting because you're in *their* memory. And that is the future—things quite in the past, growing, waiting. That's why I'm angry.'

'That's scary,' I said.

'Yes. Everything is scary. And the other thing—David—this is the longest, this story you told me on the train, that was the longest I've ever heard you speak uninterrupted,' Alin said. 'Do you know that? Your story. I've known you twelve years and that's the longest I've heard you talk.'

'I know that.'

'You should tell me about your sister.'

And I did. My eldest sister.

On my arrival in Edinburgh the first thing I'd done was seek out my nephew. James is a comedian who works the winter months in the north then returns to New Zealand to write his podcast and recover. I found him at a bar the first morning and we exchanged embraces then sat down to watch a game of rugby on the big screen.

Seven hours before flying out from New Zealand, Laura and I had been to the funeral wake in Petone for James's stepmother, my sister. I'd spoken on behalf of my mother and brother, my two remaining sisters. My niece read out a message James had emailed. It was much funnier than my ten-minute speech in the middle of one of multiple three-hour funerals held for Ros on successive days. James and I had found each other, held each other, trying to locate that shared passage of energies that articulate the miserly things of grief. We gazed at each other, looked away. We laughed; we weren't sure how to cry at that point.

I spent my time in Edinburgh resting, visiting sites with Alin, seeing other writers—Álvaro Enrigue, Brix Smith Start, Anne Applebaum—but my mind was always on my sister.

There was so much to say about her but I remembered so little as I tried to talk about it with Alin. Just that Ros was the smartest of all of us. Knew things encyclopaedically, gave precise readings on political situations and went to places where women and men were under the squeeze of immense social inequity. Went to the Solomon Islands. To West Papua, Vanuatu and Kiribati. I never saw her in these places, but I knew what her touch could bring. Like my mum, she was a reverend. She lived at the Pacific Theological College in Fiji before she came to stay with Laura and me while receiving treatment for the cancer that had metastasized and got into her lymph system. It has always been easiest for me to make things up. But this is true.

'There's only a few people we can trust to live forever,' I told Alin.

Neither of us understood what I meant precisely.

I told her of others dead. Friends, close and distant. My

father, Henry. David in the mountains. I told her about Deborah.

'That's horrible. The poor girl.'

'She had wild hair, amazingly wild tight-curled hair, and I kept thinking of that.'

We went mute, listening for something in the sparse peace of the house. We listened for changes in the space around our forms, the way they spoke of ghosts and the air-shaped surge of their reports, the tinnitus remains of long ago.

Alena

Alin eventually went back to bed and I intimated that I'd soon be doing the same. However, as I sat there I noticed a picture I hadn't seen earlier among the rows of photos. It was Alin's mother. She was young, likely in her early twenties, an intelligence in her eyes setting off the things we tend to gauge as beauty. I looked again at the images, followed the path of ages. Alin and her siblings. Lakeside scenes, Christmas and Carnival, the hubris of occasion and memory. Alena's model-like stare.

I'd learnt years earlier that Alin's mum had grown up in communist Czechoslovakia. As a young woman in the early 1960s, she was permitted to visit her aunt and uncle in Gmunden. She had family at the lake, separated of course by the weight of the Iron Curtain, but there were provisions for Czechs to leave the socialist state to visit family for short periods. Alena spoke no German and arrived in Gmunden the year following Jörg's run-in with the GDR. She enjoyed the lake, swimming in its cool waters and sunbathing on the wooden jetties that jutted into the ancient glacial cleave. And that was where they saw each other for the first time. Jörg and Alena. And that was the word Jörg had used when he told this story at dinner: saw. And see. *We see, we saw*, he said, and gestured at his eyes and then mine. They had no language in common, Jörg said, but for their eyes, the way they moved, the way they responded to their eyes with body movements and shifts in the air around them. *We see, you understand, we saw each other and*—he pointed to his eyes and smiled. *Seeing and*—and there was a quiet then, a pause where we were supposed to understand that silence was the only viable mode of expression for their experience.

At that moment I thought how, when I am ill, deeply ill, all I have is my eyes. All I have is pain as my body tries to correct the unseen, then all I have is my eyes and all I can do is look. The indescribable discomforts, those that make me groan. The disease too is a language, I realised. And like language it recalls thousands of years of repeating pain, it morphs and squeezes and destabilises the accepted and acknowledged. A talk that few can hear or read. A dialect of unreplicable repetitions of pain.

In Gmunden I'd smiled and laughed and said I understood, for we all have eyes and we all understand things with our eyes. Alena had stayed quiet through this story. She collected up plates and glasses. There was something very sad about her, despite obvious joys. And this exhibited itself as a seriousness of character and thought that felt as if it had never been translated from her old life. She never returned to Czechoslovakia after she married. She never had a chance to speak her own language and trust in the ligaments of that philological home, how it had held her previously. Her father was a goalie in the famous 1947 World Champion Czechoslovakian ice hockey team. He was arrested by the communists after accusations of planning to defect to the West. He was sentenced to fifteen years and spent time in forced labour at a Czech uranium mine. The experience harmed him deeply, and affected Alena also. He died aged forty-six, and she took his haunted self with her into Austria. She learnt German via Jörg's letters and a German–Czech dictionary. The fascists had left Czechoslovakia, but a sense of them remained extant in her need to speak their language. Word by word they got to know each other, and she prepared herself to leave Prague forever.

She told me that she often felt removed, left out, that there was a part of her that her family couldn't connect with. She liked to sing and dance; she also loved quietness and didn't always understand other people's need to make noise with their mouths. She'd shown me about the house, taken me to her studio where paintings displayed an acute anger and need. She pointed at a piece above the stairs, full of vicious lines and hard colours yanked across the canvas. It was my favourite and I suspect hers. She said, 'My family, I—' and she made an exaggerated slash in the air as if cutting something out of the house's dust-thick atmosphere. 'Very angry. I was. Errr.' And she made the noise again. She then rushed me to an atlas, found the Italian peninsula, and pointed to Palermo in the west of Sicily. *I just go. I go.* And we started laughing. She was so fed up at one point with her daughters', son's and husband's noise that, without telling anyone, she took a plane to Palermo and stayed with friends. And though it was Jörg's story that had woken me, it was Alena's that kept me awake. Alena had stayed angry for years, through weddings, global events, christenings, grandchildren. The collapse of the regime during the Velvet Revolution in Prague enraged her, but not before the wall in Berlin had fallen. She was so angry and I imagined her taking the car and driving to the centre of that story-split city, young Alin in the front seat beside her, and shouting at the crowds gathered in wrought celebration. For a long time after, she was in a deep depression, waiting for something to come right with the world so she could remain the same. The girl in the picture, the girl in Jörg's story, she hadn't seen any of this. Not the lake, nor the eventual collapse of the impermanent empires.

I slept the last half of the night with the sense of dawn pressing in. And as I lay in bed I had the urge to stroll out on the islands I'd seen as we arrived at the lake. I wanted to look back at the shore and imagine how this was before Alena and Jörg, in the days when brown shirts arrived to bathe in the spas and all the rest, because this was an area of Nazi sympathies in those years. I wanted to imagine what it was like because when you come from the opposite side of the world, you tend to lean in and imagine the notorious and vainglorious histories that dominate and burgle the sense of place from the near environs that actually have their own story to imagine over and over. Then you look. You stare and attempt to witness within one's unconscious the minute variations of juxtaposition that tell the story of place. And that was what had really awoken me— the knowledge that there was Jörg's story, there was Alena's story and there was the story I desired to hang over them all, the haunt of an unlived life known from simplified sources. It was the desire and inclination to pattern, pattern with strictures born out of morbid fascination.

I wanted to know what was wrong with the world and what was wrong with me, and know in easy broad strokes.

A year later I would be in Toronto, another view out over another lake carved during the last great ice age. Whilst the other festival writers went on an excursion to the Niagara Falls I met with Eric Beck Rubin, a Canadian cultural historian and novelist who lived in Toronto. We went for a drive out from the city centre and found ourselves splendidly lost while trying to find a path to the lake in the far western suburbs. Eventually we departed the streets and walked a trail down through gold-shot maples. Eric expounded on the thesis of his doctoral work. He'd been for years authoring a treatise on the history of Holocaust writing in fiction and the encroaching conservatism that had gradually developed in fiction and film since the end of World War II. To his surprise, Holocaust writing had become less liberal and less experimental the further the war receded. He suggested to me that this was a result of fidelity to the idea that there is a single interpretation of the Shoah, a creeping desire for unison over its meaning, how the depth of its horror must have only one, singular effect.

As I lay trying to sleep I speculated what my inclination to hunt out signs of tragedy really was. Twenty years earlier I had been in Belgium with Michael, the German manager of the band I was touring with. We were billeted with a Flemish couple living near Liège. They introduced me to Duvel at a roadside bar where bikers hung out and looked heavy. We managed to get a small drunk on before driving back to the house. There the conversation slowly edged towards the war, and I encouraged it there. I asked how the war was taught in Germany, how it became knowledge. I wanted to know how it was to learn about this, how it entered the mind and how it exerted itself. And Michael attempted to answer with detachment and decorum and describe the manner in which the young German has to enter various stages of cultural and personal reconciliation. He stated that there was a need to continue, to go on in a manner that continually addressed and worked through the war. Our Flemish host became irritated, began quarrelling, asking for a kind of bowing down before absolute fury. Suggesting that this kowtowing was the only acceptable response, to relent in the face of ongoing and justified rage against the *events*. I could only imagine that the solitary possible outcome of this desire was the dissolution of the German and Austrian peoplehood. The argument fascinated me, seemed to justify my desire to see, to look, probe with the intention of observing old facts. And that was why I used the word 'victim'; my desire is the quarry of an encroaching conservatism of history as extant and whole and present. A rock face of names and deeds and recriminations rather than the evolving knowingness and continual exchange, virus-like, streamed. Indeed, this dogmatism felt like the after-effect, the post-viral dead-space of cultural malaise. An illness all of its own.

I went to the balcony, 4am. The mountains lit in the fading smoulder of the moon. On the boulevard before the lake's water I saw a shape, a dress. A woman walking slow with her white-coated dog. She seemed to dance as her companion ran, stopped, barked. A sudden waltz like she'd been hit by something unseen and the dog leapt, sprang around her and turned, made circles until it became a rag in the lake's breeze. The woman slowed till she stopped. Then the light too vanished as clouds came over the moon. Then, so desiring of being a ghost was the woman that she managed to fade and reappear in my sleep, whispering of a strange, defiant violence.

My twin woke before me, dressed and brushed his cold teeth.

Haus

On the Sunday, Jörg took the Volvo out of storage. We drove through the town, the narrow streets into the hills above the lake. We stopped outside Peter Fabjan's residence, where we were to pick him up so he could take us to his half-brother's home in Ohlsdorf-Obernathal. A vast homestead that now sat empty as a part-time museum: the Bernhard House. Jörg was an old friend of Peter's and knew his half-brother well enough to have opinions of him away from his reputation and texts. In fact, Jörg had made Thomas Bernhard's dentures when the writer's teeth finally gave way during the rounds of chemotherapy he underwent for the lung cancer that eventually took his life in the winter of 1989.

Fabjan shook my hand and sat in the front seat, and we drove the rest of the way to the achingly old buildings just a few kilometres from the lake. I'd expected forest, a hardness in the air, an architecture of sorts that spoke to Bernhard's novels. Spoke of them, debated and imbibed some spirit of old Roithamer and the ever-perfecting cone in his 1975 novel *Correction*. Spoke in the specific language of Wittgensteinian despair and hope and despair and ultimate modification of life into its sure-handed death. Instead, we arrived at a group of houses in the countryside. There were trees beyond, but nothing of the darkness I desired, nothing of Kristen's ruins spanning the globe to here—only the young conifers holding the line.

As we came upon the building I was surprised by its size; it felt like a fort, a moated property full of resident troops and deliberating horsemen. But there was no moat and certainly no defences, only a sense of stillness, somehow cruel and against the right a writer takes with them wherever they go, the right to morph and adjust and, indeed, revise until it kills you. Large wooden doors opened to reveal a four-sided yard, properly called a Vierkanthof, a square like the piazzas of Italy and France. Built in the early seventeenth century, it was surrounded by a barn, servants' living quarters and, to the north, the actual home. Echoes and time. All the buildings were under the same roof, encircling the square. I took a photo of Alin, Alena and Kaspar seated in the sun before I was shown around.

There was a tractor in the barn, and I recalled seeing a photo of Bernhard seated at its wheel. The other side of the barn had been converted into a theatre. I do not recall whether Bernhard or his half-brother had built this, but I could see evidence of seating and a stage. Light and farm air poured in through the arched doorways out into the countryside beyond the old construction. Beneath all this was a basement whose access was a series of long stone stairs. Though it was still early autumn, the air was chilled and smelt of a close, loose rot. The basement contained bottles of what appeared to be spirits, and the heavy chain hung from two stays in the roof made a V in the air. The chain had me think of words, unrelated and certain. The simplicity of its linkages. It made ghoulish sounds of grinding, chiming metal. These resonances and accompanying death smell gave an impression of an ever deepening and biased grief. I believe this was the case because if this were the building where Bernhard wrote his 1970 novel *The Lime Works*, surely this was the basement he sat in to imagine his opening. The scattered remains of his heroine's skull and the frozen remnants of her killer husband maddened by years of doubt, by a mind fragmented by an inability to begin what he must begin.

Alin hadn't come with me down into the basement and I stood there for some time on my own imagining the use of the place in Bernhard's mind when he bought the estate in 1965. And wise that Alin had declined Peter's invitation to explore; the chain also reminded me of all the places one doesn't wish to be caught and forgotten about. It smelt of nightmares, those dreamed by prisoners caught in unimaginable places. I thought of a statement made by Bernhard's narrator's doctor father in *Gargoyles.* He says of the man who'd killed the innkeeper's wife in a brutal assault, 'Crime in the city, urban crime, is nothing compared to crime in the country, rural crime.' True, I thought, true. For I am from the city and cannot imagine the crimes of the country. The only crimes I regularly imagine are those occurring within me, those genetic trysts.

Peter Fabjan later explained as we stood in the halls of the living quarters that Bernhard had envisioned a country estate suitable for 'memorial dungeons'. Two words I couldn't get my head to explicate in a clear and ex-translated manner. And perhaps these two words sum up my experience in the basement: it certainly memorialised something; it felt both near to and distant from the author's intent for the building. When Bernhard first came across the estate, it was a decrepit early fourteenth-century farmhouse filled with debris and rotted roofing. It was redesigned by Bernhard over ten years, and while he maintained its extents and architecture, the building was, and remained, as Fabjan put it, 'the sophisticated manor of a loner'.

Every room a story or a line to be told over and over until it becomes the ruin it once was.

Bernhard desired the buildings' renovations to produce a kind of theatre backdrop: as a result, the rooms in which he lived contained multiple stage props as they had appeared in his plays. The house was populated by a grotesque array of antiques which served as his everyday utensils for living. An ancient bed, desks and paintings of gentry and the over-class. Bernhard's boots and coats and pinched Tyrolean hats sat near the front door, untouched since his death. In the Empfangszimmer was a beautiful emerald green ceramic fireplace whose chimney rose up through the walls of the house. Alin explained it was a fireplace similar to what would become central heating. It fed smaller versions of the same thing through the house with warm air. Peter took me through Bernhard's office space, his bedroom, and finally, past the upper northeast corner of the building, he showed me the room and working space Thomas Bernhard had built for young writers to come and work and study on a form of fellowship. He thought if he provided this space, writers would come and he would be giving something back to the youth he himself had struggled with. 'But,' Peter told me, in a sorrowful and practised voice, 'nobody ever came.' And he turned and walked slowly from the top floor, past the offices, down the strangely organic stairs Bernhard installed in the late Sixties, around the time I was born, into the body of the house. Death occurs in many ways, the house seemed to say.

At the end of the tour Peter gave me two books of Bernhard's, both translated and published by the same German publishers who were, at the time of my visit, busy translating my first novel into German for publication in 2017. I felt like a charlatan then; my presence there, the fact of my novel, how these were connected seemed impossible. I felt haunted by rumours about myself I hadn't managed to get up close to, a mirror-me of vastly greater capacity in all regards. Peter also handed over a book about the house decorated in pictures and text. And as I handle that book now, I wish it too could be translated, for it is full of information I cannot recall from my time at the house. It contains pictures that replicate the pictures I took on my phone. Shows the layouts of the rooms I remember well, the elegant arches of the ceilings and the modern bathroom of the 1970s I've quite forgotten about. I recently asked Laura if she could translate it for me, but it was a jagged recounting and we soon gave up. The house remains over there, solid in someone else's imagination.

That afternoon I slept once again in my small room below the kitchen where the previous night we'd been speaking about my book and its translation to German. At one point, Alena had looked at her husband and they'd started a conversation away from Alin and me. Jörg then picked up his phone and spoke German for a few minutes with the person on the other end. I heard my name spoken several times, then what sounded like the bargaining of various windows of time. He'd then hung up and put his hands beside his face, looked at me and said, 'So, tomorrow morning, David, yes? We pick up Thomas Bernhard's brother and we visit Bernhard's house.'

My face felt like a boy's, my expression borrowed from a time when I didn't know how to contain unexpected excitements and their accompanying anxieties. Alin explained to me her parents' relationship with Bernhard, and she started smiling for me, that tiny bite on the corner of her lip. Bernhard had no simple relationships, nothing less than complex. I laughed for her, to say that this was just grand.

And true, it was amusing for other reasons. Chiefly because I had been meaning to ask on the train ride west whether she knew anything about Bernhard, but we'd been busy with Kaspar and Martin and that other mirror life of youthful discharge. I'd had no idea about his life in this tiny town in upper Austria, had no idea that he lived in a farmhouse not far from where Alin had grown up. That he'd had a tractor, and re-accented rooms full of antiques like queries back and forth between his lonesome existence and a past that looked for answers in the present, for an extant history in a one-sentence conversation written over and over again, and again.

I'd been meaning to ask because I'd only really just discovered his existence a few months earlier. I hadn't asked Alin, but Bernhard had somehow appeared among all the shared voices we'd spoken, among the stories and paintings and hand-gestured conversations. Jörg, Alin and Alena, her small voice and delicately ferocious artworks that answered more for me than any question I could have posited towards her about life in the Austrian countryside fifty years absent from her home in Prague.

This, of course, reminded me there was a part of Alin that I couldn't access, though knew was present. A part left behind by her recent admitted struggle with English and my inability to pick up her language, any language, to learn it and summon it. For years, she'd told me in Edinburgh, she'd had no reason to practise English, no reason to practise thinking in that voice. Over the span of years she'd written several times that the language was leaving her, taking with it a part of her mind, a section of her history in New Zealand and Australia. Her life existed purely in German now, and mine in antipodean English. I imagined this loss operating as a low-grade brain damage, its tissue shifted or absent. There was a whole other person wishing to speak amongst the wiring, but was here tampered with. Still the person that existed when we hung together, but now seemingly absent. We looked and lamented the absence of ourselves, the certain knowability in the complex practice of our tethered presence, being and animation. It all felt loosed, like a knocked tooth shifting in the gum.

Then, as if to accent this, she said to me as we stood outside Bernhard's house:

'I think in your book, you might have to die.'

'Perhaps,' I said.

'Over and over.'

That afternoon the three of us went walking along the shore front. The lake and sky separated by the massive structure of rock heaved up from the ocean millions of years earlier, deep forest and the haze lifting from the lake's surface. An arc protruding from the western edge: a fountain shooting a spray far into the air, where it all fell apart into a flailing cloud. To the west sat Schloss Ort, the eleventh-century castle set upon a small island linked by a bridge upon whose boards horses once clattered. I walked and marvelled at the body's ability to meander despite its ruin. In fact, had I known this walk was the beginning of the last weeks of a period of reasonably good health I'd enjoyed for eighteen months, perhaps I would have run on the cobblestones and felt their uncomfortable twist and knobble on my feet and ankles, let my knees remember how they used to hurt and flex on scar tissue, but instead I walked slowly, happy to watch the distant castles announce their peerage and tell me I knew nothing, not really, of this place and its cold past.

And as we walked, Kaspar exclaimed he wanted to walk in the water. Alin spotted some other children, a boy and girl each a few years older, doing the same. She acquiesced, led him down the stone towards the water that lapped at the slipways, and he stood quietly ten or so metres from the other kids. The water reaching around his blue rubber Wellingtons, the calm of old waters and new boots. He kept turning and looking back at his mother as if he didn't want her to watch. I felt nervous for him, for myself. Like with heights, I can't deal with water; I fear it. It's a drowning, sucking thing. The other children slowly came over and stood with him. They talked, that infantile mumbling of observation and greeting. They stayed quite still, all three of them statued by something remote and telling. The sun caught the air behind them and blackened their features into shadow.

I'm not sure which child started first, or if there was a first. It's possible they started simultaneously. That high whine before the buttery run of tears. The whinnying. All three of them in a synchronised wail.

The two parents rushed down the slipway to assist, to cajole this sudden plague out of their babies' systems. But hands were shrugged off and the wailing broke into a coughing, choking weeping. The girl was picked up first, but she struggled from her mother's arms and fell into the water and stood quickly before running back to where Alin was holding Kaspar's shoulders and whispering in his ear, improvising the magic phrases to lead him away. But he stayed put, shouting. The children screamed as they were separated, faces ruined in the muscle collapse of inconsolability. Mouths open, teeth, tongues and throats, saliva down their chins.

Volant

It is not the idea, the intellectual fact of the cliff, precipice or whatever else. Nor is it threat of falling—the danger that you will, if you've edged too close to the lip, be obligated to fall. Nor is it the fear of that drop, that passing through of the air and the somehow knowing terror at the end. It is none of these things. It is something quite other and unknown to those who do not go through this affliction. It occurs at the elevation of a ladder, the edge of a cliff, building, wharf, roof, at the pause of a rollercoaster at its peak. Height vertigo is the sense that you have, already, begun falling despite being quite safe. That you are in a continuous forward motion out into space, that you are, in other words, falling. You're passing through the air, you are descending, in descent. You are heading towards the last gasp of air before the earth. And this is a continual thing. It doesn't stop when you tell yourself it has to stop. It doesn't break when there's a large plate of glass between you and the air. The best mechanism to halt the sensation is to lie down, lower your centre of gravity so that the needy part of your medial prefrontal cortex calms, settles and knows it can't possibly fall. And then, once all is normalised, you can observe the view, the glorious width and bloom of scape and survey.

This happens to me when confronted by the loom, the weight of high places.

And the sensation has no logic, can be triggered by observing a person climbing to lofty spaces.

Various films are unwatchable: *Man on a Wire* is terror. I get degrees of physical anxiety just considering the stages of work they went through atop the Twin Towers to make the Frenchman's walk possible, the rigging of the roofs, the bow and its arrow's arc across the divide between the north and south towers, the multiple clandestine trips to the roof of the buildings to probe logistics and scope the angles. It is a film far beyond the fictional horrors of masterpieces like *Alien* or *The Exorcist*, *The Blair Witch Project* or *Caché*. Because, quite simply, I am falling when Philippe Petit is not. I'm tumbling out into spaces. The awed space between these parallel structures down at the western edge of Manhattan Island.

My friend Matthew once climbed the seventy-two-metre Makōhine Viaduct near Mangaweka when we were on tour in 1992. It was summer then and that was the only excuse I could imagine for why he'd do such a thing. I was the single sober person in either of the two vans needed to take us and our support band to Auckland. I kept fondling the keys and walking to the car park. I stood at the van, sweating, then returned to the picnic tables, where everyone was watching.

I looked up with my mouth open, tongue dry. And for the entire duration of the event, every instant of the act he was falling, clanging his head on the girders on the way down in a rhythm set to our various utterances.

Matthew ultimately made it to the top and had to hang by one arm in order to pull himself over the lip of the viaduct that strutted out wider than the actual superstructure holding the bridging up. I would later put this scene in my second novel, hoping that some of my terror would come through, but little of it did. It takes a much deeper immersion in the language of dread, horror and fright to overcome the page's aversion to pain. Indeed, the page resists pain so earnestly. It seeks easy linkages and sweet rhythms and rhymes. That kind of sung excursion into the known. Pain is what occurs in spelling mistakes and bad grammar.

My fear and pain occurs in a kind of churning repetition, run over and over, such as we might find in Thomas Bernhard's later works. The continual regarding of clause, seeking out its ultimate iteration. Inversion, repetition, perfection, correction and eventual destruction.* This is terror, literary terror. These are *Correction*'s words concerning the drive towards the construction of a home in the forest, the flawless edifice designed out of love for his sister by the scientist Roithamer, who spends years building the structure in the shape of a geometrically perfect cone, only then to succumb to suicide at the project's end:

* In Bernhard's *Correction*, the narrator's Wittgensteinian obsession with language sees the narrative dominated by the obfuscating and ever self-correcting play of language and the ironies of language in its state of performance. They present as a continual attempt to amend, revise and improve the propositions in the text. These series of corrections, however, do not imply improvement, but rather, as David Sepanik states, 'an irrepressible compulsion for change, change so devoid of meaning it becomes repetition, repetition so inevitable that it inspires horror'.

From a certain unforeseeable moment on, young men, mostly those getting on toward thirty-five, tend to push an idea, and they push that idea so far until they have made it a reality, and they themselves have been killed by this idea-turned-reality, I said. I see now, I said, that Roithamer's life, his entire existence, had aimed at nothing but this creation of the Cone, everyone has an idea that kills him in the end, an idea that surfaces inside and haunts him and that sooner or later—always under extreme tension—wipes him out, destroys him. *Natural Science or so-called natural science* (Roithamer's words), I told the Hoellers, had served as a preparation for this idea, everything in his life had served only as a preparation for the idea of building the Cone, and then the outward spur for building and realising the Cone had been Hoeller's building of his house, on the one hand, I said, looking at those death notices on the wall opposite me, the idea of building deliberately in the Aurach gorge, while on the other hand the idea of building right in the middle of the Kobernausser forest, in the other case to assert oneself at last in the teeth of all reason and all accepted usage here in the Aurach gorge, in the one case the same process by other means, but from the same motive, in the middle of the Kobernausser forest. A man has an idea and then, at the critical point sometime in his life, finds another man who, because of his character and because his state of mind answers to that critical turning point in the other man's life, brings that idea to fulfillment, finally perfects it in reality.

And this perfection, well, just look to the epigraph at the head of this book. This kind of phrasing seems a pointer to the pulse of height-induced vertigo, if not its content. The mind's molecular rectification of idea, the on and on of location and time and intent and sentence, its relocation and retrieval that ends in some ill-gained demise, self-inflicted and terminal. My friend Matthew is, at the time of writing, an English professor in the United States, and I wish this meant something to the story, made it grander somehow, linked my horror of height-induced vertigo with literature in a way that made for Bernhard's prose to be considered the greatest of all writers of terror and pain. But it doesn't; it only links attribution to attribution. However, it does tell me that literature can never be immune to its own propensity to derange the real and make it strange. Besides, my fear of heights doesn't compare to my fear of water.

Combined they feel foetal and fatal.

Combined they feel like the root of some unnamed horror disease that eats blood.

Ganglia

The greater parts of our lives, my cousin Rachel once wrote, are often situated in the worst places. So, it seems necessary and vital that we find beauty in the indefinite and awful. As such, we can be found when we feel we have abandoned the best of ourselves.

I repeated this for her not long ago while she was telling me about the years spent in Brandenburg with her close friend, how the filaments of their friendship coalesced and cracked while decorating the apartment they shared.

She sent me an image of one of her paintings, a two-metre rendering of a giant, distended ganglia. I felt then a belief in her work, that, in the process of painting, the work itself will solve the illness, that escape is at the end of the correct brushstroke. Indeed, what is art but an exercise to find out the questions you couldn't otherwise ask?

Deep Rock

The train travelled north out of Milan's immense railyards and headed for the Italian Alps, the lakes and those kinds of villages and towns in the south of Switzerland you wished only for yourself and those you loved. Capolago, Melano, Maroggia. But before those towns we paused at the station in Milan and I tried to look outside the walls into the invisible beyond. Tried to get a glimpse of fame, of La Scala, of the Duomo, of the Castello Sforzesco, of the garage where Mussolini had been hung up by his ankles in April 1945. A bullet to his head. I wanted to imagine men in fine suits, women in frocks cut just so, but instead I had that fascist ass roaming my head. But soon enough he vanished, because mountains, mountains and lake and sky.

We entered the tunnel at Pollegio, southern Switzerland. The Gotthard Base Tunnel, fifty-seven kilometres tracked under the Alps in two sweeping swathes of parallel tubes. The entire massif above as the train hoofed into the dark, lights smashing at the walls and leaving not a trace of proton or wave. The glide-through ran two kilometres deep beneath the plateaus and peaks. Enough earth was shifted during construction to build the Great Pyramid of Giza five times over. Six colossal boring machines—each four football fields long, immense and clawing at the face of the rock like a fist turning against skinned white bone—worked in immense heat.

By the time I was on board, ten thousand passengers were riding the train daily. Despite this number, I managed to concentrate hard enough to feel like the explorer of some new and deft real. The tunnellers had put their machines deep into the absolute nearness of space. Its weight and heat, its compressed prison of ancient sediment and time. A sheer proximity to the unknown and known. We were inside the room of the atom, the mind of the atom, the space where presence becomes non-presence, where observation is the critical factor. Deep inside the mind travelling at ridiculous pace.

Speed, coffee and pastries. Families and businessmen, their newspapers and laptops. Tablets and iPads and Androids. The things businesspeople read and study, the graphic intent of stock pattern, the sense of other futures. Children in the aisle played a version of hopscotch as we travelled at two hundred kilometres an hour. Feigned tears and mirth, forced laughter with the aim of hurting feelings. I wondered:

Where's their sense of awe?

Despite all this enumeration *my* initial awe at the tunnel's numbers slowly slipped out seven and a half minutes after entry and I began reading my book. It was the hardback copy of *Here I Am* my old agent had given to me when I was at his offices in Pimlico three weeks earlier. Rooms so densely packed with books it felt like there was a magnificent shift imminent, a war perhaps, some great tear in the norm. And on that cue Caspian told me the best insulation from radiation fallout is believed to be books. Hardbacks, preferably, stacked against the wall in their thousands. He waved his hand around from out of his blue suit and offered me any book I liked. At my indecision he picked up the US edition of Jonathan Safran Foer's book and put it in my hands. 'Great novel,' he said, and I realised he must have sold it on from the United States in some deal. It was the very same text that would set Eric Beck Rubin and me talking in a year's time. Safran Foer's novel was at once hilarious and infuriating. It stole from everywhere and nowhere. In Eric's dissertation, he used Safran Foer as an example in his argument that Holocaust writing has become conservative and unwilling to experiment, that the days of Imre Kertész and Georges Perec are over due to forces of religion, tradition and the authority of witness. 'The works of Kertész and Perec,' he wrote, 'treat their subject [the Holocaust] as "free-flowing" or open, where Safran Foer treats it as "wrapped-up" or closed off.' I found myself opening Foer's novel to the middle pages and then turning to the back cover to read the precis again and look at the author's photograph. Study his brow-line. I'm always taking a look at the brows of writers, the exaltations of thought. Dana Spiotta and her mindful high forehead. Lydia Davis's above her close-set eyes, saying something, something you'll never think on your own. Richard Ford's threatening and grand.

Every minute or so I looked up to concentrate on the flash and run of architecture supporting the tunnel, the immense curvature of bends angling the machine north, then back to the west.

Flash-flash-flash-flash.

I calculated the lights on the right-hand side, how they were ten metres apart. And those on the left, one hundred. And at every third light an emergency door, green and blinked at repeatedly, over and over. Fing, fing, fing. I tried to read the writing, every few seconds trying to see the next letter in the deep blur produced in the merge of luminosity and speed. I imagined labyrinths beyond, and stairs, ladders taking one to the snows above. Two thousand metres of climbing, limb over limb as the heat slowly eased and reduced to a temperature which supported ice and snow and their strange-shaped molecules.

I read, then stopped after a few sentences.

Why aren't we forced to wear seatbelts on such a thing? I wrote to my wife.

I watched a woman and a chap talking, the simple ease of another husband and wife, or girlfriend and boyfriend, or perhaps the front-end of a new friendship. I began another email to Laura, trying to explain my thoughts on Thomas Bernhard. *There's a distinct connection between* Correction *and illness,* I wrote. *Can you, hon, read a little of it for me? And tell me what you feel like. Read for an hour and tell me how you feel. Do you remember anything about what you were doing beforehand? Do you feel a certain dizziness or vertigo?* I wrote that I was allowed to stay in Bernhard's house for a night. I told her I was haunted, because that's the kind of thing we say and like to hear.

And as I hit send I felt the train slow. Felt the sensation of blood pushing from back to front. To my face and eyes and fingertips. Cellular shift, and my ears began doing odd things.

We were slowing and everyone was looking up from their toys. Voices began to surround us, speakers in discreet spaces emitting Italian, then German. Everyone standing up, looking around, asking each other what was happening. Then English, but by then I was listening to the translations hooping about the carriage, the rumours quickly induced. A man stood at the front and encouraged everyone else to sit. Calming motions with his hands.

I heard a male voice behind us. A pleasant Scottish brogue I'd become familiar with a few weeks earlier. 'I do believe—'

'What's this?' The woman beside him. English, northern.

'We're to be evacuated,' he said. 'Or, rather, the train's to be evacuated, of us.'

'How's that?'

Silence then, or not silence. Just that I couldn't hear them for a moment as voices rose around the carriage.

'Underground shelters?' the woman said in reply to something unheard. 'You know this?'

A coughed laugh from the Scotsman.

'Bullshit,' the woman said.

'I read the brochures,' the man said.

'Brochures?'

'Highly complimentary of the systems, emergency contingencies. Shelters.'

'Marvellous. Do we take our hand luggage?'

'We're talking Siemens, doll. We're talking computing power and surveillance technology enough to direct total war. China *and* the Russians.'

'And the Russians! Well, I do—'

I think they were flirting.

'Aye, there're emergency stations, so we don't worry. Three of them.'

'Three? That's an investment in the assumed value of life.'

I found this oddly uncomforting, perhaps the use of the word 'emergency', perhaps the fact they believed they had to allow for contingencies in the first place. Or perhaps the possibility our Scotsman had to make something up to make himself feel better. Planning for disaster suggests its inevitability. The train slowed until the walls of the tunnel became clearer, their details exact. The repetition of componentry and cables felt precise, human and comforting; the sight of a walkable path alongside excited me. None of the words I believed to be words uniform on the walls were words, but logograms of some other language. I wondered whether there were ever downtimes in which guided tours were taken through the expanse of the tunnel. Troupes with walking sticks promenading single file, a chaperone pointing at the greyed matter of porous rock, man-made features, and explaining the density of the different strata of geologic form.

Then instructions.

Instructions as we stopped. The man at the front was replaced by a figure in hi-vis emergency orange. The doors opened and he hustled us out. We all nervously stepped onto the walkway and to green doors opening into a passageway. We appeared to be following lights or something well thought out and practised, because we seemed to know what to do without instruction. We moved through into a long red corridor lit by subtly blinking, ankle-high neuronal flashes. Slowly I realised there were calm-sounding voices in speakers looking down from the ceiling. They were giving tuition on how to walk calmly and towards certain safety. The Scotsman was just in front of me; the woman he'd been talking to was at my side. She was tall, a couple of inches taller than me, and I felt at ease. That thing I often found within myself around people of height; I felt calmed by the sensation they couldn't possibly want or need anything from me.

'Container fire,' the Scotsman said, turning and not breaking stride. He was a doctor; this knowledge seemed everywhere now, though I'd no idea how I came upon it.

'What's a container fire doing in a railway tunnel?' the woman asked, turning to me and in doing so proving it wasn't a question but rather a plea for the man not to go on as we shuffled down the hall. The bodies of many. The victims of approaching dread.

Despite all, the doctor went on. 'Aye, fuck, you see. Most of the traffic is containers, containers on freight trains. We're secondary cargo.' He explained these weren't allowed to travel at the speed of a passenger train. He gestured at the lights, depressed evenly in the grey wall. Said that if there was a fire or other in the lanes up ahead we were to be moved to the southbound tunnel.

The woman had deep black hair that hung straight and smelt of coffee. She introduced herself as Linda. The man turned and put out his hand and said his name was James. As he introduced himself to the woman I realised they'd only known each other a few minutes longer than I them.

'Money's on chemical spill. Then it's on a spark from the tracks. Inflammation of hot air. Eruption, indigo flame. Maximum heat warp. Paint stripped from walls. Our eyes can't see this kind of heat. It burns in frequencies outside our powers of sight.'

'Good Lord. Will you listen to that,' the woman said, again turning to me. She seemed to enjoy this act of turning and demurring.

As we were moved into a room large enough to fit a hundred people, we were separated. The room felt claustrophobic, hemmed in by its rectangular exactness. This wasn't architecture of compassion or hope, it was about containment. It spoke of its surroundings, the compressed inwardness of granite, spoke of the rock's hope of collapsing back to the seafloor of its origin. The lights spoke of emergency, said: *You're lucky to be here. That we thought of this. You're lucky to be alive. We thought of you and this is what we think luck looks like.*

Oddly, I thought of Alena then, Alin's mum following narrow roads through lower Bohemia on her way from Czechoslovakia to Austria. The deep drifts of snow and the massing pines on either side, forest darkness and the sudden border in the middle of a plain, hill-bound road. The way the paving improved as soon as she was allowed through on her temporary visa. It was the way she was altered in that moment of movement, the letting go of her language and the weight of the new. There was a link I wanted to make but couldn't quite fuse with bare thought. I'd driven the same road eighteen years earlier when heading to Berlin from Vienna via Prague. We became lost on the way to the border. All I recalled was trees, vast swathes of pine and the exactness of the roads that bored through the ancient forests as if insisting there was something beyond nature.

The room seemed to fill with people then empty.

Earlier I'd seen Linda shifting about, walking a few steps backwards and forwards like a smoker. Now she saw me and began to slide towards me on the tether of prior connection. Words spoken here meant we were nearer than acquaintances. She moved through a family of five who were quietly talking their twin toddlers into standing up and moving around.

'Is this as bad as we think it is?' I asked.

'I don't precisely know,' she said. 'How about you? Any intelligence?'

'Hardly.'

'What are they saying? Do we know?' She looked past my shoulder. 'I'm always worried I'm missing out on translations, yeah. I look like a chicken poking my nose in.' She turned her head and connected with a seriously puffy-looking woman wearing a yellow raincoat. They went through a series of nods, trying to see if they had anything in common.

'I got nothing,' I said.

She smiled—an easy thing, given and taken. Long arms, her handbag at her chest. She had black nail polish and a hint of old-world goth at the tips of her eye make-up. She nodded at a couple in the corner talking. They were older, late sixties, mercifully unconcerned. 'What do you think they've got to jabber about after all this time?' She sounded dismissive of her interest in them, but keen on knowing all the same.

'Maybe they've just met,' I said.

'They're married.'

'They're married?'

'There's a familiar slump,' she said. I watched her talk but stopped listening for a moment. I imagined all of the old couple's conversations, spread out over years, compressed into a page. Their entire life, it all suddenly felt like one of Bernhard's sentences—the end doubtful, death certain. She stared at me, finally, and when I didn't react she started laughing lightly, like she'd just discovered she could. I joined her for a moment and felt like a thief. 'So will we be offered bread and water at some point?' she asked.

'Once we start peeing in corners and chewing each other's hair.'

'Where's our chap from earlier?' she asked.

‘The stress got to him. He returned to the mothership.’

‘Stress is underrated and oversubscribed,’ she said and then looked away, as if to discard the statement.

I made a comment about stress making me sick. That for years it had been breaking down various parts of my body. It’s a simple claim to make, but most don’t believe it, because most don’t believe the things they can’t experience. Like depression. Like ME. Like anxiety. Like addiction. Like belief. Like war. Like crime, and total death.

‘Oh, don’t,’ she said, and smiled. As I predicted, she thought I was joking.

People were leaning back with their phones, trying to find space away from the room. Trying to find relatives and news, football scores and some hint of everydayness occurring beyond this now. Reddening eyes glancing, grasping and hopeful.

The same Wi-Fi password as on the train.

‘What’s your line of work?’ she asked me.

‘I’m a writer,’ I said. It was true for the time being, though I still felt nervous saying it, as though someone would point something out I hadn’t yet considered.

‘So, David, perhaps this is a useful thing.’

‘How’s this a useful thing?’

She held up her phone. ‘I got a theory that storytelling makes a comeback when we run out of batteries.’

‘For sure,’ I said.

‘The future belongs to disasters,’ she said. ‘We owe them our full attention.’ She looked around the room, dulled eyes, voices mimicking old rejoinders in the fibrous glow. A couple hopping on the spot in an anxious fitness routine.

‘What do you do when not frequenting . . . caves?’ I asked.

‘Journalist. Correspondent. Travel writer. I get per diems and end up in bars.’

‘Huzzah.’

‘Good thing we’re both here then, right,’ she said.

‘You think we’re at the disaster stage yet?’

She shrugged. ‘I’m just worried someone’s going to come by and say we’re going to have to walk out of here. Twenty miles. I’m sorry, but I’m not sporting the footwear.’ She nodded at her feet. She was wearing slight heels designed for high-tech office space.

‘How deep are we, under the mountain?’ I asked.

‘Not sure, though it’s mountains,’ she said. ‘Multiple peaks, glacial debris. Thirty kilometres, over halfway. If this were a brain we’d be somewhere near the interior cingulate cortex.’ She had an ability to avoid eye contact while maintaining the sense that I was the only one she was interested in talking to. Which made me think she should be on TV, a reporter from foreign climes, rich with local ambiguities and resentment, nearby children playing games in the dust. ‘I’m not claustrophobic,’ she said, ‘so this doesn’t concern me. I’m here for three weeks and I’m fine. This is merely fascinating. The others kill themselves arguing over how they’re getting out.’

‘A cheese sandwich is found and it’s carnage,’ I said.

She continued to look around the room, nodding at a small boy who had a stripe of what looked like mud on his cheek. This room was so cut off from the actual dirt and rock I was in slight awe of the fact he’d managed to get dirty so quickly.

‘I have a bag of chips,’ I said.

‘Oh, well, we’re fine in that case.’

I felt myself nearing the announcement I always have to make at some point, that I wasn’t fine despite all the conversation, despite the fact that I was standing and talking and for all appearances, fine.

‘You okay?’

I bobbled my head.

'You'll be fine,' she said.

I bit my lip.

'What were you doing in Milan?' she asked.

'I was in Austria, Venice, then I went to Florence, on to Milan. I never left the train station.'

She nodded.

'My mechanism of travel planning,' I said, 'is I look at the map and make assumptions based on proximity to geographic features, the roads in and out, what I know about the food of the region. This tells me what will be interesting about the place. Were there major battles fought here? Wars and trade routes. What was their position on slavery? What were the Romans up to? I arrive and then I look up things to do. It's ingenious in that I see very little of what others see but avoid the queues at museum gift shops.'

'What about Venice?'

'Oh,' I laughed. 'I spent my two days in bed, listening to the water. It was very—it was highly therapeutic. I can recommend it. That and Ravenna. I was there for a month. I took one photograph and wrote about the Rubicon for days.'

'When do we get out of here?' she said, turning to look around again as if there might be news in the way people were postured or gesturing. 'And where?'

'We exit at Attinghausen, eventually.'

'Which is what?' she asked. 'I never look at maps. The whole cartography thing. Terrifying. Borders, barriers.' There was a glint about her. A flash of pale hair over her face. 'Where are we now? If we weren't in this room.' She glanced upwards, through the ceiling, through the steel frame, granite, water, ice, snow, blue.

I followed her gaze, then looked around for the Scotsman. 'I suspect Tujetsch, or Sedrun. The Canton of. We're at multiple borders,' I said.

We ate my chips.
The potato and oil mix.
Sodium ruin.
The fascination of other chemicals.

An hour passed. The family of multiple children led some of our cohort in song. Massed singing. Almost harmonies. Then further minutes, and the woman and I played a game of Scrabble on our phones. Back and forth. The strategy of micro-word versus grand nouns. Pi. Xu. Ch. Spittle sounds, words outside language just sitting around. Then, then quietly, there was unspoken movement, and without instruction we exited the room, following a man sporting a weighty moustache and carrying a heavy torch. He limped and aimed the flashlight at the floor and corners, despite the glow of the guide lights set into the walls at ankle height, which sent rude shadows of us to the roof. We reappeared as creatures, staggering, strange proposals for the dead.

Linda and I meandered at the back, drifting behind the singing chorale. We followed the tubular walkway onwards in the wake of song. I wondered how many tunnels they had to dig in order to make things function. How many tunnels for emergency actions and rescue operations, how many for water management, how many for balancing the air displacement of rushing trains? I wanted to know if there were follies, ghost cuts into the mind of the rock, never be to accessed. Foul, empty memories. One hundred thousand euros per metre. Grottos covered over and forgotten about, except in plans and theory hidden in darkness. All of which reminded me of the little peeking words of our Scrabble game, the little technologies of breath and world construction put to use once, just once and now abandoned to game play and the obscurity of the points on offer.

This was the cavern of some always shifting mind.

I said to the woman, 'How many tunnels till we can announce there's a labyrinth going on here?'

She didn't reply. We were hurrying now, to catch up and not find ourselves alone. We heard the sounds of machinery, the echo and ping of metal and hammer.

I said, 'That's the sound of trapped workers.'

She ignored me. 'So, if they stopped digging here a year ago,' she said, 'this means this place isn't actually infinite. Which is certainly a plus.'

I shrugged, with vigour, so that she would see it in her periphery.

'I'm mostly interested in things that don't claim to be infinite,' she said. 'Someone says "infinite wisdom" and I don't finish the drink they bought me. They say "infinite complexity" and I'm out of my seat. Out of the bar and I'm jogging down the street looking for a shop to buy a Mars bar and chat to the shop-keep about the weather. Which is one of my favourite topics. You know, David, all considered, there are ten fundamental types of clouds. Ten. Take that infinity. Bam.' She laughed. 'I generally like small-minded people so I don't have to think too much.'

I'm generally easily impressed, excited even, when I meet someone who carts information around so effortlessly. Puts it all into sentences without fear of being wrong.

I've had a tendency all my life to mix the truth with whatever pops into my mind, because I assume that others, like me, are not really listening and instead we're talking for reasons of assembly and warmth. But this isn't true, not really; people actually listen! I've known this off and on for years. And I really came to understand it when, after a spell of life-threatening depression in 2015, I was diagnosed with Attention Deficit Disorder. The test of which I passed with flying colours of extreme chromatic instability. *But I write books!* I exclaimed at the specialists. *This can't be!* And then, of course, they told me a bunch of data I didn't listen to. But what I did learn is that people with ADD and its cousin ADHD* have an ability to concentrate immensely on a specific task. Bore in on it. Stay there at its head until exhaustion kicks in and the shell of its thoughts lie in pieces on the screen. Specific tasks. Prior to ME, I tended to drive dangerously fast, because to drive fast meant I was forced to concentrate, and without this concentration I felt I was a danger on the road, absent and paying sparse attention to the things around me. Speed slowed everything else down for me. Simple jobs I was no good at. I was, in my late teens, a postman. I was fired two months in, because I couldn't get my head around what I was supposed to be doing. Generally I sought out menial jobs and lost them just as quickly due to incompetence at the simple things. I then sought out complexity because it seemed to map what was going on in my head. University was a relief and a joy, because I could write what I wanted. I was less interested in studying for exams, because knowledge retention was a problematic task. Instead, I

* Strictly speaking, I have ADHD without hyperactivity. When driving around the country, Deborah used to encourage me to go faster than I already felt a compulsion to drive. *Faster, faster*. Deb quiet, and me hooked into this state of speed that calmed the ADD mind into a state of concentration that, these days, I feel when writing endlessly and endlessly. It was the only way I felt safe. It should have come as no surprise to me when, nearly two decades later, I was diagnosed and prescribed Ritalin. Speed saves the strangest of us.

wrote well-received essays and flopped in the exams, which was all fine because I was good at the part I wanted to be good at.

For the first time, I felt I might be useful.

I was twenty-eight when I had this thought. Then, seventeen years later, this diagnosis helped me understand the world in a way previously inconceivable to me. People are really listening and communicating, not just nodding and thinking in sparks about whatever is in that flash and flicker. Those bursts of neuron unable to connect to the next set of neurons. People are actually listening. It was a discovery of embarrassing density. What the world must have thought of me for all these decades.

And now there I was in conversation deep in these tunnels under the peaks, and soon this woman would realise there was a grand absence, a disconnect at the level of logic extension. That the conversation ultimately wasn't going anywhere.

For a long minute I felt the air pressure change, tighten that delicate intrusion of other airs coming in from disconnected atmospheres. I lost sight of people out in front. We hustled, I felt the stretch of Linda's legs, that she was about to break into a trot. We took a corner into a long stretch of corridor. A perfect equilibrium of light and architecture. She skipped beside me, almost running, because there was no one out in front, just the long extending tunnel. One of the hundreds of ankle-high lights flickered, and Linda stuttered. She said, 'Oh.' Like: *Ooohh*. Like a long series of zeros, each individually falling over and collapsing in a row of *oooh*.

I put my arm out for her to take and we started jogging.

'Have we been this slow all along?' she said.

'We have to catch up.'

'We have to catch up.'

'There haven't been that many turns, have there?' I asked. 'Any junctions we missed?'

'I don't think we should turn back.'

'No. We keep going.'

'Good because I'm not sure. Going back is like, what's it like?'

'We keep going because then we come out somewhere.'

'We come out somewhere.'

'Do you run at home? Like, do you keep fit?' I asked.

'Do I keep fit? This is me keeping fit. I'm a blinking travel writer,' she said. 'I run to catch trains and sit places and write about the goddamned coffee. Do I keep fit?'

'Just that, I'll have to stop soon. I jog across the road once every six months,' I said.

'Let's. We can walk. We'll get where we're going by walking.'

I stopped running and felt the surge hit me, the pull and shunt of enervation. The rush to light, my face feeling as if it were the snow hardening above, that our feet were treading upon it in cold, crystal air. I put my hand up and put it down again as I started to sit at the point of the flickering light. The sudden dulling of nerves, the loss of feeling in my hands and the sway, the sway like chains. The way there was no actual way to stay standing.

‘Just a moment,’ I said.

‘Just a moment,’ she said.

‘Just—yeah.’

She knelt down. Then, after several seconds passed, stood. She ran to the corner and called out. I looked up to watch her become a narrow band, a wick of candle light. I noticed things about her that were obscured before. The way she leant forward when she called out, as if she didn’t want to be impolite by raising her voice. There was something athletic in her movements, something unarticulated previously.

‘Just a minute,’ I said again. Everything sounded like smeared newsprint.

Like she was actually a sports person one time previously. Soccer. Volleyball.

She ran back. She seemed shorter, as if the dimensions of the tube and the bend of the lighting had reduced her somehow. ‘What do I do?’

‘Nothing,’ I said. ‘Just talk. Tell me something.’

‘Tell you something?’

‘I don’t know,’ I said. ‘I’ll be okay. Tell me a story.’ Other lights flashing, internal and deep and all around her.

‘A story.’

‘Just.’

‘Tell you something. What?’

‘. . .’

‘Okay. Okay.’ She sat on her haunches and clasped her fingers together just above the knees. ‘The last time I came through here, this is years ago, okay. I was doing a piece for the *Guardian* on Zurich. Okay. And I was driving. I love driving on the right-hand side of the road,’ she said. ‘Everything is elevated by the extreme need to concentrate. It’s the reinvigoration of space. I think space is the word. Does that make sense?’

I nodded. Her hair was paler now, browned by the light, or by her story, its giving over. I felt my face twist, gargoyle into that of a mouth-breather as she spoke, a half-monster with saliva collecting under my tongue. And as she talked and talked about driving, I was slipping. The first time I drove on the right-hand side of the road, we were in eastern Germany, that same tour through late 1998. I'd left the band I was working with in Wrocław, Poland, and headed to Dresden with a lighting tech and his van; the idea was to get the studio in order to record an album in an old bomb factory. We didn't say a lot. He drove, and I examined the unchanging landscape. Then, just west of Görlitz, the tech asked if I could drive. His eyes like wet grey stones. He pulled into an Esso and we swapped sides. I practised changing gears with my right hand, then pulled out into an autobahn for the first time. I accelerated into the flicker of cars and trucks all headed towards Dresden and on. The machine behaved as it should've, but as I aligned the vehicle in the lane something wasn't right. My body rejected the attempts I made to ease the van to the centre of the road. I was drawn to the right by an instinct I'd never felt before. Horns blared, doppler effect as they passed in afternoon light. By the time we hit Dresden and I'd taken us through onto 170, I was sweating despite the air roaring cold through the cracked window, the van dangerously positioned towards the parked cars. My companion woke as I was navigating Louisenstraße, a narrow two-way street in Neustadt near where our host lived, my hands unable to shift the wheel and take me away from the side of the road where Audis were parked among Volvos and Volkswagens. The vehicle clipped a wing mirror, then two, then each of the parked cars on the right were struck. A clatter of plastic and glass as I eased down the cobblestones. The tech shouting, his hands in the air in protest. But in all the noise, all the shouting and gesticulating, I couldn't move the wheel. I went past his house until there was a wooded area and a set of children's swings swaying in the breeze. I stopped the engine, left the tech shouting and got out and walked away, uncertain what had put us there in north Dresden beside a trail of glass. The whole city felt like an unfinished thought, piles of rubble amid reconstructed magnificence.

David! You fucking. You fucking. Et cetera.

A decade later, the source of my confusion was exposed: I'd had an insentient belief that the van existed to the left of me, as it did when driving at home, as if the van bulged unseen into the oncoming east German traffic. To slant the vehicle in this direction would've been to head the van's ghost twin into a collision between the hidden and the witnessing world. And I couldn't do it, because there's something about ghosts when they're tied so tight to the real.

All true, this story.

'I was heading north out of Italy,' the grey woman said, 'mountains, tarns, lakes, passes and the medieval. All that blimmin' crap.' She looked over her shoulder, hopeful of voices, but there wasn't anything but her own speech. The nervous dis-calm of her short silence. *Where were you?*

'I was driving north in the rain and I had to get some petrol. I filled and there was a man, a young man in a Yankees hat. He had a sign that said Zürich and he was obviously trying to hitch a lift and had given up because of the rain. It was peeing down. Cars crawling before the pass. Why are people less likely to stop for pedestrians when it's raining? That's a thing. Anyway, he was sitting there and he looked miserable and I offered him some of my hot chocolate. He asked that I give him a lift and I couldn't think of a reason not to. He had a nice smile. *A nice smile.* I bought a big bag of cheese snacks and told him to get in. He was about my age. He was nice, quiet. German, but with a fine, feathery English. He was trying to get to the Opernhaus Zürich for a performance by the Kronos Quartet. He was a cellist, he told me, and was a fan of Sunny Yang, who, incidentally, I'd met one time without knowing who she was. That was in Manchester. After that I didn't much hear from the guy, yeah? His head fell into his hands like a small boulder. We passed over the mountain into the valleys and he became very quiet. I was driving in traffic and he started, in muted grunts, to moan. Just a kind of—' and she started mimicking his moans '—and I tried to take looks at him to see if he was all right. I pushed his shoulder to see if he'd react. He just rocked. His head lolling. I started driving faster. I kept saying his name. Shouting his name. His hand came away from the back of his head where his cap had slipped and there was blood, blood. Then the tunnels and then the city. I crossed the river to the hospital, drove straight and insane into the emergency department. I have a little German, it's enough to get by. They rushed him into surgery. And, then, then, he, this guy, he flipped. He died about an hour after I brought him in.' *He died.* 'And they gave me his wallet and phone. This odd ceremonious moment. They asked me questions, questions because he'd been attacked, they thought. He'd been hit in the back of the head by something heavy and hard. I asked what I should do and they said to get some rest because the police would want to talk to me. And when they said this, I had a sudden urge to contact his family and tell them I had his possessions, I'm not sure why. So, I hunted through the numbers on his phone for a name matching his and I called the number. My German's okay, but I sound like an outsider. I called five, six numbers. Spoke to people who were eager to talk to someone, and then others who wanted to know who the hell I was. I stopped dialling. I asked myself what I was doing there, I thought I should find somewhere to sleep. But before I did I called a couple more and left messages on answering machines. It's funny, huh? We say answering machines, but there's no such thing anymore. It's the same word but there aren't any machines whirling and taping, just servers and code. And then I went looking for a place to stay, David. A cheap hotel. Somewhere in Langstrasse. When I'm on the job like this, I'm always looking for the centre, you know? I'm always looking for places with a whole lot of noise. I like the rotten districts.' *Where were you?* 'Night spots with that kind of nerveless vice.' *It feels important you say where you were.* 'Langstrasse. When I'm in a foreign city I can only sleep when there's a lot of noise, street noise, like, if I'm nervous at home, I get the worst anxiety and sometimes when I'm at home, I go to the hall and turn the heat pump on, yeah, wind it up to full, I wait till the machine has started up and then, I don't know why but the white noise of it, it soothes some part of me, keeps me calm, my husband has no idea why I do this, he gets shitty for wasting electricity, but it's a little whispered hum, a little song in my ear and for God's own reasons, it keeps me calm.' *It keeps me calm too. The noise.* 'I went out walking. I walked amongst the drunken, the girls in their little bonk-me skirts, the guys with their hideous I'll-be-a-fucking-you leers, awful, I loved it, hair cut violently short at the back and sides, hard eyes and the smell of piss and bars behind doors you don't know are doors until something leads you inwards, and, of course, the thump and thump of house music and techno beat, I found the 25hours Hotel on the main drag, a Sixties build, cheaply renovated, I opened my window on the fifth floor and let the noise pour in, the haze of it, the shouts and countering voices down the block, and the trains, the all-night trains not thirty metres away, I felt myself fall into a sleep rocked gently by the specific rain of the city, the way it tumbles its contents around you, truck, cry, voice, but then, I was woken by, by a dream but also by the phone, the dream, the young man dead in my car and also my phone, I'd assumed it had run out of battery and gone to sleep with me, but it awoke and woke me, I answered it and a voice started talking, it was one of the names from an answering machine I'd left a message on saying, "If you have a relative named Johannes Wiseman please call me back," and I'd left my number, then I found myself talking with this young man, we talked for an hour, I plugged my phone into the USB socket beside the bed and lay with my head on an angle as we talked about his younger brother, I barely remember how the time passed, just that it was four by the time he decided to train up to Zürich and see Johannes, "Where are you coming from?" I asked, he told me he was living in Rome, that there was a train in an hour and he'd be on it, I took a sleeping pill and woke with a knock on the door, it was cleaning and I needed to be out of the room, I headed back to the hospital, to the ward where Johannes had died. There was a man a few years younger than me, with prematurely whitened hair so he glowed a little under the lighting, he wore a square-shouldered suit jacket with a little bird-shaped brooch, and because of that I knew it was him, he told me he'd begun wearing a brooch rather than a ring when he got married, he heard my accent as I said his name, saying it wrong, saying it like an English girl on holiday and not really sure what was happening, I spoke with him, gripped his forearm when I told him I was so sorry once again, and he said, "Life is coming and it is going. If it's doing none or either, we have nothing," and he said my name, pronounced it well and I realised he was someone who'd spent time out of his hometown, maybe even educated in England somewhere, we spoke in a mixture of Italian, German and English, he was your height and seemed nervous about being with me, so tall and all, I went with him to the morgue, stood beside him as we took the elevator down into the morgue, a place devoid of smell, a gloved man presented the naked and cold body of Johannes, the boy's eyes closed, a kind of pained expression exaggerated by his straight mouth, which appeared abnormal, as if someone had tried to reset his natural smile into something more befitting the dead, but nothing befits the dead, right? nothing befits, but then it happens and it's completely—so I drove the guy to his hotel, this brother of Johannes, he was so kind and we shared his hotel room, and it seems perverse, but I watched him sleep, but before he fell asleep I learnt the things that we'd tell the police, that Johannes had been in an argument with his landlord, a man living illegally in Italy for decades, that the landlord hit him, whacked him on the back of the head with a mallet, a rubber-headed hammer, and Johannes had laughed and woken up bleeding, it must have been odd for the brother, having someone watching over him like that when sleeping and he didn't even know me, not even remotely, but I just felt like I had to watch over him. That he needed to be seen. His eyes seemed to blacken in the evening as it dimmed and cooled, he started to talk, his voice arranged by words I didn't quite understand until I realised he was talking about his brother Johannes, saying the same words, over and over in a different order, then he was quiet, exhausted by this odd fact, I continued to sit on the bed watching, I think I just wanted to be there in case—in case he started talking again, and there was someone there to listen. "He's a perfectionist," the brother had said earlier, "perfection was the thing that made him, he was the voice of his efforts to be perfect, he was kicked from the orchestra for studying just one piece and perfecting just one technique and was always killing himself and his teachers, which was what killed, what killed his career and why he worked as a lab technician and kept getting sick, always getting sick and then his landlord, he came with a hammer and with the hammer, they argued and the hammer . . ."'

Then she was behind the Scots doctor.

She came into view. She loomed. She was stout now, expanded at the waist and trotting towards us with two others I recognised from the song circle earlier. I looked up at the Scotsman as he finished telling her story. How it was his voice and her story. The way they marched towards us, foot to foot, necks a-bending, jaws a-jutting, to peer down at me. The way people squint in moments like this, telling us something of their concern.

'I watched Johannes's brother in case there was something more he wanted to tell me. In case there was something he knew about himself,' he said. 'Which, which reminds me of a couple I treat. This couple with two teenagers, twins. One of these, the boy, was hit by a car while on holiday. It wasn't fatal; the boy lived and everything remained the same for him,' the Scotsman said, 'everything but the way he experienced time. You hear of people waking up from a coma speaking a new language, losing their mother tongue and overcome with a new reality. This wasn't the case here. Instead, this kid woke up and time had changed for him. He suddenly experienced all his past moments without sequence, all of them at once. That's what I think of when I think of him: life and its people compiled into one, new, infinitely heavy instant. The kid watches himself, watches from outside time.'

The song people had their hands out, palms up. I saw their mouths move to some dreadful song as Linda rose once more to her full height. The six feet of her. The straight back of her.

The blackening of her hair as others gathered around to tend to my slump and ask all the questions and lift my dead weight so I was being walked down the tube, the angle-less hall but for the walkway, a grill that looked down below to bedrock, and we walked upright, arms under my own, the careful hands extricating me and helping me towards the end of the tube where we turned and turned and slipped through light and were sat on a train, a new train, soon slooting through the tunnel in what direction until there was light and the tall woman beside me was directing me to sit up and take on the herbal tea that had come from some place. But I lay still, dense and done. She seemed nervous and smelt of a familiar brand of perfume I think an instructor of mine at university used to wear, I would smell it on my essays after they'd been returned to me post marking and I would think of those essays fondly until I left the institution and they were placed in a box I'd forgotten about until this moment, tearing through mid-Switzerland, the broad stretches of ridge meeting lake, peak hitting sky, and the way the city came at us bulging, inflamed by light. I'd forgotten how smell corrects the senses when whole parts of you are lost, how you begin to see the things that might well have been there all along.

Passe-partout

During the last leg, the aircraft went through a patch of rough air rising off Taranaki from the sea. The plane dropping and righting. Ryan, Michelle's neighbour in the middle seat, said he was continually frustrated by the effort airlines put into shielding passengers from the elements and noise. He told Michelle about the Soviet answer to the Concorde, the Tupolev Tu-144.

Why are you telling me about this?

This was a horrible machine, he said, straight-faced.

Sure.

A brutal aircraft.

Yes, but faster, Michelle interjected. She said it was faster than the Concorde. She'd come across this information on YouTube. She'd spent a day rifling through mini-docos like magazines, with her son at her shoulder saying this and that. She looked across the aisle to where he sat with his sister and dad.

Faster, yes, but awful, the man said. The beastly thing needed a parachute, to land.

Yes.

The word 'beastly' made her feel heavy, like she'd have to carry a carcass of the word for the rest of the flight and then the drive home until there was the couch and some brandy and no more planes, no more—

Had ejection seats—for the passengers, Ryan said. Imagine that. Ejection seats. Two crashed. No survivors. But. But, it had one advantage. It was incredibly, incredibly loud.

He laughed, almost secretly.

She realised how nervous he was, that this speech was a kind of discharge of those nerves, like jokes made in place of a sense of safety.

Horrible to fly on, Ryan said. Shook like Saturn V. You couldn't talk. Had to pass notes. One flight an alarm went off, a warning to the crew that the landing gear was damaged. Imagine a civil defence siren, and nobody knew how to disengage it. Stayed on for the entire seventy-five minutes. Heaven.

It landed safely?

Oh yes. Landing gear was fine. Just made a horrendous noise. Imagine a hundred detuned guitars, a thousand broken amplifiers.

He was smiling through a dilapidated mouth.

Plus, he said, imagine the dollars saved on insulation if they left you to the elements. Flight should be a remedy for economic decline and a fixer of futures—instead, you land on the far side of the world and you have the most desperate sense of having a half-death.

Across the aisle, her husband, daughter and son were quiet and happy, her boy marvelling at the sights below. She told the professor she'd always worried about supersonic flight, that the speed of travel from one place on the globe to another made her suspicious of herself. She feared she was more likely to make generalisations of the approaching continent and people living there, due to the lack of effort she'd put into the expedition.

He laughed. But don't you think, don't you think there's a need to make generalisations, to stereotype, in order to find out what we really need to think?

She shook her head. Her son was looking at her.

Generalisations are essential, the man smiled.

Michelle wasn't sure how to interpret the grin. It was like a map full of spiders.

They're like temporary, interim borders—necessarily separating uncertainties, he said. They're a part of science: you make a proposition that stands till it's tested, proved true or, most likely, otherwise. The universe is fixed until we need it to shift. Don't you think?

No, Michelle said.

The woman in the window seat with a head of wilding grey curls asked if they wouldn't mind standing so she could squeeze past.

But yes, Ryan said as they got up.

The aircraft hit dirty air, and he talked through the shaking until the woman returned. Vaguely articulate provocations, and the whole episode reminded Michelle of something. It was the effect of a pair of contrasting thoughts that she at times figured were the key elements in her specific persona. Since she was a girl, she'd always felt the dubiousness of this kind of speech. This custom of saying something was this, this and that. Since she was young this hunt for exactness had troubled her. Something inside her thought processes was convinced that nothing is ever properly certain. But something else in her, some frightened creature living deep within the act of thought, within its patterns and waves, was determined to hammer everything down, lock it down. Box it in. Manipulate it into confines where the minimum amount of attention would keep it fed. It was as constant as her conviction was false. She feared both ends of it. She used to think, in times of mental liberation, that this particular stress was the root of all illness.

And perhaps. Perhaps this was true, has always been true, but there, on that plane, the root was something else, something in their breath and in the way they, the three of them in the row, Michelle, the man, the silent woman at the window, they held it. Held it and held it and then let go as the plane dropped, dropped and seemed to drop forever.

Royal Free

During the mid-1930s, a series of outbreaks of a previously unnamed malady were recorded in certain unlinked localities around the world. Swathes of people, mainly women, were affected. Severe lethargy, terrible pains and what appeared to be a breakdown of the nervous system were prominent presentations. The illness was initially diagnosed as poliomyelitis (polio), but it was eventually discerned as something separate and received the designation 'epidemic neuromyasthenia'. By the 1950s the term 'benign myalgic encephalomyelitis' popped up to reflect an outbreak at the Royal Free Hospital in London. As the Institute of Medicine's brief history of the disease suggests, the details of each outbreak varied, but in general, patients experienced an assortment of symptoms, including malaise, tender lymph nodes, pain, and encephalomyelitis, indicating a swelling of the brain and spinal cord. Although the cause of the condition could not be verified, it appeared to be non-infectious, the term 'benign myalgic encephalomyelitis' was selected to reflect 'the absent mortality, the severe muscular pains, the evidence of parenchymal damage to the nervous system and the presumed inflammatory nature of the disorder'.

Then, in 1970, two UK psychiatrists, McEvedy and Beard, reviewed reports of fifteen outbreaks of the disease, concluding that these 'were psychosocial phenomena caused by one of two mechanisms, either mass hysteria on the part of the patients or altered medical perception of the community'. Indeed, this charge of hysteria was the prevalent attribution from that moment on for several decades. McEvedy and Beard based their conclusions on 'the higher prevalence of the disease in females and the lack of physical signs in these patients'. They also recommended that the disease be renamed 'myalgia nervosa'.

So, madness. Madness and myth. This was, by the enlightened Seventies, a disease of the deranged, the uncoupled, the hysterical. Interestingly, my cousin Kimber recently had a hysterectomy but still suffers from the same lingering elements of the disease she did prior to the operation, though the fits of screaming seem to have stopped.*

'My doctor stopped giving me appointments,' Kimber once told me. 'I'd ring the medical centre and the receptionist wouldn't give me an appointment. The guy had decided it was all in my head and the best treatment was just to ignore me. That that'd somehow cure me. I was living on the smallest allowance from the government, I couldn't work and my doctor refused to see me. ME in the 1990s, you see.' It turns out this was a common approach and 'treatment' of the disease back then was ignoring patients. Kimber said she guessed ME meant, to her doctor, that she was weak-willed and needed to get over herself. Which was interesting, because on the strength of her will she's climbed multiple mountains and walked the Pacific Crest Trail, which

* My cousin has never suffered from fits of screaming.

took her and her partner five months. Campo, near the Mexican border, up to Canada. Four-thousand-plus-kilometres. She once told me how the two of them sat on a narrow rock ledge above a swollen river for days, waiting for the waters to subside. That, she'd said, made her nervous. Her feet like cinders by the end of it. She's cycled New Zealand. Travelled throughout old communist Europe because, why wouldn't you? She was held in a holding camp for dissidents in Romania, I think. That made her slightly nervous, too. She has a will. Too much of one, and I sometimes suspect that's what made her sick to start. What has made many of us sick. We push ourselves to ridiculous levels and the body responds in cruel ways.

I told her that my doctor expressed to me she hated the term 'chronic fatigue syndrome' because it was so *unscientific*. So, I just started not seeing her.

'That's the thing, right.'

Kimber has always had a determination beyond the ordinary. As has everyone else in my family. Mountains to summit, continents and divides to walk and ride. Odd bouts of intellectualism and dabs at artistic intrigue. A type of perfectionism that doesn't always lead to excellence, but to another less anticipated place. I began forcing my body for the first time when I was forty-three. It cracked after a few months. I was a half-year into writing *The Invisible Mile*, and everything since has been created in a pained, wrecked blur.

'At least I got a few years use out of mine,' Kimber joked. She was talking about her body—which, I am pleased to say, is mostly better these days. Which gives hope.

My cousin Rachel, too, she was always after a form of perfection. She's a painter. For years I have been looking at her artworks trying to understand what the figurative aspects of the pieces were. Something unseen and within the surface of being seen. Her works are huge, mysterious, beautiful, illusive. Last week she read the first sections of this book and made the comment that they reminded her of the moment she started to paint the interior parts of her sick body. She's over sixty now and still working at it.

Indeed, she asked to the world that she be an eminent painter, then decades later inadvertently bought the house next to Bill Hammond's on Canterbury Street in Lyttelton. After several years of the disease easing off, her body cracked. She had been trying to learn how to be the great artist's neighbour, how to be a painter of exactness and meticulous intent. Now she can't even make her mouth say the disease's name. It's too exhausting to get through the twists of vowel and consonant. Thirty-two years for her, as it stands. Twelve for my sibling before she gradually stepped out of it. Eighteen for Kimber. I'm at eleven as I write.

It's a disease with a naming problem in the same way as it lacks a proper medical attribution. For years it's been plagued by poor data and poor interpretations of data, both clinically and anecdotally. In 1988 the condition was given the term that's so prejudiced Kimber and Rachel's physicians: chronic fatigue syndrome. Which would be a fine term if it were merely fatigue that affects us. That we are merely a little tired and in need of a rest, just a little in need of a place to lie around and recover. That'd be great, though unfortunately there is no recovery; sleep does nothing but put a small gap in the rounds of physical pain, the very real mind pain that sits alongside the cognitive ineptitude, the confusion and obliterating tiredness. And it's a disease with another naming problem. With a head affected by the swelling in the brain that is a hallmark of the illness, one can't possibly get through its Latin designation without pausing for some time, taking tea and ignoring the issue of returning to its pronunciation. Myalgic encephalomyelitis, the words my cousin and I struggle with so badly. Impossible. As a result, it's almost as cruel in its medical appellation as it is in its physical form.

And according to the US Institute of Medicine it's an interim name, imperfect, and the hunt for a new one goes on. Lately, the term systemic exertion intolerance disease (SEID) has been suggested. Dr Maureen Hanson has another decent one: enervating neuroimmune disease (END). None of these has the adequate poetics or stark brevity needed to describe such a thing, not really. Without an established name it feels wordless, shapeless and wronged by language.

I have often wondered how long we have to say a name before it becomes something else.

Like a love story, one that's gone horribly wrong.

We use words, though it's only the body that's ill. Or am I wrong about that? Is it the language too that's sick? I used to think all words were perfect until used in a sentence. All bodies too, until sentenced. We're pure body when ill, pure body, and there's no mind but the one that stands beside us trying so hard to replicate who we are.

'We've become other people,' Rachel said to me not long ago. I'd flown south to visit her and her husband there in the main crater of Banks Peninsula, where she and my sister live on opposite sides of the harbour. 'We have others' lives,' she said, 'and it pisses me off.'

And it's true, our stories are not the ones we imagined for ourselves. But, as she suggested moments later, we must find ways to tell them outside of the obscurity and allusions to the hurt we can't isolate or name. Outside of the fact of time and how much time has been taken away. She said it's necessary we find an image to match the complexity that resides in the lack of words.

'When I die,' she said, 'I want people to know I've struggled. I want people to know that every day, I've struggled, that despite this, despite all the pain I look for beauty. Just in the smallest things I look for beauty. This way the struggle doesn't define me. Instead I'm defined by what I look for in people, in the world.'

The two of us were positioned beside the fireplace at her house in Diamond Harbour. The July cold and the mānuka smoke caught in our hair and clothes. I recorded our conversation on my phone. She asked why I was doing it. I said so we could remember what we'd said.

'When I die, I want people to know how hard this is. You'll make sure of that, eh?'

'That is my goal in life.'

'That this is just so hard and that I've really struggled.'

'And that you've struggled and you're pissed off.'

She laughed. 'I'm not pissed off. Not at all. That's your emotion.'

I agreed that that was likely true.

She said, 'You know, David, I think about this and I don't feel bad or guilty, but it'd be so much easier being dead than alive. Don't you think?'

I nodded and we felt the quiet like the quiet itself was felt. Rachel had first become sick while punishing herself with a diet of chocolate and coffee while living in Wellington. On occasion I saw her, Rachel, all beautiful and raging with thoughts of paint and canvas.

'We have others' lives,' she repeated.

'And Steffen,' I said. 'This isn't the one he asked for either.'

'No, not so much. But I was like this when we married.

When I met him. But, Laura. That's another matter.'

'Yes.'

'This isn't the life she'd a right to expect, not when she moved in with you.'

I didn't have the energy to explain, to tell her about my wife's own struggle. That there was by then a known pain, an exhaustion beyond the exertion of just putting up with me. By then we knew she had Sjögren's, another systemic malady, an autoimmune disease affecting the entirety of the body. The sum of our illnesses had begun equating to an undiagnosable loss of energy between the two of us. Sjögren's syndrome.

Another unwieldy set of words.

This made its first appearance in 2020 while I was in a brief moment of reprieve—a drug that kept me high for a few weeks, then faded. Then, just a few days into this break, Laura began exhibiting all the signs that follow me around. She was exhausted and caught in bed for days without sign of a cold or flu. Her mind faded in and out, and she entered peculiar moments of miasma.

Sjögren's. We pronounce it show-grins. But it doesn't operate like that; there's little joy in any autoimmune illnesses.

It could have taken years for her to have got a diagnosis but for the fact her specific malady is hereditary, and her mother, she has had Sjögren's syndrome for decades. And now, now it's in Laura and she goes to work each day and the pain of this, of her doing this breaks my heart.

Whenever I head south to see friends and family, I stay with Rachel and Steffen. Sometimes there's other people there—her brothers, old friends, Gretchen from Brandenburg or Andrea from over in Little River. But mostly it's just us. We like to share our anger and laugh at the whole impossible thing. In summer, her house is cool and airy; in the winter it's in a constant battle against the cold, and the fireplace is hungry and constantly fed. We make dinner, eat, then talk lying on sheepskin rugs.

She tells me about her young niece, a professional acrobat who Rachel fears will also succumb to this blood-fed feast of fatigue and pain. She has the same urge to work and punish and work and not rest, this urge like a diabolical rage, until there is only the body depleted and done and done.

'I watch her, and you should see her in her art, David. She's beautiful, so beautiful—I watch her and see her overcoming seemingly everything, every everything to become *body*. To be everything, all beyond thought and become only that singular physical form, and it terrifies me. I'm terrified watching her—that she'll become *me*.' She paused and pushed hair off her face. 'A version of me, the me watching her in the theatre. I love her so much and I fear that love too will be, that it is too much, and she will become the will of the audience because the audience is always watching, secretly waiting—'

'I know.'

'I was going to say they all wait for her to fall.'

'I know.'

'They all wait for each actor to fall, fail, melt into the stage.'

'But that's not true,' I said.

'No.'

Rachel suggested then, in an open thought, that the audience doesn't exist but for the artist's pain, for all their suffering. 'They, we, are a product of pain—of joy also, but mostly pain. So, they, we, want the pain and suffering to go on. Just on and on. I watch and I don't want to watch,' she said. 'I don't know, is that true? I feel, just like I'm a product of the event. You watch a film, read a book and you're a product of an event of some kind, right?'

'And you want me to go and see her?' I asked.

'Yes. But you remember Jung?' she asked quickly, as if he were a shared acquaintance from years past. 'Good old Jung. Him of the foreboding forehead. I think he suggested at one point that we're born with the recollections of our forebears, and so on, buried deep in our subconscious. Apparently he said that.'

'Really?'

'I think so. He, or someone after him, they suggested these memories are imprinted in our DNA. Which sounds ominously simple, but it's not a simple thing.' She looked up at the ceiling danced with light from the fire. 'What he or whoever meant is we have instinct, which, you know, can be thought of as a form of memory. But memory obviously isn't a precise thing.'

I agreed with her.

'There is no ur-memory. No such thing.'

She laughed at her use of 'ur', as if it was a word she used every day and here it was, adding itself to the conversation like any commonly practical prefix. She again pushed some hair off her face as if there was something telling in her eyes.

'So, I mention him for a reason, David. I watch my niece and wonder about the hit and impact of traumatic goings-on, events. That perhaps these are the things that leave traces in the descent of physically received memory. This, you know, instinct. That these are the kinds of things that break into, I don't know, these little streams of knowing that we forever seem to take with us everywhere. Knowledge about what to fear; what to walk unimpeded towards.' She frowned at herself. 'Like these little hurts we take from lifetime to lifetime. The little ructions of life, you know. Like a dispute in our instinctual flow, and these ructions fuel little bust-ups, thereby, you know, David, creating new-fangled instincts.' She gazed at me, large brown eyes similar to mine, similar but quite different. 'I wonder if these, these specifically, are the chemical imprints on our particular DNA. That our bodies, their memories, they're the end result of really old hurts. Our sickness is the result of ancestral error. I think about this but suspect it's something else I should be thinking of. I don't have an answer.'

I reminded her of the thing her late father, Jim, once said to me when I was much younger. He was kind and, like his daughter, vastly intelligent, but he never showed it off, just shared and queried. I once asked him whether being a professor and a philosopher entitled him to solutions to the world's questions. He shook his head almost instantly and said, no. 'Oh no. I have many answers to many things. But I can't ever know if any of them are right.'

Rachel missed her father terribly and I felt sad bringing it up, but it was, oddly, one of the most humane things anyone had ever said to me. The words meant a great deal, those short sentences, and I carried them around like a relic, a talisman that would keep me safe from false promises.

'How are you going to finish your book, David?' Rachel asked.

'I have few answers,' I said, and she laughed. She turned to the fireplace and fiddled with the damper. Something wasn't right, and she opened the begrimed door and a shadow of fine white dust puffed into the room.

'It has to be about the body,' she said.

'I don't know. I'm sick of talking about my body.'

'It has to be about the body. We're only body.'

'Why?'

'It has to be about the mind. It has to be about the undoing.'

'That's a good word.'

'The undoing, yes.' She paused. 'Of logic forms, or—you know how we have a serious cell receptor dysfunction? That at our core our cells are inherently stuffed? You know what I mean?'

I shook my head. 'No.'

'Well, we're far more likely to have nucleotide polymorphisms, like DNA typos, in our genetic codes for certain cell receptors. This is depressing.'

'I know.'

'I know. It's horrible.' She laughed like she was stuck in a lift, that she knew it would be a long time. 'You know much about this?'

I said no, and she said she forgets most of what she learns. We reached for our phones for that's where so much of our memory resided. We traded sentences quoting essay and text. Learnt this receptor was called 'transient receptor potential melastatin 3', or TRPM3. That when inside healthy cells it transfers calcium from outside its wall to the inside. That's where it regulates gene expression and protein production. This wasn't happening for us. Calcium ions aren't making it inside our immune cells; the cell's functions are weakened.

'We're screwed, David. This is why I started painting cells. I wanted to look at what we can't see.'

'. . .'

'Our entire bodies,' she said, 'are the equivalent of old wives' tales.' Her laugh is light and specific, has a distance on it, as if she was smiling just for you from across a dreadfully crowded room. It somehow accessed the vaguely humorous values we have to find within the disease.

'Don't worry,' I said, 'I'll come see you when you die.'

She chortled.

Our phones explained more, that the activities of these receptors clarify why so many of us come up against the worst of the symptoms after a traumatic event, or after an acute viral infection, or something other. Like after just a bit of exercise. They said this class of receptors, the one TRPM3 belong to, are known as 'threat receptors'. These are upregulated when the body is under any kind of threat, such as infection, such as environmental toxins, trauma, or even something like childbirth.

She spoke, then paused.

'This is the undoing,' I said.

'This is the undoing, yes.' She looked at her phone. A bone-like silence. 'They predict—' She paused. 'Look in this article, David.' And yes, they predict that it's this upregulation that triggers the defective genetic receptors to get over-expressed and then take over, messing up the calcium transfer in a range of cells. Immune cells are being seriously messed with, but not just them, a whole range of cells. This is why we get so sick in the face of threats. Imagined or real, doesn't matter. Physical or mental.

'We put our bodies under stress,' she said, 'and they capitulate. This is the undoing.'

And true: sometimes we went walking, parked the car and walked till one of us sat down.

The undoing.

We repeated the word multiple times, the two of us trying to understand what it meant beyond the obvious and why it was the perfect word. The fireplace was just inches from us, turning the wood into heated dust and throwing our shadows across the room so they landed on the walls, furniture and ceilings, pale puppets of failing thought.

We talked about the metabolic trap hypothesis. About the widening possibility that within a single gene the answer to our malady sat shaking.* We talked about the Itaconate Shunt

* The metabolic trap is a recent hypothesis proposing a new etiology for ME. It revolves around three key elements: the genes IDO1 and IDO2, and the essential amino acid tryptophan. Tryptophan is vital to the production of precursor enzymes for neurotransmitters such as serotonin, and for the metabolite kynurenine. Kynurenine and its by-product NAD are vital to the production of energy in cells, while serotonin is fundamental to the mind's ability to process information and directly linked to happiness and, when missing, its inverse. What has been shown to occur is that there is a substrate inhibition of IDO1,

hypothesis, though neither understood its proposals.

We talked more, words handicapped by volume, by the energy it took to speak and hear. Disposable words seeking poetry in the ash that kept falling from their excursion into the room, slight white in our silvery hair.

'All I know is it'll be a cryptic book for a cryptic disease,' I said.

'Call part of it *The Undoing*,' Rachel said. 'That'll be my offering to your book.'

I said, 'Sure.'

'Just one word. You can write the rest.'

'. . .'

'Then you can tell me how long it takes, to write one word.'

---

and it is possible that this has a 'dark side and may be involved in the pathogenesis of ME/CFS'. Lemme explain. IDO1 allows for the production of tryptophan into kynurenine and serotonin. However, on occasion the level of tryptophan becomes too high and IDO1 effectively switches off and stops producing its vital components. This substrate inhibition is the metabolic trap; a saturation of enzymatic catalyses occurs, and it shuts down. All's not lost, as this is when IDO2 kicks in and allows for the process to continue and the tap to energy and well-being to open once more. This is what happens in healthy people—if and when this saturation occurs. However, a certain percentage of the population have a set of mutations of the IDO2 gene. Having any one of these mutations means IDO2 won't cover for IDO1 in its weaker moments. IDO1 is on its own, and the inhibition continues. This means, in the case of saturation and inhibition, that the production levels of NAD and serotonin become dangerously low. It is believed all ME/CFS patients have this gene mutation. (See Open Medicine Foundation, 'Robert Phair, PhD | Metabolic Traps in ME/CFS', 3 October 2019, youtube.com/watch?v=d9oVHDh8rjk.) This is the metabolic trap hypothesis, and as of writing testing continues.

Though

I'm stuck again. Three weeks in bed now. Three and they keep coming. These two paragraphs are all that's been written since I completed the first draft of this book. I want to say, want to say, want to say how heavy, how many kilos my head weighs now, want to say how much more than before autumn came around. Weight feels like the correct measurement of illness. *Dr Coventry, I'm afraid your sick weightage is over the #$#@#$& kilos allowed in this hospital. Go home to your people. Die among the clouds.* There hasn't been a sicker moment in memory, no moment in my life where I've felt closer to dying. Three days ago I was unable to move, speak. I needed help—it took me twenty minutes to write that word on my phone: HELP. Another thirty before I had the energy to reach and press send. Laura came and gave me water. She had 111 dialled on the phone. I shook my head; nothing of the event seemed real. I thought afterwards that I should probably see a neurologist. Or thought that at least someone should suggest I see one. That would be the right intervention, right? Someone should suggest that. A doctor or someone. Doesn't seem to be a thing.

I wish I could describe the weight of illness as noise. I can describe noise. I understand noise. White noise, pink noise, graduations of serialised tone. My computer contains words from another book describing such things, though right now I can't see the screen.

Despite this I feel I know the content of that 'can't'—that it's the space that needs to be elucidated. The great *perhaps* in the valleys between facts I write and the fiction I seem to live through. I remember so little this modicum feels like a fabrication, the aura of the rest seems most certainly so.

Amongst the Stone

Trains in September, just before they shut them all down once more. Trains, cities, boats and an island in a series of islands. Each volcanic and each in different states of living and dying in the afterlife of eruption. Great black rocks jutting from the sea. Dormant bodies just waiting. We sat on the beach with the hurting hulk of Isola della Scogliera Rossa behind us. The island, the maddened island of half-desert, the island of imperfect refuge. My chin rested on my knees as we talked, each pulled tight to my chest. I slowly straightened my limbs and brushed out the creases in my cotton trousers so they wedded evenly with my legs. I'd brought them with me from Wellington eighteen months earlier, they had a pebbly colour and merged with the cluttered stone glistening near the waterline. I watched Rachel side on while she spoke. When she went silent we looked out towards the yachts, the way families called to each other over the paned water. Kids diving in the sea, sleek and suddenly long and perfect as they appeared in a different section of the bay.

I spoke about a camping trip taken by a lake when I was small. Rachel stopped me as I described leaving the house at dawn and arriving at some place to the north. She asked where, specifically—as if the answer might explain a little of why we were still seated on that stony beach. I told her I didn't recall exactly but believed it was somewhere in the Wairarapa, north of Wellington, that we had a rugby ball and a net Henry had put up to play badminton. I described how my siblings swam—for that was the crux of the story. How I watched my brother and sisters and thought: *How? How do they know how to do that?*

Out by the yachts a girl yelled, and as I looked I saw her arms fling outwards, rapidly rotating trying to realign her centre of gravity, her brother shouting, guffawing. These would be their days of sun stunned memory, of jumbled lives forgotten and recalled. There a beach, there a horizon, there the habits of continuation.

After the sound of her splash died down I told Rachel how on the second morning my father took me to the water's edge, then said, 'Walk in.' I asked why. My father, I told her, said, 'Walk in. Just a little. I'll tell you when to stop.' I took off my sandals and started walking on the soft stones. Walked up to my knees, up to my thighs. I walked on until I was up to my waist. I waded, waiting for my father to say stop. I heard families on the shore, I told her. Games and laughter and I kept going. My dad had said he'd say when to stop, so I walked slowly and waited for him to say something. At one point Henry yelled out, 'This was how the others learnt.' I kept going, up to my belly, expecting some kind of intervention, a knowledge of some kind. That suddenly I would know, my body would know. I'd swim. Just like that. I'd start swimming. Arms out in front. Ducking and diving like my sisters and brother. This was how people find out the divine, and there I was in the water, up to my neck. And I stepped and stepped and then suddenly I was under. Fighting. Throwing my arms in the water. My knees grazed on the stony bottom. Everything black because I didn't know I could open my eyes. Black. And I was, I told her, so alone—I thought that this was death. A version of death.

And that—that was why I don't swim. The story I tell of how I don't swim.

Rachel swore in appreciation.

She watched my face until I wasn't sure what she was looking at. Relatives are strange in a way—that we're free to stare and find the things others can't. My eyes replied in kind. I saw the illness in the areas she hadn't aged, life in the defiant wrinkles. She's nine years older than me, but there was something equalising in the way my eyes struggled to find focus. I wondered how I looked to her, what traces of malady she saw that I couldn't. A person is imperfect as a mirror, but after a while you realise their flaws can't be argued with.

Eventually Rachel expressed deep concerns about the event and I explained how my father was interested in an intriguing version of control, in the gratification of using his mind to make the self a mechanism that obeyed every thought. And he used this extraordinary control to drag his children to extraordinary places. I always suspected, I said, that he was the kind of man who would build himself up every day then destroy what he'd made by the time he was in bed.

'Your dad was always, he was always so fascinatingly distant,' she said. 'But I liked his smile, you know. Sometimes you look like him, but only sometimes. And the way you get grumpy, that's kind of the same.'

I laughed, then opened my satchel and looked inside—old papers, stapled and pen-marked from my time in Potsdam and

Berlin. The posturing of history, its unplanned gifts from the ages. I felt unkempt, my beard now beyond what looked good. Earlier, back at the cottages, I'd told her I had always disliked well-groomed men—that there seemed a spitefulness in all the small things they miss. A single hair on a chin could make the whole event of shaving seem suddenly hideous. Remembering the conversation made me smile as we sat on the beach far from the strict streets of the city. So many on the island were now in a such state of frazzled lazing that I almost felt the opposite. Men walking the boulevard beside the port with hair knotted by sweat, sea and time. Women in cafés, their shirts stolen off the line of a neighbour, the billowing white of some discontent. The smell of both, a vast uncomfortable perfume distributed through the old streets. It was an island famous for the city, for the basilica and museum, for the painting Hannah spoke of, and the forms, for its mysterious, unseen exhibits, famous for its place names, words from lost languages many thousands of years old kept in the mouths of the marooned and permanent. Words immaculately living while bodies remembered what it's like to be untended. Women and men, hair and clothes returning to rags.

We watched birds spiral and float, hang then dive at the sea.

Rachel ate a small carrot and I stared down the extent of the beach. The steep incline and the open sea, exhausted and flat. It was easy at first, the walk down from the road. An odd broken set of stairs, rain-washed and crumbling at the once smooth edge of the southernmost cone. Then it was barely a track at all. Sections of path bored deep from shoes and boots and feet stepping one at a time over hundreds of decades. Bored by herders looking for errant goats, by the partisans of old, by that invisible force who sought refuge in the caves below, by those searching for lost ghosts amongst the stone. Paths shaped by water and rain, the runoff sand distributed to some other parts of the world.

As we walked, Rachel fell often, catching herself and correcting. And I did the same. The two of us paired by weak limbs, untried for so long. We were surrounded by cacti. Needles at eye height. Footholes that came up to the knee. I had to lift my foot to find the next placing, as if climbing stairs. It was exhausting but we went on. Muscle step and deep lunges, blood and circulation. It took us forty minutes to hike down. Now we lay on the rocks, and I felt heat in my muscles. Small groups, loners, and the odd couple came by. Women and men making themselves naked in the serotinal light, swimming loudly in the water. None stayed too long because of the heat, no one but an older woman in a mask who seemed to know the arc of the sun and its shadows. She sat reading in the lean of a rock, shifting with the shadow before the shadow knew it had moved. But she too eventually got up and left as two helicopters with decals of news outlets from the mainland flew overhead and my question went unanswered. The machines lowered, rose like lonely hawks as we bent our necks, and glanced upwards. We waited until their noise vanished and we continued talking about the things that vexed us. The voices of us sometimes made indistinct, not by topic nor agreement but by the sound of two drained people in conversation; the incompleteness of us blurred which mouth was stating what word. Hours became ours, frowns shifted into nouns.

We had a weakness, I suspected, for the stories that displayed our various hurts as if they were victories won in terrifying circumstance—but victories over what, neither could say. One of the helicopters returned, scanning the beach for evidence of peculiar acts. We both waved, hopeful of something in reply.

At some point one of us will suggest we leave.

Dead

In the late nineteenth century, the French neurologist Jules Cotard met in Paris with his fellow members of the Société-Medico-Psychologique. There he gave a report listing the case of a forty-three-year-old woman who believed that she had no brain matter, nerves, chest or intestines, and that she did not require sustenance nor care. The woman said that she did not require food or drink, light or air, as she was, she claimed, already dead. It was reported she asked that she be burned alive, and that she'd already made several suicide attempts and believed that neither God nor the devil existed on this plane or other. She was, in all reality, she claimed, skin and its accompanying bone.

This, in June 1880, was the first instance in the literature of what has become known as Cotard's syndrome, and also as Cotard's delusion and walking corpse syndrome. Rare to announce itself and often undiagnosed, the condition's pathology remains a mystery. Debate has ensued over the last 140 years as to its provenance, whether it is a locatable dysfunction in the parietal lobe or, indeed, a nihilistic element of depression within good old melancholia—that breathing, seething thing.

Whatever the case, the phenomenon continues to occur in patients in multiple countries and across diverse cultural divides, gaps, schisms, rifts, divisions.

For example, in 2015, a woman in her sixties presented to the department of psychiatry at the Medical College Kolkata in India. In the preceding six months, she had developed a depressed mood, become lethargic and lost interest in daily activities. She articulated an expanding sense of desperateness, worthlessness and suicidal intent. Over the last months of this period, the symptoms intensified. She began to testify that she had cancer in her head and abdomen. She stated that her brain had rotted away due to this phantom cancer and expressed deep reservations about the possibility of harming her family; the infectious nature of the disease was sure to afflict them. Indeed, she started believing that she had transmitted the infection to her daughter, that her entire family was going to die due to her contagious state. For the last month she complained that she was indeed dead. In the final fifteen days of this period she was unable to distinguish her close acquaintances from others. She displayed a severe retardation of psychomotor activity and as a result the patient's speech patterns were near to disengaged. A physical examination did not reveal any significant abnormality.

Cases like this have come and gone, with quotations attached such as: 'I can't cry because I don't have tears . . . I don't have lungs, I don't have intestines, I'm empty . . . I don't exist . . . I lost my spine . . . I don't have the mind . . . My soul and body are dead . . . My heart, brain, ears, lungs, oesophagus, stomach and intestine are gone . . . I am not allowed to die completely, and have to suffer forever.'

On 'n' on
The phenomenon

Before the medical fraternity re-christened the illness in Cotard's name early in the twentieth century, the syndrome was first offered the title 'the delirium of negation' by the doctor during the 1880s. These are, in isolation away from illness, spectacular words.

The Delirium of Negation

I recently quoted this term to my physician when visiting for a mental health check-up. I was struggling to speak, slurring with that broken brain aspect I'd been carrying around for some days. I announced these words and she looked at me with the eked-out concern of a doctor perturbed that I was reading literature on such a disturbed thing, something so spectacularly unrelated to my own neurological ills. I said, 'June, PhD research.' And she nodded in that bird-like manner that deploys when something touches the stems of her intelligence, feeler-like and subtly nerved. I told her I mentioned it because one patient in the literature had shown improvement with the administration of venlafaxine, the drug she was threatening me with to dull down my own negating symptoms.

'It's related,' I said.

'To what?'

I told her the syndrome was believed by some branches of the medical fraternity to be directly related to depression and its close friends dysthymia and seasonal, general, manic, psychotic, dysphoric depression, all the -ics of cheerless ills. This perked her. Mental health happened to be her forte within the speciality of general practice, and we discussed the various accents of despair, how within moments of its actualisation it feels like a manifestation of specific annulments, a reduction and loss of the ability to reason and construct thoughts, a loss of the base technologies of the self.

She said, 'And—okay, it's interesting, isn't it?'

'Mmhm.'

'It's really interesting.' She spoke to me, but mostly she spoke to the part of her mind that lines things up for later mulling. 'Parts of your physical whole do give the impression of a kind of malicious disappearing act. Right?'

'Right,' I said.

'And it makes sense,' she said, and found some silence for a moment, then spoke over me when I tried to return us to course. She described the whole manifestation, the goo and ooze of the mind and its misfirings. Our collapse into states of incapacitation. She excitedly described depression in regard to this word 'negation' as she fussed with things on her desk. A new term for relating the manner in which the self is no longer capable of being held in its whole form. The manner in which the self is reduced to a state marked by the paralysis of thought and hope, in which the major delusion of personhood is this: the dysthymic state is the *ur* state, the original condition to which we all fit, an inverted world of joylessness and hatred in which happiness is the drug of falsification and its proclamations the work of strawmen and, and, and—'What's the word?' she pondered.

There are no words.

'How are you feeling?' she asked.

I could smell alcohol and swab.

'I haven't been great, June.'

'Mmhm.' She listed other options of medication and therapy.

'Perhaps I just need to see the sun again.' It was winter.

'We could all do with the sun. No, let's try . . .' and she listed remedies, both folkloric and pharmaceutical.

'Where'd you hear of this condition?' she asked eventually again.

I handed her the article I'd printed off that morning and was reading in the waiting room. 'It's ancient and documented,' I said.

'Sounds like a horror film.'

'Sorry?'

'The delirium of negation. Sounds like a horror film.'

'Sounds like a forgotten death metal band.'

'What's, what on earth is death metal? Not that I have anything against any forms of music.'

'You have other patients, June.'

'True, true. I'm over-inquisitive. Costs the practice zillions.'

For some reason I stayed sitting for a moment longer. And she didn't hurry me on.

She just looked at me, then said, 'What do we know about the brain, David? This is the question, and I don't know. We have these pills, and they do stuff, but we don't know why. Psychiatry lags behind all the rest. Here's some analogies,' she said. 'This is what I've come to believe. Imagine heart surgery, this lives in the city. It has a shiny apartment overlooking the harbour. People come and go. Heart surgery lives next to spinal surgery and bone setters and urologists. Psychiatry, however, lives in the woods in the country where it's mostly dark and they don't really know which batteries fit which torches. A pastoral analogy, sure, but what the hell. We basically have no idea how the brain works. We treat it with our eyes closed. Iron gloves.'

'What about ME?'

'Don't ask.'

'I'm enjoying your attempts at analogy.'

'ME? Ha, well. We're in a basement of a dungeon beneath a collapsed castle in the black woods of deepest darkest arctic Siberia. Or maybe not Siberia, somewhere else and it's hot. It's leaky and smells of rats. Nobody enters because, fuck, would you enter?'

I always liked it when my physician swore. It took a few years for her to step over the mark, but once she did, our world seemed to change.

'This is the true delirium of negation,' I said.

'Myalgic encephalomyelitis,' she said. Though she didn't

really say it. She mispronounced it, as everyone does. It means the swelling of the brain, in Latin. Or close enough. Which I think I said earlier. It refers to pain. It refers to a chamber of hell. It refers to debilitation on cognitive functionality. It refers to the breakdown of the nervous system, of the immune system, of the gut, cells and mitochondria. It refers phonically in a perfect physical analogue to the inability of its victims to form thoughts, create narrative about the world and those in it. Try saying it out loud. See? Try again. That's what it's like when we try normal sentences. It takes effort and time. Indeed, to think oneself is to remember oneself. Someone said that.

Did Foucault say it? I don't remember.

She tried it again, sounding like she had a mouth full of snakes, and from then on she just said CFS, an acronym referring to those faithless words: chronic fatigue syndrome. Which is possibly the most condescending name ever given to a disease. It's as helpful as calling multiple sclerosis by the same name, fatigue being one of the many symptoms of that awful, debilitating illness.

Dr June and I kept talking about the delirium of negation for another minute longer because we couldn't help it. *Delirium. Negation.* How marvellous they sounded when placed together, how homely they rang, and in such a way that suggests desire and dance, a kind of dervish fling for reversal, for a physical inversion of the instant. I thought of Bernhard's novella, the one buried in my imagination. I imagined a short book in his style, a dungeon place wild with his unstoppable voice. Women in the prison, a scattering of men. An open door through which they can't leave. I imagined a short sharp ritual, an act of singing and dance that would reimagine the exploits of others who they believed had once escaped. The words that undo the done and extant, open the spiritual doors to realms of liberty and emancipation. And perhaps I'd name it in honour of this disorder.

I left Dr June's surgery determined that these harmonically pleasing words had also been used for means other than a rare and horrifying condition. I was quite sure that amongst the realms of hard rock, punk rock, of heavy metal and hardcore, this phrase had to have been utilised at one point or another. I can't have been the first to see their potential; this was a certainty. Indeed, on inquiry there have been at least two pieces of music given this name by bands whose particular strength, potency, force might be said to belong to the sub-genres of death and black metal. And indeed, it is the latter's extreme Norwegian manifestation which is of most interest to us here.

Pelle

Per Yngve Ohlin was born in January 1969 in Stockholm, all of about nine months before I came into the world that October. As a young man Ohlin was known as Pelle, a sweet enough name for a blond kid with a sharp jaw, prominent chin and ice-blue eyes. However, it is rumoured that from a very young age he suffered from sleep apnoea and would often wake struggling from deeply heavy sleeps. He would later state that he was, since the age of three, supposed to be dead; that life was a kind of inconvenience prior to what would follow. At the age of ten he was placed in hospital with a ruptured spleen and internal bleeding which occurred, according to his brother, after a series of beatings at school. For a time he was, in fact, clinically dead. He recovered and became obsessed with two things: death and its relationship to him, and (of equal importance) heavy metal. Bands came: Black Sabbath, Judas Priest, Motörhead, Venom,

Iron Maiden, AC/DC, Sodom and Mercyful Fate. These goliaths poured their weight into his life. In 1986 Pelle became the frontman for the proto black metal outfit, Morbid. There he took the stage name Dead. This was the name by which he would become known, and he continued to use until it became his prophecy. After recording an influential demo album, *December Moon*, Dead resigned from the band due to what he saw as commercial inclinations within the group. A few months later he wrote to contacts he had for the Oslo group, Mayhem. He sent the band a demo tape, a letter outlining his plans for the future, and a small, crucified mouse. He was immediately hired as Mayhem's new vocalist and moved west in the winter of 1988 to join guitarist Øystein 'Euronymous' Aarseth and bassist Jørn 'Necrobutcher' Stubberud in Norway. Drummer Jan 'Hellhammer' Blomberg joined two months later and, with fate on its side, the seminal though far from most notorious line-up of Mayhem was finalised. And, as such, so began the band's slow descent into carnage, murder, arson and suicide.

Pelle kept dead animals under his bed. Buried his stage clothes in the woods so they would rot in time for concerts. He carried a dead bird around in a bag and would take great lungfuls of the decomposing stench to get himself in the mood to perform. He starved himself in order to get, as guitarist Aarseth described it, 'starving wounds' on his body. He was, as noted by his friends and band mates, extremely depressed and pushing for physical and psychic annihilation as a form of self-realisation. He encouraged people to take pills and smoke marijuana because he despised drugs and believed it a good habit for people to imbibe the things that made them feel and act terrible, which could destroy their lives. He claimed that he longed to torture people and animals. At the few shows he managed to perform with Mayhem he threw pigs' heads into the audience to ensure only the devoted would stay. Hellhammer once stated, '[He] asked us to bury him in the ground—he wanted his skin to become pale.' Others described him as sweet and shy. He killed himself in April 1991 and left this note:

> Excuse the blood, but I have slit my wrists and neck. It was the intention that I would die in the woods so that it would take a few days before I was possibly found. I belong in the woods and have always done so. No one will understand the reason for this anyway. To give some semblance of an explanation: I'm not a human, this is just a dream and soon I will awake. It was too cold and the blood kept clotting, plus my new knife is too dull. If I don't succeed dying to the knife I will blow all the shit out of my skull. As yet I do not know. I left all my lyrics by 'Let the good times roll'—plus the rest of the money. Whoever finds it gets the fucking things. As a last salutation may I present 'Life Eternal'. Do whatever you want with the fucking thing.
>
> Pelle.

In the wake of Dead's suicide, the black metal scene in Norway descended into a movement marked by megalomania and overt narcissistic sociopathy. Many books and articles have been written on this period of personal, societal and media-driven insanity, the music itself and the legacy of Dead. Simply put, multiple church burnings and the murder of Aarseth by the band's temporary bass player probably should have ended the group in 1993. However, the remaining members managed to release what some still consider the reigning masterpiece of Norwegian Black Metal: *De Mysteriis Dom Sathanas*. (My favourite came out a few years later, but that's another story.) It features Aarseth on guitar and his murderer, Varg Vikernes, on bass. A union Hellhammer famously promised to erase to appease the guitarist's family, but left intact. The presence of Dead is there too, by way of his lyrics sung by a young Hungarian vocalist from the Budapest band Tormentor. The lyrics to the song 'Life Eternal', gifted to his band in Dead's last act, seem an anodyne meditation on his hunger for passing the hell on. The words are easy to find and don't need repeating here.

Unsurprisingly, perhaps, it has been suggested on Pelle's Wikipedia page for many years that he suffered from Cotard's syndrome. Indeed, an intriguing paper alluding to this very thing was published not long before this book was sent for its final edit. As Sanches et al state, there is no definitive evidence for the diagnosis other than anecdotally, and from his statements that reflect the delusions that mark the illness. However, the authors do suggest that, if he did in fact have the syndrome, the very sociocultural context he lived and worked within might well have masked the illness. Norwegian Black Metal's celebration of death, of depression and pain, as a tacit rejection of Nordic societal mores could be said to mimic Cotard's symptoms in such a way his pathology may have been invisible to those around him. He once claimed the blood in his veins was frozen. He once claimed he belonged in the earth, in the rot of the woods outside the house he shared with Aarseth. And if we take from this some measure of proof of pathology indicating Cotard's, I can only make the claim that, in this negation, this cognitive delusion of decay and absence, there points, via the laws of continuance, a line towards a confirmation of something actual, a future of other souls, all quite living.

Hardback

Laura enters the narrow lane that curves around the base of the fortifications. The smell of jasmine and exhaust that seems peculiar to Isola della Scogliera Rossa. For the moment she's surrounded by bright voices and leather soles tapping on stone. A group of echoic young women in masks standing by their Vespas and boys. Immaculate, each of them. She manages an unseen smile and watches how they rearrange themselves to the words they say back and forth. She follows their shoulder lines up, up through their voices and the angle of the awning and up and finally there, Cratere Museum still open for an hour—there's time. She leaves the alley for the stairs up to the old palace, to the museum, its new wing of glass and sombre, shy stone. It's beautiful, the wanton assemblage; architecture and all its ideas stacked against a bare and barren sky whose stillness is only ever occasionally ruffled by the rotor-wash of news helicopters. Crews fly over filming the locals, the quiet visitors and foreign tourists stuck here until something alters.

She takes the stairs up. Each tread has a depth equal to a horse's stride. Fifty, sixty of them, up, up. She walks in a half-silence, talking quietly to herself, taking each step until at the halfway point she stops to unmask and drink. There are drips on her chin and she wipes with her forearm and there she sees them, jutting from the wall—things she's read about, things immortal rearing out of the stone on each side of the famed staircase. The carved heads of old martyrs. Medieval fuckers with their features smoothed down to nothing. The rain, the centuries of rain, and they're still there, recognisable but so near to nothing. A nose, an eye socket. How long does it take before all humanity is rubbed from these forms and they're returned to rock and mineral? How long until we can't say what each nub of stone once was because of what it is now?

Rhetoric.

She drinks again then moves up towards the old court of Cratere. Sun and sweat and then the noise of them, a wedding party drifting into view, or into earshot because she hears them first and then sees a commotion of shadows on the wall. Noises and colour, multi-dimensional; she's aware too of cameras and a sudden drone overhead. They start towards her, a herd of frocks and skirts, of suits, shoes and heels. Wide faces with masks tucked under their chins. A bearded groom, a bosomy bride. She feels a tight panic, that each of their steps is a part of something greater and she is just going to ruin it if she continues upwards. She pushes herself against the wall to let them pass, her eyes, face, head and body glanced at and the receptor of the odd sustained smile. It's become a fad since isolation, young couples all over the island marrying, protecting themselves from the natural effects of permanence. And then they evanesce, fade and vanish. Married, perfect for a moment—then something else. The thing that comes after.

And after—the museum.

The Modern's cure for time's passing.

Laura enters and removes her mask, as all seem to do in this space. A place of odd immunities. The tall doors wide and open, the case-clothed covers of an immense hardback stacked and wedged on the side of the long-dead volcano that marks the town. Everything, the world inside, and all remove their masks. It's a new compulsion: all time is here, all the possibilities of the past.

A large man in a name-tagged suit lurks among the marooned tourists and Homerphiles. He stands beneath a large poster for the famously yet-to-be-named exhibition. The bill shows an image only, the strange forms. She asks for directions to the curator's office.

The elevator opens at a high-ceilinged, modernist-clean hallway. Wood panelling and slight rectangular windows glancing into the offices. The whole place seems based on another modernism that never existed but is suddenly here. She opens a door on the right, and instead of finding more offices she arrives in one of the myriad exhibit halls in the old part of the museum.

Endless space, gaping.

Shit.

A place of broad worship, of lost time and found things, of imprisoned time. Two film fragments by the artist playing in continual loops on the wall; 'primers', the woman had called them. Primers for the painting—which, of course, was the final thing one was supposed to see in the museum, the last gasp before the real made its return in the streets.

Clear glass cases stare wildly into human pasts as she walks. Statues and busts. Neolithic pottery and tools, hacking tools, eating utensils and rescued obsidian figures. Centuries and millennia, stolen centuries, each summarised in a single three-by-two-metre case.

This isn't where she's supposed to be.

Shit.

She feels surrounded, affected by involuntary glances. A panic rises and she just wants to walk right through, run right through and watch it all disappear, vanish like she'd imagined when she was a girl. All time and people and the rest. A sureness that this is possible, to march straight through each display and nothing would touch her, because time disappears in such places. But then she's struck by the sound, by the hugeness of the place and then, conversely, by how small it all seems. How in its desire to be *the* space, one designed to capture our entire universe of thought, the museum too becomes small. It becomes tiny and sullen against the breadth of the world it desires to project.

During the late stages of the war it was a hospital; now it seems a ward of another kind.

She finds herself at a beautifully framed window, a floor-to-ceiling doorway open to a French veranda looking out onto a garden. Beyond the trees an ordered collection of buildings, perfect rounds and rectangles. Beyond, the exact hills where the cottages sit on the side of the second volcano. Places so exact she feels they can't possibly house humans. A wide quietness forms around her, like glass blown through a tube and expanding into the room.

She aches for a breeze, a wind on her neck.

An hour ago, after a light rain, Laura pushed up from the small writing desk in the corner of their cottage and stood. Within twenty seconds she'd hooked her shoes out from under the bed and gone through the door, locked it, then unlocked it because she remembered—there was only one key. She stepped onto the tiles under the faded shade of the rooms' linking portico. Even there the shadowy areas felt bleached, whitened with the removed hue of blue, yellow and red. She walked. The flat section of the driveway. Then the descent off the southern cone. The jumbled staircase that led to the city below and circumvented the one road that took cars and bikes up into the hills. She headed past dozens of houses that cut towards the city and hunched inside the eroded crater. A path stacked with villas and apartments. The view. The great sea clinging to cliffs, to the beached shore and harbour. She navigated by things, objects at her side and in the distance.

She'd walked the city in that eerie pain that radiates up from her knees for an hour before finding the stairs that lead up to the museum. Walked in circles through the alleys and narrow byways—though she didn't think of her path as circular because she believed she was strolling in straight lines.

And now, as if to confirm this, these lines are what she sees against the blue skies. An architecture of perfect angles and linkages. She takes out her phone to photograph the scene.

The sampled camera-click her phone makes over and over. She blows on her hand because she wants to feel the movement of air, and as she does so a low voice merges with the room. She turns. A short man in a fitted suit, on his phone. He moves closer until he's a few feet away, cologne colliding with the air. Then a middle-aged woman, holding a small dog, heading through the same array of display cases. Her shape varyingly distorted by the graduated volumes of glass. She too is on her phone, coming closer, and gradually she lowers the device. The man continues talking as he puts down his phone. They nod at Laura at the window, framed by immaculate design.

'Hi hi,' the curator says, and Laura finds herself waving. 'Nice to see you again,' Gretchen says, and Laura feels a cool wash of relief drain through her.

There's a small table set by a window. The room is closed off from the rest of the museum by partitions decorated by facsimiles of paintings of cracked Neolithic pottery. The man has brought them tea on a plastic tray. Cups and a pot decorated in blue parrots.

'I'm glad you called,' Gretchen says, and puts her dog on the floor where it inspects Laura's sneakers.

'I realised I didn't know—didn't know what to do so I started walking,' Laura replies as she bends to touch the dog's fur.

'Well, I'm glad you did.'

Laura moves her eyes around the room. White spaces on the walls where paintings were once hung, rectangles bound by the light grime of years. There's a smell of hospital-strength soap.

'How long, how long's it been a museum,' Laura asks, 'the palace?' She feels a strange plainness in her voice asking this, like it's the question everyone asks, not realising its repetitiveness till it's been said.

And indeed, Gretchen nods; she's been asked many times. 'We like to say it became such over time. People started coming from the mainland during the nineteenth century on the rumour of visions. Plagues of grand-touring Brits in the galleries. Servants to such and such. So centuries and then the war and. And it became something else.'

'Okay, that's . . .' but Laura isn't sure what this signifies. She attends to her porcelain cup. It's hot but that's fine; she's always liked the heat in her mouth and chest. David's one to let his tea go cold and she feels an odd frustration at that. All the energy that goes into making it hot and then all that same energy radiating out as the steam curls to nowhere. Her husband's foolish with energy, and maybe it bugs because he should know better, because he should, know better.

'So, the bay. The Bay of Mouths,' Rachel's old friend states.

'They just up and—and I didn't think about it until I thought about it.'

'And how many have gone down there to, what? Is "rescue" the word?' the curator asks.

Laura says she isn't sure.

'No,' Gretchen says.

'Didn't you make the call?' Laura asks. She looks at Gretchen's eyes for the first time. Blue, set in dark, caked make-up.

'Yes. Sorry,' the woman says, not looking at Laura's face for a moment, until she does, and Laura feels a raw discomfort. Gretchen explains she'd messaged Laura immediately after calling the police.

'You said five,' Laura says. 'You said five of them had gone down the hill.'

'Yes. Five. They're okay, David and Rachel are really okay. Just—'

Sound then, a hint of rain. Laura looks up. Heavy tarred-black rafters repeating across the ceiling, each bent blindly downwards. Time and its ally. Gravity and time.

'They'll be okay.'

Laura glares at the door and feels an urge to push her way through the museum and return to the streets and find her own way to the path, down to where David and his cousin found themselves stuck some hours ago. And as if sensing this, the curator reaches a hand across the table to hers. It's cold, but Laura grips it with a hope this really will alter everything, change it so there's certainty in that word *okay*.

'Just stay here with me and the police will help them back to the house.'

'What if they need an ambulance? I just want to—'

'They don't need an ambulance. They just need a hand.'

'Fuck. What if they need a helicopter?'

'It's okay. Tell me about him.'

'What?'

'Like when did you guys get married? Tell me about the two of you.'

'Fuck.'

'It's okay. It's okay.'

Laura finds herself talking despite the tiredness that's roaming through her, despite just wanting to escape the hell out of these walls and find her husband. An echo of defiant strategies she's learnt in order to get by wakes her. She's talking but also drifting, uncompliant. As she tells Gretchen about their house and travels she finds herself thinking about those who were here previously, the ones who once surrendered to their bodies in this room. She thinks of facts you can't know without googling the museum, without entering its grounds. Can't know without a husband who talks about the war incessantly with locals and tour guides, and then to himself and intimates about the rumour of his great-great-great-great grandfather living on the island for a month in the 1840s. Because of his fascination, Isola's battles and past populations have entered her thoughts in a way war never did previously. It was because of the women in the end. The young women and then the men from the mountains, partisans fighting a partisan war against the fascists and Germans. She's talking about the wedding in their lounge, but somehow also about these civilians, these non-combatant combatants who held Isola della Scogliera Rossa as a stronghold, a refuge for the wounded, the haunted and hunted. Boys with old rifles, bullet belts over their shoulders, posing in the shade. The secrets of hiding, of stalking learnt by instinct. Women who knew the ways to cut off the blood circulation, hair held up by bits of string. Virgin births, because who remembered the acts of love? Its voice. She says she barely remembers the wedding, but there are photographs so something must have happened, says it but is thinking about the end—near the end of the war, a wretched battle. An internal violence that left bodies in the streets. A skirmish broke out between the communists and a group of belligerent anarchists, men and women who'd rejected a return to the mainland. Women died in here. Men too, brothers, sisters, mothers, daughters, sons and fathers killed trying to protect the island from itself. When Gretchen asks about David's illness, Laura tells her of their journey through Borneo in 2012 before they both became sick, talks about how overweight he was in the heat and how he decided to get fit and pushed himself and pushed himself until—'He has, or his body has, developed a bad habit of repetition,' Laura says.

'Yes.'

He has a habit of repeating things, Laura explains. She pauses and glances again at the door. She has no desire to be sharing any of this, but she hears the words come out of her mouth like sharp rebukes against something purely her. She says how these reiterations, how they begin to feel like an error of memory. 'And he repeats the things that cause him and us harm. But such is the harm . . . he doesn't recall any of it, how something as simple as reading might put him in bed for a week. How denying my opinion can cause me a harm he doesn't seem to get.'

Gretchen nods and glances at her phone as it suddenly vibrates on her lap. 'It's nobody,' she says.

Laura looks at the phone and then the curator's eyes. 'Fuck,' she says.

'You know the question I felt inside me over and over when I was a physician?' Gretchen asks. 'The one I'd ask myself was what do we really know of memory? It's a pitiful question because there's no real answer.'

Laura nods, an impatient movement, not entirely without spite. 'Because he does shit like this, and why doesn't he remember? Like what's happened right now, he'll barely recall it, even though it's happened before. Even though he's come home from a walk a hundred times and collapsed on the couch so he's unmoving and kind of ridiculed. He won't remember the collapse, only the walk. So what's the point?'

When Gretchen asks what was the point in what, Laura just shakes her head. She makes to stand.

'Just sit. We wait, okay.'

Laura repeats the words in her head until they sound like a chamber of maddened consonants.

'I should go,' she says. 'I can't wait here having this conversation.'

'I've seen Rachel paint the same artwork multiple times,' Gretchen says. 'For the same customer, and months after she'd delivered the first.'

Laura stares at her. She feels an anger that has no known source but she feels herself start to blame the curator for keeping her there. But nobody's keeping her there, though something seems in charge of her status. She can feel it in her arms and legs and chest.

'And she can only sell it once,' Gretchen says. 'Every piece must be original. You've seen their house? It's full of cast-offs.'

'Can we just go?' Laura asks. 'Can we just get out of here and find them? 'Cause I don't really want to be talking like this, not right now.'

'Let's just wait for the police to call back, okay?'

Laura frowns at the walls. She feels embarrassed about having said the things she'd said. This isn't her talking, she thinks, not really. It's all a figment of another's thoughts.

A weight of clouds make their way past the island. City-sized shadows in their wake.

'God, I'm sorry,' Gretchen says. 'I keep talking. I keep trying to say something that'll make it okay for us to just sit here.'

'Do you have any idea why it's called the Bay of Mouths?' Laura asks.

Gretchen repeats the words without affect.

'The Bay of Mouths,' Laura says again.

'No, I don't. I mean, it's just—rocks.'

'Have you been?'

'Have I been? Yes,' Gretchen says.

'What happened?'

'I dreamt I'd been attacked by invisible men,' Gretchen says. 'I went down and returned, and these dreams. It was awful. Like I was someone's cursed widow.'

Laura nods and her mouth moves and they both find themselves then giving over stories of their attempts to get to the beach, recall the depth of the gullies, the impoverished grottos where the partisans once lived. How everything was exaggerated by steepness and the colour of the darkened rock. Says how they'd spent the next day asleep and dreaming.

Laura watches Gretchen, the way she goes silent after her words get tangled. Goes quiet like disease when disease is just waiting.

So, silence.

A sizeable silence then destroyed by an expanse of black rain hitting roof and windows.

'Fuck,' Laura says and Gretchen stares upwards.

The curator drags a long, clear fingernail around the rim

of her cup, then stands as her phone hums on the table. She answers and walks to the other side of the room and leans the length of her arm against the steel of a spiral staircase that heads to the ceiling trapdoor. She speaks, sits on the first stair.

Laura gazes at the nothing of the painting-less walls. She stands and moves to the window. Rain smashing blur after blur onto the glass. The hill in the distance hunkering down under the weight of the grey. Below in the city, smudged souls scamper on the streets. Somewhere out there people are making their way to where her husband waits unmoving in the downpour. She feels a hard regret, that she'd said any of the words she'd shared. So often, speech feels a like betrayal, a deception of the desired self.

Just an Interruption . . .

David didn't like to use ropes while climbing. He liked to climb solo and without assistance. My brother Simon told me this two weeks ago, as I was doing a final read-through of this book over Christmas in Timaru. While Simon barbecued steaks one evening at the house where he and Esther had raised their kids, he told me the reason. David was climbing Mount Aspiring with a friend during the early Eighties, the two of them roped together as they made their ascent. As they neared the summit, one of David's crampons came loose from his boot and he slipped on the cornice. In the moment, in the precise instant, he believed he was dead. He said goodbye, to what I can't tell you; he felt a peace with what only the gods know. But what I do know is that in the next moment his friend, feeling David fall, threw himself off the other side of the mountain into clean air. In this act he counterbalanced David's weight and saved both of their lives. Below them air, air then ice, then rock. Death would have quickly announced itself to them both, such was the steepness of their climb. They managed to haul themselves back up the mountain's sharp ridge. In the years after, he disavowed ropes, because had his friend not made that insane decision to jump off the mountain, David sincerely believed he would have been responsible for the friend's death. He believed this because earlier that morning he'd not attached his crampon correctly, thus leading to the two of them hanging off the mountain like fulcrum weights.

Several years later, and after saving my father's life, he died, of course, falling into Fox Glacier. I visited the glacier recently; there was very little of it left. Indeed, the equilibrium of fate is impossible to countenance with reason. It's easier to say there is no balance, not really; only a continual struggle to live up to the wholeness of the word's promise—and that the promise is seemingly everywhere.

Play

We both knew we'd struggled during those early lockdowns, when cities around the world went quiet and skies cleared and streets became a vast network of silence. We knew that when the virus first hit, Rachel and I found ourselves on the rack, twisted by a psychic disquiet as airports closed, as heroes were made out of the kids delivering food, who stood in supermarkets helpless as the strain began killing. We hadn't been in the same city to talk about it all, and on the beach we tried to make sense of the people we'd become in our separate towns. Our voices unbalanced when we tried to speak. Initially I shrugged when Rachel asked how the lockdowns were in Wellington, then I said, 'It was like an abominable one-act play.'

She was quiet for a moment, then asked over the surf, 'You know David, I watch movies and there's the whole three-act thing, isn't there? Three discernible acts. But I have never ever been able to tell where one starts and the other ends.'

'Neither,' I said.

'There's just lots of acting.'

I laughed. 'There's also the Acts in the Bible. That's when they get up to stuff and the pricks blame the Jews.'

'I've never read the Bible,' she said.

'Neither. You know I just watched way too much YouTube, I don't know, kibble,' I said. 'Fun with pets and birds. Then I found myself watching videotaped rats for hours at a time.'

'Oh David, that's—'

'They become fine actors after a while.'

'That's quite gross.'

'Well –'

I explained I had been going through a period when we all closed our doors and put teddy bears in the windows. It started in late March, but for me it had begun in February. I'd been at home for a month already without leaving, and then lockdown was announced and—

'And, it was like everyone was coming home to join you?' she asked.

'Yes, like everyone in the country was coming home to join me, and something about that—and I couldn't cope, not really. Everyone in the world. The sense that all were as sick as—and I was paralysed. It was the stress, obviously. Cinereal stress.'

'Like continents grinding up against each other.'

'Yeah.'

She turned as birds hustled in the bushes behind us. Rocks fell from the red cliffs and sent up a plume of bird life.

I asked her if there was madness.

'. . .'

Because I knew she knew there was a madness.

'A drop, yes,' she said. She joined me by moving her knees up to her chest and hugging them in tight. 'You know: the body is, the body signifies. Mind follows in step.' She shrugged and picked up a stone, dropped it, then shifted it back to where she'd first touched it. The sounds like a footstep, someone near. 'And I guess the opposite is obviously true, too.' She told me how for a time she revelled at the peace that came over the peninsula where she lived. That there was a beauty in those noiseless spaces designed for noise, a beauty in the reclamation of the air by birds and song. Voices, words, how all of us seemed to live in spaces between them as our texts, conference calls and desperate shouts to the outside world made narrow pathways through the new sky—those songs were all she needed for a time. Though she was aware something of the inverse was at play. There was disquiet in those temples we make in our hearts, she said.

I wondered if 'temple' was the right word, or if it was 'heart' that was somehow wrong. I then settled on the idea that it was the verb that was out of place. That we can't build anything near our organs without catastrophic failure. I didn't tell her any of this; instead I told her I'd stare at the empty streets in Berhampore that could be seen from our house. I'd wait for an hour until the view was spoilt by the sight of single car and then feel the destruction of something, how this whole two-second-long event would challenge my whole day. The calmness became a kind of broken affect. A pained vagueness, a mental lag and limp. I explained that on the surface I appeared quite calm. I believed the government was doing the right things and I still believed that; I felt safe. But somewhere internal there was a quaking, an agitation that made me very ill. I didn't write a word, did no work on this book for many months. 'Four or five,' I said. 'It was a madness, but how to give it a name, I'm not sure. Even after the lockdown was lifted it was another month or so before I could leave the house.'

'Yes.'

That was me, I told her. Laura did splendid, I said. But me, I was a wreck.

Rachel nodded into her narrow hands.

'I thought, I thought I'd died at one point,' I told her. 'I thought I'd died. I was okay with it. But annoyed too, because to die unwillingly, it seems such a waste, you know, of volition.'

It took a moment before she laughed. She said her father would've had something to say about that.

I suggested that surely somebody by now, somebody famous, would've said that if free will were really a thing, half of all deaths would be suicides. I said this out loud and Rachel didn't move and I wondered if she heard me. And then she took my hand and held it gently.

'You know Gretchen's never been through a holding,' she said. 'She's been here the entire time. She came to interview for the curator's position and that was it. She stayed. She's terrified in fascinating ways that it'll all fall apart.'

I laughed at that. Gretchen was someone Rachel had often spoken of back in New Zealand; I'd even met her once or twice before coming to Isola. A person of mythic thrust, a young woman in the stories told, and on meeting she was quite the opposite, sixty-four and quite real. Laura and I were reintroduced to her back in June before the island was cut off from the rest of the world. We ate dinner at her house, which overlooked Cratere, along with Rachel, and Gretchen's small, untameably friendly dog. The city's lights glancing through the tomato vines that festooned the balcony, illuminating the contents of our glasses with shimmers and unrepeating code-like flashes. Rachel had a newness about her in Gretchen's company, their shared proximity seemed to reproduce the agencies of youth. I'd enjoyed Gretchen's stories of the museum where she worked. The various queries of time its halls and rooms produced. She was only marginally, she said, in control of the visitors' experiences; the rest was in the infuriating unknowns of the guests' thoughts. She made a comment that the margins are where real power lies. At first I thought it was a joke and felt uncomfortable when nobody else laughed. The sound of a car then echoed out of a gully and droned into oblivion, and I watched the curator fork aubergine into her mouth and eventually smile as she finished chewing. I had the thought it was a look that had, by fortune and timing, no link to the awful realities endured back in her hometown of Potsdam where an entire public garden had been dug up and filled in with bodies. She was released from Europe's travails by her arrival here, immune to the questions of survival. She drove everywhere in a red Fiat and spoke about the painting like it was her own deranged child. Rachel mentioned we'd been at the museum for three hours earlier that day but had avoided looking at the piece. Gretchen then went into defence mode, summoning the artist's name like a spear and spitting it through the hovering light.

At the beach, Rachel and I didn't speak. I was recalling the questions Gretchen had asked that night. I was also intrigued that I couldn't recall the answers we'd offered as we ate fruit and cream. I remembered the table's surface, its mosaic of painted pebbles and shells, the limestone bowls and white outlines of the walls behind us. I recalled the thirty-degree heat, the asymmetrical geometry of the houses stacked below like discards. I remembered the curator's intrigue at our states of being, and fought for an image of the way we'd answered. But nothing, just the smell of herb and heat.

'But I don't know. The second wave, the delta wave, I was okay,' I said suddenly. Rachel looked up from her hands. But then, I explained, Laura, she had a hard time. She knew she had her own illness by then, so it was the two of us. And the two of us sought refuge in opposing regimes of creativity and isolation.

The two of us stewing in sickness.

I felt the hard sun as we went silent. I put my hand up to protect my eyes, my heart barely beating in the heat. Time then, and time seeking itself, asking for answers, answers as to how it passes without speech to catch it and count it. Devouring the tail of instant after instant till it gets its answer in light, the way it clings to skin, beckoning a slow, altering burn. Rachel had been on the island a month when the sweep hit the mainland; Laura and me just days, and those days morphed into months. Marooned days waiting. Waiting until they were all we wanted, this strange salvation. Then the waves of madness that swept the island, the protests, the sacrificial protests. A man jumping into the sea with his daughter. They died at the bottom of the cliffs trying to get across the horizon to the mainland. The great peninsula where everything but the island waited. They fell amongst the rocks, split skulls like jackfruit.

My father always said survival was based on two things: good decisions and luck.

The shadows between the rocks seemed to bind them all together as the day wore on, a strange cement of sentiment and illusion. An engine began vibrating and I watched as one of the yachts moved windlessly from the bay. Birds called uncoded warnings and salutations to the afternoon.

'Anyway—' Rachel said.
'Yes.'
'What are we going to do?'
'I don't know,' I said.
'You don't know.'
'I don't know.'
She looked to where the gully narrowed like a wishbone high in the hills, a bone merging like a thought you wished you'd never had. Perhaps the one that had convinced me to convince her to come down here. I had a thing about battle sites, and there was once a skirmish amongst the trees, amongst the boulders and strewn rock. Fascists vs Partisans, if I can break it down so simply. It was also a beach where I imagine one of my ancestors landing on his return from Africa. And perhaps that's it, beaches are the gathering point of so much of the world we resist imagining but do so without moral opposition.
'And you come to the beach, but you don't swim?' she said.
'I go to the airport, but I can't fly,' I replied.
'Strange the things we inherit and don't.'
'. . .'
Instead of replying, I explained again how I thought I'd died during that first lockdown. That my mind had lost its connections to its body. All transmission had vanished. I explained how I eventually lost all sense of self. A complete collapse of ego, and I could only imagine myself as the worst creature that had ever lived. I reimagined every interaction I'd ever had with anyone as vicious, as psychically violent, as malicious and brutal. All my loves, all my dearests. All the good in me vanished from my memory, sucked out, and this person left over just a moronic, this moronic piece of meat. A fictional fragment of base humanity.

Rachel didn't reply; she just picked up a warm stone and placed it against my cheek.

'I've never been there before or since,' I said.

She looked out at the bay. A heap of clouds barging across the horizon.

'Everyone I've ever known despised me,' I said. 'That was my, I guess, madness.'

My cousin placed the heated stone against the back of her neck and I had a sudden sense of a pain there.

'We learn about others' fears,' she said, 'and imagine they're the same as ours. As exact. But that's never actually true.'

'No,' I said.

She smiled. This time it seemed to be camouflaging something, and I didn't know what.

I watched the angle of the old volcano. We both watched till it finished speaking and we turned again to the water. I thought then that my father, that he didn't quite understand fear, that there was only will and how will might bend. I too picked up a sea-smoothed stone, slung it, and we watched it skip through the tide, dialling a temporary code to the bay for whoever might want to trace our path to here. We watched the stone on and on across the glinting sea, how at some point it missed its last mark and sank.

'We wait for another boat,' she said.

'Yes,' I said, and we spoke again, retelling the stories that had put us there. They became less innocent that way, the repetition placing a parasite at the raw of them, eating out each bone until they were dissolved to the short whispers I couldn't distinguish from sea-wash and bird song.

James

In July 1996, I left Beach Road in Auckland and drove the work van south with my friend and sound engineering colleague James. We'd been working together for a covers band for six months. An unspeakable horror of drum machine, keyboards, sequenced bass, guitar and two singers with such twee voices. We played weddings and corporate events up and down the country.

It was a time of great darkness.

James and I stood to the side and watched families and sons and fathers split and fight and hold each other screaming; we watched CEOs drunkenly dance with ties strapped to their heads; we watched two women with a hand each in the flies of a waiter; we watched, we watched the scattering dance in the low tidal sweep of cover band morbidity. And all for fifteen dollars an hour. That July I told management that their next show in Wellington would be my last, and there I would stay. Wellington would be my hometown once more home.

So, we drove the Hiace south.

James would, many years later, find a legacy as the bass player in the fantastic sludge metal outfit Beastwars, but now he was just starting out as an audio engineer, the thing that would become his career. And at that instant in time James was going out with future novelist Rachael King, whose band had shared the bill with mine many times at the Auckland shanty-dives of post-punk and the slow-core we were deep into. The future existed, as we have now proven, but just how was a nervous proposition. I was somewhat blue and not sure how I would get through each night. In fact, let's say overtly blue. Blue, black and bleak, heart-torn blue. An atomised, stigmatised, fragmentised by the everyday of simple things blue. The blue at the threshold of space blue, the border of atmosphere, ozone and oxygen blue. Blue that's so far gone it's mistaken for obsidian black blue. The cobalt hue of blood vessels lurking too near the surface. Blue like illness blue. The colours of a mind fluctuating from functioning to inoperative blue. I was not sure how I was going to get on with things in Auckland.

There was an evening in August the previous year during which I'd stopped talking. Halted. My mind went cold with the kind of shuddering that accompanies the bodies of the deprived in the weaker weeks of winter. The whole thing went opaque, for thoughts usually represented light, no matter how beaten up they may be. Couldn't actuate idea or impressions of my surrounds, couldn't interrupt the conversations of my friends with my own allusions. I bewildered Deborah, and broke us with this sudden distemper. Bust into friendships and stole the parts that held them together.

This kind of lapsing, this rolling on into mental crisis had been going on since I was fifteen, though this is the earliest I can recall with clarity the physicality of a breakdown. The rendering of synapse, enzyme and neuron into waste, and the sense that something was terribly, terribly wrong. The world smelt of gas and all thoughts ached. It was like trying to walk on a broken ankle, or two (as my father had in fact done). Which is not simply negotiated.

We drove to Wellington at 1am after packing out a show at a hotel near Auckland Airport, where the band had played to trade delegates and partners. Somewhere near Matamata I fell into a deep sleep rocked by the road and the effects of the previous night. I hadn't slept but for an hour after the sun had risen.

Twenty-four hours earlier I'd arrived back at the warehouse flat on Beach Road at midnight to a phone message from Deborah's mother. She sounded panicked, rushed through with an anonymous anxiety I hadn't heard in her voice previously. I held the phone to my ear and listened to the message multiple times. Three months earlier Deborah and I had broken up. We'd been together for four years, two in Auckland, the rest in Wellington. I'd given up on myself after my band had split and there was no possibility a relationship could sustain itself through the misery I was inflicting on us all. Her mother spoke for some time on the answering machine and said I had to call her back, it didn't matter what time I returned after work.

Wake me at any time, it's very, very important we speak.

It was nearly 1am. I sat in the huge space that served as our lounge. White walls and sparse furniture. Nobody else was awake; the room ached with the kind of quietness that was so rare for our flat—the seven of us were art students, band mates, drunks, users and fused minds. We'd had gigs in there, parties of hundreds. Forged joke bands out of bad inclinations and made local super groups on the fly. Themed gatherings where the marginally insane strolled about with begging eyes. And there I sat, in the depth of silence, the corporeal remove as I waited to call her back. I feared death, not mine, but Deborah's. That something terrible had happened. I waited in the summoning well of this potential, the draw of gravity and tragedy. I imagined an incident, a car crash. I cried, for I was certain. But it was so late, and her mother was old. I couldn't bring myself to call. I couldn't break her sleep. What if it wasn't anything? What if she'd just said those words without knowing their potential?

I sat in the same place for five more hours, letting the rush of thoughts flee from hard logic to the specious. That Deborah was dead; that she wasn't dead, that she was sleeping in our old bedroom on Karangahape Road, stunning as always and calm and snoring because God she could smoke and drink; that she was in a ward and needed me to hold her again; that she was snoring like she snored and she hadn't thought of me since we'd said our last farewell two nights earlier; that she was bent up and crying someplace; that she'd be getting out of bed in a few hours to go to her job; that her ribs had broken through muscle and skin. Over and again, the worst and the mundane. I imagined deep bruising, the turning of sores as she ached, the change of pallor and the arrangement of tubes around her bed, the way they said life is simply wayfarers from this heart to this cell to this lung and to this hand as it remembers how to guide us through. I imagined she needed me to come back, that this was the event that would let us reconcile and live out life.

At three I opened the phone book and looked up the entry for hospital admissions and wrote it on the back of my hand. At four I lifted the handset and dialled the number for the hospital.

I was surprised, shocked by the fact it worked. And then there was an answer and I hung up because, I realised, there is no real beyond midnight, just the imagination and its distrust of science.

And the distrust of science, this comes with the ruin of rationality, and in the stony ruins are as many beautiful things as terrible.

Eventually the light began to change in the room, huge shadows appearing under the tall windows. The time was near to six and I knew the sun was coming up. I called then, rang her mother, filled with fear and the strictions fear makes on your desire for peace.

Twenty hours later, in the centre of the North Island, James woke me. The vacant dark spreading through the van. I looked around, I didn't recognise the surrounds. He was driving very slowly down a village thoroughfare. Eventually he stopped a metre from the kerb. His head slumped.

A streetlight hanging a distilled light over the windscreen.

'You have to drive, man,' he said.

I made a groaning sound like I'd been hit, roused into a stream of fists thumping on my face, or not my face but the will of something. 'What's the fucken—'

'I have to sleep, man. You have to drive.'

'What's the time?' The stereo was still playing. We had a box of tapes, each poorly labelled, each stretched and damaged by lousy tape machines, capstans and rollers.

'I don't know. Four-thirty. I can't drive. I'm seeing shit in the trees.'

'What's the problem?'

'I need to sleep,' he said.

'What shit in the trees?'

He shook his head. Then he said he was seeing things, that they kept jumping out in the road in front of us and vanishing.

'Have you been falling asleep?'

He nodded, affirming that he'd been the host for that worst thing, that dark sleep that no one is supposed to wake from. Road sleep, the sleep of torn metal and death in a ditch. We sat waiting on an answer because something had been queried. A question of survival without eyes, without consciousness. The van ticked in a side street, one of the unseen roads that fill in the towns we'd driven through dozens and tens of times. It felt obscured by the expectation that I knew the stretch that ran south from Auckland like I knew the shape of the sun. The things one can't see directly are always broadest in our imaginations, and I felt run through by the panic that had been expanding since August last year and shocked open once more by the previous night's ransom of my senses. The idea that Deborah had somehow died hadn't left; it ached in thought and movement.

She was fine, of course. I'd rung her mother: she'd just wanted to say goodbye. Deb was fine, and her mum just wanted to say goodbye. She'd cried and said goodbye, farewell. And afterwards I sat in the huge lounge prolonging the moment in which it would occur to me that there was never going to be any reprieve, there was not going to be a return, that I was alone.

I whispered, 'Where the fuck, James?'

He blew air out between his lips. The air of compressed thought. I tried to rouse myself, to undo the weight of waking. I undid the seatbelt and got out of the van. It was cold, hard on the skin, the grass at the verge crystallised under the streetlight. I didn't recognise anything. I walked twenty metres up the road and came back.

I went to his window.

'Is this Taupō?'

He shook his head. 'I don't remember.'

I tried kicking the cold out of my boots. I walked back around to my side and got back in, only to find myself staring at the ice on the windscreen as we each waited on the other to say the thing that would allow us to leave. That specific combination of words that would key back in the real, for it seemed oddly transplanted at that moment at the side of the road. James was always talking about chaos theory, quantum mechanics and event horizons. He liked hard science, but he also liked its edges, where it spoke into unknown panoramas of time and the gaps between things, hence these versions of physics that said that nothing belonged to the world in the way old narratives said they would. All as if it spoke to the similes we tried to make about our own lives, in violent pop songs, punk epics of distortion and hackneyed fury, the rotted-out homes only good for the vanishing and departed. I wondered if this pause at the side of the road in the absolute freeze of July was a broken gateway into the odder dimensions necessary for all James's physics to function as they should.

We sat still in the van, waiting until one of us was ready to drive. The two of us heavy, staring through the windscreen, trying to breathe. The near terror of closing space, our incapacity to drive out. It was freezing. A heavy moon sat at the head of the street. We swapped seats and I put the key back in the ignition but couldn't turn it. Something was waiting for us in our breath, a wakefulness, a return of distance. It had all come in so close and I realised then that this was the make-up of fear: the compression of far-off things, of time and its reckoning with mortality, into the simple plane of now.

Eventually, after an unremembered period, we found ourselves back on State Highway 1. I still don't know which town we were caught in. James slept and I drove up onto the plateau and watched the cones of Ngāuruhoe and Ruapehu glisten in the once-reflected light off the moon. It was eight in the morning by the time we hit the narrowing outskirts of Wellington. I ejected the tape from the cassette player and the mimed voices of radio broke out of the static. It was RadioActive waking up. The first thing out of the speakers was the morning music news, a pre-recorded national scene update thing, and on the bulletin was an announcement including my name. David Coventry, they said, was moving back to Wellington to start a new band. Which was good to know, positive, restorative and quite extraordinarily up with the actual truth of the moment.

Porcelain

When Laura was four, her family lived in a two-storey house on a hill above Aro Valley. Her mother taught her how to walk the staircase that led from the bedrooms up to the living space. She wore red tights, little brown shoes. She learnt the way to balance herself at the top, how to step downwards and wait until she had sure footing, then the next step, all with a sense of a coming avalanche. At first her mother held her hand, then she walked beside her, ready to grab her if she did in fact fall, a safety net of fingers and forearms. After a time, she could do it herself, learnt to run the stairs, careful, purposeful strides. She conquered the rises and steps until she had absolute confidence. With this learning complete, she found herself unexpectedly fearful, as if such sudden confidence meant a change, an alteration to the things about her. She became fearful of her confidence. That with it came the ability to enact unalterable modifications to the known, that with such self-assurance came belief, and with belief the ability to annihilate the world's ability to tell stories and recall itself. Hence, within a thought she imagined the vanishing of fundamental things.

Stairs.

For years she was too terrified to think a determining thought, to enact a thought that might bring disaster upon the world. Until she did, one day, think. A hard, brutal thought she wished forever she could take back. She spent weeks scanning newspapers, watching the news for the terrible things she had imagined into fact. Now, in the silence that comes after Gretchen finishes her phone call in exclamations of both Italian and German, she turns back to the white spaces on the wall and wonders where those paintings now lived, wonders what the nature of fact really is when you only know something by its absence.

'I met her at a hospital,' Gretchen says as she walks back across the room. 'In Paris, thirty-five years ago.'

'Rachel?'

'I was an intern and I met her in the psych ward. They'd tried to section her after an ambulance brought her in from the Metro. She was found on a train; she'd been going around and around for most of the night. She was—she wasn't absorbing nutrients, couldn't speak, the blood flow to the brain, of course. Everything about her dangerously decreased. She was dying, basically, and they wanted her in the psych ward. I realised something was wrong. That was where she first got sick. That's when I was still a doctor.'

'That's pretty, that's awful.'

She shrugs. 'It was. It was awful,' she says and grimaces, then says, 'That was the police, by the way.'

'. . .'

'They say in an hour, maybe.'

'Okay.'

'An hour to bring them up.'

'Okay. Have they reached them?'

'They didn't say, they just said hours and minutes. Laura, I'm sorry. The best thing to do is wait.'

Laura looks down at her tea and feels like she has been hijacked, held ransom here in this room and conversation. 'What was she doing on the train?' she asks, but for a moment she isn't sure who asked the question or why. There are bigger questions to ask but she realises she is frightened of them and these are instead the words.

'Just going around and around. She couldn't move. I just

despise disease, if I'm going to be an honest person, I hate all kinds of sick. I used to love it. I trained to be a pathologist. Spent three years training to be a pathologist in Paris, loved disease. A fascination with its structures. Then I realised something awful about myself: I hated all the people who were dying, detested every one of them. It was a dark—'

Laura watches Gretchen in her pause. Looks towards the spaces on the wall. The white gaps where a hundred portraits of the landed by a hundred white men sat on the walls for decades, fading the truth of time.

'And I had to change.'

'Was that after you met her?'

'They brought her in. She was inert, barely a word on her breath, and barely breathing. And they thought she'd lost her mind. I don't know what would have happened to her if I hadn't— We started living together in this, this shithole apartment.' She laughed. 'And we decided to do it up. Or she did, I don't really remember.'

They watch each other. Laura again feels the need to stand, to threaten all the grandeur of this place with her leaving.

The curator turns her cup in her saucer.

Laura again tells Gretchen about her walk to the beach. This time including the fact that by the time she'd returned, they'd stopped the ferries.

'It was that day?' the curator asks.

'It was that day.'

The mainland closed down while Laura was walking, all its doors shut and Isola della Scogliera Rossa was beyond being an island, all free to do as they liked. Free, though they were marooned. The island became an island twice over as the surge raged around them on the mainland and time seemed to stop and become like water, drifting to unpredicted bays and beaches.

Laura watches the peppermint leaves in the cup, the way they seek the surface and sink all the same.

'There's nothing you could've done,' Gretchen says.

'I know.'

'They'll bring them back around to the port.'

'I know.'

'And he'll be fine. And Rachel will be fine.'

Laura shakes her head and feels a red anger, the kind that forced stasis produces, like at the end of a runway, an error in the manifest. Red like when the day surrenders itself and the sky makes its threats.

'Do you want to see it?' Gretchen asks.

'What?' Laura asks, her eyes focused on the walls.

'Do you want to see it?'

'What? The—'

'Yes,' the curator said.

'Oh.'

'It's supposed to open when the island reopens, but—I can show you. Now.'

Laura sips from her cup, carefully as if the birds decorating the porcelain were readying to fly, wings at the lip. 'Yes,' she says.

Waiheke

A few days after arriving in Wellington, Paddy, the drummer from our now defunct band, took me up to RadioActive, the student-run station, where he was working as programme director. We just wanted to hang and drink tea. Along with Charles we'd played together for over five years, learnt music and constructed a way and form, a language that provided for our limitations and created something just a little larger than their confines. There was a sadness, I believed, for that part of life that couldn't exist outside of certain years, and we were trying to find a way around it. On the way up the stairs in the Student Union building, a sharp-eyed young woman hurried past us and said, in a way only minorly sardonic, 'Urgh! Rock stars!' She was smart, had dyed red hair and immediately we were friends. She also recognised that Paddy and I were, after all those years, now merely old comrades, demobbed from active duty. That we had now to endure the timidity of life after a band. It was also that she knew my name before I knew hers. But that was Mena. We became drinking buddies and a few months later I asked if she would manage my new group. She said yes. We didn't achieve anything, but, as far as I know, that was her start in artist representation. She went onto a career guiding bands in New Zealand, then San Francisco and New York. She now sells vintage and antique clothing and I am still awfully fond of her and her fledgling family, despite whatever difficulties we now face. Though, in truth, for the last twenty years we've seen each other perhaps a half-dozen times.

The last time was on Waiheke Island during the summer of 2018. Laura was heading to Auckland for work and unexpectedly I found a break in my schedule and so made a week of it in late January. Mena asked if I'd like to visit Waiheke Island, where she was living in a small cottage, and stay a night with her and her husband and daughter. We arranged to meet at the ferry terminal on the Wednesday morning and travel the forty minutes across the harbour. As I walked towards her, I thought of my conversation with Alin on the train fifteen months earlier. Telling her about my life in Auckland when I was twenty-four. How the two of us seemed so certain something was about to befall us.

I wrote to Alin on WhatsApp.

I'm about to get on a ferry to Waiheke. I'll tell the captain I can't swim.

She didn't write back for two weeks.

Instead, Mena arrived quite hungover in a dress that seemed five sizes too big for her. Alongside her was a bald intense man with an eastern European accent. He was, it turned out, a friend of hers from New York whose band had played the previous night at the Kings Arms. His name was Attila Csihar and I realised quite quickly he was in another band I rather liked called Sunn O))).

We spent the day at the beach, eating ice-cream and fish and chips. The beach a perfect sweep of sand, full of swimming kids and dozing parents. Attila and Mena swam, and we talked. By the afternoon we retired to Mena's rundown old cottage and sat out on the porch in the heat, Mena still wet from the swim, and Attila's jeans soaked. They talked about people they knew in New York, and I listened. Bands, musicians I knew of. The people he'd worked with, who he'd like to work with. They talked about the tour so far, and eventually I asked him how his show the previous night was.

'It was, yes, good. It was a good show, yes. Late night, very late.' And he laughed, and Mena shook her head before smiling out of her hangover.

'I was so damned pissed, David,' she said. 'I thought I'd stopped getting so, so stupid smashed, but Christ almighty.'

I remembered then that when we'd first met one of the prerequisites for being a friend of mine was to keep up with my capacity to drink. And I could drink, dangerous amounts. And so could Mena. Before Waiheke, the last time we'd seen each other we'd drunk ourselves to tears and knew something was changing. It was 2009. That was the end of it for me, of drink and the rest. There was another life to have. A writing life.

'I don't miss drinking,' I said. 'It's one of the things I don't miss.'

'Ah, well. Fuck you then,' she laughed.

'Was it packed?' I asked.

'There were mountains of beardy dudes. Sweet, scary punters, stinky dudes. Heaps just hanging after,' she said. 'You know? Just like—a really adorable vibe of old metalheads. All sweaty and gross and sweet.'

'They were really nice,' Attila said.

'Right,' I said. 'Right, I saw a crowd of them crossing Great North Road.' I had. Kids with painted faces, corpse paint, as Laura and I were heading to dinner with Kristen. I thought: *Heavy metal.* I thought: *Fucken eh. Heavy metal show*. 'I didn't realise it was you guys,' I said to Attila. Even though I'd realised by then he was kind of famous, I still didn't quite understand who he was.

He smiled. 'They're a force. They are there, everywhere in the world,' he said.

'They're the dark blood,' Mena said.

'They have my heart, yes,' Attila said.

I leaned against the railing of Mena's deck. Beyond, thick grass.

'I kinda wished I'd have come along,' I said.

'I wish you had. I've become kind of enamoured with kids who get dressed up for their favourite bands,' Mena said. 'You know what I mean?'

'They pay the money. They buy records. Get drunk. Get dressed up. They have my heart,' the Hungarian said.

His voice kind of soft, intelligent. He reminded me a little of James. Like my old friend, Attila had trained as an electrician before music altered him for good, and I imagined the two of them talking. I imagined their philosophies of science, the bicker and sweep of knowledge outside my own. But more, I heard James's excitable voice as they spoke about frequency and heavy metal. It was never my thing, though it interested me now on a theoretical level. I wanted it to be something I liked, but there were always things I struggled to get past. The showing off, the comedic posturing and words, the reliance on technique and ridiculous narratives. I preferred punk's incidental brutality, quite often a result of incompetence, of a mind keyed into the desire for noise over prearranged harmony.

Mena turned to me. 'He hung out with these kids for hours. We're talking a massive bogan contingent.'

'Ah—they come to the show. I like to hang out afterwards and talk, you know? It's part of the whole thing. The others in the band, not so much. But I like it. The fans, they remember the old stories better than we do, so it's always entertaining, hearing about your life.'

'You should have come, David,' Mena said. 'Attila does these things with his hands when he sings, it's quite . . . maybe show him, Attila.'

'It's just the show,' Attila said. 'I do these things.'

'Yes, but he does these amazing things with his hands. It's incredibly, it's a kind of, I think, both melancholic and discomforting. I don't know, a kind of demented trance. Demented isn't the right word. It's like you haunt some part of the sound, Attila, that no one else can hear. Yeah?'

'It's—thank you.'

'But the kids, they desperately want to hear it.'

'You know the hardest thing?' Attila said and started to laugh. 'The hardest thing with this band is that I never get to take a drink. I get so thirsty, but I can't take a sip of water.' He gestured with his hand to his mouth with a phantom bottle.

'I kind of understand,' I said. It always felt like it was a dereliction of duty taking a drink during a show. Like there was something I was breaking when reaching for a glass. There's something obscure in performance that doesn't wish to be disturbed.

'Attila has his face masks made by a guy in Cairo. Is that right?'

'My corpse masks, I have a man in Egypt who creates these things. It makes it very hard to drink. Also, I feel like I'd be breaking Mena's trance. I want it to all be spell.'

'I understand,' I said.

'Anyway, they were brutal,' Mena said. 'If they were a cult, the villagers would come after them with pitchforks.' She laughed. I'd always liked that she loved extreme music, its physical and mental force. She liked the bruise of noise, of hard dissonance, but also liked Fairport Convention and Pentangle. I've always found it odd, though, that there are people who know music so well but don't play. In fact, it was something that made me wonder if there was another thing wrong with me. I could barely play, never could, but was obsessed with playing music for ten years, making it on stage and recording, despite never getting anywhere. In fact, I still am. I've recorded a dozen albums never released.

'It is brutal. Yes,' Attila said, and laughed.

We spoke about some of his other projects outside of his current tour. He was sought after, an experimental vocalist who'd worked with a dozen other groups and performers. It was fascinating to listen to his plans for his solo performances, loop pedal and accents on Mongolian throat singing, which he learned back in Budapest from the lead performer in a cultural group visiting from Ulaanbaatar many years earlier. I asked if it was the end of the tour. He said, 'I fly straight home to Hungary. Auckland, Abu Dhabi, Budapest. It's going to be cold.'

I made an *argh* sound.

'You want to know how cold it is at home right now?' He pointed at his ice block and started laughing. 'It's snow everywhere. It's like this, without the sugar, lemon. Hungary is the coldest place in the universe in January. I'll do nothing for a month, and then, we'll see.'

I made a joke that he'd be in his soaked jeans for the entire flight home, that he'd freeze on impact with European airspace. *Dink*. He laughed.

We took selfies in the shallows of the rocky shore at the north end of Oneroa Beach and then he had to leave for his ferry and flight out, and it was just Mena and me.

We listened to records and tried to rehydrate in the heat. She asked if I was feeling okay. I told her for the last month I'd been feeling relatively fine. The previous year had been awful, but for the moment I was okay.

'Just say if you need to take a lie down or anything,' she said.

'You'll know when I need to take a lie down. It isn't terribly voluntary.'

She smiled at me for a long time. 'How old were you when we met?'

'I was twenty-five.'

'Twenty-five.'

'You were twenty-one,' I said.

'I was twenty-one? No wonder I don't remember. I remember jack shit.'

'We were drunk all the time, that's why we don't remember shit.'

'Drunk all the time is a good reason for not remembering,' she said and laughed. 'Isn't it? God, I'm hungover.'

'But only if you had a good time.'

'Did we have a good time, David?'

I didn't say anything for a moment, because I realised that for the first time since I'd left Auckland in 1996 the city wasn't impinging on me. I wasn't run though with unease about the place. Every time I'd visited in the last twenty-two years I found myself hurting, triggered into states of anxiety that only had one source. Heartbreak, and its invalidation of thought and action.

'Fuck, I don't know. I was wrecked when I arrived in Wellington,' I said. 'Paranoid. I would have gotten into fights had anyone let me.'

'I know.'

'Paranoid and fucked.'

'Weren't we all?'

'Yeah, but. I had nothing. Just nothing.'

She nodded. 'I never really knew what happened to you. You were just this nice guy I'd seen play who was around suddenly.'

'Wasn't I nice?'

She laughed.

'I wasn't always.'

'No, well, no one is always nice, otherwise we'd kill them. What happened?'

'I was with a girl for four years and then it fell apart. We made no attempt to fight it, just let it happen. I was very depressed during that period and after. But I'd no idea what that meant. I didn't use that word, depressed. But I was, dangerously, and I didn't have a word for it. The only way I could get to sleep at night was imagining a knife entering the back of my neck, just below my skull, as I lay down my head on the pillow. That was my strategy for sleeping. I imagined being dead. Not being dead, but dying, peacefully. Then I could sleep. Released certain endorphins that let me relax.'

'And you used to sleep with the light on,' she said.

'Yeah, always. How did you know that?'

'I crashed at your place once and the light was on all night and I asked you about it the next day and you told me you couldn't sleep in the dark. I thought it was funny.'

'I mean, of course it's funny,' I said. 'But, yeah, I couldn't sleep with the light off. It was a tricky means of fooling myself. I wasn't actually trying to sleep. I was just saying to myself I was having a lie down.'

'Smart.'

'And then the knife thing, and maybe I'd sleep.'

She paused for a long while and I lay down with my head on some pillows she'd pulled out onto the deck. 'Tell me about your heart attack,' she said.

'You want to hear about my heart attack?'

She shrugged. 'Sure.'

'I was reading a book, that was it, then bang.'

'Bang.'

'Not *bang*. More like: *I need to lie down.* That was me having a heart attack.'

'That's scary, David.' She watched me, looking for some kind of confirmation. She sounded close to these words—that these were the words she was supposed to say—but there was also something else she wanted to express.

I said, 'A little scary. But I didn't really feel any worse than I do normally, so.'

'Still. I don't like it.' She was looking at the gate that led to the car park. I realised then she was thinking about her daughter, the time of day, the coming of evening and how she'd organise the family. 'Tell me one more thing. Were you in danger?'

'You mean, from the heart attack? Was I in danger of dying?'

She nodded.

'No. Not at all. But it made me very sick. Only a month ago was I able to get out of the house again. No. People make a big deal of these things, but really, really I'm in far greater danger of dying because of despair. Of having enough of being sick. It's far more dangerous than a measly heart attack.'

'What's it like, I wonder.'

'Dying?'

'Aha.'

And I told her.

Path

By 1995, Rachel was living in Potsdam, a large apartment near the university. The building it sat within was a quarter-of-a-millennium old, with a view to the Templiner See. People stood outside on the street with cameras and guidebooks, gazing up at the building's ancient window boxes and summoning architecture. This was a survivor of bombing and fire, of the Prussian purge and unification; it was also where, after two years of stability, Rachel became seriously ill for the second time. The first wave—if we can use such language for the disease—hit while she was living in Wellington in the early Nineties. It faded just enough after four years that she was able to journey to Europe and see friends made during earlier travels, people who would put her up for days or weeks. She met Gretchen and Jim, Gretchen's white-coated kuvasz, in Paris when Gretchen was an intern.

They fell in. Two doubters who discounted truth in the conversations around the dinner table where they'd share bread, cheese and meats. Their voices ranging, adding a new beauty to the world as they talked of cities, of summer and love and its incompatibility with so much. They moved into Gretchen's house together after her internship in Paris was done, and in the winter they'd huddle in the same bed, fearful of the cold's murderous clutch. During the spring Gretchen made the decision to renovate the apartment with the money she'd received from her deceased grandparents. Death money, she'd called it. Made during the war, made during the exploitation, the punishment of the skeletal who roamed the country at the end of a rifle. Probably, she added, admitting she didn't know for sure.

Men came, measured and left. Secret conversations with space, with walls and stairwell. The first architects came, and Gretchen quickly fired them. She became intent on doing the design herself. She'd sit up late at night after long hours at the hospital and draw and cross out. Redraw, and stare at corners of a room, willing it into a new shape. She hired a series of builders to begin work on her design. From the first moment, Gretchen had issues dealing with these professionals. She believed, she'd tell Rachel late at night, that they were intent on destroying all her ideas, that they'd be single-mindedly determined to undermine her plans for the apartment. She'd cry and lie awake at night pondering, changing the sketches in her mind. The builders' destruction of her ideas, she believed, was at the behest of their belief that all was theirs to manipulate and confiscate. Rachel believed her friend had lost her reasoning in the gathering tensions. Indeed, Gretchen gave the builders only one part of the plan at a time. Rachel wrote to her family in postcards, saying it appeared that her friend had slipped the bonds of sanity. The contractors never had an idea of what they were building, where they were building to. Gretchen had the idea that she should leave each thought and the idea in its isolated cell until it reached the utmost degree of realisation, that perfection had been touched. Think how many, she'd say, will go on to live off our idea, the idea we had, if we'd share it all in any moment before its realisation. That ancient Potsdam mansion was a palace originally, then a warehouse. Then bombed in the war. Local royalty, three hundred years of them. Then Rachel and Gretchen, they lived in a construction site, the hard-hatted men coughing in the dust and heat. Partitions smashed through, lungs straining against the chant of hammers and saws. A hole sat untended in the exterior wall for a month while the contractors were on strike about something. Dust in everything. It was summer, but the winds. God, the winds. The constant flapping of the tarpaulins. Despite Gretchen's belief in her methods, there was a storm and the tarps were torn away and replaced by wind and rain.

Rachel found an excitement in this existence, the caffeinated stream of days that twisted about them, the voiced exhalations of builders staring at incomplete, always altered plans. Humans blocked from their purpose by a young doctor certain of her method. And the dust in her eyes and her skin. Rachel didn't want to go back to New Zealand. But the dust and powder of old mortar, of moths, thousands of moths and insects. Gretchen insisted they live there, that it would make something of their scepticism, break it or make it a new defiant truth. They instead became a continual argument. Always modifying their retorts, redefining the terms of aggression. It was impossible for outsiders, for the builders, and for themselves to tell where the two of them and the argument began. And Rachel became ill during the third month of turmoil. She woke on the morning of the 27th of September 1994 after falling asleep during a horrible storm. Gretchen was in Austria, a mini break by a lake with Jim the dog, and Rachel was on her own. The house was soaked, water running though, and she couldn't get up. She was on the couch, and her clothes were in a pile beside her as a wind shredded the plastic holding back the weather. She didn't remember undressing, but she was naked and freezing and couldn't move. She was covered in dust, trembling. Everything covered in debris, the carpets and walls. It was like a kidnapping, Rachel said much later, but inverted. And as she'd said these words to her husband, she learnt how this was Gretchen's idea of precision. Her friend's idea of perfection. This whole thing. It was her idea for the two of them. That in the process of constructing this apartment, they would be led to an exactness, as people.

'What does that mean?' I asked.

'I don't know. Just that we'd be amended by all our efforts. Made whole,' Rachel said.

It was then that we stood slowly and made steps back along the beach.

Laura and I had come to Isola and Cratere in June, the trains and ferry across the strait. I'd stood on the deck in the sun, the glow so bright all colours seemed to withdraw and contract. We'd come to stay with Rachel while Steffen looked after an old friend in Frankfurt, a soul who'd developed dementia in his late sixties. A memory like those hues, each retreating from the now's bewildered brilliance. That was four summers after the first wave had caught, killed, shuddered and quit after three years. When it woke again, each of us became an island among islands, and this island, Isola della Scogliera Rossa, became an island a dozen times over as the holding measures went into place on the mainland. Cratere was cut off, no one allowed on or off the island. Only supplies came in. I tried not to look for the mainland wedged in the horizon, tried not to recall how it was there. Instead, I kept the dark glow of Rachel's brown hair in my periphery as we walked.

'And I left,' Rachel said as we stepped around boulders. 'I crawled through the soaked apartment in a robe. I left everything and called a cab and drove to Gretchen's mother's house. I arrived and her mum didn't understand that something had happened to me. I didn't understand either. Her parents had seen many things, but not this. The first time I got sick I hid it from everyone, like you do when you're young. The second time, David, I just couldn't. And then I returned to Christchurch and New Zealand and everything. Europe was over. Even as I sit here now it feels like a ghost, running between my various minds. I wouldn't trust Gretchen—maybe I would with my life, but not with my living arrangements. But she was fun.'

I turned and looked out at the boats, how simple they seemed sitting in the water, each an idea, drifting out of focus in the heat. Kids playing at volume, the echo of them in the saplings behind us.

I paused at a large tree trunk we hadn't noticed earlier. 'What?' I asked.

'The kids,' Rachel said.

One of them was filming us.

'Are they allowed to do that?' I asked.

The boat from the mainland was there for the coves, for the sense that all was right with the world. Two teenagers scanning the beach from the deck seventy yards out. They'll be fined when they return to Genoa.

Rachel sat on the log at the join where branches once separated.

'They can do what they like, as long as they don't come within a hundred metres.'

I turned so I was facing the cliffs behind us, trying to imagine what they were filming. The island had its city, it had its sea-dazzled villages perched on stone levelled out of the rock. It had its scattering of ruins, of ageless streets crooked through the sculptured stone boxes, it had its money-machines and restaurants, it had its shades of blue that had been painted on the walls of every home since the end of the war, a marker of grave intent. Endless lines of washing waved at the scented sea. Terraces trimmed in white where the besotted stood and watched the distance, the rise and blast of Kónos's vents issuing to the sky raw signals only the future can untangle. The people who lived off the fishing boats, off crafts and pottery, off the ships that came with tourists, off the museum's funding, off scooter rental and the letting of rooms, of houses to people like Laura and me. There was an English language bookshop, second-hand and new. On a shelf near the door, the spine of my wife's first book could be spotted among other literary offerings with the same last initial and when you opened the door you appeared sudden in the rush of the city's main boulevard, the haze of exhaust in your nostrils and shouted conversations somewhere between your eyes and ears. Locals in cryptic exchange. Fingers pointing and laughter outside the miniature churches that lined the opposite side of the road above the port. The way the streets bent up and away, hiding their contents from view. There the True evaded the sightlines of seekers such as us, pushing out the shopfronts that begged we take the potters' and weavers' simulated neolithic wares as the face of the true city—while the city at your back, the one hidden off the tendrils of the twisting streets, lurked silent, pretending nothing, observing all. And there, there within was a mania, a specific malady amongst a percentage of Isola's population you couldn't see in a lens, a skittering desire to escape and enter the skin of the plaque.

At first the city's madness was wrought out in dance, in mass dances, streets filled with music-less parades of women and men, day and night jigging. Then a week of suicides, then the madness of youth and elderly bonds, peculiar unions across the island. Old friends marrying, first kisses walking into bright chapels, florets held at breasts. Then the onlookers, desperate for something to bond each vision to the Great Memory. Cobblestones and sleeping under the stars. Work shirts and aspirin. Cogito ergo sum and baskets of wheat. Wind shifts, and that first taste of coriander, of espresso, the one that altered your take on a certain music at sixteen; the colour of granite and the way your father used to walk, that certain gait that made you believe there's something about the deep past, the way it ricochets around the genes till it lands in your muscles, fomenting that one ache; five people standing at a lookout, the bled white sky and the eerie scenes of family dead dancing their minds; the shapes, the faces, the arms and limbs caught in obsidian, and the endpoint of a dirt road you took the summer before last because you liked the way it bent off the narrow-hipped highway near Lake Tekapo; cities you've spoken of for hours longer than you ever spent within their walls, and the one time you went to church with an open mind; Diamond Harbour and the rubber soles of shoes that you bought in Palermo and still wear; the sad fusion of land and awakening statehood; Potsdam, the child wriggling wild in my ancestor's womb, Potsdam and an ever-widening hole in the wall of an apartment shaking with the wind, a stretched open mouth breathing life into my cousin's sickness. *The insanity of time*, I start to say, I start to say, *the insanity of time, of its desire to be something else other than years and seconds*. I start to say.

'But you know, David, I forgave her in the end. It's possible to forgive. We learn this, don't we?'

'Gretchen?'

'Yeah. And I think perhaps I forgave her because after two years, she finally finished the work. I have photographs that prove it. Photographs prove everything if you grant them that power.'

I turned and watched the teens filming us. I smiled and felt us wave. The young woman with her iPhone, the lens dreaming of our forever place in those vast vaults of time, the creatureless data centres and earthbound clouds. And in that gesture, that effortless wave, something seemed to vanish—we were overcome with invisibility.

'What do you find yourself scared of, like, if you ever get scared?' I asked.

She bunched her shoulders. 'Just being scared really. I'm scared of being scared. I'm scared also that when I die people will want to know what I went through. That scares me, that all this and nobody will know how hard, just how hard. You?'

'I'm scared that I'll never finish this book. That it'll be published and I still haven't finished it.' I stood up as I said this, and the log shifted. 'I don't know what this will mean. And I'm scared of that.' For a moment I stood in silence. Birds darted from the trees behind us as Rachel stood beside me.

'What are you thinking about?' she asked, then said it herself. 'The path?'

I nodded.

'Yeah,' she said.

Some hours before, we'd stood on the side of the road that tours the outer extents of the island and stared down into the gully. From there, at the top of the trail, you could see the desert on the far side of the cones, but we didn't look in their direction, just downwards. We waited entire minutes in the heat, wondering if we should save the journey for another day, or just step off. All along the island there were plaques stating the events and their tragic sources. I was taken with the printed plate that commemorated the end of Isola della Scogliera Rossa's resistance. It read:

Seppellire lassù in montagna
Sotto l'ombra di un bel fior
Questo è il fiore del partigiano
Morto per la libertà

It was on this road that a quick battle had broken out between the factions, the invisible politics that construed the small, determined army defending the city and shores. Death and blood, red on the cobblestones. It was halted by a woman and her beau, and it is to them the words were dedicated. Now couples raced past on mopeds and bikes, oblivious. I read it quietly out loud as I stood there, my voice in pieces. I finished and glanced down the track, the chasm that led to the Bay of Mouths. My hair felt hot. I could feel the sun put its burn into my skin. And while staring down I saw movement, a sudden family stepping through the shadows and cracked stairs towards us. A woman, a man and a toddler. To let them pass I stepped back onto the road, and instantly there was noise—a Volvo honking violently, and the voice of the driver. Everything seemed a bright red. Red and removed and real. The bumper, the car's bumper hissed by my right leg. It missed and it didn't miss. There was noise and colour and it seemed, it seemed to pass right through me, through my knees and legs. I shouted, gave a shriek. Several extra honks. It seemed to pass right through me, but it didn't. I felt my heart, sensed the nearness of the vehicle's bumper, just this whisper of hot wind and specks of dirt on my knees and calves. It was horrid. I turned back to my cousin and the couple. *Almost there*, Rachel said quietly as the car decelerated. Her voice seemed slow. A heavy blood shifted through me. I continued to feel it: the car or some part of the car, the machine, enter my bones and muscle, then exit, tear out of my skin. I felt the whole wash of my history and how simple it was to bring it up, how guileless it was as it vanished. People, their lives, gone. Laura was there and not there, and I was suddenly terrified.

You're almost there, Rachel said to the family.

It was a Volvo, no passengers. I'd felt it hit my leg, then felt how my knee crumpled, but didn't. We heard the couple panting, chortling as the car's brake lights lit up. The couple saying: *You don't want to do this.* Saying: *If it weren't for little Cillian, we'd still be down there building a shelter, becoming locals selling—I don't know. What would we sell, Lorcan? Selling cockleshell necklaces for a sun-sick cult of sunbathers.* They were laughing, hot-faced and damp from exertion. *If you go down, make sure you have a backup plan. Or a helicopter, it's fucking—abyss.* The woman's voice went up at the end and I knew she had no idea that they'd seen us before. Then, as Rachel started to explain about the boats, another voice interrupted. The man in the car yelled a local variation of *arsehole* my way. It was horrible.

The glistening woman asked what had happened, and the car started off again, bumping into the distance. She picked up her toddler. The boy wrapped his legs about her hips as she touched my shoulder. I said I got called an arsehole for almost getting killed. An idiot-oso, driving a whatever. The woman wiped sweat off her boy's face and stared in the direction of the car. *He almost hit you?* I held up my thumb and forefinger. Then squeezed them to nothing so the space between the layers of skin were inseparable from light. Everything felt inseparable from everything but light. The woman wiped at her own face, pale as if resistant to tanning. The boy twisted. I managed to smile and as I smiled I caught the little boy's eye. He stared at me for a long moment as if he recognised me, or the space around me. Then he curled into his mother's arm, his hand in her hair. The woman started saying something, but she was interrupted. The Volvo had turned and was driving slowly towards us. The driver with his head out the window, staring at me. The sound of engine and exhaust as he accelerated and the car raced up the north end of the saddle. Tire noise and we all watched him go. Again, I felt something brush against my leg, like air was whispering in the space between moments, distant and close moments. The gap between belief and after belief.

We only went on once it felt like there was some distance between seconds. Finally, after we'd said goodbye to the family and begun the trek downwards, I started talking. We sat on the log and I told Rachel it felt as if time had been squeezed into a single instant. One of all pain, all delight, all colour and everything that constantly turns invisible. We stepped down the anfractuous path, the one we should never take but take just the same.

'We should go,' Rachel said again.

We started to move away from the tree trunk and felt it roll backwards as a band of rain hit the ridge to our right, sudden. I glanced at the boat. The teens stared at the rain, confused.

'I thought,' Rachel said, watching the rain, 'that when I went back to Potsdam something would be altered in me. I kind of hoped for it, you know, David. I hoped seeing the house completed would change something in me. We wish for things and . . . instead I went there and all I felt was anger at all the change. I was furious. It was only later that I realised I wanted the apartment to be exactly the same as when I'd left. I wanted a dingy little museum to myself. Or something. Instead it was full of light and a polite mixture of new and old things. It was the politeness, I guess, that made me furious.'

'We could hollow this out if you want. Make a canoe,' I said, and tapped the log with a stone. It responded in a surprisingly musical timbre, a note from a harmony left here long ago.

The Kids

I told Mena how, years earlier, while with friends in Grey Lynn just before I left Auckland, I'd stayed up late. I could be panicked easily by the way friends interacted. The way people talked. The way they joked with me. As if making a joke would somehow ease my panic. Jokes don't work that way; they become cruel, forcing you to hunt for the thing that's impossible at that moment, which is happiness. That drug has been dragged out of you. And here were people, and they had no clue, no knowledge of what I was incapable of at specific moments. We were inside. My friends were drinking, and I went outside in the rain. They were saying: *Buck up*. They were saying: *Let's drink.* I went out into the rain in bare feet because it was summer and I sat down in an old chair. I said I just needed air. I sat for the longest time, breathing. Breathing in and out. A cycling of rapid inhales and exhales. I thought, *I can do this. I can do this right now. Just by breathing, just by letting the life out of me.*

'I told myself to die,' I said to Mena. 'To shut down and die. So, I did.'

'Fucken eh.'

'Yeah.'

'We don't have to talk about this,' Mena said. 'We can talk about other things.'

'No, it's okay. It's interesting.'

'Yeah.'

'First my tongue. This is how I did it. First my tongue. It seemed to get really big in my mouth, then the thing started to push out between my lips. Soon the whole of my tongue was protruding. I felt things start to turn off. You see, I believed I could just kill myself with active thought. The muscle of my tongue getting huge in my mouth. Then my eyes, bulging. I was grotesque in the rain. Hideous. My eyesight went first, then I stopped hearing. I was excited, for the first time in months. My heart was racing. I was excited and I was going to die just by thinking about it. A pain in my chest—I was going to burst my heart out, was how it felt. And my head, my head was pounding. This is desire. This is the work of desire. Thoughts were slowly harder to come by and I had only the one thought: *Keep going.* And I did. I kept trying to push the life out of me because I was sick of living, sick of being sick. Exhausted from the fight. And because the fight, because it's so damned physical.'

'Jesus, David.'

'But—and of course there's a but—something intervened. Something pushed its way to the surface. I realised how much further I had to go to make this thing happen. How much pain I was about to go through. I realised it was huge, a cascade of tearing and breaking as everything switched off. So. And life felt suddenly enormous. A mass of deep physical energies. Colossal. An extraordinary thing to overcome, to beat with your mind and teeth and mouth and tongue and whatever else I was trying to do. It was too much, too big. Life was too big.

Instead, I turned everything back on. One by one. Gradually I heard my feet standing in the rain, the micro movements, the crunch sound of wet grass.'

'You think you could've?' Mena asked.

'That's pain, if you want it. I know I could've. It's not a doubt I have. I felt like a, like a faltering hydroelectric plant. Manned by white-coated lab technicians. Studiously watching dials.' I laughed.

'How can you laugh?' But she knew why, and asked, 'Why'd you stop?'

'Human momentum, I guess. The complexity of physical being, how hard it is to stop once it's going.'

'And now?'

'Now it's years later and we're talking about it,' I said. 'You're the only person I've told this to.'

'Really?'

'I'm too relaxed.'

'Waiheke's doing it for you.'

'It was just before I left Auckland, so just before I met you. Also . . . I stopped because I knew how much pain I would have had to endure to get the job done.'

'. . .'

'I have this sense, Mena, that I could have another heart attack just by summoning up the will. It's strange, but it doesn't leave.'

'What doesn't?'

'The sense that I can die just by thinking about it.'

We fell into silence. I thought about a few of the people I used to know in Auckland, lived with or otherwise. Some I stayed in contact with, some drifted off and I heard stories of them occasionally, others still vanished. Some died stupid deaths. James told me that one of them, Richard Lyon, died with a needle in his arm as he shot up at a friend's house. Kids running about his feet as they went cold. He was someone I was really close to, then that closeness vanished, then he was dead. I could never figure out what that meant. I looked at Mena, wondered if she'd ever come across him. I had a sense then that her daughter was due home, that we couldn't keep our conversation going in this mode for much longer. She started taking the washing in off the line, the hardened swimsuits and underwear.

'How'd you meet Cliff?' I asked.

'It's so long ago.'

'Yeah, but—'

'His band, of course. He's minorly famous.'

'Sure, of course.'

'They were on tour and I did some shows for them. He's super cute under his beard. It's insane how many people I've met just from shows. Hundreds and hundreds, and I'm supposed to remember them all, yeah? So many. Same with Attila, he's another cat out of the blue. I know half the universe and who cares? Do you know what I mean?'

'Maybe.'

'I love them all, but sometimes it's really damned hard, you know? Loving people is hard when there's just so fucking many. That's why we moved back here.'

'Really?'

'I don't know,' she said. She was distracted. Her daughter was due home, and something in me deeply wanted to see her, just to see Mena with her daughter, to see her being a mum. I've always loved watching those I feel closest to loving those they love. Something deeply affirming in the whole act. Eventually she said, 'You know about Mayhem, right?'

'Mayhem?'

'Who was playing last night. Attila's band. Or the band he works for. I'm not entirely sure of the arrangement.'

I shook my head and showed my teeth in mock mortification. I'd had no idea what the band was called. I had been too embarrassed to ask.

'You probably know about them,' she said. 'They're from,' and she slowed right down, 'Nor—way.' She squinted a little, and then, as she saw I was nodding, she too started nodding.

'Fuck,' I said quietly.

'The whole, you know, the whole black metal thing. The whole—'

'I know about *stuff*,' I said, and I too was slowing down, each word. 'Everyone knows about Norwegian *stuff*, right? In Norway. I know about one—one band.'

She kept nodding.

'That was Mayhem?' *Mayhem.*

'The whole, the singer killed himself shit. Guitarist murdered by bass player. Arson. Insane as fuck brutal fuck me in the mouth Satanic metal. That's Attila's band. Dead. Necrobutcher. Hellhammer.'

Oh.

'Jesus *and* Christ.'

'You heard them?'

I shook my head. 'Not really. I just always thought it would be silly.'

She shook her head. 'No, it's. It's fucking great.' She stared at me. 'Okay.' Mena ran inside to get her laptop and we sat on the porch watching live footage of the band until her daughter got home. They were prodigious, a kind of dissonant drone forced out by dual vibrato guitars, massively heavy with blast-beat drums against the slow charge of the chord progressions. I'd never heard anything like it. James used to try and get me to listen to this when we went out on tour, but I was devotedly anti-metal, immune to its posturing and infantile lyrics. The lyrics were still infantile but masked by Attila's extraordinary penumbral whispering and grunts. The invocations of the dead.

And, and the things he did with his hands, tiny, subtle movements, quick and random like movement glimpsed from another space and time entirely. Or we were glimpsing into another space, one where life is much like dying.

The Forms

The two of them stepping down through the layers of the museum. Key cards and doors opening to sucking sounds of new air pressures. Time, and it goes so slow here. They come out into the light. A veranda sidles around the west side of the building.

'So,' Gretchen says. 'The contemporary wing. We go in, yes? And through.'

'It's beautiful.'

'Yes, a kind of beauty—stupid money gets its own kind of beauty.'

They're rushing, striding through doors, stairs downwards. Laura's knees ache but there is little she can do. On they walk, the dog's claws slipping and scraping on the floor. They head down through the museum's internal layers, doors and short-tailed vistas into the exhibits and time, and then the flickered fluorescent lights of the halls and stairwells, and she can't help sense, sense and think of time. Broken time, and the power of a foreign city to make you talk, because time.

'Are you okay?' Gretchen asks.

'Yes.'

'You seem, you're limping.'

'Yeah. It's okay. It's just a thing.' Just a thing. Just a thing. She thinks of the final lockdowns when this really had become a thing. A kind of invisible crisis of trust as her memory turned to vapour and she became, she became very small with pained limbs. She found her various selves, the state of their self-knowledge, shrunken and isolated. It was an unreported violence. It took time for David to notice, far too long, and what was there he could have done?

'Everybody and their things,' Gretchen says. 'If something's wrong, just tell me.'

'. . .'

'Because I'm not perfect, but I worry about everyone,' Gretchen says. 'Which isn't much of a cure, I know.'

'Thank you.' Thank you, and Laura wonders if our loves are always hurting the most because we feel them the most. She wonders too if madness catches. If the two of them caught it half-living in the same house, the months of it. She feels a lone fragment of him in her body, in the sharpness of hurt that kicks up through her knees, and she imagines his legs and torso bent at queer angles.

'You know, there was a time,' Gretchen says, looking over her shoulder, 'in which I didn't really believe Rachel, that she was truly—sick? I rather dislike myself sometimes. She had outrageous symptoms and, well, something in me just couldn't believe her. I thought she was an actor and we were in a terrible film. I came to realise I was just protecting myself. That it was easier not to believe. That her weight loss, God, and verbal incoherence and pain, that if there was a voluntary aspect to her symptoms, that meant it could be stopped. I'm guilty of that. I told her once.'

'How did that go?'

'She was furious. *How?* she asked. *Can you tell me? How can a person act pain like that?* And it was horrid. We were both hurt awfully that day. We came back from it.'

'I'm sorry.'

'So, that's why I'm asking if you're okay. It's important that I ask.'

'Thank you.'

Gretchen shrugs. She nods slowly as she walks on, and as she walks she suggests that perhaps there's something in comparing the bodies of the ill with actors. 'Not actors swanning at home, but those in action, in a play or film fighting, fighting to become *body*.' She uses air quotes and hard emphasis. 'That in the act of performance they'll overcome their own body and become the realised *body* of—but then I think the only people who truly know *body* are those who are leaving it behind. The dying, maybe. Or someone like Rachel, I don't know. Suddenly I get angry at actors, that they've no right. Maybe that's why I gave up being a doctor. There's no room for fiction in medicine.'

'I don't think that's true,' Laura says. 'Fiction's everywhere in practice.'

Gretchen chortles.

Doors, windows, then just doors.

'It's just up ahead,' the assistant says. Laura hadn't noticed him until now. He'd joined them invisibly on the stairs as they twisted slowly down the layers of the building.

Laura finds herself talking, telling Gretchen how several years earlier in Shanghai she'd taken David in a wheelchair from gate to gate. Before departure, he'd been ill in bed for days and didn't know if he could fly. But fly they did, and though he was much better once they cleared the New Zealand airspace, they thought it safest to take the wheelchair. Laura pushed him through the airport queues and kept banging into knees and shins. She explained they never knew when David could walk. Or, more precisely, never knew what the effect of walking would be on his body at a later time. He hadn't wanted to find himself extremely sick on the flight to Zürich, so Laura pushed him through the queues. It was precautionary, she tells Gretchen, as much as David was incapacitated.

Gretchen nods, glancing back at her.

Because she was pushing a wheelchair, nobody seemed to mind. She wasn't in control of its momentum, just banging into them with the footrest and so on. No one seemed to care. 'I suspect there was a level of pity, or concern,' Laura suggests. 'When a wheelchair is involved, there is little choice. You become kinda invisible.'

'It's the collective fear of the disabled.'

'Something like that. But also, this was an act.' David could walk; he chose not to because of what *might* come later, because of what had gone on in the days before. But the wheelchair, it signified malady. People would've been furious if they had known, would've felt duped. He was a sick person acting out a potential future moment. 'It was a performance.'

'The true threat of most people isn't what they do, but their lack of empathy,' Gretchen says. 'That's the cruellest thing.'

They re-enter the building, dark then light, and down further, further until the sun is replaced by iridescent bulbs spaced at even measures. The dog, the assistant and Gretchen stride hurriedly in front, their shoes tapping on steel stairs. Then the basement and a workman's door. A short passage and a curtain. The assistant pulls it back. Tugs at it to reveal another room curtained off from the rest. The drape to the light is shut and they're in a dimly lit hall. An airlock between spaces. A light-lock. The next curtain is pulled open. All in front of them is impossibly blank. Forms vague in a space made hopelessly invisible by the previous room, its total intensity. Laura battles, trying to see through the eidetic dark, until an image of an image ranges out of the dim. She feels a hard, absolute panic. It's the lack of reflecting surfaces, the absence of grasping patterns, and now what feels like the muscles of her heart, they begin constricting, tightening till her blood feels full of tiny, enraged cells fighting nothing. All as if without light there's no thought and no body.

Stone.

The glisten of stone now, as if wet—not wet with water but a material that imitates a memory of water, how it runs and collects and freezes. It's stone, or a kind of stone, the emergence of obsidian and all its frightened black, and she stops when she sees it—them. The cinder people, as they'd come to be known, grotesquely and inaccurately known.

'Should have turned the lights on. Sorry,' the assistant says from the corner where he is bent over a switchboard.

'And, yes, this is it,' the curator says. 'I thought you'd like to—I'm never sure which verb is appropriate. See, not see? Observe?'

"Thank you,' Laura says.

Thank you.

Five human figures, bent and curious and huddled and wretched. A family of farmers caught out in the open, a clutch of Neolithic souls instantly fixed in a hail of hot ash, fallen in a cruel rain from the rage of Kónos then submerged in black lava from the last of the living volcanoes. Here they are in half-form, an inversion of them. The four-thousand-year-old rock which froze about their remains. Held them there in imperfect animation, and then, as their remnants decomposed and vanished over time, the shape of them hung on, sealed inside the glistening rock.

'They often strike me as beautiful,' the curator says. 'Then I'm horrified. I come in here at odd moments and see what I guess is pain, then I see the flawlessness of their absolute rage. I vacillate between these interpretations.' Laura senses the woman looking at her as she moves about the darkness, glancing at the black glass then back to where Laura's eyes remain fixed on the forms. 'Perhaps I have to give in at some point,' Gretchen continues, 'admit that it is neither and I have yet to find the correct set of words. It's like I want to help them, but something in me that I don't believe in is stopping me. I hate that we haven't yet found an adequate name for them, but this is—'

The assistant explains the provenance and discovery of the figures. In autumn 1944, a young captain in the resistance was returning from a day fishing off the coast near Cala Fico, on the west side of the island. The boat was her new responsibility after escaping the mainland, where she had helped organise the factory strikes in the north. Here she was a piscator, fishing in the peace of the big blue. She was coming into the cove where she often anchored her vessel and slept under a tarp. She heard a shuffling, then a muted roar. She turned and saw dust rising off the nearby cliff face. A post-rains avalanche, dumping a ton of soil from the hillside. The avalanche stopped. Curious, she took her boat close to where the cliff entered the sea. That was when she saw what seemed to be a perfect profile of a face peering out of the rock. And not just a face but a neck and a torso and an arm. The rock had cracked open, split along the median line of a woman's body, held in old black glass.

She kept the secret for decades, until she was in her nineties. She finally told a great-grandniece about the faces in the cliff. The story came out with many other tales of her months as a resistance fighter. It almost got lost until the niece was on a boat with friends and she remembered and they found the spot and light glanced out of the cliffside.

They stay at the exhibit for a long moment, one which Laura feels she needs to break out of, run, sprint from, but she can't. Neither the curator nor the assistant seems immune to the stare of the inverted figures. The exhibition is yet to receive an official appellation. Archaeologists and PR consultants shouting over the boardroom table till they are silenced by the return. The Return. Eighty-three dead. The virus, harrowing its way through the population until silent. The germ famously-mysteriously vanishing from the island: smoke, opium fume, a tiger zipping into its camouflage. Twenty-two imprisoned for trying to gain access to Isola's, a three-mast boat gliding in the merciless night quiet.

Laura's eyes catch on the light and at times the faces and bodies seem to bulge outwards, casting humanly rendered shapes into the room. The adult and adolescents in terror, the child with a rent face, a serene scream filled with ash. Then they retreat into their cavities, terrified and suddenly alone. And in these moments, she realises it is impossible for them to leave the island. And not just the island, but the account of the island.

Exhaustion runs through her. A crippling weight of tiredness as the faces look back at her and through her.

'People go to where they were discovered,' Gretchen says. 'Go to where the woman found them. They pray. Chant phrases. They make the site somehow—there's something calming in this. I've been going there myself, in the last weeks. Just to see what makes them return. The problem with knowing things like the past, like having all your history written down, is it mucks with time. It completely messes with it. This here is isolated memory. It's troubling, so we make generalisations about it when we talk, which is what makes this job so hard.'

They head through other exhibition spaces. They point and mention specifics, but Laura doesn't stop and look, she only wants to depart the museum now and find where the boat will come in. She feels cloistered, trapped by the size of the place, by the vision of those people caught in glass. Souls so close to being real they're beyond the hone of bone and rock.

'They were duped, but also right,' Laura says.

'Sorry?' Gretchen says.

'At the airport in Shanghai.'

'. . .'

'I was essentially an actor, speaking of actors. I was pushing him through the crowd as they parted.' It was strangely revelatory, she explains as the assistant turns the lights off. The way the crowd of travellers moved in unison as if they all were experiencing something higher than that moment, lost to something larger than simple observation. 'But there's an irony to this,' Laura says.

'Always ironies.'

'I, I had a migraine. I had to stop to vomit. He didn't know but I had a migraine and I left him in the concourse and went to the toilets and vomited. Then, then I had to find some water and it was—urgh—it was warm, like swimming-pool warm, lukewarm. Which didn't help. So I was sick, pushing someone who was capable of walking.'

'Yes.'

'And I just felt so rotten.'

Gretchen makes a low noise. 'And despite it all,' she says, 'sometimes we become invisible despite our better acts.'

'Tell me about it.'

Thieves

That night Mena, Cliff and their daughter slept in a tent in the long grass so I could use their bed. The cottage was tiny and this, it seemed, was the most obvious solution to the issue of size. And as they went off to sleep I stayed up, reading about everything I placed at the head of this narrative—the screeds about Mayhem and the arson, murder and Dead. I read interviews and articles and watched video after video on YouTube, including the murderer's own channel. The deep history of Odin worship, the juvenilia of Satanism. Nationalism. Fascism. The hype, and the band's recovery, which ultimately brought fame and respect, both musically and institutionally; national music awards for their extraordinary fourth album *Ordo Ad Chao*. For the hundredth time in this story, I didn't sleep. I shifted restlessly in the voluminous heat. I thought of Attila, how he'd replaced Pelle, taken over from Dead, and in doing so somehow repudiated the young man's act of negation. I thought of Attila pointing at his ice block and how calmly he'd walked the beach as the waves ate at the shore. I suddenly had so many things to ask him, so many things to tell.

In the evening we'd walked down to the shore with Mena's husband and daughter, and barbecued meat on the gas-powered grill the council provide for beachgoers. Pork sausages, lamb and chicken, smoke rising off fat. The cries of children at the edge of the sibilant sea, where they swam and pushed one another down.

I found myself telling Mena about that car journey south with James twenty-three years earlier. I told her about being caught at the side of the road in the heavy cold. How I still didn't know what town we'd been in.

'Sometimes,' she said, 'when I was on tour in the States, places would just appear out of the darkness and then they'd go. They just appear and disappear. Whole cities.'

'Yeah.'

For years, Mena drove bands around the great swollen provinces in the name of punk rock and never once was she driving legally. She didn't have a driver's licence of any sort and didn't get one until she returned to New Zealand.

'Once I was on tour with some cats from this other band, you know. And I got us lost driving somewhere in Pennsylvania. This was before Cliff and I moved to Nazareth, and I really didn't know what I was doing, driving around in the winter. We came across this place called Blackwell. Just a nothing town with a few shops and half of them closed and whatnot. I remember how we watched this old dude in denim dungarees playing his guitar in front of a bodega on the corner. The singer from the band, Joseph, he watched the old guy from the back as we went slowly by, just unable to turn away, you know? Despite not being able to hear him, Joseph watched the man hammer out his song and then, then he started in singing, his voice matching the rhythm of the man's, halting but smooth and flowing. He knew what the guy was singing just by looking. That was something beautiful to watch. And we watched until he was out of reach, and Joseph continued on, serenading the shop fronts and empty windows. He had a beautiful voice when he wasn't screaming.'

'That's kinda beautiful.'

'Yeah, exactly. But that was around the time this guy, Joseph, he started seeing things. He started seeing his brother who'd, I don't know, just—he started hearing from him at night and stuff. Joseph was a dark soul, but beautiful. I don't know, I love these people, but. Anyway, it was kind of creepy, hearing about it.'

'. . .'

'People talking about twins always makes me, I don't know. You know?'

'Started hearing him, how?' I ask.

'I don't know exactly. Not sleeping, kinda fucked-up visions. They were doing lots of speed and they all got weird, if I'm honest. Anyway, then the road went angling into these old hills and I was really lost.' She said how the odd building leaned in the afternoon. There a fence and a gate, there a jackalope mount leaning against a fence, and they all stared as they went by. By then, Mena said, they were all singing, repeating six lines over and over. They sang at horses, beautiful auburn things walking slowly at the horizon. Signs and then signs. Then the next sign and it was for the dumpy old highway. Joseph reached over and ruffed up Mena's hair. She drove them down the long twists and cracks, wondering how you christen something when it's never the same, never repeated except in some crude simulation.

'So, the ghosts of implied authenticity,' I said, then laughed.

'Yeah, something like that,' she said. Eventually they saw smoke, a mile or two out from the town they thought they were looking for. Smoke shifting sideways through those old trees. They expected to see a crowd, a truck or fire appliance. There was no one, just an old store half burnt out. Mena stopped the van and opened the door for Joseph and the others. They woke up and stepped out, saying nothing. She led them around the van to the store.

'Half the siding had burnt out, and we could see inside. It took a minute for us to go in. There were burst cans and cracked preserving jars. Melted bags of potting soil. Vegetables burnt and baked.'

Joseph stood by a table tilted on its side. He picked up a potato, burnt and raw, and bit into it then dropped it on the floor. A wind hummed in through the windows and made the shelves rattle. Then Joseph walked out of the store, nodding at the others to follow. They caught up and found he was carrying four bottles of singed bourbon. They ran back in for more and came away with two unexploded boxes of beer and, from the far wall, ten M-80s, four bricks of crackers and fifteen skyrockets that had inexplicably survived. Mena took another jar of ancient preserved peaches and that was it.

'I drove out, newly crowned thieves with bounty in the back.'

'Awesome. Perfect.'

'And then as we were driving out, right, Joseph said: *Thieves aren't the root of evil; thieves are the key point of survival. 'Cause once all rules have changed, there's only survival.* That's what he said, something like that, and I didn't reply because he was seeing the dead more than the living at that point and I didn't know how to take it, didn't know which rules might have changed for him at that stage. Could have been anything, you know? The rules.'

I told her then about the young man, the one who'd died in the car. The young man in Switzerland just waiting to get to the opera house to listen to something eloquent and beautiful. I told her about his landlord, the trial that had the Englishman exonerated. The problem was the dead man wasn't able to corroborate this story.

'It's all about whose stories we believe, right?'

'My biggest fear,' I told Mena. 'What horrifies me most is that one day I might vanish because someone out there is telling the wrong story about me. About everyone with this kind of shitty disease.'

Rebus

Laura angles through the museum, empty now and somehow smaller for it. Walks towards the stairs that will take her down and spill her out through the huge doors into the city. The grand case she spotted on the way in, magnificent; balustrades like time's various vines. But instead of the stairs she finds the lift, its steel doors closing then opening as she comes near. Gretchen had pointed her this way after offering directions to the port because the port, the wharves and all, that's where they'd arrive.

'I'll see you there in half an hour,' the curator had said. They were standing at the archway cut into the wall of the original stone exterior of the old museum. Beside them played another primer: a fragment of Aleksandr Sokurov's film *Mother and Son*, the son seeming to walk willingly into that 1818 scene of Caspar David Friedrich's. 'I have calls to make, to the mainland and so on.' They stayed still. Elsewhere in the museum, five other fragments played voicelessly on the walls. 'I need to talk to her specialist,' Gretchen said, and as Laura patted Gretchen's dog goodbye her left foot slipped a little and she felt herself fall, slip the unexpected two inches into the old building from that startling new edifice built post-war, her ankle twisting, and she'd felt like she was falling forever, until she wasn't. 'I'll see you,' Gretchen had said as she fell. 'They'll be fine. I'll make my calls and they'll be fine and I'll see you at the port and we'll get a boat to go get them. We'll get a boat to them.'

Laura's ankle.

'There's nothing wrong; they'll be fine,' Gretchen had said. 'That's the doctor in me. Never really goes away.'

Laura enters the elevator limping. Her ankle twisting and landing her strangely on each step, exacerbating the pain in her knees. The joints and how dried out they've become, her eyes too. There's not enough fluid in her body. The door closes, hushes, and everything is quiet, just as it is on the mainland, where they're all in silence in their small rooms and apartments. The whole world islands now, tiny and huge and each cut off in its own way. She presses the down button. Nothing. She presses other buttons for other floors. She imagines the voice of the specialist, muted and staggered by the great quiet. The dead sound of the carpeted cube. *Fuck. Fuck, fuck.* The doors stay closed until, *fuck*, they open.

She walks the halls then stairs, the main stairs and the front doors. The large things that once opened for a local lord like the arms of some corny Christ. But the doors are closed. She yanks at the heavy door handles. They stay shut, only shift in the space between the lock's bolt and its encasement. She finds herself sitting on the marble stairs.

Fuck. Fuck you.

There's a breeze. A breath of outside air on her shoulder and neck. It touches her and she stands and turns. She walks into the air, the little rush of scented wind, and down another short spiral staircase. She balances herself with the centre pole, takes small, precise steps. There at the bottom is a door open to a garden. Flowers, unnamed and unmanicured. She looks up and sees the shape of the buildings she'd wanted to photograph earlier against the sky. A basking blue after the rain. But that desire to capture has run out of her now. Then there's a gate, and she recognises the shape of the area beyond. It's the medieval church she and David visited some days ago. A thing of past belief excavated in the fifteenth century, when the current church was built. They'd stood in the columbarium focused on the walls, recessed to receive the ashes of the dead.

The rain had made its way down here, puddles glancing

back at the sky.

She bends down to retie the laces of her beaten sneakers. She's exhausted, for herself, but also for her bloody husband. For and by him. That combined body sense. Life should be simple and calm in his absence, yet it's many things not yet described. Shc thinks of other words for *invisible*, because that's the state her own pains take on—especially now. They're amplified, poured into pools of clarity too deep to see. She bends, and the shadow of herself is busy until the sky, the wide width of it, is caught blinking. A great eye shutting out light and returning it. Noise. The giant weight of a noise not yet word, not yet anything, low and colliding, and as she's looking up from the ground she catches the tail of a huge jet not two hundred metres above, the ripple of heat and decibel. The tail, then gone. The sky shuddering. A pierced silence. She stays staring at the sky, then stands and runs, staggers through the bay-leaved gate at the south end of the garden, her heart manic and marvelling in fright as she goes through the greenery. She rushes around a small fountain where water is flowing, vanishing into another time.

The floor of the church is covered in petals—red, recent. Sun through the front door. She finds herself running into air, light. She looks for smoke, for a massive pall, the haze of spiralling souls caught in fire and fireball, because what else? What else could that have been? Only sky, and how free it was of anything. There's a silence, silence exacerbated by the echoic stairs to the old city.

At the bottom she walks down the damp path, turns left because that is the way to the wharf. The path is quiet. No kids leaning on their mopeds, no tourists. She rushes, taking glances skywards and sideways. The wide blue city and a sense of terrifying emptiness, windows and doorways previously obscured by people, emptiness pouring through the narrow-gauge streets, a vacuous emptiness she usually leans into to listen against the noise of life. The buzz before the people, the dawn expectation, but it is way into the afternoon and the anticipation is that there should be noise. Noise and smoke and someone to ask in a broken voice: *Dov'è l'aereo?* There should be people but there are none. The lane curves through shops all quiet, and nobody is at the counters, the shelves or the display cases. Doors are open, fans are on. Air-con breeze and the scents of whatever—food and soap and wine.

It's here, she thinks.

It's here from across the horizon.

An opening. There's a narrow stair down off the empty street. She steps, her hands out on the walls. Graffiti. Spray, and swayed words, words in no language she can read, though she mouths them. Vowels, consonants; she feels her lips pout and draw.

She feels each spray of paint through her palms.

Words, uncontrollable.

Terror is the uncontrollability of the end, all ends.

Something dumb, he would say.

Something said in place of the actual thing.

But then the real thing, the port, open space, and she turns, turns until she sees the sea. Smoke, direct spiralling smoke rising from behind the east hills. She runs to the boardwalk and glances around the headland. Kónos. Kónos always smoking, taking a puff out of the earth. The slow rise, time teetering on time.

It's here, and all are in hiding, women placing blankets against the windows, counting cans, apples and jars. Children playing a version of some tweaked real because that's what children always manage to do. Men being large, silent and in denial of something. But that doesn't feel possible. Even in hiding, people can't help but be seen, heard.

Something is here.

The silence makes its own echoes through the streets, a deep chorded nothing. Instruments lying waiting in a room. She fears all she can't see. She fears shadows and marks on walls. She asks herself whether she's inconveniently sidestepped time into a real where nature exists without women and men, that exists just to show something of the ease with which one moment in time can operate without human interference. Exists without the naming and claiming and renaming and the whole war of words used to summon and destroy. It exists beyond language, which is an idea she has some trouble with, but she walks amongst it all and feels an urge to rename everything, because words seem to have abandoned this place.

There's only colour and the slow movement of colour.

Words have vanished.

There are daubed hills, and she has no idea which one is hers, which one their cottage sits on and which mark is their room and all their belongings—if their belongings even exist there without them—and which is the donkeys', dogs' and chickens'. There are so many animals at the cottages. The donkeys make so much noise. Donkeys come in pairs; they get lonely otherwise. Deb told David this a few months earlier. *You can't have just one donkey*, she'd said. *They start to break apart if left on their own.* It became a kind of mantra when Laura decided on this place while David tried to understand Berlin. She hadn't wanted the donkeys to get lonely without them. She remembers the animals, fears their disappearance. She feels surrounded by things without names. Anonymous husks.

She watches the streets' corners. Looking for spare verbs, adverbs and nouns.

Shifting brushstrokes and errors.

Again, she walks, higher.

Always watching, always looking.

Streets, streets named after members of the famed. Men in revolutionary beards, women in blackened overalls. Wounded partisans who'd seen off a seaborne approach by the Wehrmacht, shattered steel with two small, stolen pieces of artillery and a dozen high-calibre machine guns.

She walks among the names, and this is what she imagined.

Imagined as a girl.

The absence of all, and all sucked from the universe, spiralled into galactic nothing.

She turns to the harbour and stands on a marble table. The impossible still of the sea. The impossible still of everything, because this is madness—a blatant insanity that she's here, awake and breathing in and breathing out air and thoughts. Madness that all other thoughts have taken themselves to the horizon and slipped.

How still the sea is.

She feels all the colour of her skin vanish.

Perhaps that's it. Or perhaps something else.

But perhaps the town is here, here and real and bustling, perhaps and she can't be seen and she can't see.

The water utterly and penetratingly immobile. She scans it for signs of the boat. The craft she was told would sail around the headland and bring her husband back. Nothing. Nothing. And how does she know this word anyway, 'headland'? Hasn't it all, hasn't everything been annihilated?

She stares at the horizon, the pale slit beyond the harbour.

The hazed horizon. Flat, lifeless.

Her gut feels like the cracks of marble that ruin and make this place.

She stares at the horizon. The boundary of two blues. A gap between fact and fact. This makes an anger stir up from her heart. She swears at it in the back of her thoughts, like: *How dare you?* Blue and blue, the vague layers of the sky and secretive sea. Actually, her stomach feels like eels, and fuck them if they don't stop cramping and biting. She watches with her hand on her sick belly. She stares at that awful gap. *Why are you?* she asks. Squinting, trying to see something. Something, anything that'll tell her where she is and how to be scared. *How dare you be a word when you're not even—a thing?* Did she say that out loud?

She gives it the finger and feels a little mad, happily crazed. She tells it how it's just a passing thing. Just a temporary thing. The provisional word for the never-was and non-corporeal.

'God, I'm tired,' David had said as he sat with her that morning. It was just a thing he couldn't help saying. Now Laura says the same. I'm tired. I'm tired of this, I'm tired of being tired. I'm tired of the interim, of the interim of tired, the bitsy in-between and all its states, and I'm tired of being tired. Tired of tiredness, tired of its volume and manifold states. Tired of feeling no right to this word.

She turns to look back up the hill. Above her the labyrinth of alleys, of houses and paths, of empty shelters and skies. There's a road, and on the other side a path, reckless, to the sea. She begins her walk.

Smith

Two days after my time on Waiheke I met with Marcel. We'd made some albums together in the late 1990s and thought we'd try again. We'd lost touch as we'd headed off to do other things with our lives. He was married now and had four kids; I was on holiday from real responsibilities and had been for quite some time. Marcel was well known in experimental music circles for constructing his own instruments, shim saws, he called them. He was a civil engineer and built these theoretic implements out of various gauges of metal and hunks of wood. Some were enormous, but most were about the height of a seven-year-old child. The instruments' sounding boards were made of pieces of stretched shim metal, and he would play them with violin bows, altering the metal's tensions through methods he'd perfected over the years. He had no interest in playing the guitar or piano or drums, just a fascination with sound and the tones he could build out of these machines. Often he asked other musicians to play his instruments, seeing what could be constructed out of his improvisations.

We'd come back into contact the previous spring and decided if I was ever in Auckland we'd record a new album. He knew of my physical limitations, that he'd have to carry everything and do all the physical work. We set up in his father's factory in a light industrial estate to the south of Mount Roskill. The place was called Bear Hotmelt and there, in the week hours, they'd adhere glue to wood veneer. I'd done a few days' work there in the late Nineties when I lived in Auckland a second time, and much like when I was eighteen and a postie, I was incompetent and soon not called back.

But in this summer, I believed I could play for a certain amount of time before the lights shut off and I'd need to head back to the house in Western Springs where Laura and I were staying. I had a plan that we'd play to certain tunings based on the fundamental frequency given off by the shim saws. I tuned my guitar to this and we improvised for an hour before

I needed a break.

As soon as we stopped, we heard the rain: a storm had hit, tremendous thunder and immense noise on the roof. We opened the front door and slipped a couple of chairs out under an awning. He handed me a coat. I put it over my shoulders, the arms hanging by my sides. I felt pebbles and gravel in the pockets. He brought out some snacks and drinks. We sipped tea and watched as the car park exploded. The whole area filled with fast water gushing from here to there.

Marcel asked if I was all right. I told him I was holding up. The previous night the world had learnt that Mark E. Smith of the Fall had passed away in Manchester. A small number of us, Rosy, John, Kiran, Laura and I, had gathered to listen to Fall albums as they all got drunk to the attack and warble of the music world's greatest non-musician. Marcel came over also and saw how shattered I was by the time it was 10pm and I was trying to order a cab on my phone. My hands like oven gloves and my face like wool. Laura got me outside, and Marcel stood with us on the street waiting for the car to come.

'You'll be okay tomorrow?' he asked.

I shrugged. 'Tomorrow doesn't matter. I take painkillers, I get through.'

'What scale?'

'Painkillers? Large scale.'

'Large scale.'

'They are, they're just another mechanism of getting through, Marc'.'

'What flavour?'

Laura stepped back from the road as a car came by, honking at the unseen.

'Codeine, usually,' I'd said.

Now out in the rain I removed the cap of the small urn I

kept them in and asked if he wanted any.

'Yeah, nah. Prefer chocolate.'

He asked if I wanted some of his Whittaker's. I told him that, like caffeine, sugar knocked me out.

We watched the rain. The mounting tide slowly forcing its way towards my shoes. We kept edging backwards, picking up the chairs and dragging them along the asphalt to a dry spot. We laughed often. I had a rudimentary sensation that I was stoned, high, opiated, whatever. And I was, but it's different when there's no intention of actually getting stoned; the effect here was one of distraction, not joy. The world felt closer but also distanced by the drug's effect. People were rumours, traded for ideas of what truth they might hide behind their teeth.

'I was listening to this doctor,' he said. 'Like, I don't know. This was ages ago.'

'What are you going to tell me here, Marc'?'

'No, like I heard this doctor talking about it. He said he was dubious about it for a time.'

'Well—'

'No, I'm just telling you this.'

'Do I need to listen?'

'This is the story of a suspicious physician.'

'Yeah, well. He can go back to medical school, can't he? Start again. No, he can start high school again if he has a record of being that stupid.'

'No. It was that he was dubious and then he said he learnt more about it and he gave in and made this big hoo-ha. That it was this disease and everything.'

'Okay. Hurray. We give him a prize.'

'Let me finish. And you'll, I don't know.'

'And I bet he's never apologised to anyone he's denied the thing to previously.'

'Probably not.'

I stared into the near distance like I was talking to someone else.

'Doctors can actually be complete cunts,' I said eventually. 'Which, you know, isn't harsh.'

'Cunt is harsh.'

'Well, no. If there was a harsher word, I'd use it. I have a permanent belief I can change the world by swearing at its problems from a distance.'

'He was like: *The science hadn't caught up with the disease. So, we treat what's in front of us.*'

'See—cunt. Where did you hear this?'

'At a seminar. He said it was at the time just depression. First of all, it was polio, then something else, then it was hysteria, then depression. Now it's a fully acknowledged disease, albeit one with near zero funding—which seems to be a metric. I was thinking of you.'

'Aha.'

'It's good to think about people. We think, we heal—at least part of us.'

I was quiet for a time, then told him about those who were humiliated by the health system before me. I said I couldn't imagine how it was for them. I described how ME was a disease fomented by men into a joke because it affects mostly women. 'Misogyny's been driving this thing for decades,' I said. 'So don't think of me.'

'Yeah. But I thought of you because of depression.'

'Why?'

'I couldn't help it.'

'The depression link is, it's an absent causality, Marc'. Like butterflies in Beijing and a hurricane in the Caribbean.' I described to him how I'd tried to kill myself twice, with varying degrees of success. Both times because of depression. 'And you wanna know?' I asked. 'I'd take depression over ME any time. Swap them just like that.' My face screwed up as I said this and I felt a little demented. 'I've had multiple kidney stone events. If I could exchange that pain for an hour a week, swap it for ME, I'd take the fucking stones. I'd have a heart attack a day, and you can have my ME, burn it at a stake—they're arseholes.'

'My point is not every doctor is an arsehole.'

'For a while, you know, they tried to treat the disease with actual exercise, just a few years ago, treat it with very thing that makes us sick—they'd do better with leeches for cancer. They might still be doing it in some countries. No proof of effectiveness, other than further fucking sick bodies.'

Marcel laughed sympathetically as the rain intensified. Gutters spilt the overflowing water onto the windscreens of cars and a curtain of it formed in front of us. For a time, Marcel had wanted to retrain as a doctor because he had wanted to heal people. He had a healer's soul and a healer's heart; he just happened to have an engineering degree. 'I've often felt,' he said suddenly, as he ate a square of chocolate, 'that the medical fraternity is so gung-ho after perfection, so whatever, and it forgets about what it leaves behind, leaves on the floor because of this—this drive, reach, not sure which word. It's sad, makes me sad.'

We watched the water rise.

I told him I'd met Brix Smith Start, late of the Fall.

'Oh. Oooh, Brix,' he said.

I laughed.

I explained she'd been at the Edinburgh writers festival at the same time as me. There to talk about her book, *The Rise, The Fall, and The Rise*. That she was as small as imaginable, as pocket-sized as I'd ever conjured from video and stage evidence.

I told Marcel my heart rushed for her a little as she'd walked in, that she was an ancient crush with her black eyeliner and the Rickenbacker that always looked so huge on her. Through various stages of my life I've had grand preoccupations with the Fall, ignored them, obsessed with them again and again, given up only to find myself once more listening to album after album on the long walks I'd take in the Wellington hills during my remission. I told Marcel how I'd listened to her tell humbling stories of rock 'n' roll oblivion, her relationship with her guitar, with Mark E. Smith, with the violinist Nigel Kennedy, with her American family, and with her new band with ex-members of the Fall.

There was an unexpected hippy vibe to her, I said, a desire for Californian equilibriums of body, spirit—the whole mind–soul thing. She was a celebrity, it seemed to me, because she believed in that part of herself that longed to be known. I'd liked this a great deal. I kind of admired her will to stardom; she was known to millions and had an indelible part in one of punk's utmost acts.

What I didn't tell my friend was that as I'd watched her, I'd had the strange sensation that a little over a week earlier my sister had still been alive. She was dying, but alive. Ros was racked with a cancer that had metastasized into her lymph system. Run her down to the point she could barely speak but longed to speak. I didn't tell him how almost ten years ago to the day my father had also died of cancer. We'd gathered around his bed and watched the life slip out of him like a rag. And thirty years ago, in the same month, Ros's old boyfriend perished on a glacier in the Southern Alps. And as I sat listening to Brix on the stage, I wondered how many kinds of life we have. How many versions we live before that moment. I wondered why illness doesn't attract the same kind of fame as film and dance, book and song. I also wondered what had happened in the decade when no one in my family died. I had the sensation there was an unknown, an eclipse I hadn't clocked or fully understood.

I told Marcel how once the session ended I snuck through the crowd, crept up alongside Brix and walked out into a roar of sunshine that greeted us. And as I walked beside her I felt the urge, a kind of hapless confusion with normality that said: *Do it, say hello*. I stayed at her side, her cheek inches away.

I leant in near her ear, and I started to say, started to whisper, 'Thanks, thanks so very much,' when she turned and her mouth kissed against my nose.

I jerked, a surprised stupid spasm.

'Shit. I thought,' she said. Her Chicago accent.

'No,' I said.

'I thought you were someone else,' she said. 'I thought you were my agent.'

She smelt of warm perfume and wine.

We laughed then.

I said, 'Well.'

The two of us turning to stone, as something had to happen next.

'Well, nice to meet you,' she said and leaned forward. The warmth of her and I felt well within her aura.

I kissed her cheek and she touched my arm.

I kissed her cheek. She didn't pull away, or jerk like I had. She turned and smiled. I wondered if she knew the kiss was as much for Mark E. Smith as for her. I marked a little of my saliva glistening on her cheek. I pulled away and saw it there and thought impulsively how close DNA is to life, how it is we throw it around with such abandon.

Brix smiled as she was led off to her signing session. I hadn't yet bought her book and had no intention of getting anything signed. Being near her was more than enough. 'There's something urgent in the famous,' I told Marcel. There's something that asks we maintain a distance, I said, and experience fame through the act of seeing. Of looking, and respecting the awe we replicate over and over as they stroll on by, being famous, their shadows the weight of stone.

Marcel laughed.

'How'd you manage?' he asked. 'Like, talking. Doing talks.'

'It's, I don't know. It's okay.'

'Talking isn't your thing, eh?'

'It's okay, actually. I walk into a room and I'm suddenly on the other side of David, of me. I'm someone else. I'm the guy who, I get to play the part of being the author guy. And, of course there's no such thing as an author anymore. There's only readers, and I get to be their invention for a while. I'm not a sick person, I'm something else. Which is really nice. The only problem is that I write books that nobody really reads.'

'I'm never going to read your books.'

'Why not?'

'In case they stink.'

'But you're in this one.'

'Not yet.'

'Well, they're all the same essentially, so don't worry. I'm just trying to perfect an idea, if I can. Which is basically one definition of insanity.'

'I make shim saws, you write books.'

I told him how fed up Laura often got with me, that I do things over and over, say the same things, write the same shit, cause the same offence, do things over and over again that are obviously going to make me sick. That it's like I don't have any memory of outcome.

'You've always been kind of infuriating,' he said.

'But it's not that,' I said, ignoring him. 'I don't have any memory of doing the things in the first place, the thing before the outcome. My life is full of endless ellipses I can't see. It's maddening.'

'Where are they?' he asked.

'But she's right, being fed up. I have a moment of wellness and I get so excited, and she gets so fearful. It's not a way to live.'

'Okay. I feel for her, when you put it like that.'

'She says thanks.'

'Anyway, this doctor,' Marcel stated, 'he said when he realised what a dick he'd been went back and wrote a paper on diseases through the ages poo-pooed by medical ineptitude. He said his wonder at the end of it all was how many are left. How many, you know, are yet to be found.'

'None,' I said. 'This is it.'

We went back in and realised we'd left the amps on, with the guitars and shim saws shaking and humming. I woke up the computer, busied the screen and went to hit record so I could capture the sound of the room, then I discovered we'd never turned it off. Half an hour of rain filled the silence. I took two more codeine pills that tasted like chalk. The drug seems to ease the pain that starts to grow in my head when engaged in something like this, something physical and mentally arduous. They seem to reduce the inflammation that causes the falling fog, the massive exhaustion and shutdown. Or they just reduce the stress on the body and mitigate the likelihood of inflammation. It's guesswork. I stopped and started the machine recording once more and we played on. Huge drones, echo units and feedback. I had Marcel's amplifier, a 100-watt

Concord from the Sixties—as thunderous a thing as has ever cracked the sky. Marcel had made adjustments and replaced the speakers. When the distortion was let loose it was immense, surrounding, a form of light that filled the ears and blood. I've always loved vast measurements of noise, the weight of it, the physical totality of volume and chord, the invention of notes no one in the room is playing. The way you move your head and the sound shifts, the way you struggle to move through it, the pummelling of watt and decibel.

We played for hours, this music of electron and wave. Tearing steel out of the speakers, lightly shifting them into binary code.

Of course, my body began its processes of shutting down. First to go was the cognitive faculties, the ability to hold thought, logic and memory. A kind of dense vapour pulls in around the edges of the conscious mind and begins its work. In moments of physical and mental stress, strange things start to happen; the mitochondria in our cells become exhausted and energy production is quickly shut down. Then, it seems, the body's immune mechanism makes the assumption it is under attack instead of just having a nice time. It activates all its systems, causing inflammation throughout the body and particularly inside the brain. The physicality of which feels like a massive, dense trauma. Soon the ability to actuate movements is retarded by the mind's new inability to make complex thoughts, and then, later, thoughts of any kind. The pathways of neuron and nerve begin to slim until the point coordination is limited to short, stunted movements. I knew going into the session I would damage myself; I'd done it before on numerous occasions in order to see what would happen.

During the writing of my first novel, I became ill. After I came down with the syndrome, I was reduced to small amounts of activity that put me on the couch for the next few hours, or days. I would write for ten minutes each morning, and that was it. But somehow it was enough. After a year of this, it came to the point that I had one major scene left to write. I had put it off for months, because it involved imagining a leg of the Tour de France in which my narrator tracked down and duelled with the race's leader, and I knew I needed reserves of energy I just wasn't able to produce.

Then, in October, Laura was away in San Francisco on business and my friends Matt and Hamish came over to eat pizza on my birthday. We had a nice evening, and they left early, as it was obvious I was fading quickly. I found myself couch-bound, caught by the expansion under my cranium, drooling and unable to take myself to bed. I stayed there into the deep night until I was able to move. At 3am I stood and went to my laptop and opened a new document and forced myself to write this scene. I wanted to see what would happen if I went beyond the edge of the illness. I imagined myself pushing so hard I'd disappear; I'd vanish in a round puff of vapour. I put the Fall on in my headphones and went to work. I couldn't see the screen but for a slim slip of light between the blurs my vision had been reduced to. All as if the flanks of my peripheral vision had bent all the way into the centre and what remained was a line of sight similar to what I imagine devotees see when they put their hands up to pray and the light that slips through is the only light. The keyboard was a smear of black and grey. The whole world vanished and I typed blind and in a great deal of pain until it was finished. I completed the scene and went to bed, assuming it was terrible and full of appalling typos and the spelling mistakes of a child (which is the way I have always spelt). Two days later I was able to turn the computer on once more. There wasn't a single error, and later the section was published more or less as I wrote it. It was the utmost achingly painful thing I have ever done, and that includes all sport, all recreation, all operations, heart attacks, kidney stones, depressive episodes and breakups. And all the while, Brix banged her guitar and sang 'C.R.E.E.P.'

I haven't done anything this extreme since. And not because of the pain, but because to think myself into this kind of action is a kind of insanity I'm not interested in. It'd be like killing myself off in this book to see what effect it had on the narrative. Which Laura says I should do.

But I did try it to a degree while recording with Marcel. There were things I wanted to try to get done, dabblings with tunings and microphone techniques I'd thought up over the years. I kept trying new things, banging my guitar, running this modal scale, and it was horrible, broken, foozled music. And putting myself through it was also an experiment, an experiment of body and what kinds of things it would produce. You can hear it on the recordings: I'm trying to strum but I'm so out of time with myself it's almost intriguing: you can hear my body slowly working itself downwards; you can hear the distortion between mind, thought and body control. This disconnect between my brain and hands became a kind of babble that fascinates me now, but I doubt will be released. I have another fault: I demand a kind of control over the chaos unless the disorder sounds like it derives from an intellect that desires it, and I have no desire for this form of chaos.

And it happens without warning. Sitting on a train; waiting for the lights to change so you might cross the road; standing at an EFTPOS machine; the middle of a conversation. The resulting effect can be as simple as forgetting how to cross that road, how to exit the train, what it is you're supposed to do with the card. It can also be as frightening as forgetting how to eat or speak.

Just yesterday, while working on this document, my body went into a state of fatigue-induced shock. The nervous system crashed, producing a state of frenzy. I lay on the couch shaking uncontrollably for twenty minutes, my feet, arms, legs kicking. Then it just stopped. I found then that I couldn't speak. Laura was worried I'd had a stroke; she asked if I could manage a smile. I was able to raise the corners of my mouth in an even manner and this told her she didn't need to call an ambulance. Instead, I picked up my phone and typed out that I just couldn't speak. I have no idea why I could type and not speak. Most things are unexplained. There are still no doctors for this.

The Rise

After a light rain, the sun.

We made for the path under the wide arch of a rainbow forming above the hills. The island rose in runs of sable shadow and bright rock. Rachel and I moved slowly. The yachts, the runabouts, the cruisers and weekenders had pulled out with the sun's disappearance. Months ago Gretchen told Rachel it was an unwritten rule on Isola: if people couldn't walk back up the hill, boaters would be obliged to help them out. Hence, boats and people in some exhilarated exchange. The stranded could be seen hitching rides back to the port with day trippers. It was a thing since the war, Gretchen told Rachel, a thing since necessity and survival linked arms. Citizen soldiers would smuggle their wounded and their mad hither and thither from the port to the Bay of Mouths. There, partisan youths hid in the grottos, their imaginations destroyed by visions of blood and bullets. The people of the island reinvigorated this trade when Cratere's island population stopped shifting with each ferry and people would walk down and hope for escape. Many found they didn't have the heart to walk back up. Boats were hailed from the shore. A short swim to their sterns. Hallelujah.

But this old, corrugated path, this was the way back now. The only boats in the bay were yachts from the mainland and even if, even if they weren't there illegally—I couldn't swim out. I just assumed there would be a jetty or a simple rowboat; instead all that came were the stories of us.

We came to a dip in the trail. I stepped down and up, climbing in my loose-footed way. I heard Rachel stepping, following me. Slow. We climbed, gradual and easy. Our words vanished into the hills around us. Phrases hanging then swallowed by vegetation and gullies. The echo trail of diminished afterthoughts as we walked. And it wasn't the fact of not listening that caused our words to vanish. No, words are pockets of energy if they're anything, and they were failing in our bodies, vanishing entities as we stepped forward.

A hunk of flat rock.

I moved gradually on. My legs, my wet back. The only sound was my boots on the stone. I half turned, my eyes leading my head. My body felt slow, unwilling to take the step my head asked I take. Gradually I turned. Rachel was sitting on the rock twenty metres back. I glanced at the tremors racing in her hands. I asked something unheard by either of us. I walked back until I was ten metres distant. My shadow leant towards her. I felt myself call out. Everything felt measured in distance. Each word the length of a run race. There's so much energy in spoken words, how they agitate long after they've been said, vibrating and forging paths through and on, and my body—its organs and cells, hips, thighs—it couldn't maintain the trembling of others' thoughts.

Rachel didn't reply.

I looked up at the sky and repeated something.

'What do you want to do?' I asked.

Birds flew across the track, squabbling nervously over unseen food.

My cousin's hands shaking.

I stood next to her.

She took out her phone. Waited as it recognised her fingerprint, linking up with cell tower and systems, worldwide complexes of word and text. I sat gently on the track. I waited and watched her. I leaned in slightly as she tried to speak.

She looked past me out towards the sea, the phone at her cheek. Large cacti ranged up behind her. Two-inch needles, each ready in defence. We'd lain on the rocky beach for an hour before the drizzle. As we watched boats shift in and out of the bay, we spoke as we had for decades. When it was time to leave, she explained we needed to swim out to the boats. I'd stood at the edge of the sea surrounded by water and stone. That was how I came to tell the story of my relationship to water. Quite untrue, of course; the real story involved my mother and a bath when I was ten months old. An event I have no memory of, so I tell the story I tell—that it was my father, because I needed to remember my father.

Rachel put her phone in her pocket.

On the beach I'd said I'd thought there would be rowboats, that it would all be as simple as stepping off the ragged shore onto a boat with splintery oars, but then the story of my father, and time passed. There's something cruel in the story I tell: I shouldn't have to lie to make the truth, but I can't help it.

Now Rachel tells me she'll try a little more.

I helped her up, tugging her from the wrist. The weight of her head, my legs just nerves, just the flickering of nerves like light, like tree-filtered light, shimmering so it seemed to have no source. We'd spent an hour at the beach. Sharing our versions of the madness this disease effects. The surety of this state, of being alone, being locked in, of the invisibility of self, being invisible to others and to one's own senses, to the things that produce self. We told stories that try to tell the sickness; their failures are always a part of the truth. The small deaths of the everyday, when every day you cannot finish a thought, the one that'll have you stand, the one that'll let you speak, the one that'll let you remember self, because to speak thyself is to remember thyself. Then I told Rachel about Laura, the small and brutal attacks that were going on inside her.

Now we walked.

Twenty-five metres. Twenty-eight. I stopped.

Sat.

I was mumbling, the grey sound of voices, voices not in tune, desynced, so I was just phase noise and syllables. I watched Rachel count the spaces in between, watched her watch my mouth for evidence of other languages. But nothing. She bent down. She put her shoulder under my own and lifted my body, drawing me up off the ground. But then she fell and we were both on the track.

Time, an hour.
An hour of time.

And after an hour I stood. I said something distant, put her in a fireman's grip. I lifted her, walked her in silence to the first climb proper. I rearranged her and took two steps up, steadied myself. Three more steps, the ground suddenly four metres below. We got to the plateau and that was it for a moment.

The weight of breathing, her chest, how it pushed down on my shoulder.

I went on, stepping until a rock face. I hefted her again. She watched the earth jerk and move each time I took a step. A blur and up, up.

Up.

My eyes on the ground, no energy to lift them above the dirt.

Dirt, swaying dirt.

Rachel sounded out.

And then the dirt was moving, shifting in a new way, shifting as if sucked in towards us. Rising.

The earth rising and the world failing in the peripheral black and white. We were in flight, falling. Falling, drifting, and I felt myself counting the hours until this collapse was complete. Down, air rush, and so quickly groundward. Down and then not down because the hit, the weight of the hit. Then another, other-bodily hit: the heft of my body and the upthrust of the rock and earth and it was just Rachel between these two things. The grunt sound of our bodies collapsing in the earth and I remembered gravity, remembered the truth of it. My satchel landing beside Rachel's head. Thudding there like a secret organ nudged from my insides by our fall. Now it sat in the wet dust. Paper, writing in disarray.

Oh.

We lay like that, the two of us breathing. The sound of us breathing and nothing else, the two of us before I moved. I made a shy, groaned noise, then rolled so I was leaning against the rock face. There were abrasions on my face. Cuts in my arms. Everything was dust-strewn.

The alien sound of us breathing.

'Your shirt's torn,' she said.

I glanced at the tear. 'It's been through worse.'

She moaned as she moved. She reached and touched my sleeve.

'It's been through worse, Rach.'

'Yeah,' she said.

'Much worse.'

She tugged at it. Her eyes squinted.

'You know, David, I was at the oncologists, I was there with Gretchen. Two years ago. I picked up a magazine and I read that article and you were wearing this same shirt.'

'Yeah.'

'The picture of you and you were wearing this shirt.'

'It cost thirty-five dollars in 2003,' I said. 'I get fat, I get thin, it seems to remain the same relative size.'

I put the heel of my hand against my forehead. Then looked at the transferred blood. Red like a butcher, red like a hunter's hands. I made a series of noises. Low-grade, bruised sounds. All around the sense of people watching, listening.

'I saw you wearing it yesterday,' Rach said. 'I thought: This is maybe the same person, but it can't be the same shirt.'

'It's the same shirt.'

'And you can guarantee it's the same person?' She coughed. She was shaking her hand out. A finger looked bent.

'Don't know. I feel kinda, I feel kinda—'

'I feel a thespian's urge to be someone else right now.'

'What do we do?'

'Don't know.' There was blood on her arm and her knees were cut up. My body felt light, as if it were another's, Rachel's—transferred, swapped out with hers. I said something dumb. She said it only hurt when she bled, then she laughed. She managed to get herself into a squat. She leaned towards me, wiped the blood on her skirt then shook out her hand again.

She looked past me.

'What?' I asked.

She stood, achingly, on a rock, and gazed at the sea.

I turned my head. A salt-scented serein wafted in, holding all the light like all had a halo. I felt momentarily like I did when Laura and I visited galleries and museums. We'd exit the rooms and halls and forget what city we were in. People appeared vague to us. Extra mundane, and the two of us feeling quite beyond the world we'd exited as we'd stepped into the museum. Or sometimes the opposite—folk suddenly vibrant and full of colour. Or sometimes we didn't see anything, nothing, and it was as if the world didn't give a damn. We'd just have to believe what we'd read and been told about all those famous articles of virtuosity and perfection dead in our eyes. Experience isn't always truth.

'It's one of the weekenders,' Rachel said, crouching, 'from earlier.'

'Which one?'

'Don't know. Does it matter?'

'What colour?'

She stood again.

'Blue,' she said. 'The one from before, from the mainland with the kids and camera.'

'. . .'

'What do I do with you?'

I shook my head. 'Can you walk down?'

'I just leave you?' she asked.

'Correct. It's easy to do.'

She turned once more to the boat, nodding. Her bottom lip out, a pout like she knew something only she could know.

'I've no interest in leaving you here,' she said.

'Well.'

'I need to rest anyway.'

She stayed crouched and then sat. The two of us quiet for what seemed like the rest of the day, but such is time; it was only minutes, and by then she was up and moving slowly, limping through dusty rays cutting light across the path, each moving so easily out of her body's way.

'Cheer for me madly,' she said.

I was in deep silence, involuntary and gaping, as I lay back. The rock, it seemed to grow around me, mould over my form. My arms pinned to my side, the rock cold and growing. Seeping into my skin and over my neck.

'Cheer for me madly,' she said again. 'Cheer—' but then she saw it. She stood still then and watched it grow, folding over my chin, into my mouth—the rock. It had been on the move for thirty thousand years and you could watch me on a screen if you were able to find one. You'd see the thalamus inflamed, the amygdala and hippocampus rife with whatever chemical mediators and expanding. Evidence of chronic neurological deficits. Look inside the cells and you'll see mitochondria, heads lowered in pain. Find a big magnet. Lie me down, set the MRI clunking, watch it all on the screen. The anterior cingulate cortex. This, the seat of travail. Inflammation, fluid, patterns of destruction and replacement, neuronal damage, and all from a walk, a walk to the sea. Inflammation and silence. An un-tender silence. And within this friable silence the structure of sentences evaporated. I grunted, my mouth opened to strings of saliva as a heavy rain began to patter and splat around us.

'You got to move, David.'

She loomed in her words, a giant blur, and she seemed to realise I couldn't see because I couldn't then see; she touched my hand, and our fingers felt shapeless. The rock warm as it settled my body into the earth.

'Cheer for me,' she said.

The rows of cacti pointless at the side of the track, seemingly warm to the touch. The new rain collided with our sunburnt skin—hushed now, hushed and voiceless.

Starling St

I returned to the house on Starling Street where Laura and I were staying with old friends. They were up north for a day at the beach. The tips of my fingers couldn't feel the key they'd given me to get into the house; all sensation in my face had disappeared. I handed the keys to Marcel and he managed to get the door open and I went to the couch. The deep suck of cushion and spring, leather, and a flopping cat the size and weight of a rug.

The tunnel is simple; it's all walls and light. I said this to my old friend and watched him watch me.

'You going to be okay?'

'I'm used to it,' I said. Which wasn't necessarily true; it's always different. I watched him glance around the house, the foreignness of other people's ways and doings, all of it amplified by their absence. English ivy climbing near the windows. 'I have a distant ancestor,' I said, slurring. 'This old baron and knight and doctor. A Tory twit, or at least I make the assumption. We have these people in our unseen pasts, right? Just some overblown personage we can't make sense of. And he's the guy, the one I'm named after. My middle names at least. And my dad, Henry, was named after him, too. He was like, he was this doctor to three kings, and then Victoria when she was a pup.' Marcel indicated he was listening by touching the chrome knobs of the euro coffee machine on the kitchen island, then turned to me when nothing happened. 'But, who knows,' I said, 'who can know if he was any good. They all died, these kings, under his care, you see. Like, awfully, so I suspect he was a bit crap.'

'Like, died how?'

I took a moment, then, 'One of the Georges, the fourth, maybe? If you know the kings, you know he was a bit shit. Plus he was fat. He was massively, terminally fat and bleeding inside. He had a heart three times the recommended dose, a tumour in his gut the size of a melon. My niece Danielle and I, so we've got a little conspiracy theory. It's that, like, according to Henry Halford's biography, he was a firm believer in euthanasia, he thought it best to help people's suffering pass quickly and with timely intervention. I don't know if this was ever something that happened, or occurred, but. But I sometimes lie awake and imagine this man.'

'The Henry guy?'

'Yes. This baron. I imagine he has a mallet of some kind. That he's this guy and he stands over these regal figures when they are in their last agonies, and in a dark palace chamber he smites them. He lifts this mallet and splits them open. Renders them in two, and just for a moment they're living and dying in separate instances. Two of them at the hilt of life. One goes over into the nothing and the other lingers for a split second.'

'A mallet.'

'A sizeable mallet,' I said as my eyes closed over, 'with special, you know, properties.'

'Where is it now?'

'The mallet?'

'Yes, where's the mallet.'

'There is no mallet.'

'So—okay. I thought you might have inherited it.'

'No, just his name. It's just, just, when I'm like this, there's a hammer.'

Marcel mumbled a laugh and in my half-sight I saw light glint off the bald part of his head. I closed my eyes again. Marcel seemed not quite certain whether to speak.

'My point,' I said in a half-voice, 'is that when I'm like this it's hard for me to follow facts. Follow them down their path to the end. I think it's the same for anyone involved in this to do the same. Like, you always trust your doctor, but don't. You know what I mean?'

I heard him say something.

'I have this urge,' I told him, 'to go someday to Germany. Go and spend a long period there, particularly in Potsdam and Berlin.' I told him I wanted to research some of my ancestors, the folk who came from there. I told a story of my great-great-great-great-grandfather, while talking about something else. I was talking about his wife, Princess Marianne of the Netherlands. 'There was something likeable about her,' I told Marcel, 'but it isn't her I'm related to.' She was said to be artistically minded and highly intelligent. She found the Prussian royal court in Berlin to be repulsive—increasingly oppressive and dark. Her husband was remote, engaged in multiple affairs. This husband, this ancestor, Prince Albrecht, was said to find interest only in army drills, horses and the bodies of his various mistresses. I explained that this abhorrent tradition of the Hohenzollern men taking mistresses didn't sit well with Marianne, and she rebelled and indiscreetly took lovers herself. Which went against the acknowledged protocols of the time. Even though the couple were now living apart, Prince Albrecht was furious when he learnt that he was being deliberately betrayed in front of his family, court and regiment. On a cold night in late October, Marianne made her bed with her horse master. On learning this was taking place, Albrecht tried to get into her bedroom while they were in the act, naked and full of themselves. A guard outside the room barred the prince's entry, a lance at the ready. They argued. Shouts echoed through the halls and into the room where the pair continued at their pleasure. Albrecht's temper raged, his face rent with an othering energy. He unsheathed his sword and struck the guard, putting him to the floor. Albrecht then beheaded him in a horrific flash of steel and blood right there in the hall. He entered the bedroom and tore the pair from the bed. He attacked the horse master, beating him with the blunt end of his sword. The horse master collapsed as the blows broke ribs and shattered his forearm. Albrecht refrained from killing the man and put Marianne and her lover out of the Prinz Albrecht Palais on a starless night. This prince, this sociopathic entity, likely knew of his wife and her lover's intents and choreographed the event to place fault for the failure of their marriage squarely on Marianne. That she was disloyal, adulterous and eager to besmirch his name.

Soon after, the prince was summoned to court by his brother, Kaiser Friedrich Wilhelm IV. They had a dramatic altercation, shouting accusations at each other inside the king's vast rooms, until the king instructed Albrecht to leave Prussia, travel to the Mediterranean, land in Alexandra and join an archaeological expedition there, all in order to let events back in Prussia calm and resuscitate the affairs of the crown. So Prince Albrecht and several fellow officers left Berlin late 1842 to join an expedition led by the well-known Egyptologist Richard Lepsius. They were there to gather antiquities and, of all things, look for the route of the Exodus. 'They spent six months,' I said, 'doing scientific studies—whatever that means—of the pyramids of Saqqara, Giza, Dahshur and Abusir. They uncovered sixty-seven pyramids lost centuries earlier to the wandering desert. Then the prince returned via Italy to his palace. There he had a liaison with

Caroline Henriette Wagner, who died in Masterton in 1912, forty-eight years after giving birth to their illegitimate son.'

I said to Marcel that I wanted to learn about these events, about the vast underlying baseness of these people. It'll be a book, I said. Or, a part of one. Or, I believed I said this and something else was going on.

Voices adrift, made incomplete by the interplay of outsider sounds, a cluster of sighs as cars exited neighbouring driveways. 'I want to know about the guard. The murdered man, the man killed in the hallway of some arrogant toss. What of his family? Did he have a wife, girlfriend? What of her? What of her story? I'll talk about history. Say how it's a clutter of privileged pricks getting away with horrendous acts and we forgive them in the manner in which we tell their stories because we believe, despite ourselves, there's something bigger at stake.'

'Okay,' Marcel said.

'We walk amongst their buildings, participating in and replicating the aura and awe that only exists because—there we are. I find it revolting, but I keep talking about it.'

'Who'll die in this book?' my friend asked.

'Everyone.'

Marcel was silent for a moment and we shared the room's stillness. He told me something as I lay still, that he'd bumped into an old friend of ours from when I lived on K Road, back when bad things stalked us and we let them because that was what we believed living came down to. That Marcel's and our old friend's daughters went to the same dance class. I drew in the news like it was air into a vacuum, a hissing sound through my mind, and I couldn't tell if it was coming in or escaping out.

Marcel made tea and I listened to him talk and ask questions, and when I didn't answer I felt him move about the house, his location evident in footfalls and floorboard noise. The echo and response of some mammalian throwback. The house, and the way it let in air and sound, and how air and sound surrounded distance and its inverse states. I heard other streets; I heard the scraping of shoes on an empty court. I heard mouths shouting voicelessly at the lines of the sea lapping at stone. Eventually I heard the front door and the ignition of his car. His people mover, I think it was a Toyota Estima. Earlier we'd talked about his Alfa Romeo. The thing he'd bought in his early thirties and driven around with the back seats down so he could listen to the exhaust. I'd remembered then, as we talked, how he'd helped me move back to Wellington in February 2000, after the second time I'd tried to live in Auckland. We'd packed up his car and he told me I was driving because he wanted to see what that high-revving Italian machine could do with someone willing at the wheel. I'd moved north again to be with Sarah, but the city was ghosted by old versions of myself. I'd see people standing on street corners who weren't there. I'd see faces who were there and I wanted to run. Each time I walked out into Grey Lynn the smell of it would transform into the mortar of anxieties, fixing me with their certainties about this city—its mounts and heat, old volcano rock sidings and constant rising wet air, its money and poor and bars and bands and old friends and old hells and walks, and the way a city is marked, given consciousness by ancient desire lines, the pathways through grass and park, through car parks and back alleys, and the way you always believe this way is quickest and this way is the only way and the only way is always moving like the oil of the mind shifting to its promised place. I had to move home again. I could never explain why to Sarah; the lack of explanation caused a hurt that I'll never know how to ask forgiveness for. I sometimes think forgiveness can only be given when the understanding and its opposite are equal. I don't know if that is true.

I lay there listening to Marcel, his engine start and the automatic transmission clunk. I heard him head off in the heat, and I imagined driving, that it was me behind the wheel of his car, only it wasn't the people mover but something big-engined and powered by the will of unnecessary horsepower. I imagined the road out of Auckland, the highway and the route we always took through Matamata so we didn't have to pass into Hamilton, because Hamilton. I knew the straights, the long-arced bends and the continual wait until we clocked back onto State Highway 1. The power of the machine and the weight of the steering. I fought it until it got dark, and I remember after that the drive was all peace, the drift and glide at one-hundred-and-eighty. The flow, dream shudder and pull, the discourse of road and rider. Flashed wethers, the rhythm of high beam on, high beam off. Eyes on the road, staring things. Houses and shops, vast fields of livestock, then the bare acres of hillock and sparse sheep-trailed mounds. A farmer at a gate, the ghost form of country and inhabitants caught and lost in the headlights. Then hitchhikers misplaced on the outskirts of Tokoroa, where I neatly turned off so to raid the roads on the west side of Taupō. A woman and a man, sworn to their own secrets. I thought of Martin, then thought of the young man bleeding through the back of his head somewhere in Italy. An argument, argument and scuffle. A man with an actual hammer and money, an argument over months of missed payments and actual payments. And maybe that's why I told the story about my ancestor Albrecht: you're always filling in the gaps. I felt empty at the thought.

There was nothing legal in the way I drove back then, just

a calm desire to always get there, running through the gears as hard as my body would let. Claiming time for one's own as I rushed headlong, trying to grab its tail. After all, it's the integrity of time that keeps the mind alive, the body willingly intact.

I listened until Marcel had turned around and his engine had merged with the street sounds of summer, the chatter of nuance and cicada, distant city noise and a party three blocks over whose excitements rose and subsided on the will of the wind and the thickness of the heat bands roaming the suburbs as the neighbour's dog barked at its nerves and permanent anger.

I believed my eyes were open, though I was shocked by the blackness, how cheap the parts of my body felt, its bone. The house full of murmurings, the pipe drips, the shifting cat on my shoulder. I bored into each ridge of sound, the heat warp bang of the iron roof, the flicker of a breeze caught in the blinds, the creak of the sash windows—every one of them lifted, inviting other breezes and haunts—the thickness of the leather as I shifted. Shoes clapping on paving stones, clapping in time, to time. I knew someone was talking. I heard breath and the ticking of a tongue on teeth.

I understood breathing; I knew its life in my lungs. I knew it as breath shifted through the sinuses, trachea and bronchi, touching the alveoli and running on, back to where it came from, over and over again. The last refuge of the body, its closing conversation as slow as ice.

There was a thickness in my head.

They weren't speaking to me, these people. Though I knew their shape in the reverberations from the walls and windows, the furniture and floors. I knew their names but couldn't speak their initials; they knew my name and spoke it. And whispering, because they thought I was sleeping, then the normal complex chatter as if I were awake, which I was, I'm always awake. I heard sand as they removed layers of clothes, tiny bits of beach showering the rimu floor.

I struggled to stop interrupting their sound with repetitions of Attila, what he had said three days ago at the beach on Waiheke, and the trees and how we kept seeking out cold drinks, fried food and popsicles: *They remember the stories better than I do*, he'd said. *It's always fascinating, hearing all about your life after so long.* And for so long, so long he'd been the substitute of Dead, that's what I was thinking. For so long merged with the inner distemper of a young blond boy from Stockholm whose disease goes unmarked in journals and is heralded by the estranged and wan, the longhaired, corpse-painted, the fearful and knowing, outcast and near insane, by metallers for Satan, by punk rockers all up for their experiment of drone and speed, their intellectual intrigue of pure weight and force, by the narcissistic and hungry, angry and depressed, by the pure force of a ravelling narrative, its constructions and salutation of a scene desirous of connection.

I wondered as I lay there what it is that happens to the annulled elements of us when large parts of self are the product of others' accounts. What happens to those parts that are voided in this act of real-time reincarnation? Are they incarcerated within the walls of a great unpicked narrative, a story told by the desperate and hurt? I decided they're retold in others' lives, in the hidden lives of others. We just can't know when and how.

I couldn't remember then if I'd yet had the dream about Bernhard's novella, or if it was still to come. I just knew it existed somewhere in time. When everyone else went to sleep, I found the rooms silent. An echo of sentiments from earlier, when I was alone and waiting for bodies to fill in the areas around me and remind me I was living. I sat up and found a cold cup of peppermint tea beside me. I drank it in two takes. I opened my laptop and began to write it, my novella on behalf of Alin's near neighbour in Gmunden. Thomas Bernhard's fight against the remaining elements of a hard right he believed still extant in strands of European society, those not wiped out by the war. A fight against the false presumptions of blood.

Roaming

Laura in the vacant streets, in the culverts running seaward. Her eyes hurting, dried out and heated. They have a burning sensation most of the time, like someone's been directing a hairdryer at her face. Now they also hurt in that other way—she needs to, or the world seems to demand that she must, cry.

She's lost.

Boats in the water behind, rudderless now and coasting in the soft wash as she walks upwards. She's lost in the empty streets and realises it's people she fears now, actual people stepping out of the stillness. She fears they are nearby, close but invisible. She feels stalked, eyes in street corners. Wanton murder in their judgements. She feels the great pain that pushes up from her chest, the ache before tears. She sits momentarily on the edge of a fountain. She tries to think and imagine. A dog seems to bark, but immediately she knows it's the creak of a sign hanging in the breeze. Maybe, maybe everyone is at a gathering that happens on this day and only this day. A celebration that demands full participation. A day of national pride, spiritual connection and elation. Art and song. The blood effect of absolute participation, a hymn sung brightly through their veins.

She knows this isn't true. Though she also knows nothing is no longer true.

She wants to creep back to the museum and ask Gretchen, ask her every question ever thought. She wants to hide in the museum's secret places. Nuzzle into time and time's terror. Oh God. She wants to recant on ever having left the museum. They'd talk again.

'Days like today should simply be heaven,' she'd said before leaving. 'I shouldn't have to think about him for hours and this should be—'

'And now the hours, here they are,' Gretchen had said.

'. . .'

'He's okay. They're okay.'

'He does this intentionally,' Laura had said. 'I'm certain.'

'Yes.'

'I've dialled for an ambulance. He can't speak and I'm asking if I should call and he's gesticulating, making strange noises till I realise he's just asking for water.'

'And have you ever let it ring through?'

'. . .'

She walks again and finds herself at an open piazza and sits once more, sits because she can't remember where she's going. All around her is space, space remembered by its human affects: church, restaurant, a Vespa resting on its side, ticking. Jesus. What is ownership in such a place? What is it to give your whole self?

It begins then, first in her body, then her face and eyes. The hard effort of tears when she can't produce tears. The logic of them, the memory of tears, and the memory that there's a little hit of opiate in every run of them, that in a crisis there are tears, and how utterly practical they really are, and what kind of crisis is this?

She's shaking and turning her body to look. Her eyes searching out eyes. Everywhere a potential eye.

'Have you ever just let it ring,' Gretchen had asked, 'ring till there's someone else's voice?'

She stares at the old white of the church walls, earlier so happily full of wedding parties and now empty; she sees how flecked the paint is, how the white is chipped in some places, wrecked by mildew in others.

Bible and clock.

The crying has an effect. An equalising effect. She scans the area for movement, but nothing; sees only abandonment and markers of the past.

She stares at a memorial set high on a plinth; she thinks she might have it seen before. A woman and two men, sacked youths who came here to protect Isola. She can't help but stare at it now, and seemingly for the same reason she used to ignore such things. What did Gretchen say at that dinner at her house? What did she say about them when Rachel said none of us wanted to see the painting? 'It's heartbreak, this island is born to break hearts. Everywhere, everything. Those brave loves, those boys and women. Lost it all, didn't they? Lost it,' she'd said as she poured wine, 'lost it when the stressors of it all, of the war. I don't know. It was like when their clamber for what I've often supposed or imagined was a combined ideology, for coherence amid the blood carnage, this spilt their appetite for harmony. These are the failures of youth, yes? Tore it and placed a fever at the heart of all they knew of their resistance against all that immense hatred.'

Laura wasn't listening at the time, but now she realises she was. She stares up at the bronzed figures. Melancholy postures against unseen threat, brave jaws, legs splayed in uncertain stances.

'They fell apart because they were trying to defend this place and ended up trying to protect themselves. Everything is madness. So many of our efforts are born to fail.'

Now, in the damp evening, the warriors are surrounded by fruit stands and fish, postcards fluttering uninterested in the wind. Above them balconies stand empty, washing waving white flags. Laura has a sense then, a sense of how inept we are at memorialising youth and what youth means. Because it's always the destruction of youth, isn't it?

She feels the emptiness of this place. Of sacrifice and hope and need, of the half-love we fall into when surrounded by unheard silences trading echoes with the emptiness. Empty, the whole place empty, until a flash, a light in the corner of her eye.

A red flash.

She walks through the piazza and into the lattice weave. Dark doors and their dark mouths. The distance between details condensed, reduced to the span between two things no longer paired by difference. Clothes racks and hats. She jogs. Runs past the strip of cafés, the alfresco arrangement of tables and chairs, velvet ropes trying their best to separate the co-mingled seats. The smell of herbs, the hint of seared meat reek, everywhere everything searching shadow. She runs, ten, fifteen metres past the open doors and shadowy interiors, runs but stops. Some scarlet glow. She stops, walks back hunched and searching.

It's a restaurant spanning two storeys, red and green livery. *Il Grande Odisseo* says the sign, an eatery festooned in flowering vines. So popular and now empty. Laura stands at the top of the steep staircase leading down to the eatery in the basement, a glow in the frame of a door to a back room. 'Hello? Hello?' Nothing, just the pulsed and shifting light of the room's glow.

She asks of the room again, 'Hello? Hello?'

The seats abandoned, no evidence that anyone has ever eaten here but for knives and forks set in place. She moves between the tables and through the swinging doors into the kitchen. Then she's at the entrance to the back room, the place where meat is beaten on a board, chooks throttled and plucked. She sees a table, a chair, and there a large door frame like that of a painting discarded and leaning against the wall looking back at her.

A doorway and a basement beyond.

And in this doorway—a canvas of air filled with a dozen naked women. Women and a scattering of men, each of them in pain, lying under a tree in the large patio surrounded by the high walls of the museum. They're emancipated, arched bodies groaning. Breasts and genitals, ribs and hip bones, beards and a vast stillness. Desert sores in hidden places. No one moving, no one but the painter—though there is no painter. No painter, but it's a portrait whose love is pain and humiliation. She's seen David stare at such works hanging in the halls of museums, splurge on them when he's too exhausted and all there is is pain but, like the rest of the world, he's somewhere else now.

She opens her mouth; her lips stick then peel.

In this foul mud-strewn scene, every movement seems agony. Eyes deep in their sockets. She's seen them but they react without betraying their instinct for survival; they reach for a pot of bad water. Their bodies, their insides in states of invisible wreckage after prolonged days of serious thirst. A dehydration in the heat radiating from the desert beyond the walls, and their organs are no longer producing energy. Without water, without fluids, the vital chemical responses in the body, all those metabolic ructions involved in the production of energy, begin to shut down. She watches and there's barely a sound from these souls but she knows the noises they make by the shapes of their mouths and the lines on their faces. Lines deep beside hollowed-out features, eyes and cheeks, and beyond this room is the town and the town, she now knows, is empty.

The town is empty.

The town is lost, mislaid in the rain.

She moves closer until the whole of the basement is gradually unveiled. Closer, their groans suddenly words, though a language she can't hear. And everywhere the scattering of mice, secretly appearing and vanishing. She sees the beginnings, then, of a foot, the shape of its arch and ankle suspended above the ground. A leg, knee and thigh of a body hung in chains that are looped about branches. She sees the trace of blood at the hips of a man and the gash where a cock once hung. A violent rip where genitals previously swayed. The bulge of a weighty torso, then the neck, hair and bearded face of a man whose mouth has been desecrated and all his teeth knocked out clean. The man's eyes held open with small stick and an agonising death stare. He's not long dead, or not dead at all. She watches for movement, for pain responses, replies to his vile moment. She looks about him, seeking evidence of how and who has done this. His clothes, his shoes, his shirt in a pile lousy with mice. Then: a small glass urn slowly filling with rainwater, pink now for the blood, pink and a smashed white. These, the remains of the man's teeth.

She feels the violent upheaval of bile and sick. Her hands at her stomach and mouth.

She wants to run.

She wants many things but stays in this terrified moment.

Laura looks to the corners of the court—limbs, severed legs and arms. She knows she's crying, she knows she's screaming, she knows she can't move. A torso, a woman's, breastless, and a face without eyes. The stench reaches her, the aberrant odour of torture and death. Her eyes cling to the scene, for it is unyielding in its grip. The slow walk of a woman, her arm skinned and fly-struck. Another with a makeshift broom shushing leaves. Laura turns, in every direction she turns, and horror, death and wreckage. Bent corpses, the shuffling dead, the hurt of abandoned violence. A woman with a gash in her side trying to stand. A girl stubbornly attempting to walk towards Laura on smashed out knees. And there, there in the shadow behind the door, an intact woman, her eyes wide and seeing, seeing only the stones riding up the side of the city's walls, for she has long turned away from this all. Her face true to something, and then a word, a plum tone is pulled from her cracked black mouth as Laura moves towards her. The woman's white dress brown now, and she clutches at Laura's torn skirt, takes it in her hands and to her face.

The smell of iodine from somewhere. Laura tries to pull away from the woman. She pushes at her head with her palm so the woman falls backwards, a pack of bad luck cards landing strewn among the mice. Laura screams at the woman but only dry air escapes her mouth. She must run, she must escape this dark, dank room. Her legs suddenly cementitious. Dream heavy.

'They,' the woman stammers. 'They said they're coming back.'

Laura lurches out of the way as the woman grabs at her once more. Then, then she runs. A terrified motion of legs and tears and the smell of sick.

Her body seems to melt as she runs from the basement to the stairs, to the alley.

Her heart red and pounding like that's all that's left of her. She runs, lit by all terror, the absolute weight of it.

The alley. The *they*. She runs so her sneakers grip on the cobblestones, runs so she's hit by bands of sunlight again and again. Her face, her arms assaulted by the beams slanting through the gaps in the building. The they. The road. There's just one, and she takes it. Up. Running, panting, wet shadows everywhere, eyes, and where are they hiding? The great invisible I.

Dislocation

The last time I saw James was when I went to pick up a piece of recording equipment in Newtown, near the old SPCA, where he was tracking in a studio hidden in a row of ancient, rotted warehouses. Though hardly any distance from my house, I drove our Honda down, parked and went inside. There's that which comes after energy. That's what makes me worry when I leave the house. That there's always something beyond tired and something beyond energy, and when there isn't, I'll be the one to know. I hadn't been in a good place for several weeks and worried about having to talk with my old friend. I bumped into the band's guitarist as I entered the facility. He nodded me into the control room, where I saw James. He spotted me, and instead of his usual grin he looked grey. He stood and hugged me in the doorway. As we went through the hall we talked through various greetings.

'Hey.'

'How are you?'

'Yeah. How you man?'

'Ah. How are you?'

'Yeah.'

Neither of us had the usual response on hand, that we were good and all, that we were all the usual so that we could finish the ritual and get on to business.

I made a statement, said, 'You're not okay, are you?'

And he wasn't.

A month earlier, around New Year's Eve, he was working at a music festival up in Hawke's Bay. He told me he woke on the last morning and went to his work van. He opened the door and found a friend dead in the driver's seat. The man was sixty years old and had just simply passed away. James explained that in the last weeks he'd been unable to think, felt decimated and rankly out of kilter. He was unable to bring himself up for the simplest of tasks.

'Then another friend,' he said. 'She died of cancer the same week. She was fifty-seven.' He nodded back at the control room, where his band were searching for the right guitar sound. 'I haven't done a thing for this song. I'm just . . .'

He started crying then. A raft of tears came out of him, and in the hallway of this hidden place, he cried and I held him.

'It's a month ago, man. And I just can't. I should be better but I'm just not.'

It was summer; the hall was dark but warm.

He told me his father had died three years ago and he felt like his life, too, was somehow ending. I'd never seen him like this, his face and his mouth. He walked me to my car, which I'd had to park up on Mansfield Street. He helped me carry the road case because I was struggling with its bulk.

'I just feel nothing,' he said.

'I know, man.'

'Just nil, nothing.'

'But nothing is something.'

'Yeah—but that's not what I mean.'

'. . .'

'It's like—to die willingly is extraordinary,' he said. 'Any other way feels a waste of life.'

Across the road sat the Newtown Park stadium. I had a sudden memory of being ten and losing a gumboot in the mud on the far bank as my brother ran the fifteen hundred metres at the national championships. I remembered the sound of it, the sucking sound as it was removed from my foot and lost forever.

'But it is something, you're right,' he said. 'That's how we get dark matter.'

We laughed, a weak laugh, a sad laugh.

'It is something,' I said. 'It's a negation—of self. Which is the worst kind of self. But it's a kind of self.'

He nodded slowly. 'Hey, Deborah died, eh,' he said.

I nodded.

'I heard, like it was a few years ago.'

'Few years ago, yeah.'

'I read about it. Or, I don't know. I just knew about it.'

'Yeah.'

'That stinks.'

'It was heartbreaking, man.'

'I saw her name in the paper. I thought—fuck.'

'Just—heartbreaking. I couldn't stop thinking, you know? About her husband, about Mark and their son. And, Jesus. And I couldn't stop thinking about what happens to us when we stop trying to love people. That's a really bad moment in our lives.'

'That's the negation.'

I raised my eyebrows and repeated the word back to him. I told him then about Richard Lyon, that he hadn't died like we thought he had. He was living out west and had kids. Marcel had seen him. He hadn't died with a stupid needle in his arm, lying there amongst someone else's kids while looking after them. That was what James had heard and told me years earlier.

'Fuck. News. Good news.'

'Let's take it, eh.'

'I swore he was dead. Like, I was certain.'

I reminded him of that drive south a quarter of a century ago. How I was haunted the entire drive by a sense of Deborah being dead, and though she was quite alive the sensation seemed to live on in me. A viral haunting that hadn't ever really left.

'People never leave,' James said. 'Not really.'

We hugged again and that was the day.

We made actual plans for two weeks in the future, set a time and a place to play some music together. I bought new strings and cleaned out the sockets of my pedals on my board, replaced the patch cables which had cracked and tested all the equipment and made sure it functioned. I tried to recall some of the riffs and rhythms I'd been thinking of for a while. I played until I was exhausted and waited.

It's foolish when I play music, to play and expect something of it. It's physically very difficult: The brain doesn't send signals, or it does, but they come in slow. My nerve endings are sluggish; they don't recognise the urgency. They only feel like half-signals anyway. Rhythm is impossible, fingerings clumsy. Ears are blocked, but I do it anyway. It's a response to another fear of negation, of the mind my father and grandmother ended up with before they died. Dementia and all that it entails.*

I fear what was happening to my dad before the end. Each time he told a story he would start from the beginning, and if

* And now my mother, too. As we edited this book, my mother rapidly developed a form of vascular dementia. It was heartbreakingly destructive. To exist in the world we narrate ourselves, our surrounds and past. Much of what she believed near the end didn't exist; it was a reality of stories unhitched to her love and family. But stories are stories, so we listened and tried not to correct too much; there was something she needed to grasp in order to be. She passed away two months ago, taking a glimpse of my mother with her.

interrupted he'd begin again once more. It seemed the only way he could recall things was if he went the entire way through a narrative. A simple mountaineering story could take hours. He seemed to have no cognition of the fact he was doing this, repeating what he'd already said without correction. I fear this very much, because it happens with me. I have so little memory of what I have written in this book, or any of my books. In reading it I have to start from the beginning and finish it before the sickness gathers. I haven't yet managed a full reading. I can only get so far before I'm sick and horizontal and it's as if my memory is wiped and no book exists.

I found Richard Lyon on Facebook. He had eighteen friends and was not active in any way. I messaged him and we talked like twenty-five years hadn't passed. And then I told him about Deborah and that was when we decided we'd form a band. And we did; he sends me songs and I mutilate them, then go to bed.

Some years prior to contacting Richard again I'd walked to our window that looks out over the mountains to the east of Wellington. The Remutaka range, slightly snowed from a storm that had barrelled up from the south a few days earlier. I answered the phone. A call from Auckland. An old friend, a love close enough, near enough, aged enough to call kin. I stood in the same spot in which I'd taken a selfie with Deborah only a few months before, when she and Mark, son and new puppy visited on their way back from summer holiday. It was a nice photo. The two of us smiling and looking full of summer like we might have twenty-three years ago. I was standing in the same spot, in the same place where her brother-in-law had called me.

We were silent for long periods, Hayden and me. Periods of breathing and waiting. The waiting for that impossible moment. That undoing of the information into the actual, physical. It was with Hayden and his band that I'd travelled to the USA, UK, Europe and South Asia back in 1998 and 1999. We knew things of each other because of that time. Unnamed things. He's married to Deborah's sister, Damaris. She too was on that tour and knew things about me, the messed things.

'We didn't know how to tell you,' Hayden said. I could hear his stubble rubbing on his phone. His hand swapping the mobile from hand to hand.

Whatever my reply, I sounded weak.

'I'm so sorry,' he said.

I waited. 'How?' I asked.

He sighed, which told me he didn't know how to tell me. All he'd managed so far was a noun, an old noun.

'How's Mark?' I said this softly, transferring concern to those who really mattered. Deborah's husband had always been kind to me, even if I hadn't always deserved it, such was the state of my jealousy back a couple of decades. Such was the hole that I'd let our break-up tear through my life and render me useless and express the hopeless in the things I'd say.

'Mark's . . . I don't know. He's—what else would he be?'

'I know. I mean, I don't know.'

'He's bad.'

'Hayden. Where's Damaris?'

'Oh man.' He sounded sick.

'Maybe I'll call him.'

'Give him a few days.'

'Of course.' I paused. I waited.

This was the impossible conversation we never have, never practise.

'So?' I said.

Hayden sighed. 'Have you watched the news?'

'I never watch the news.'

'Look on your phone. Actually. Don't, don't do anything.'

'Hayden?' I sounded trivial then, a small, startled version of myself. I sounded like a little boy, that something was coming at me through imagined pasts. I recalled a television programme I'd watched as a kid. A boy was trapped in a room and outside were stones in a field. Every few minutes they would come closer, closer to this house. Shifting invisibly across the field. I remembered the boy's terror, and my own fear, how they felt linked by the utterly unknown force of these stones' movement.

'Kaikōura,' Hayden said. 'You heard?'

'Fuck.'

'Yes,' he said.

The noise I made had no letters, no form, just unpatterned air passing out of me in desperate affect.

Deborah had been working in Kaikōura for eighteen months, a comms expert as they rebuilt the town, roads and railway after the earthquake. Pictures of her on Instagram in a yellow hard hat beside a helicopter. Pictures then of mangled land from several hundred feet up. I'd spoken to her only a month earlier. We'd become a bit incompetent over the years, never entirely sure what to say to each other, but we liked to say nothing anyway. News and strange occurrences. Her book club had had a session dedicated to my novel and I remembered waiting for her report, far more nervous than I was for the book awards, which I had to fly up to Auckland for the following week. I laughed, remembering how she remained dedicated to that small part of us that lingered after decades. She was the best kind of love to leave behind.

'Oh, this is hopeless,' I said. I could hear Hayden was near tears. Those damp man tears that are so rare and soft. An echo of far past youth, when we were held on to by our mothers. I realised Damaris was standing next to him, listening, waiting and wanting to say something. 'I want to come and see you and Damaris,' I said.

'I know.'

'You know?'

'I know.'

'I want . . .'

'I know.'

Breathing.

Time.

'I'm broke up, man,' he said.

'I know.'

'I'll tell you when the funeral is when I find out.'

'I'll come, of course. Laura and I will come.'

'It'll be good to see you both.'

'I love you guys.'

'Love you too.'

'. . .'

'. . .'

'Fuck, Hayden.'

'I'll tell her parents you'll be there,' he said.

'Yeah. Thank you. I'll try to get my head around what I could ever say to them.'

He went silent and we stayed that way, waiting on the impossible, the words that would correct something that now seemed vapour. Now seemed mixed with a quarter century of passed time and doubts and certainties.

I hung up. I stayed standing by the window. The tight June air, the ranges of hills, the patch of harbour and the rise then of mountains. The climb to the peaks and the white patches on the hills. The snow that only ever hangs about for a few days, then goes, runs off to creeks and rivers, dams and turbines and the new electricity that'll run through our bones once the tears are all done. I kept seeing the event as it played out in the new. I kept seeing it. The machine. This fuel-eating thing, this mile-hungry gadget of engine, light metals and speed. I kept seeing the colour of the silver, the flash of light, although I can't tell you what real colour. I kept seeing the uncoupling, the simplicity of aerial derailment, the suddenness of stressed noise. Of vocal cords and steel and glass. The absolute howl of metal and the buckling of instant into—into—

I kept seeing her face. Her fine features and mouth. The way her back, how it would have straightened and snapped to, every muscle hardened. The way all eyes in that cabin would have looked up. All of this. The rapid passing through of all events, through her eyes and face and every word spoken, the screech of voice and how quiet she always was, always had been, the silence in which she greeted everything, until everything was falling around her and she had to speak. How every vein was pumped full of adrenal reflux and I recalled, God, I recalled how small she was. How light she was. How easy she was to pick up and throw around and make laugh and all that and I felt the terror of this, of other arms, invisible and unimpeachable, lifting her and loosing her into the wreckage. And then the hiss of it, the mangle and eventual, utter silence of it. I remembered my backyard then, I remembered the rain, I remembered its suddenness and the suddenness of life, the surprise of its readiness, its willingness.

Today, This Week, This Year

Six fifteen and it's not light yet, not really. An almost-light beyond the ridges, talking, saying wake, wake, come to the day.

So, I wake. I wake first. I wake and I have the sensation someone has jumped me in the night.

At best I feel assaulted.

Last week I was sleeping through, right up until the sound of the closing front door stunned me awake. The door shut and I heard my wife's shoes on the path outside and I was jolted into this state of consciousness. I would stay in bed then. For the whole week I let the heater switch on and stretch the air through the room, finger its way through bedclothes and curtains. Then it would click off. I'd let the day creep like the eyes of a stalker. Black, hurting pupils peering over the hours and then it would end with time sullied by fear of the room and smell of the room. My mouth open like a sound was trying to escape, an already nullified scream. But now, it's six fifteen and I let Laura sleep until her alarm rings.

I head to the shower. We redid the bathroom eighteen months ago; there's a bulge in the wall above the shower unit. I keep telling Laura, I say: *I'll call MCLEAN & SPOUT*. That's the company who did the install and the plan was to get them to come back and seal the gap between the PVC unit and wall, for them to repaint, and then everything would be all right. It's a phone call. It's trying to remember how to say what the issue is, where we live and so on. I put the water temperature up to fifty degrees and loosen the tap as the extractor fan comes on. Water and air. My expectation is the shower will wake me, and the stronger the flow the more awake I'll be when I exit the bathroom and try to ascend the stairs. There are stairs everywhere in our house; it's a place overcome with stairs. I turn the temperature up so I can put more cold water into the stream and make it stronger. The muscling of water, how it stuns the skin, and the skin is where the nerves lie and nerves tell us how we feel. I find myself sitting on the floor of the shower and let the jetted stream impact my neck and back.

In the lounge, with the stairs overcome, I sit on the couch for ten minutes. Each of those minutes feels like a migraine, though I rarely get headaches—I'm lucky like that. Others of my kind are racked by them, lanced to the temples by unrelenting pain. I stay looking at the phosphenes dancing in the place of light. It's the weight of my head. It's the sense of pressure on my occipital lobe, one of the lobes. I find myself in the initial movement towards the kitchen at the back of the house. Feel the thought being made, a palsied effort felt by a mere half of the necessary nerves.

A matutinal light is hinted at on the edge of the Remutaka range in the forested east. I watch the clouds, the black weight of them slowly reducing until they puff above the ragged line of the mountains.

The cat is somewhere nearby.

An awareness of movements in the steady reverberations of morning. I try again to organise the motions needed to make myself breakfast. It's simple: The fruit bowl sits on the table on the way to the kitchen. Pause. Pick up a banana, an apple, then remove the bread from the fridge and place it in the toaster. This is simple stuff. The thin-cut wholegrain I've been eating most days for the last five years since this thing came back with such viciousness. Surface area and absorption factor. So: Table, stand, walk to the table. Pick up fruit, move to kitchen. Open fridge.

The sun between the hills and the cloud. In winter, when covered in snow and wind, we call them mountains; in summer they are hills.

Is that what you call them?

Yes.

The cat melts at my feet, then stretches up onto the couch beside me so she's lying at the col between my neck and shoulder, where nerve damage lurks. There's a white spot under her chin Laura and I always seem to be reaching for, as if it's asking for the kind of attention we can't help but oblige. As if we believe there are nerves beyond those resting throughout the noiseless continuation of the animal's body, that she desires us to touch them.

The hills separate Wellington from Wairarapa, but most days we don't know this.

Apple, banana, fridge, toaster. I'm showered, smell of skin and water. I'm wearing the clothes I took from the bedroom to the bathroom.

We don't have a bath, only a shower.

The base rule of language is uncertainty.

Now Laura is sitting at the table when the seeds crackle inside the toast. She's listening to soft music. We try to keep the house active with sound, until we forget and it goes silent.

'You sleep okay, honey?' she asks.

'I don't know.'

'When did you wake up?'

'. . .'

'I slept in,' she says. 'But I'm . . .'

'What's the time?'

'I kept hitting snooze. I kept rolling over. Then I realised you weren't there.'

'I was in the shower.'

'I know.'

How often I wake up surprised my wife is still with me. And not because she would ever desert me, but because I imagine all things in my life vanishing. Most others have disappeared, the people and the things that once held us close. I need to thank her for so many things.

The kitchen is just off the lounge. The lounge looks out to the Pacific and the mountains. Mountains because it's winter and there's snow over that way. The house smells of bread and sunlight. We didn't know what the walls would look like when we painted it last summer, plastered the rooms in a deep, dark green. In summer it feels cool, lighter than previously; in winter it feels close and warm.

I stand beside the table. Laura in her red gown.

'What's today?' she asks.

'They sent through another version.'

'How does it look?'

'They just sent it through.'

'You okay?'

‘What time did you get to sleep?’

‘I slept really well.’

‘Good. Good, good.’

The room is shaped by sound, the smallest sounds we don’t know we hear. People move about inside it, wary they’re disturbing us.

I eat at my computer. CricInfo, because somehow cricket in the northern summer while all else are at home, because numbers, and these numbers are human numbers and I can stare. News, and I just look at the headlines. The great nothingness of politics and the distant, great disaster. This many dead, this many infected. This many dollars. Email. I leave it open and stare at the words. I wrote nothing during the first lockdown and it was mere months after that that Laura became ill, and this seemed doubly cruel. Who wants to know you’re sick when millions around the world are dying? I’m not sure, but I do know illness doesn’t wait its turn. There is no queue for the undoing.

There’s a form of focus. Inexact. Last week, I think. I think it was last week, and last week I found during every second morning I couldn’t see the screen. I could navigate the house but the inflammation back there in the occipital lobe sometimes causes a situation. I assume the occipital lobe; I have no proof because I don’t have a positron emission tomography scanner to peer into the ends of my soul and extract data, but this is the theory I postulate. Actually, it’s more likely it’s just other inflammation somewhere in there causing disruption. That day my mind wouldn’t let a focal point form, a locus of clarity and clear vision. I watched a Tom Hanks film instead of working. A man and some people. He wore a hat. Then his plane crashed.

I hear the double engine sound of the extraction fans in the bathroom.

Two fans counting off.

Then the shower sound.

I hadn't seen Laura pass by. My office is adjacent to the stairs and bathroom. Just across the hall.

Sometimes I think my wife has an invisible self.

Email and I can't read just yet because there are ants on my desk, slender lives I watch helplessly.

Letting life live is so simple.

It only takes the suppression of base rage. I had a lot of rage when I was younger. A lot of small things in my blood.

When COVID hit, it felt like all people were at once present and missing; all people had joined me at home, were sick like me or waiting to be sick. That they were dying and half refused to acknowledge it. I didn't write a word for this book during the first four months.

Now the way the sound of the water changes as Laura moves in the cubicle. The shape of her body visible in the sound of water. A sonic locator of her slight size, and I seem to know she's washing her hair. Which means it's Thursday, or a Monday and I forgot to have a weekend. But it's Thursday, because today is the day we leave.

I don't believe in the past anymore. It's a lie.

Food makes me feel sick, but I'm always hungry.

I'm at my best when I avoid raw food, which is annoying. Sixteen hundred calories a day. It's hard to maintain.

Time

The usual count is an hour, an hour and a half before I can focus enough to read what's on my screen. For the muscles to pull and for my eyes to remember, or it's not my eyes, it's something else. I explain it like I know. I don't know. I just understand there are things that swell in there and sometimes they don't perform their operations in a way that makes time pass in the way time might normally pass. I wait; time passes. I work, or I go to the couch, or bed.

Water sound, and I imagine a perfect shape shaped by the water.

Time occurs, I think, only when we're working.

This other passage is something else.

'When will I see you?' she asks.

'I'll be there.'

My wife looks sleek, hair wet and combed back. I see her before I hear her, a peripheral movement that makes me startle. She works most days, whether well enough or not.

'Can you leave the extractor on?' I ask.

'The fan? Why?'

'Yes. Just leave it on.'

She appears inaudible. A wave form that refuses sound, which makes her half invisible.

'I'll be there at quarter to,' she says.

'Okay. I'll be there exactly then, give or take. Just leave the fan on.'

'Have you found out if we can sit together?'

'I just want to make sure all the steam is out of the room.'

'Okay.'

'I just want to keep it dry.'

'Can you give them a call? I want to sit with you on the plane.'

'Are you taking a taxi?' I ask.

'Of course.'

'Is it supposed to rain?'

‘I think, maybe. How are you feeling?’ she asks.

‘I’ll see you at quarter to. Are you going to eat beforehand, or?’

‘Probably not. I’ll be nervous.’

‘Sure.’

‘You okay?’

‘I’m okay.’

‘Okay. Love you.’

‘Love you, too.’

‘What’s the guy’s name?’

‘Who?’

‘The guy . . .’

‘Khiem?’

‘Is that it?’

‘You talking about the painters?’

‘Is Khiem the guy we decided on?’

‘I don’t know.’

‘You don’t know,’ she said, standing there in her towel. ‘I’m thinking about somehow killing you. Gently.’

‘Yeah.’

‘Mildly,’ she said. ‘With—I don’t know—dusters.’

I open two documents on my desktop. There’s nothing there, and the cat stirs on my desk. She watches me with green eyes and sometimes she brings in her favourite toy and starts crying. A small blue fish on a string. Now she’s happy sitting on top of the papers I printed out before I went to bed last night. The fan turns off and I get up and go to the bathroom, open the door a crack, reach around and turn the fan back on. It takes a minute to engage. The builders have installed a two-motored extractor to make sure as much moisture is taken from the room as possible. Otherwise the steam builds up in there and finds its way into the rest of the house. The bathroom smells of towels and I take the basket out and leave it in the hall.

The MetService says a twelve-degree high.

I find myself upstairs with my empty plate.

The heater turns off automatically in the living area at 9am.

The TV comes on when I touch my phone.

A film by Angela Schanelec.

Maren Eggert and Dane Komljen talking in the street.

Everything I say and have said through my life is a singularity, a drone navigating poorly lit rooms. Everything is always changing without me.

The Willing

Up. Upwards. We'd climbed, bodies and shoulders. His legs, his steps shook. The weight of David and me, of our combined selves. A step, a footfall not quite exact, his sneakers, how they didn't quite grip and grab and—and down, backwards. Backwards and down, the earth slowly rifling, the dirt and sand sucked towards the plane of us. The length of seconds, the sound of time as we breathed, and then the speed of us as we hit. The weight of us, the light heft of me then him, and we bounced and we lay in the rock. How long before we said anything, and what words? We lay on the rain-wet rock, the small rivulets from the storm and the traces of sand in tiny, branching deltas.

Then I was slowly, achingly, up. Words.

He lay in the rock and heard me fall, just a few fine metres. I fell as if the hold of my joints had failed—and down.

We lay still, the sense of rapid entrapment, of enclosure and tightness. Of light. Of glass and light. All as if my skull was made of light and light was tightening around every thought, every hint of idea and its twin sensation glassed in, the sound of a thousand tiny bent bells. My legs, my arms. My eyes blinking, imagining time vanishing into another measure of time. Time is, and time is a symptom of despondency and unrelieving tides of knowledge and un-knowledge, the desperate accents of humanness that hold it all in place.

Voices. The soft touch of words, of a memory of words.

Six metres, seven. I got up and walked as the rock grew around him and then I collapsed, buckled from a pillar to a pile, a pile of nouns and all they take with them to keep them alive.

Now we talk again, drift; we hear and don't hear.

Can you come to me? David asks. I can't see you.

I shake my head. Shift it so I can see how much of him is now enclosed in the rock.

We talk. Wise words and fakes, spaces of rhetorical backbeat and drift, a music of trust and distrust, of loneliness and love, the shaking and weeping and the pain that has no site but body itself, body and why we walked here. What do we see when we see in the other, the mirrored life we can't expect to see because no science yet sees it? David says how he always misses Laura, always just wants her company, but knows he can't always be company. I say how I just want to correct the world with colour. I say I want to slow the undoing with great tides of colour. We talk, weep and talk just to be inside the sentence. The sentence. The way it seeks itself, its tail, shaped like a question curling, curling till it's its own answer, an agitated stillness surrounding everything.

Time is such that the movement of the earth's crust can be seen; it's observable, a sight neither of us can turn from. My arms now surrounded, my legs too, and the red-rocked cliffs join us.

Previously

Two contestants have been voted off the island during an extra-long episode. Which is exciting. The cat finds her way back to me as the episode ends. Fifteen minutes into the next episode I roll over. I make a sound, a kind of long grunt that she imitates. I stop the show and replay the tribal council of the previous episode. I don't recall who was voted out. The files I download have the *Previously on . . .* cut out, which is the way I prefer it. Then, there he is: a man my age who said nothing as the council ejected him and sent him to another island. He has regrets and unmaintainable anger. I don't remember his name. I give up and lie still with my mouth open. If my head makes a sound it's like an elongated drone, continuous after a hard, vast metal has struck it. But there is no sound, just the sense of it. An unlocatable pain hums in its place. By midday it's cold, and the TV is still showing images. I turn it off and return to my office.

I hadn't closed the files and bring up the first. The sentence my eyes fall on won't settle. I go back to the beginning of the page and read out loud. Sometimes that helps, like the eager ghost of a former self is there in my head to lend a hand. I come to the sentence I started with and highlight it, start typing over the top. Sentence followed by sentence. I let them come out, tapped and rhythmic, though I stop because again I can't see the screen clearly. Twelve hundred words. I don't know what chapter I'm writing.

There's a text on my phone from Hayden: *See you at the café!*

So excited. Where's it?!

I call the painter. He said he'd be back with the final quote by the fifth, which was a week ago. I say my name and address and he sounds excited to hear from me, then hangs up. Since COVID, since the lockdowns have been lifted, every painter in the city has been putting me on hold.

'Can you give me a rough idea?' I ask when he calls back twenty minutes later.

'Sure.'

'. . .'

'Can I call you back?' he says.

'I . . .'

'I just need to call June at the office. This for the interior?'

'Exterior.'

'Exterior. Did we do your lounge?'

'Yes.'

'Of course. Of course we did. I need to call the office. I'll call you back.'

I read the overnight emails and respond to one from my editor regarding changes to the cover. I scroll down further because the number in the upper left-hand corner says I have seventeen unread messages. Some are from Dictionary.com. Word of the Day. Phrase of the whatever. I keep words on hand if they look like they might warrant future use.

[**ahy**-l*uh*m]

noun

the hypothetical initial substance of the universe from which all matter is derived.

ORIGIN | EXAMPLES

LOOK IT UP

There are notes to myself sent from my phone, queries and answers to issues of plot and theme. Three a.m. desperate; midnight certain. One in ten contains logic, and implementing logic means drastic rewrites. I'm always writing two books and they always overlap. I borrow lines, see which text they work best in. There are casualties. At any one moment I can't tell you what I have written already and what I haven't yet written. I have accidently written chapters twice. There are many things I can't know.

Khiem. An email from Khiem the painter from a date earlier in the month.

I print out the attachment.

He sent the quote two weeks ago. I've already responded to him; we accepted it, but who knows what acceptance means.

I call him back and ask if the quote includes paint.

'Great. Yes. All materials.'

'Materials?'

'Yes. All materials.'

All I can think of when I hear the word *materials* is that of cells. I read stuff, all the partial glimpses at articles my eyes will allow. I open articles for my PhD, and I read half a sentence discussing the way my cells aren't behaving. My eyes stop and I'm left with images, visions of cell walls crumbling, whole parts of me fragmenting in my blood, dying proteins disassembling. The materials of living mater in free fall from some height, the elevated horizon where we place the living. The small rectangles of mitochondria with rounded corners, all the information of energy and drive falling downwards in sequenced spirals.

Dizzying.

The Faces

The weight of footfalls in the rain, heavier now. The coarse shambling of boots, the noise of approach. The coming. The singular sound, human-heavy. Human in the trace echoes through the dirt and rock. I feel them and feel the unfolding of the tell-tale telluric forces that announced the day's completion, the last beat of time as the sun begins to hit the sea.

Get up.
Get up.

The gully wants to be empty, hollow, a vacant place of near sound, but it keeps being filled with foreign noise, occupied with sound, with boot sound, the emptiness and the sound, the light and the spaces between ellipses of light, of echo and echoes because of high-hanging rock, because pockets of gorged-out stone and the ancient grottos, hiding places of soldier and lover, child and partisan, silence then echo then silence, then the scrape and the drag and scrape and then a couple, a woman and a man stepping down the path from above. A child piggybacked by his mother in the light from the beach. They nod hellos as they come closer, eyes seemingly untouched by the buried sight of us. Boots and shorts and a daypack on the man's shoulders.

They're there to remember us.

I feel David track their eyes and mouths. The man says some hello or other and they speak. He has a gentle west Irish accent and he talks as he fidgets with the top of his water bottle. But he stops as an interruption comes from his little boy. First words, now tears. The boy starts crying, twisting, burrowing into his mother.

They're yet to remember.

'Hey, little man. It's okay,' Mum says.

'You on your way up or down?' the man asks.

David nods upwards from out of his enclosed face.

They're yet to remember. Their eyes, the thousand ways to look. They're yet to recall. The moment when they'll see my face, see his face, see us replayed in an alignment of synapses—that will come later.

'It's okay. Hey, hey, baby boy,' Mum says.

'No,' the boy says. 'No, I don't want to!'

The kid's face wretched and pink in the hot day, eyes shocked red. His mum struggles to hold his small body as he bends this way and that. The absolute noise of him, screaming, really putting his back into it. His legs kicking like he wants out.

'Sorry,' the man says. 'To be honest, this doesn't happen, not usually.' He bends down to his child.

Time, the rippled sheet after waking. Time, always waking.

'It's okay,' David barely says. 'Just whatever he needs.' My cousin looks over to where I sit.

'He's usually so calm. Most of the time. Not rowing like this.'

By the looks, the boy just wants to slip from his mother's pale arms and hammer himself on the rock, mash his face, just so that they would know, that his parents would know just what it is to be him in this heat and the rain, the new rain. Because this is a new downpour and it's really trying to articulate itself.

'Okay, okay,' Dad says. 'Home soon. Home soon.'

They'll remember, when the sheet is pulled tight. Time suddenly time.

'Baby, baby boy,' Mum says softly. 'Come on, baby.'

'Get him his water bottle. Here, splash it on his face.'

'No, God, Lorcan.'

'Come on.'

'Good boy, Cillian, good boy. Come on.'

I watch them, this battle, this boy's determination in the rain, his amped heat ready to rip him from their clutches and damage himself in front of everyone. David says my name and I'm supposed to react, but my arms are quite pinned to my sides.

'It's okay, it's okay,' the mum says again.

David lets them be. He still has fingers free and he lifts them, making a sign. I'm yet to learn its meaning.

'Good boy, Cillian,' the woman says. 'Good boy. Stop that now.'

'On my shoulders,' the dad says. 'Up on my shoulders, come on.'

The man crouching. David tries to push out of the stone but just makes noises instead.

'Come on.'

'I'm too heavy,' the boy shouts. His face harassed, twisted with tears and dread.

'I'll get you up.'

'I'm too heavy.'

'Rachel,' David says.

I look up, look.

'Rachel?'

I give a slow blink. I feel myself glance inward, a glance though to some lost penetralia at the centre of me. A cold gasp. I give David a last look, and what cost, that word *last*?

'I'm *too* heavy,' the boy shouts. Shouts, and this is the end. He falls, his head, slipping his mother's arms and then, his head and face—faces. The faces. He falls screaming through the rain, wretched, eyes and nose first. The blood thud of bone on rock.

David shouts.

'Cillian?' the father asks as the boy goes silent.

'Cillian!'

Silent, and my legs vanish and I sense us compacting inwards.

'Cillian!'

My eyes closed, their fixed stare at all the lights dancing. How *strange* the choices made at the end. How strange it is we must even say, *the end*.

'Rach?' David says as the boy goes silent. 'Rachel?' The red of the boy spreads so quickly from his rent mouth and his parents' screams hit the walls of the tight canyon, ricochet through the rain.

Mum and Dad shouting. There's blood, blood running with water.

The echoes bounce downwards, upwards, voices and generations.

My eyesight now, the peculiar lack, the vanishing of all.

'Cillian!'

'Rach?'

'Cillian?' as the boy sits crumpled, ghost quiet. His parents speaking, just dialogue. Or they're not speaking and it's something else coming from their mouths. David trying to stand again in the rain but there's only stone. Bird sounds, like I'm hearing the fall of the glittering phosphenes behind my eyes.

Then—then the howl, the noise of the boy. How it spreads so quickly from his blooded mouth and hits the walls of the tight gullies. Hits the glass and stone and ricochets into each corner and out again, rebounding on and on; it has no limit and the rain seems to pulse and pause. Pulse and linger. Appears to stop, midfall, and hang like a thousand lit globes in the afternoon.

The smeared child, he slowly stands achingly up and begins his walk from it all, ambling in a queer wobble through the stalled rain, and each drop has its own sound as his body, face and arms tap at each glittering jewel, and his form, it makes a path through the frozen light, a child-sized tunnel cut out of time.

Television

I wonder if there's another episode and do a quick search. I started watching *Survivor* the year I finished with work, or my body finished with work, or my head. It's tricky tracing the pathologies of viewing habits. I enjoy *Survivor*. Have found other writers and artists who like it too, so I don't feel so alone in my weakness. There's nothing to follow, really, but the editing of people into personas, TV-ready and trustworthy, or (and this is vital) otherwise. Somebody always wins, but I don't know who.

It's day twenty-seven on the island.

The episode finishes and I watch *Naked and Afraid*. Exposed and terrified people near killing themselves, nude in the desert heat. One paints with mud on a cave wall.

I imagine the conversation we'll have when Khiem calls back. That I've already accepted the quote and he'll give a start date and I'll write it down and try to memorise it like I try to memorise people by the things they might have said years ago and how that forms them into current people, for it has been some time since people came to the house.

On March 27th, ten years ago, I went home from work. I seem to recall that date effortlessly, like a birthday or public holiday. I went home and never returned. Eventually people stopped coming to the house.

My doctor said five to seven years is the average length of the illness. It's day 3782 today. I'm beyond average now. Back then I couldn't imagine it. It gets easier, simpler, I tell people. Only Laura knows this isn't true. This book wouldn't exist without her; many things wouldn't. Ideas, their contour and width; the house, the electricity in its bones. When she leaves, something rushes in, a silence, an emptiness no visitor quite fits.

But I lie. I lie. Some do come and visit. Two weeks ago, Kristen came to the house. Our old friend, who Laura and I both knew before we knew each other. When she visited, we managed a conversation about ruins and how casually they seem discarded by time and traded empires. I'd made the empty comment that New Zealand felt lacking for its absence of grand, physical discards. We'd been talking of Rome and Greece and all the rest. Kristen made the observation that we too lived amongst ruins. In Wellington's hills were the fragments of another life, of deep forest left from the time before Europeans, before axe and fire and gorse and pine and suburb. The culture of replacement was deep in our own land, she said.

We had lunch, then talked, then the three of us watched a horror movie.

I remember this because I'm looking at the trees in the hills. Or, no. No, I'm remembering this because it reminds me of the last time I went further from the house than the letterbox, which was the day before Kristen came to visit. I'd headed out for blood tests. Some days I'm reminded how long it's been since I left the house. Sometimes it's months, but I don't seem to mind.

The noise from the door interrupts my attempts at giving articulate instructions to my body. I want it to roll over because I'm not comfortable lying the way I'm lying. My arm is pinned under my body and has gone to sleep. But noise and banging, a kind of hard knocking. I'm trying to roll over but suddenly I'm standing and I make for the stairs. Once you get to the landing, whoever it is peering through the front door can see your feet and they know you are coming and they stop banging. The front door is mostly glass.

'I was driving by and so I stopped. I thought it might be simpler to come by the house.' It's Khiem, hulking in the front door. He's a large man, moved to New Zealand when he was twelve. By the time he was thirty he had a crew of fifteen fellow Vietnamese and they were never out of work.

'Sorry. I must have fallen asleep,' I say. Though this is never true; I only fall asleep at night after taking various concoctions and pills.

'I remember you saying you work from home.'

'Yes.'

'I thought it would be easier if I just came by.'

I say it's fine and invite him in. He takes off his boots and I open the bathroom door a touch and turn on the extractor fan again and close the door.

He stands inside my office as I sit on the chair listening to him.

'The only problem I see is, is the tree,' he says. 'The kōwhai.'

'Yes.'

'We need to remove some branches and all the foliage at the side of the house.'

'It's the neighbours',' I say.

'Okay. Is that going to be a problem?'

'I doubt it. They hate trees.'

'They hate trees?'

'It's the only one they haven't cut down.'

'Okay. Okay.' He shrugs his enormous shoulders. 'Some people are just the people you'd never think to meet, aren't they.' He makes a *hm-p* sound. 'Anyway, I thought I'd just come around and say about the tree.'

'I'll get our gardeners to cut out the foliage.'

'Great. Should be fine. As I say. I was in the neighbourhood.'

My office is lit by a narrow beam leaning across a bookcase, sliding and eventual, heading for the afternoon. I type CALL GARDENERS into the middle of a word in the middle of a paragraph.

'And you work from home?'

I nod.

'I'm not sure I could do that.'

'You'd be surprised,' I say.

'I'm not sure. Getting in my car and driving the neighbourhoods, I'm up at dawn doing this. I couldn't imagine not seeing how everyone lives.' He chortles.

'Sure.'

'What do you write?' he asks after nodding at the screen. He looks around at all the books.

I tell him.

'Okay, right. I had a friend once. He tried to write a book. Didn't get too far.'

'No.'

'He thought he had a story. He wrote a page and that was it. He realised he'd told the story in half a page and the rest was nonsense and he stopped.'

'Sure.'

'So, I'm guessing there's more to it than story.'

'There's motivation,' I say, 'there's consequence and theme. There's making it remember itself. That's mostly it.'

I see him out, close the bathroom door.

Then close it again because I come back to my office from the kitchen and it needs closing.

Motivation and work. Repetition and its consequence. I tell people a novel, the writing of a novel, is essentially a thought carried out over several years. I didn't say that to Khiem, but that's what I usually say. It is never instantaneous; it learns itself through the passage of both time and extraordinary repetition. Brain-numbing repetitions of the same phrases and sentences whose origins eventually become lost as their secret workings take over from the mind of the typist. Cogs and steam. The process is effective, a continual reminder that mirroring and facing up to one's difficulties doesn't guarantee their release but does allow for the possibility of movement toward the eradication of time as the necessary ingredient in revelation.

It's all I can do to stay extant in the world, to make comments like this.

Yes. Put some music on.

Thanks. Okay.

My office is due to have its windows replaced with new frames and panes, double-glazed. A whole three-metre unit looking at the Pacific. I'm hopeful this will stop the drips of water that come in through the architrave and fill the cups I have arranged on the sill. I don't complain because beyond the window is the ocean; even when foul it is a beautiful life.

I pick up a piece of paper to file, but the filing cabinet isn't where it should be. It's black and three-foot tall and heavy. Some things can only be moved by the mind.

I'm on the couch. I don't know why. After a few minutes I realise there is a plate beside me. It's dirty and I think it's from breakfast. I must have brought it upstairs to put in the dishwasher. It's too warm since everything was double-glazed upstairs. There's a piece of paper in my pocket. A phone number. I call it.

'David?'
'Yes.'
'Hi.'
'Hi. Who is this?'
'. . .'
'Oh, hey you.'
'Hey!'
'Hey.'
'Is it okay if you die in my book?'
'Eh?'

Then, I don't know. I recall calling and now, now I only recall remembering calling. The name gone like breath on the winter windows.

The house makes itself known often. Usually through various odours, sounds and flickering lights. This latter habit ceased after the rewiring of the house last autumn. But before that, Laura put a call through to the fire service: there was a smell of burning somewhere in the house. Three fire appliances arrived. Men and women in thick clothing and heavy boots scouring our rooms, peering inside our walls with heat-detecting devices as I stood outside with my laptop with Laura apologising to the neighbours. Nothing was found. The week following, the electricians came with their rolls of wire, with snippers and cutters and multimeters and strippers and screwdrivers and nut drivers and a new fuse box to replace the old Fifties model lurking in the hall. Men in matching T-shirts stretching inside our walls, reaching, pulling, cutting. In the stairwell they pulled out blackened wires. Held them up for our inspection.

'Near thing, this,' the apprentice said. A long, drawn face. I imagined him aged before his time.

My office is too full of books to be useful to anyone else. Their order flows through the rows on the floor up into the shelves. There's an occasional moment when I find a duplicate and I never do anything about it. There's an acceptance of absence of reason and humanity that only the presence of so many well-organised words can imitate.

I open the Air New Zealand app and find my ticket information. I tap *Manage Booking.* I'm taken to the website where after several links I am able to request assistance at the airport.

Rain, suddenly. Sudden rain. A southerly bearing in from the Strait.

I type for a moment.

Then I go back to the website. I click the box again. Then a few more times, then get back to writing. I sometimes I write things, chapters, people, twice. I don't realise it until later, sometimes years later.

That eager stream of words that feels much like the syncopation of harmony when you kick your guitar in a corner. Always have your machines tuned to something interesting. That's the trick when you can no longer play the things that bring that other kind of joy.

I stop and check Facebook because there was something I was meaning to check.

It's black now, which is interesting and feels mean and economic.

There are a few words left of *Dance Prone* to write. I don't know what they are. The book feels dangerously unfinished without them. It's signed off on in London and I'm terrified about these words. That someone else knows what that they are, and I don't.

Where are you?

Me?

Yes.

I'm on the stairs.

How did you get there?

I was trying to work.

I'm sitting on the stairs. The front door is in front of me.

I'm waiting, aren't I?

Are you?

There's something coming.

You got an email?

Yes.

You opened the email.

Yes.

You opened the email and it told you the couriers are on the way.

Bookshelves. I'm waiting on bookshelves.

Good. Then you'll get back to work?

I'll get back to work when they come. Unless—

Unless they don't come.

And then you'll get back to work?

Work?

You're looking at the front door.

Yes.

Looking through the glass at the path alongside our house.

That's what I'm doing.

Water is collecting in pools.

Which is true: an imitation of the major flooding occurring across the city. Which is what FB told me. Flooding.

And then you'll get back to work?

Work?

Work.

I wish I understood work.

I don't understand work.

No.

It is just something that has come over my life.

I understand that, he says.

Of course you do. Let me tell you this, I say.

Tell you what?

Just this thing, this small story.

Yes.

Let me tell you.

. . .

Just this thing, a small story.

I know what you're going to say.

Of course you do, I say.

At the age of twenty-seven you spent four days awake in your appalling house in Kelburn.

Yes, that's what I was going to say.

That's what you were going to write, isn't it.

Yes.

This was many years ago for you.

It started with an all-night drinking run. That's what I was going to type.

But you're on the stairs.

Yes.

You stayed up and the night continued on until the morning and the next night. Then you had an essay to write for university.

Correct. You know this story.

And again, you stayed up. The night following you played a gig with your band, and none of you bothered with sleep. And again, you stayed up through the night staring out the window at the ships at port. Great things, sulking that they were tied up at the wharf. You stayed sitting in the same place.

Yes.

A stillness came over your body and you knew you weren't going to sleep for some time. The days after were extraordinary things of illusion and revelation, that's how you like to phrase it. Though you have never told anyone this. Your mind began to fall off the edge of reasoning. You felt like after that nothing was the same. Much like how people talk about drugs and their effects on consciousness, you knew the nature of exhaustion, its habits amongst your body. So you're used to it, primed perhaps. It was the disassembling of thought, the inability to count change at the dairy. You went to buy a newspaper on the fourth morning and stared at the things in your hand, not understanding their link to anything. Everything seemed to suggest common logic was being replaced by another form of knowing. You believed you knew things that didn't yet have a language. Your body failed. You became a set of lines tangled in the mind of what seemed a new, annoying kind of deity with a dicky name. For the last two days you didn't eat or drink. You found massive pleasure in the experience. Your limbs stopped working; your mind became mush. Ligaments like loosed seraphim, muscles intercessory prayers. This was real work, you said: fighting to stay cognisant. Any work done since, it just seemed the mechanism of others' lives. Yours felt elsewhere. Impermanently locked, with no hint as to when the impermanence would reveal itself. This is the way you wake in the morning.

Every morning.

Every morning, this is how you wake.

Sometimes he looks like me. Sometimes I recognise his voice, his eyes. My eye colour seems to change between brown and green depending on the light. His eyes don't have a colour, more like a frequency, a number. I don't mind him here. I like his anger.

'Honey?' Laura says on the phone.

Yeah.

'Khiem called me,' she says.

Oh?

'He said you told him to call me.'

What did he say?

'He said he believed he could get the whole job done while we're away.'

That's good news.

'It's fantastic news.'

They'll start tomorrow?

'Yes. No. The day after.'

Good. I'm thrilled.

'Yay. But why did you get him to call me?'

I don't recall.

'He said you told him to call me.'

. . .

'He said you gave him my number. It's okay, I was just surprised.'

I don't know.

'Okay. Honey, I'll see you at the airport.'

Yes.

'You okay?'

I'm fine.

. . .

I've packed everything.

'I know, we did that last night.'

Okay.

'Okay.'

Rachel

'Rach?' David says.

He sounds peculiar, and I imagine my cousin as the noise of the parents and their son grows distant. I see David rising, fully upright, out of the rock as they lift him, standing as he says my name a last time. There are arms about his body, his own on their shoulders. Hi-vis arms. Glinting, false light. Imagine his legs first, then up through his hips, up, and they have him up out of the stone so easily, and then the walk. The walk to the sea and a yacht, a cruiser. The path, the walk. Local emergency personnel with their arms about his waist and his on their shoulders, walking like that, the three of them trying to understand how the other strides. The blue horizontal sea as a medic attends to the child up the path and then to the last of me. A woman calmly asking questions, asking what medical conditions I have, and I laugh a little, just a little. She has a scent about her like she's just eaten an olive. I imagine David moving to the horizon as the medic speaks—I can tell she enjoys speaking in English. He's walking to the beach in the downpour. The water dripping from the woman's nose. There a boat, there a set of sails. Imagine people waving, waving him towards them in the rain, their eyes. Waving him towards their eyes as the medic becomes serious, speaking Italian now, hailing others. She uses a little axe from her pack to hammer loose the stone from about my body, the rock clinging to my skin. She shouts, and there is a rush of boots, and I know the water will soon be at his feet, rain in his hair. He moves to the precise edge of the water. The strength of water, the weight of it around his ankles, shins and thighs, and it's all Italian now, his belly and chest and the rocks, the wet rocks and this step and how the ankle, how the ankle twists as they gesticulate to each other, bone and stone, and he looks up, trying to see, and how the stone rolls and the world swallows—its tongue.

Painter

The Remutaka. The ranges dominate the view. They sit below Mount Matthews. The large hill that separates Wellington from the Wairarapa. I stare out there each day, promise myself that when I am well I'll climb it, and once there take a picture of the knobbled hills where Laura and I live, twenty kilometres away across the harbour. Something will be perfect then. Still and complete. A photo of Tapuae-o-Uenuku, too, for my dad.

I glance at the voice; he begins again. The voice and the form that comes with it. He's my height but appears small. Reduced, fractioned by each sentence he speaks. I imagine him telling someone else's story, but he's always telling me mine. Though it's not like he's talking to me—more to the room as if full of people. Laura and I got married in this room. I was healthy then, was operating amongst people for the first time in a couple of years. It was June but winter forgot this fact. Our friends got drunk and rowdy on the deck. I can see this figure amongst them, at times taller than he should be; I see his mouth moving but no one engages.

You spent the summer on your bike, he says now. Or not now. You spent every lunchtime on your bike. At first, it was just two kilometres, because you were unfit. You were obese. You lost ten kilos in three weeks. Every day, twenty kilometres, thirty. You lost fifteen kilos. The bays, out to the airport and then to the Hutt Valley. You arrived back in your office rinsed in sweat. Your fitness rose and you imagined running, you dreamed of running. You went everywhere in these dreams in a noiseless glide. You ate only salad, lean chicken.

I lost thirty-six kilos.

But that was eventually, I'm talking about the days.

Yeah.

Even in the rain. You'd walk from Taranaki Street down Courtenay Place, then straight up Majoribanks Street into the hills. Straight up the paths amongst the pines to the top of Mount Victoria, then back down to your desk in the vaults. Days were about getting to that hour so you could ride or storm the dark hills on your feet. The body became everything: the force of it against years of nothingness, of inactivity and attention to the mind, which too had become slothful.

A kind vagueness of his movements. He sits *in* the couch, only he seems to hover above it, all as if he is settled into another seat, but here, this is him. Here, he blinks and the whole of his body vanishes and returns.

Light then light.

And then, you were talking to your boss. She told you how unwell you looked. She was concerned, suggested you go home. And at home you lay on the couch, and it started, didn't it? It started.

I watch him. Every word alters his form; his hands expand and withdraw up his sleeves.

You lay on the couch, mouth open. You couldn't close it. You wanted to leave the house and ride. You wanted to head to the coast and ride, you were angry that you were stuck at home for the afternoon. You told Laura you thought you might have a cold. In the morning you told her you thought it might be the flu. Two weeks later you knew. Every morning you woke feeling as bad as any day in your life. Fourteen years earlier a doctor came to your hotel room in Kathmandu and treated you as you hallucinated. You writhed in pain as parasites reigned in your gut. Saw faces in the walls. Every morning you felt this same distance from life. An unlocatable, red agony.

I ask him who he is.

I'm the knowledge of you, this part of you.

Or that's what I feel him say. His voice is distorted. It holds harmonics, detached from the movement in his throat. I ask him again.

You don't know me. I'm the memory of you.

Where are you?

Behind me a mountain, before me the bay. I'm waiting for someone.

Who?

Someone who's going to die.

Who?

He told me I had to leave.

Yes.

I put on my suit jacket, the one with the tūī brooch I pinned to my chest on our wedding day, and lock the front door. I hear noise on the path. Voices and footsteps in the rain. I start towards the commotion with my suitcase rolling behind me. Shadows then faces. Men in overalls.

'David, hi!' the first man says. He's my age, short, sun-damaged and alert. 'We thought we'd make a start this afternoon.'

I look at him. A vague flash of recognition that quickly vanishes behind my retinas.

'We won't do much. But we had an early finish down in Berhampore.'

I don't know his name, but he's English, I think.

'So, we'll bring in some stuff.'

'Did you talk to Laura?' I ask.

'We talked a few weeks ago. We thought we'd start while you're in Auckland. It's Auckland, yeah?'

'I'm confused,' I say.

'We emailed and talked on the phone. I came to the house. We decided on Maraetai for the weatherboards.'

'Maraetai, yeah. I'm just getting in the taxi. Can I call you?'

'We don't have to start today,' he says. 'We'll start Monday. Like civilised people in civilised countries.'

'Eh?'

'. . .'

'Shit.'

'Shit?'

'Can I call you from the airport.'

'Of course. Do what you need to do. It's raining anyway. We'll just leave some equipment in the basement, if that's okay?'

'Thank you. I'll call you soon.'

'Of course. You have health things, am I right?'

'Ah—yes.'

'Just call me from the airport.'

'Or maybe when I get to Auckland.'

'Auckland is fine,' he says. He laughs. 'It's always fine in Auckland.'

'Yeah.'

'My wife and I head to Greece every August,' he says. 'I'm enamoured with the whole thing. Flying, there's a rhythm to the whole—and then you're there.'

I nod, say, 'I tell myself it's just time and that's it. A day of awfulness and that's it. Okay, I'll call you.'

'And then you're there and I feel like the worst things about me should've been cured, but they're not. You travel the world in hours and all you get is a lousy cold.'

'. . .'

'What about the key?' he asks as I begin walking through them towards where the path slants down off the hill.

'I'll email you the key,' I say. 'We'll talk.'

For years I had a red Vespa, which is the ideal way to pilot the narrow roads in Wellington, to get through the traffic. I felt safe on it; I didn't feel sick either. The tiredness would vanish as I navigated the hills; it was the only time I felt awake. But then I was knocked off the machine on Brooklyn Hill by a driver not looking. It was written off by the insurers and we decided to buy a car with the money. I no longer feel the calm and freedom, I no longer have the moments I once had.

Now my taxi edges out onto Farnam Street. I watch the GPS map on the driver's phone. Watch as it takes precision interest in our whereabouts. Then as we go past Liardet Street Park I remember the painter, recall him from several months ago, as if the satellites above had conspired to redraw him in my mind. He'd come with his dog and stood inside the house and talked with me for half an hour. The usual, and I'd told him I couldn't talk for long as I wasn't well. Which is always a prompt, because it encourages a sense of familiarity. I'll never absorb this information practically. He quickly learnt I had ME. He took interest and soon told me he had a niece with the same illness.

He spoke, impassioned. They were close, the two of them.

'Ah—and if she ever tried to get out of bed, well, her body would collapse,' he said. 'Just the effort of trying to stand sent her into a state, she'd pass out. Horrific. She couldn't deal with light, sound. For two years she needed a drip because she couldn't process nutrients. Death's door. They lived down in Wanaka by the lake and it was hard, especially in winter.'

'. . .'

'So, I know your pain.'

'Thanks. Yeah. I'm lucky, I've never been that bad.'

'She ended up trying to kill herself,' he said. 'Three times.'

'Oh.'

'Yes. She was so sick. So, I know what's happening with you.'

'Is she, she okay?'

'She's, yes. She actually came out of it. She's in remission, as they say. She's so beautiful, full of life. She put on ten kilos and looks like a normal girl. She's thirty-five, but I say girl every time. It's a—I'm an old man.'

'She's okay?'

'She's okay. She failed, each of those attempts, each time she tried she failed. She says she's grateful for that. But she said she never really had the energy to get the job done anyway. Which is something I never understood; she always had a sense of humour.'

'No,' I said.

'So, I know, kinda,' he'd said. 'I know what you're going through.'

'Thank you.'

'Have you ever tried regular fasting? I do it every second week. I don't eat for seventy-two hours. It cleans me inside and out, I swear. My girlfriend says my skin glows after.'

I told him I'd tried, and I did feel less ill and inflamed after a time. 'Like when a flu lifts suddenly, and you can move around again, can think and speak. But then, I have to eat,' I said.

'It's the gut, isn't it,' the painter said.

'Part of it. It's the brain, it's the nervous system. Yada, yada. Sometimes we think it's the house. Sometimes we think it's the interior of the house that makes us sick. Sometimes it's the only thing protecting us. Or, the whole house that's . . . the interior, the exterior, we don't know. Where it is on the hill. Could be anything. We don't know. All the books. What did your niece do? What made her better?'

'Nothing; she just got better.'

'Yeah,' I said. 'That's usually the way.'

'Maybe her body got sick of her trying to kill it.'

I'd laughed; it was a horrible sound.

'Maybe it decided, *fuck you*.'

As he was leaving, I told him Laura would call him. He smiled, like that was all he'd wanted to hear. A few days later he sent a text message. It had the paint name Laura and I'd agreed on and its serial, along with his niece's phone number. I remembered staring at all the digits, the strange sense that there was a code somewhere in those numbers. I called her, his niece, listened as I stared into the view as the phone rang with possibilities.

Island Bay

The taxi goes down the hill into Berhampore. I tell the driver to take me around the bays; there is plenty of time. I take out my phone.

'Hey?'

'Oh, hey.'

'How are you doing?'

'I'm good. I think.'

'You think?'

'The dog ripped up the couch and I'm staring at it thinking—*Maybe this is a good thing?*'

'Sounds like a—is it a good thing?'

I see their couch briefly, in that corner of my mind dedicated to old rooms, furniture and teacups. Their house in Beckenham, south Christchurch, under the hills. A haggard old horsehair thing, buffed cushions and split leather. The thing you'll never throw out until it's been destroyed by fire or other. My first memory of it was from Auckland twenty years ago.

'I'm online all day. I'm looking at sites across the universe trying to figure this question out.'

'The answer to the universe is in online furniture stores.'

'Exactly.'

We laugh a little. Then silence. A known force.

'So, I'm writing this book.'

'Yeah—yes you are,' Deborah says.

'No, this new book. It's like, memoir but fictional.'

'Cool.' She plays this word out like it has twenty syllables.

'You're in it, of course.'

'Of course. Better be. But you told me already.'

'But here's the thing.'

'Yeah. How are you?'

'I'm, hey. I'm okay. Hey, so. I was just thinking.'

'What?'

'I was just thinking. In this book I'm writing, this autobiography thing. It would be really useful if I could, like, kill you off. For narrative reasons.'

'Kill me off. Like, kill me?'

'Yeah. Because, for narrative reasons. Can I kill you, in, I don't know, a train crash or something? Laura thinks I should die, but I'm thinking you.'

There is a long pause. Over-long, and I think: *She's left me*. And not just like how we left each other when we were twenty-five, but utterly, fully. The pause means something is complete and everything, everything is regret. Then her voice, sudden and so clear: 'Cool.'

'Cool?'

'Yeah. I'd be honoured to die in one of your books.'

'It's for narrative reasons.'

'You don't have to explain,' Deborah says, and laughs. 'This is awesome. Thank you.'

'That's not the answer I was expecting.'

'I need to die?'

'Yeah,' I say.

Again, nothing.

'David,' she says. 'I would be honoured to die in one of your books. But I told you that this morning.'

I laugh.

'I'm not kidding.'

'What about?' I ask.

'You already called.'

'. . .'

'You asked me already.'

'Ah, shit,' I say.

'Doesn't matter. I like talking to you.' She laughs. 'But this is great.'

'Brilliant. You're a trouper.'

She sounds chuffed, lightheaded, and I picture her without effort. The way her eyes gain a distant, eloquent look. A hundred thoughts, each quite separate and impossible to know.

'Do you think there's many writers who actually ask their old girlfriends before they kill them off?' she asks.

'No, just me. I'm the only one in history.'

'As I said this morning, as long as I'm hot and it's a glorious death.'

'Of course. Plane wreck at two hundred miles an hour.'

'I'm so excited!'

We laugh again.

'Honestly, this is my favourite thing of the year. By the way, are you in a car? I hear car things.'

'Yeah—taxi to airport.'

'Ohh—where you going?'

'Auckland.'

'Damn.'

'What?'

'I was hoping you were going to say Christchurch. Then we can talk about this more.'

'We can talk about it more. I'm only in Island Bay.'

'I miss Island Bay.'

'Yeah?'

I've forgotten the Bay was the first place Deborah and her family moved to from the United States in the early–mid Eighties. I remember their house faintly, like ash dust.

'So, what's the deal with my death?'

'I need to suggest an inevitability—within the narrative structure of the text—of death. Not real death, but the death of knowing. Death, but narrative continuance.'

'This is the book about Chronic Fatigue.'

'Aha. It's about what a book can remember, how it can and can't. You dying kinda plays with that.'

'What's the—'

I find myself talking her through it, her section of the book. The nascent years of Norwegian black metal. About Dead, and death and Cotard's syndrome. About her mum, that night, waiting. I tell her about Italy, Austria and Henry.

'So,' I say as the taxi comes to the end of the Parade, turns left towards the actual bay from which the suburb gets its name.

She laughs. 'You were always an idiot, weren't you?'

I laugh. 'Anyway . . .'

'Yes, of course. Where are you in the Bay?'

I tell her, and she asks me to describe the drive, and I do.

'It's so pretty down there,' she says. 'An actual nice drive to the airport.'

'It really is.'

'How do jet engines work in the rain? How's that a thing?'

It isn't really a question and she goes quiet for a period of time; it's comfortable because it's as if we're both driving, rounding the headland.

'It's been a hell of a year. It's almost a relief to be killed off,' she says. 'Mark's developed, he's got this neurological condition. It's, I don't know everything yet. It's rare, it's complicated. No one in New Zealand knows much about it, that's how rare it is. He loses balance and his speech gets a bit, drunken sailor. We poke him with jokes but it's never that funny.'

'Oh Jesus.'

'Yeah—so. Kill me off all you like. Feels like some kinda cure for something. I heard a story, about a woman. She had cancer and she was dying and she had one last, I don't know, one last moment. She walked out of her house and down a hill to the beach and she just found a place where all her last energy could pour out of her. Out of her body, her mouth. Out of her cunt and face and hands and . . . she just lay down in the ocean when she couldn't walk anymore and there, peace. Anyway, I just thought of her. Where are you now?'

I tell her we've just started north into Lyall Bay. 'I can see the airport, the planes. So—'

'It's not a terminal disease, Mark's. But not a good disease either.'

'God, I'm sorry,' I say.

'You both suck. I've had two loves in my life and both have shit brains.' She goes silent, which I know means she's smiling. 'So, make sure I'm really smoking, okay? When I die. Make sure I'm really glamorous and just—sex.'

'Of course.'

'I want helicopters and detonations, beautiful explosions. And make sure, please, it's during the golden hour.'

'These requests aren't a problem.'

'So.'

'So?'

'Kill me off.'

I already have. I wrote the scene two years ago.

We hang up as the car enters the tunnel that runs under the south end of the runway. I remember visiting her parents' house a few months after they moved to Auckland in 1991. It was about to be sold when Deborah and I had just begun going out. We went there to see if there was anything we wanted before the cleaners came. The house was mostly empty but for a few small things the movers left behind for reasons I don't recall. There was a small black digital clock. Deborah didn't want it, so I took it. I had it for twenty-seven years until in 2018, around the time I started writing this book, its alarm began going off at unpredictable moments. I threw it out then, no ceremony. Just put it gently in the trash.

Void, the Rain

The rain, the rain, the flood, the rain, the rain, the skin and rain, the rain, the flood, the rain, the light, the light, the smashing of light, the rain and the flood and eyes and the rain, the flood, the rain, the rain, the hands, the rain and no further, no further than our hands, the rain, the rain, the flood, the rain, no further than our hands do we see the rain, the rain, the rain, the flood, the rain, the torrent, the rain, the rain and what rain, the rain, the flood, the flood, the rain, the gully stream and rush and rain, the intolerable rain, the rain, the rain and the voids, the voids, the voids smashed through voices when the rain, the rain, the rain, the rain

The Delirium of Negation

They did a good job when they built Wellington Airport, an even better job when they expanded the south end. It's a pleasure to leave from.

'The painter turned up.'

'Khiem?'

'No. It was another guy.'

'What do you mean?'

'Another guy. He showed up with half his team. Or all his team. I don't know.'

'What was his name?'

'I don't know. Graham?'

'Did he say his name was Graham?'

'No.'

'So, what's he doing at the house?'

'I said I'd call him after I talk to you.'

'Does he have a key?'

I put my suitcase on the scales.

'Does he have a key?' Laura asks with a lost kind of weariness. She's tired, the day too long by hours.

'I don't know.'

'Did you give him the key?'

I feel my wife watch me as I chew at the edge of my thumb nail.

'No.'

'Okay.'

'I said I'd email him the key. The location of it.'

'Let me check my emails.'

'Yeah.'

'Wait on.'

'I'll ah, I'll do the same.'

We are baggage-less, walking through Wellington Airport. The kind atmosphere of light reflected through the high windows, of soft, unheard music. Coffee, bagels. Families and the two of us at our phones.

'You okay?' Laura asks me.

'I'm good. I'm okay. You?'

'. . .'

'I told Deb,' I say, during her long mute moment.

'What? About her death?'

'Aha.'

'You're kind of a dick.'

I smile.

'I'd be so angry.'

'She's thrilled.'

'I'd be like: *What an utter arsehole.*'

'She was happy about it. Like, it was the best thing to happen to her all year.'

'You're always exaggerating. Not the best thing that happened to her all year.'

'They haven't had a good year. A literary death is just the, the panacea.'

'You should try it. Kill yourself off. See if it has any positive effects.'

'I don't know. Do we get an insurance pay-out?'

Laura goes back to her phone and I watch the rain gather on the runway.

'I told him that I'd call him when we get to Auckland,' I say.

'I'm just worried, honey. Like how many people have you organised to paint the house?'

'God, I don't know.'

'I don't want to be paying half of Wellington to paint the

stupid house. Did you pay any deposits?'

'No.'

'How many quotes did we get?'

'I sent them all to you in an email, in February.'

'Did you? God. Do you have your laptop?'

We sit at the bagel place, looking at her email on my computer.

'How many quotes did you get?'

'I don't know. Six?'

'Fuck. And you say his name was Graham.'

'He had a Graham-ness about him.'

'Grant Simonds.'

'Is that one of the guys on the quote list?'

'Yeah. God, how many did you get?'

'Grant. Yeah, I think maybe that's him.'

'Okay.'

'I spoke to his niece.'

'You spoke to his niece.'

'She, ah. She had ME. Then she didn't. So, I called her. He gave me her number.'

'What did she say?'

'She, Michelle, she said her daughter needed her attention, so we didn't talk long.'

'That's pretty weird, David.'

'. . .'

'Pretty weird.'

We'd talked for an hour.

I told her I was writing this book.

She told me she'd read it if she were in it.

We got to the point of me asking large things, asking how she'd come out of it, the illness. She said she didn't know, just that it was eventual. Slow and unnoticed until she did start to notice. She was agitated by something, and eventually there was a long pause.

I want to tell you something else, the woman said. I want to tell you about something I learnt when I was sick.

She spoke several sentences, gearing herself up. She enjoyed the telling. Michelle explained that when she'd had enough, after eleven years of being in bed and in pain ninety percent of the time, she'd swallowed pills. They didn't take. She said she tried with a rope in the stairwell one summer, when she was well enough to be out of bed for a time, well enough to summon the physical will. She told how she thought if she tried hard enough, her body would do it on its own. That when she was thirty, she woke up in hospital with this memory. Her mum was lying in a chair snoring and Michelle had no idea how she'd got to the hospital. She assumed she'd passed out from a lack of nutrition, was rushed to emergency. But slowly a memory came to her. She remembered being out of bed, that she had the strength to sit in the lounge with her family. She remembered she'd stayed up. It was Christmas. Her brothers were drinking, and she said she was going to the toilet. Her big brother asked if she needed help and she said she was okay. She went outside in the heat. She said she just needed air. She stood for the longest time, breathing. Breathing in and out. A kind of cycling of rapid intakes and exhales. She thought, *I can do this. I can do this right now. Just by breathing, just by letting the life out of me.* She told herself to die. To shut down and die. So, she did. My tongue, she said. This is how I did it. First my tongue. It seemed to get really big in my mouth, then the thing started to push out between my lips. Soon the whole of my tongue was protruding. I believed I could just kill myself with thought, and felt things start to turn off. The muscle of my tongue getting huge in my mouth. Then my eyes, bulging.

I was grotesque in the rain. Hideous. My eyesight went first, then I stopped hearing. I was excited, for the first time in, in months. And my heart racing. I was excited and I was going to die just by thinking about it. A pain in my chest; I was going to burst my heart out, was how it felt. And my head, my head was pounding. This is desire. This is the work of desire. Thoughts were slowly harder to come by and I had only the one thought: *Keep going.* And I did. I kept trying to push the life out of me because I was sick of living. Exhausted from the fight. And because the fight, because it's so damned physical. But then something intervened. Something pushed its way to the surface out of this. I realised how much further I had to go to make this happen. How much pain. I realised it was huge, a cascade of tearing and breaking as everything switched off. So. And life suddenly felt enormous. Colossal. An extraordinary thing to overcome, to beat with your mind and teeth and mouth and tongue and whatever else I was trying to do. It was too much, too big. Instead, I turned everything back on. I heard my feet standing in the grass, the crunch sound, the micro movements. I asked if she thought she could've? She said, without doubt. If she'd had the energy, without doubt.

'What did you tell her?' Laura asks me.

The bagel stand is all done up in distressed wood, like it's been brought here from a junkyard. People come and go. The place smells of espresso and bread.

'I said we were about to go on holiday. And she said, she was like, "I used to hate holidays, I always end up sick and it's awful for everyone."'

'What did you say?'

'I said I go on holiday and I take a lot of pills. Said Diazepam is helpful. Said any kind of opioid can be helpful. Then there's the comedown.'

'You make me nervous in unpredictable ways,' Laura says. 'Did she say how she got well? I'd like to know.'

'Hey,' a voice calls before I can answer. I look up. The woman behind the bagel bench leans past the coffee machine. 'Hey. Did you order a salmon bagel?'

I shake my head. 'No.'

'Shit,' the woman says.

'What?' Laura asks.

'I think the guy's gone.' The bagel woman seems agitated, as if the cost of it will be subtracted from her pay.

'Bet that happens, like . . .'

'Yeah. Stupid planes. You want it?'

I look as the woman offers the bagel. The raw pink of the salmon jutting from the side of the sliced bread. Lettuce, cream cheese.

'Ah—'

'No, honey,' Laura says. 'You don't need it.'

'You certain, you sure you don't want it?' She looks at us both. 'Most people, you know, they never come back.'

Acknowledgements

Enormous thanks to Laura Southgate—for the role played in this book's creation: practically, creatively, emotionally and intellectually. Will forever be thankful. Thank you to my brother Simon Coventry for both saving my father's life and letting me borrow and mess his account of the mountains (you can have it back now); to my sister Anna Coventry; to Deborah Diaz for so enthusiastically agreeing to be killed off; Hannah Upritchard (who's one kidney lighter); Henry Coventry (RIP); Rosalyn Nokise-Coventry (RIP); Francie Conolly (RIP); Danielle Ashby-Coventry; Esther Ashby-Coventry; Adi Coventry; James Woods; Angela Winter Means; Attila Csihar; Alin & Kaspar Sanwald; Alena (RIP) & Jörg Wisemen; the estate of Thomas Bernhard; Peter Fabjan; Kristen Wineera; Marcel Bear; Sarah Donnelly; Matthew Packer; Hamish Clayton; Hayden Kingdon, Damaris Diaz; Mark Revington; Justo & Laurie Diaz; Paul Rockel (for the invaluable information on the Germans and his account of the night of the sabre); Alan McMonagle; James Nokise; Eric Beck Ruben; Katie & Clare; Lynn Worthington; Simon Waterfield.

A massive thanks to Damien Wilkins for sharing his brilliant creative intellect to this project, for pushing me and supporting my search for the text's inner madness/logic. Thank you to Heidi Thompson, Cherie Lacey and Thierry Jutel. Thanks to all in my doctoral cohort who gave their thoughts on this book's early drafts. Cheers to Fergus Barrowman and all at Te Herenga Waka University Press, what people! Thank you Ashleigh Young: you edit and make us fuller.

I'm humbled by and hugely grateful to my cousin Rachel Thornton, whose voice, art, love and thoughts are all throughout this book. This novel's for anyone who's sick and just can't explain it.

The Undoing

Laura takes the one road up, walks in the dense downpour. Steps paving stone by foot and yard in the rain. Paranoid, fearful steps. Walks through the named streets, and the collision of her breath and footfalls eventually winds her. She takes breaks above the city and its wide view, fearful of what she might see—fragments of people, the woman, the women. Her chest empties and fills trying to catch something of the air. She looks at the villas parked on the hill, the houses dozens and dozens of decades old. The absolute fear of seeing movement. Human movement. The jumble of lives lived, broken ladders and old bikes, a washing line junked in a yard. No one. Smaller houses sit under reaching trees and trees searching for the roofs of the grander homes whose windows are the expectant eyes of all who've become immune, and inside these eyes she senses movement—but movement, she's learnt, is restricted to her now, only her. Her body feels impossibly light, but heavy too, like the weight carried by an airship sinking into a setting sun.

She walks around a large ridge that has been weathered down, down into the southern extent of the main volcanic cone. She walks higher, towards where the path to the Bay of Mouths opens towards the sea. Intense, sweeping blue. Houses, windows gaping at the world, the always-smoking peak in the clandestine distance, the fear of what each step might bring. The they. Say the words, how one sits inside the other. She'd walked up through the layers of ages, the medieval dwellings, baroque apartments and cement monoliths of the current century. Each with their shadows, each with a seasoned sense of loneliness.

She stands still. Still because, *is that sound?*

A bundle of nervous waves collecting into something human, into voices, but there are no voices.

But.

She can hear them.

Her body freezes around the sound.

Talk, conversation.

She thinks of pain, she thinks of those impossible souls ragged and bleeding deep into other lives.

The They.

Jesus.

She crouches down.

People. A voice within her says, *people*. She barely has breath in her and perhaps this is the sound of her now. Her various interpretations of sound pattern and flow, of tree rustle and gate creak.

People.

She remembers them, everywhere. She feels herself become a person who repeats the word until it's true. Repeats the dancing mantra of the world.

People.

She can hear them. Talk, conversation. She feels light on her feet at the buzz of them.

People.

People.

The smell of fruit, of a peach, people.

She stays still, in a crouch, leaning against the breeze. The houses and the sense of eyes. She hears an engine. The high whine of wheel and horsepower. People. People and people.

All the terror, and as she tries to shift herself into verges, thorny branches push back at her.

A Honda then, a moped, excited and driven hard against the hill. It comes past her. Two, two souls, a man on the back shouting into a woman's ear. Hair whipping at their young faces.

Laura wants to call out.

People.

She stands, walks quickly, past the street corner that will take her to the cottages but instead she jogs on her aching knees down the straight and through the dip in the road towards the plaque at the top of the path and a person, someone motionless at the cruel stairs. A man, immobile, gazing into the Bay of Mouths below him, waiting, paused by the unseen. By the sea and sky hazed by rain. She stops, hands go to her knees momentarily, then she's upright and trying to get air back into her lungs. The man, he steps, a shift backwards. Noise, and she turns because a car, a Volvo, is coming up behind her and she moves quickly to the right. A man at the horn of a wagon tearing out from a corner. A car, flashing chrome, and a body, the man, stepping back from the verge and the driver, the driver yelling, screaming from his window. The sense of direct movement, of body movement, of proximity and steel, of the microworld of slight distances and the end of distance.

Noise.

Noise, collision, collision and aftermath and the aftermath of time because David, his body is lifted, smashed, thrown—

then falls. He's flung up, then ragdolls downwards, falls through the outline of the wet trees, descends through the transecting line of the horizon that cuts the sea and sky out beyond the Bay of Mouths. She feels a scream, an ancient hungry voice, the wave of it at her teeth, at her face, faces for they are multiple now, mouth, teeth, eyes, a hundred eyes. She watches it all, her husband, his body, his body bent out of shape, twisted by blood force and steel and time and time, and only time knows the nature of time. She too, she screams and joins the world shouting at the violence of it all, the twists of his torso and legs and she watches, watches until from the stairs a boy and his mother rush up to the road and see this form, this strange ache twisting on the cobblestone and the boy turns, his eyes, his eyes and the worlds they see.

List of Illustrations

Notes

The Watcher

18: 'Edmund Hillary climbed the mountain in a day as an RNZAF cadet training at Woodbourne. His first real mountain, he'd famously claim years later.' Edmund Hillary, *Nothing Venture, Nothing Win* (London: Hodder & Stoughton, 1975), 33–36.

The Buckle and the Stammer

26: 'This disease, this myalgic encephalomyelitis, constitutes the manifestation of intensified nervous sensitivity, one which the science tells us is most likely attributable to a neuroinflammatory etiopathology, one that's associated with abnormal nociceptive and neuroimmune activity.' Julian A.G. Glassford, 'The Neuroinflammatory Etiopathology of Myalgic Encephalomyelitis/Chronic Fatigue Syndrome (ME/CFS)', Frontiers in Physiology 8, no. 88 (2017), doi.org/10.3389/fphys.2017.00088

26: 'It's a kind of hell, not knowing: indeed, the underlying pathomechanism of ME is incompletely understood, but studies suggest there is substantial evidence that, in at least a subset of patients, ME/CFS has an autoimmune etiology.' Franziska Sotzny et al., 'Myalgic Encephalomyelitis / Chronic Fatigue Syndrome—Evidence for an Autoimmune Disease', *Autoimmunity Reviews* 17, no. 6 (2018): 601–609, doi.org/10.1016/j.autrev.2018.01.009

27, footnote: 'According to Stephani Sutherland in the *Scientific American*'. Stephani Sutherland, 'Long COVID Now Looks like a Neurological

Disease, Helping Doctors to Focus Treatments', *Scientific American*, 1 March 2023.

28, footnote: 'According to a 2009 study, muscle biopsies taken from patients with ME'. Sarah Myhill, Norman E. Booth and John McLaren-Howard, 'Chronic Fatigue Syndrome and Mitochondrial Dysfunction', *International Journal of Clinical and Experimental Medicine* 2, no. 1 (2009): 1–16.

28, footnote: 'Another such study on ME mitochondria, at La Trobe University'. See Cort Johnson, 'Novel Approach Brings New Insights Into ME/CFS Mitochondria', *Health Rising*, 27 March 2022, healthrising.org/blog/2022/03/27/novel-approach-mitochondria-chronic-fatigue-syndrome/2022

28: 'These are genes associated with bioenergy production'. Sarah Myhill, Norman E. Booth and John McLaren-Howard, 'Chronic Fatigue Syndrome and Mitochondrial Dysfunction', *International Journal of Clinical and Experimental Medicine* 2, no. 1 (2009): 1–16.

28: 'There's a likely breaching of the blood–brain barrier by immune cells.' A.C. Bested, P.R. Saunders and A.C. Logan, 'Chronic Fatigue Syndrome: Neurological Findings May Be Related to Blood–Brain Barrier Permeability', Medical Hypotheses 57, no. 2 (2001): 231–237, doi.org/10.1054/mehy.2001.1306

28: 'The bodily conditions that allow for ME are believed to be hereditary, believed to be in the blood and genes.' Joshua J. Dibble, Simon J. McGrath and Chris P. Ponting, 'Genetic Risk Factors of ME/CFS: A Critical Review', *Human Molecular Genetics* 29, no. R1 (2020): R117–R124, doi.org/10.1093/hmg/ddaa169

28–9: 'Some suggest a connection between maladaptive perfectionism and the disease.' Amelia Wright et al., 'Perfectionism, Depression and Anxiety in Chronic Fatigue Syndrome: A Systematic Review', *Journal of Psychosomatic Research* 140, no. 110322 (2021), doi.org/10.1016/j.jpsychores.2020.110322

30: 'They are yet to misidentify (as of writing) a single ME patient.' See Ana Sandoiu, 'Chronic Fatigue Syndrome: New Test in Sight', *Medical News Today*, 30 April 2019; and Hanae Armitage, 'Biomarker for Chronic Fatigue Syndrome Identified', *Stanford Medicine News Centre*, 29 April 2019.

The Valley

43: 'ME has long been known to follow glandular fever and other systemic infections, even decades later.' Gordon Broderick et al., 'Cytokine Expression Profiles of Immune Imbalance in Post-Mononucleosis Chronic Fatigue', *Journal of Translational Medicine* 10, no. 191 (2012), doi.org/10.1186/1479-5876-10-191

43, footnote: 'a team at Northwestern University have published research that reveals differences in multiple metabolites and metabolic pathways.' Leonard A. Jason et al., 'Pre-illness Data Reveals Differences in Multiple Metabolites and Metabolic Pathways in Those Who Do and Do Not Recover from Infectious Mononucleosis', *Molecular Omics* 18, no. 7 (2022): 662–665, doi.org/10.1039/d2mO00124a

Red

51: 'These signals are made by "motor units" and such a unit consists of a single motor neuron and all the extrafusal muscle fibres it innervates.' Hayri Ertan and Ismail Bayram, 'Fundamentals of Human Movement, Its Control and Energetics', in *Comparative Kinesiology of the Human Body: Normal and Pathological Conditions* (Academic Press, 2020), 29–45, doi.org/10.1016/B978-0-12-812162-7.00003-5

51: 'They suggest central neural deregulation may contribute to this disturbance'. E.G. Klaver-Krol et al., 'Chronic Fatigue Syndrome: Abnormally Fast Muscle Fiber Conduction in the Membranes of Motor Units at Low Static Force Load', *Clinical Neurophysiology* 132, no. 4 (2021): 967–974, doi.org/10.1016/j.clinph.2020.11.043

52: 'The patterning of inflammation seen in MRIs of ME patients' brains suggests that immune cells are breaching the blood–brain barrier, and doing it in multiple areas, a flood overwhelming a dam pouring through gaps across the brain.' Cort Johnson, 'Brain on Fire: Widespread Neuroinflammation Found in Chronic Fatigue Syndrome', *HealthRising*, 24 September 2018.

52: 'Studies also suggest that the high choline signal present in the anterior cingulate cortex points to patterns of destruction and replacement, that neuronal damage is likely occurring.' Open Medicine Foundation, 'Jarred Younger, PhD | How Brain Inflammation Causes ME/CFS', YouTube, 8 November 2018.

Stone

56: 'The overlap between depression and ME is stark and present, but it is now understood that the co-occurrence of these maladies is explained by overlying abnormalities in oxidative, inflammatory and nitrosative pathways within the brain'. Michael Maes et al., 'Depression and Sickness Behavior are Janus-Faced Responses to Shared Inflammatory Pathways', *BMC Medicine* 10, no. 66 (2012): 416, doi.org/10.1186/1741-7015-10-66

56, footnote: 'I also read daily about the dreadful state of funding inequality.' See Cort Johnson, 'Novel Approach Brings New Insights into ME/CFS Mitochondria', *Health Rising*, 27 March 2022.

Phenomenology

69: 'The language of biomedicine is never alone in the field of empowering meanings'. Donna Haraway, 'The Biopolitics of Postmodern Bodies: Constitutions of Self in Immune System Discourse', in *Simians, Cyborgs, and Women: The Reinvention of Nature* (New York and Oxford: Routledge, 1991), 203.

East Atlantic

81: 'Specifically, Zeigarnik discovered that we have better recollection for the details of an unresolved task, an unfinished riddle, an unnamed psychological phenomenon, than an explained or labelled entity, item, thing.' Lulu Miller, 'The Eleventh Word', *The Paris Review*, 5 October 2020.

Eighty

133: 'The literature tells us over 80 percent of ME sufferers are women.' Michael Falk Hvidberg et al., 'The Health-Related Quality of Life for Patients with Myalgic Encephalomyelitis / Chronic Fatigue Syndrome (ME/CFS)', *PLoS One* 10, no.7 (2015): e0132421, doi.org/10.1371/journal.pone.0132421

133: 'However, a recent Barcelona study suggests that as a neuro-inflammatory process the divergences in male and female ME patient numbers could possibly reflect variances in the disease and how it advances.' ME Research UK, 'ME/CFS in Women and Men', *ME Research*, 19 August 2015.

133–34: 'The resulting effects are often extreme, debilitating body fatigue and cognitive dysfunction that can replicate the symptoms of patients presenting with damaged brain tissue.' Joanna Lane, 'How Doctors are Failing to Spot the Brain Injury that Could Be Behind 30,000 Cases of "Chronic Fatigue"', *Daily Mail*, 18 May 2014.

134: 'There is definite reasoning for this supposition: the functional cognitive profiles of ME are similar to those presenting in patients with traumatic head injury.' Tiago Teodoro, Mark J. Edwards and Jeremy D. Isaacs, 'A Unifying Theory for Cognitive Abnormalities in Functional Neurological Disorders, Fibromyalgia and Chronic Fatigue Syndrome: Systematic Review', *Journal of Neurology, Neurosurgery, and Psychiatry* 89, no. 12 (2018), 1308–1319, doi.org/10.1136/jnnp-2017-317823

134: 'Imaging studies at Stanford have shown distinct differences between brains of patients with ME and those of healthy people.' Bruce Goldman, 'Study Finds Brain Abnormalities in Chronic Fatigue Patients', *Stanford Medicine News Center*, 28 October 2014.

Haus

180: 'There was a tractor in the barn . . . mind fragmented by an inability to begin what he must begin.' This passage draws directly from Thomas Bernhard's *The Lime Works* [1970], trans. Sophie Wilkins (New York: Knopf, 1973), 4–5.

181: 'Crime in the city, urban crimes, is nothing compared to crimes in the country, rural crimes.' Thomas Bernhard, *Gargoyles* [1967], trans. Richard and Clara Winston (New York: Knopf, 1970), 3.

Volant

188, footnote: 'irrepressible compulsion for change, change so devoid of meaning it becomes repetition, repetition so inevitable that it inspires horror'. David Sepanik, 'Reconsidering Thomas Bernhard's *Correction*', *The Quarterly Conversation* (2006), archived at the Wayback Machine 12 October 2008, web.archive.org/web/20081012123509/http://quarterlyconversation.com/thomas-bernhard-correction

189: 'From a certain unforeseeable moment on . . . finally perfects it in reality.' Thomas Bernhard, *Correction* [1975], trans Sophie Wilkins (London: Vintage, 2003), 80.

Deep Rock

199: 'The works of Kertész and Perec,' he wrote, 'treat their subject [the Holocaust] as "free-flowing" or open, where Safran Foer treats it as "wrapped-up" or closed off.' Eric Beck Rubin, '"Then Cover the Abyss With Trance", an Exploration of the Novelistic Representation of the Holocaust', PhD Dissertation (Goldsmiths, University of London, 2013).

Royal Free

229: 'The illness was initially diagnosed as poliomyelitis (polio), but it was eventually discerned as something separate and received the designation "epidemic neuromyasthenia".' Institute of Medicine (U.S.), *Beyond Myalgic Encephalomyelitis/Chronic Fatigue Syndrome: Redefining an Illness* (The National Academies Press, 2015), doi.org/10.17226/19012

229–30: 'the absent mortality, the severe muscular pains, the evidence of parenchymal damage'. Institute of Medicine (U.S.), *Beyond Myalgic Encephalomyelitis/Chronic Fatigue Syndrome: Redefining an Illness* (The National Academies Press, 2015), doi.org/10.17226/19012

230: 'Then, in 1970, two UK psychiatrists, McEvedy and Beard, reviewed reports of fifteen outbreaks of the disease'. Colin P. McEvedy and A.W. Beard, 'Concept of Benign Myalgic Encephalomyelitis', *British Medical Journal* 1, no. 5687 (1970): 11–15, doi.org/10.1136/bmj.1.5687.11

230: 'McEvedy and Beard based their conclusions on "the higher prevalence of the disease in females and the lack of physical signs in these patients". They also recommended that the disease be renamed "myalgia nervosa".' Institute of Medicine (U.S.), *Beyond Myalgic Encephalomyelitis/Chronic Fatigue Syndrome: Redefining an Illness* (The National Academies Press, 2015), doi.org/10.17226/19012

230: 'It turns out this was a common approach and "treatment" of the disease back then was ignoring patients.' Jennifer Brea (director), *Unrest* (Sheila Films, 2017) and Stephanie McManimen et al., 'Dismissing Chronic Illness: A Qualitative Analysis of Negative Health Care Experiences', *Health Care for Women International* 40, no.3 (2019): 241–258, doi.org/10.1080/07399332.2018.1521811

232: 'In 1988 the condition was given the term that's so prejudiced Kimber and Rachel's physicians: chronic fatigue syndrome.' See Gary P. Holmes et al., 'Chronic Fatigue Syndrome: A Working Case Definition', *Annals of Internal Medicine* 108, no.3 (1988): 387–389, doi.org/10.7326/0003-4819-108-3-387

232: 'With a head affected by the swelling in the brain that is a hallmark of the illness'. See Yasuhito Nakatomi, Hirohiko Kuratsune and Yasuyoshi Watanabe, 'Neuroinflammation in the Brain of Patients with Myalgic Encephalomyelitis/Chronic Fatigue Syndrome', *Brain and Nerve = Shinkei kenkyu no shinpo* 70, no.1 (2018): 19–25, doi.org/10.11477/mf.1416200945

233: 'Lately the term systemic exertion intolerance disease (SEID) has been suggested.' See Leonard A. Jason et al., 'Reflections on the Institute of Medicine's Systemic Exertion Intolerance Disease', *Polskie Archiwum Medycyny Wewnetrznej* 125, no. 7–8 (2015): 576–581, doi.org/10.20452/pamw.2973

233: 'Dr Maureen Hanson has another decent one: enervating neuroimmune disease (END).' See Open Medicine Foundation, 'Maureen Hanson, PhD | Metabolism and ME/CFS', 2018, retrieved 11 September 2021.

240: 'These are upregulated when the body is under any kind of threat, such as infection, such as environmental toxins, trauma, or even something like childbirth.' Fiona MacDonald, 'One of the Biggest Myths about Chronic Fatigue Syndrome Has Been Debunked', *Science Alert* (17 March 2018), and T. Nguyen et al., 'Impaired Calcium Mobilization in Natural Killer Cells from Chronic Fatigue Syndrome/Myalgic Encephalomyelitis Patients Is Associated with Transient Receptor Potential Melastatin 3 Ion Channels', *Clinical and Experimental Immunology* 187, no. 2 (2017): 284–293, doi.org/10.1111/cei.12882

243–44, footnote: 'What has been shown to occur is that there is a substrate inhibition of IDO1, and it is possible that this has a "dark side and may be involved in the pathogenesis of ME/CFS".' See Alex A. Kashi, Ronald W. Davis and Robert D. Phair, 'The IDO Metabolic Trap Hypothesis for the Etiology of ME/CFS', *Diagnostics (Basel)* 9, no. 3 (2019): 82, doi.org/10.3390/diagnostics9030082

Dead

255: 'It was reported she asked that she be burned alive, and that she'd already made several suicide attempts and believed that neither God nor the devil existed on this plane or other.' G.E. Berrios and R. Luque, 'Cotard's Syndrome: Analysis of 100 Cases', *Acta Psychiatrica Scandinavica* 91, no. 3 (1995): 185–188, doi.org/10.1111/j.1600-0447.1995.tb09764.x

255: 'For example, in 2015, a woman in her sixties presented to the department of psychiatry at the Medical College Kolkata in India.' Seshadri Sekhar Chatterjee and Sayantanava Mitra, '"I Do Not Exist"—Cotard Syndrome in Insular Cortex Atrophy', *Biological Psychiatry* 77, no. 11 (2015): e52–e53, doi.org/10.1016/j.biopsych.2014.11.005

256: 'I can't cry because I don't have tears . . . I don't have lungs, I don't have intestine, I'm empty . . . I don't exist . . . I lost my spine . . I don't have the mind . . .' Domenico De Berardis et al., 'A Case of Cotard's

Syndrome Successfully Treated with Aripiprazole Monotherapy', *Progress in Neuro-psychopharmacology and Biological Psychiatry* 34, no. 7 (2010): 1347, doi.org/10.1016/j.pnpbp.2010.06.015

256: 'My soul and body are dead . . . My heart, brain, ears, lungs, oesophagus, stomach and intestine are gone . . . I am not allowed to die completely, and have to suffer forever.' Hiroaki Shiraishi et al., 'Sulpiride Treatment of Cotard's Syndrome in Schizophrenia, *Progress in Neuropsychopharmacology and Biological Psychiatry* 28, no. 3 (2004): 608, doi.org/10.1016/j.pnpbp.2004.01.011

Pelle

261: 'For a time he was, in fact, clinically dead.' Ika Johannesson and Jon Jefferson Klingberg, *Blod Eld Död [Blood Fire Death]* (in Swedish) (Stockholm: Alfabeta, 2011), 84–85.

262: 'He starved himself in order to get, as guitarist Aarseth described it, "starving wounds" on his body.' 'Euronymous Interview', *Morbid Magazine* No.8, TheTrueMayhem.com (1990), archived at the Wayback Machine 18 October 2007, web.archive.org/web/20071013034900/http://www.thetruemayhem.com/interviews/previous/euro-morbidmag8.htm

263: 'Hellhammer once stated, "[He] asked us to bury him in the ground—he wanted his skin to become pale".' Dmitry Basik, 'Interview with Hellhammer', TheTrueMayhem.com (1998), archived at the Wayback Machine 23 August 2007, web.archive.org/web/20070823184104/http://www.thetruemayhem.com/interviews/previous/hh-june1998.htm

263: 'Excuse the blood, but I have slit my wrists and neck.' Ika Johannesson and Jon Jefferson Klingberg, *Blog Eld Död* (Stockholm, Alfabeta, 2011), 94.

264: 'Indeed, an intriguing paper alluding to this very thing was published not long before this book was sent for its final edit'. Hugo Sanches et al, 'When Cotard's Syndrome Fits the Sociocultural Context: The Singular Case of Per "Dead" Ohlin and the Norwegian Black Metal Music Scene, *Transcultural Psychiatry* 59, no. 2 (2022): 225–232, doi.org/10.1177/13634615211041205

Path

306: 'Think how many, she'd say, will go on to live off our idea, the idea we had, if we'd share it all in any moment before its realisation.' Much of Rachel's speech in these passages is taken from Thomas Bernhard's *Correction* [1975], trans. Sophie Wilkins (London: Vintage, 2003), 129.

Thieves

331: '"My biggest fear," I told Mena. "What horrifies me most is that one day I might vanish because someone out there is telling the wrong story about me. About everyone with this kind of shitty disease."' David is paraphrasing Jennifer Brea, as quoted in Megan Moodie, '*Unrest*: Gender, Chronic Illness, and the Limits of Documentary Visibility', *Film Quarterly* 71, no. 4 (2018): 14, doi.org/10.1525/fq.2018.71.4.9

Tighten It

The quiet bulge of this sea. Sand and rock and the swim of incoming rows, the white-tops crossing out the beaches then pulling back. They catch a burst of shale out by the ranges, then the scrubland, then roads, then the blue harbour boats, the trails of a wake across the Cook Strait where the sea and ocean link their arms. The great aquatic, the Pacific and curve of the earth—then back to the sands and back to the Kaikōura. Everything goes back to mountains if you let it. They glint through the sun with a tilt on the wings, barely beings in the tumult. Some of them tourists, some permanent from the viewable land and its coasts and cities and seasons rocking back and forth below the wings bent at their tips like the flick of a pen lifted from the page. You can't tell them apart except for the clothes, and even then you'd have to account for taste, for history and what it does to taste. We wear what we wear at a certain age and nothing tends to get in the way. Nobody knows who we are, not without suspicion.

And there they are, heads peeking over the headrests. Something zoological in this, a transplant from the savannah.

A bald man two rows ahead holding his glasses as he stands and looks to the front. Just stares with a suffocated look as if his child has run that way.

'How do we do this?' a voice in the middle seat asks.

Deb points at his iPhone, but Ryan shakes his head.

'What do I write?' he asks.

Deb hunts through her satchel for two pens. The nub of a pencil. The dust in the corners from when this thing was all paperbacks, painkiller pop sheets and the stray cap of her lipstick. She takes out her diary, spiral-bound. She bought it at the terminal a month ago with a dollar coin when she was running late to catch her first flight. She only feels the urge to write things down when she's heading out of country, and now on her return flight it's full of strange words. She tears out two clear sheets and hands them over. 'I'll need them back,' she says, and he laughs without looking away as he starts to write.

A hit of cool air then, mixing with warm and the aircraft twists and rights. Voices rising, falling. People pressed.

'Christ-fucking-Mary,' Deb says.

'What do we write?'

'Write everything.'

'How?'

'Just write to everyone. Write to everyone,' she says.

Then silence, because—

'My address,' she whispers as the aircraft rights itself, putting it down on the cheap paper. 'It's a secret, so—'

'Yup.'

They get to writing their last thoughts, because this was the idea. Then hand them over as if soldiers before the howl of battle hits.

'What do I write?' he asks, now purely to himself. Or to himself and his wife and kids.

He's a character of stilted design, this Ryan beside her. Short by five inches and primed by little judgements from out his mouth. A professor of Blah and Blah University in Auckland, as he's named it. A sociology head of some sort. Or anthropological. She wants to introduce him to her husband in that odd way we want connections across our lives. She jokes a poor joke; he aims one back.

It was his idea to write these letters to their loved ones, to trade them like in war. His idea, but it's Deb who has to explain how to do it. He writes something in cursive. He looks up finally, showing a mouth blooming with the Pinot Noir pinched from a trolley after the first announcement. They'd sent it around, loaded up with beverages, apologetic cheese and crackers, crisps. All their wrappers sitting in the magazine pocket in front of them trying to scratch the screen of his e-reader.

There's a family split across the row. The mum in the aisle seat and her daughter, son and husband on their own, arguing.

And then Deb's swearing again. The aircraft shaking so her neighbour loses his phone and she grabs the seat in front. She holds on like that, as if she's shaking the shoulders of a loved one who just won't listen. She's thrown into the back of the headrest, her head jarred and ringing out. She swears, all around people swearing in their own practised ways. Whispers, grunts: the deep preparation of one hundred and twenty souls readying for the hit, for the mysterious compression of life near the hit. Imagined selves clambering for a hint of what it was all about. She half-stands. She pushes up but she's thrown sideways. She can hear her voice, the hundreds of voices.

Twenty minutes. Half an hour. The second flight attendant rushes to the front, hands on headrests, balancing and propelling herself forward. Then the third. Deb bends her neck trying to catch a glimpse of them, what they might tell us without opening their mouths. The plane bunts on the air once more and they shake, but they're still aloft, despite their eyes, despite the low circle they're tracing in the air above the Strait and how the first attendant now stands leaning ever so slightly, not looking at anyone.

The other attendants rush hither, they make announcements, they calm the panic, feel it rise again. But the first: she's still. She's been silent for whole minutes looking out the window. The way she holds herself, a bend in her neck, a tilt on her hip. Her hair, unclipped now, curls over her face and shoulders. *Tighten it like this*, she'd said when demonstrating the seat belt during the safety video. She's not saying anything now because she's already said the last things she will ever say.

And that's the cruellest guess Deb's ever made.

It feels true. But hardly an emboldening truth.

Tighten it, like this.

Deb shouts to her neighbour, and all they do is catch the edge of the other's sightline. A transitory glimpse through the unmoving flight attendant.

She's stuck, holding onto the headrest as the aircraft bangs into the rough air, the unresolving geography of cloud and contained moisture. So many stretching their necks, looking for something in her eyes or even her mouth, but she's silent, and it's a hard thing to accept because they're shaking, and I haven't mentioned a word about how they're shaking. And I haven't mentioned the noise either, the noise around her. I haven't mentioned the faces and eyes and the smell, the evacuations and tremors and the micro ache of each damned breath and the real thoughts that are constricting in her mind.

Her neighbour still writing, kind of panicked.

The boy in the row opposite says: *Aileron*, like it's his first word.

His dad says nothing. Such a man thing, to answer in silence and for that to somehow be comforting. His wife undoes her seatbelt and stands up. Then sits, all while the flight attendants are trying to get their silent colleague to move, to get her to shift to her seat at the front because there's black smoke, and parts are coming free now. The wing, splintering.

'Dad?'

'Enough.'

'What are you going to tell your husband?' Ryan says.

'Dad, I can see the sky!'

'Enough!'

Enough, dear Christ. Deb wants the kid to shout to the guy: *Where's your sense of awe, Dad?* She wants him to call out to the man and ask: *Where's your sense of fucking awe?*

They hit eddy then another eddy, pockets of air in the Pacific wind because they're coming in from the east, over the Strait now, and she can see the shore of Wellington, she can see the scrag-ends of a city and they hit cold air, bang against the floor. Jessamine's floor. For that is this craft's name: *Jessamine*. She always remembers an aircraft's name, so she knows who to blame when it all goes to pieces.

The shouts ride up. Brutal wails; terror sounds.

'Dad!' the boy shCALL GARDENERSouts.

'Buddy. Buddy.'

'Okay,' her neighbour says. 'Okay.'

They go on, rise, but not enough and smash back through cloud, mist whipping and lashing about superstructure. The distorted sea, shimmering at two hundred miles an hour. Light on glass. Leisure craft and triangular sails.

'Dad!'

There's no more altitude and there's just hills and water smashing together in the blur. The engines at full go-around. Noise and the undoing of noise. 'Fucken, fucken,' her neighbour says. Everything's thunder and it's the sound that's going to kill them that's the sense of it all, the sound and the air that comes charging, boundless and metallic.

'Dad!' The boy's nose is bleeding.

Her neighbour's mouth open.

The chanting of the flight attendants. Everything is physical—idea, thought, time—and she's shouting. Everyone's shouting, except those who are muted by the mingled bulge of people on their inside, the compression, the merge of all the botched narratives that rave on and on.

Then the estranged attendant, her hair spread out, she starts, she shouts, 'Thank God! Oh, thank God. Thank God!'

'I gotta . . . get . . .' the boy's mother half-screaming across the aisle as she starts to stand. Her face whipped and smeared as the wing touches, as it kisses the crease-line, as it touches the edge of the surf and sea and they feel the terribleness of it all, the aircraft, and their bodies stalled, the buckle and stammer of critical things.